"OH, BRET…
BRET," SHE GASPED.

Shawna's head was spinning from the effects of the wine. She opened her eyes as she felt him stand, and then he was lifting her in his arms and walking through the open door to the bedroom.

"You are not going to stop me," he threatened. "Not this time."

Shawna was unable to think about anything but Bret's lips sucking passionate kisses from the very depths of her soul. His fingers were rapidly unhooking her dress as they swayed beside the bed, bodies locked together.

"Oh, Bret, I love you so much," she whispered, stroking his smooth-skinned, muscular shoulders.

She moaned as her dress fell into a pool about her feet, exposing her breasts to the burning pleasure of his kisses. His hands slid down her sides to hold her closer against him, and the thrilling contact sent her floating upward on a cloud of exquisite sensation.

THE
FIRE
BRANDS

GEORGE
SMITH

PLAYBOY
PAPERBACKS

Published simultaneously in the United States and Canada by Playboy Paperbacks, New York, New York. Printed in the United States of America. Library of Congress Catalog Card Number: 80-22222. First edition.

Books are available at quantity discounts for promotional and industrial use. For further information, write to Premium Sales, Playboy Paperbacks, 747 Third Avenue, New York, New York 10017.

ISBN: 0-872-16765-8

First printing December 1980.

1

For some minutes the uproar below his window in the sunny drafting room of Glencannon & Sons had been tugging at the edges of David Glencannon's concentration. He finally looked up from the sail plan of the schooner he was working on and looked out the window in the direction the noise was coming from. Then he got to his feet, a tall, lean man with the features of an introspective hawk and a shock of sandy hair in which the first signs of gray were beginning to appear, and strode closer to the window to get a better view.

"You sneaking, lily-livered, pusillanimous poltroons, get out of this shipyard!" The voice was female and filled with fishmonger Billingsgate as it echoed between the sail loft and the slip where the potbellied ex-Indiaman *Alfred* was being pierced to carry an armament of thirty guns.

"You cowardly swabs! You simpering, mealy-mouthed, bastardly religious fakers!" The strident voice was filled with such rage it could have singed the paint off the sides of a two-decker at six cable lengths.

David stared at the scene below, his expression ranging from amazement to serious concern. A tall, hoydenish girl with red hair, freckles, a wide mouth, and aggressive nose was assaulting with a tarred rope end two men in the plain gray dress of Quakers.

"Get your fat bottoms off our property and take your book of spells and fakery with you!" the tall wild girl in doeskin dress and bare feet shouted, swinging the tarred rope ends at the two heavyset men in somber garb who were trying to ward off the blows with raised hands holding Bibles. "Take your canting and ravings where they're wanted, you sneaking Tory swine!"

David leaned out the window. "Mercy! Mercy! What are you doing?"

The girl paused and looked up at him, her face flushed with anger and dripping with perspiration.

"Why are you assaulting those men?" David demanded.

"Assaulting them, me arse!" the girl snorted. "I caught these sneaking, sniveling fakers snooping around the slip where old *Black Prince* is being converted to *Alfred,* a United Colonies man-o'-war."

"We came to protest the arming of that ship," one of the Quakers said. "This is needless provocation of His Majesty's government."

"We are already shooting at them on land, and they at us," David said, "so what difference if we do it at sea?"

"We are opposed to war in all of its manifestations," the older, fatter man said. "Our meeting has taken a firm stand on that and an even firmer stand must be taken against war by sea and the danger it poses for commerce."

Oh ho, so 'tis commerce that concerns thee at least as much as religion is it, me fine graysides? David thought.

"They were trying to talk the shipyard workers out of their jobs," Mercy shouted to her father. "I caught them ranting at the men cutting the gun ports in the old hulk."

"We were but trying to bring those men to their senses," said the younger man, whom David recognized as Thomas Moorcock. "We would win them away from this godless course of working on the sinews of Mars."

"That men in our own city of Philadelphia would be at this devil's work is unthinkable," the other man said. "We were remonstrating with them when this . . . this young person set upon us so viciously."

"And what might your name be, sir?" David asked.

"I am Reese Clifton, merchant of this town."

"I see," David said. "And did your meeting send you to exhort my workmen?"

"We acted upon our own initiative but within the teachings of our faith," Moorcock answered.

"And we shall certainly protest to the magistrate about the unprovoked attack this young person launched against us," Clifton added.

Mercy was rubbing a fist back and forth across her nose, and David could see her hands were stained with tar and a smear of grease covered the freckles on one high cheekbone. He could also see that her barely restrained temper was about to break loose again, so he spoke quickly to head it off.

"May I point out, gentlemen, that you are trespassing on my property."

"Trespassing is not a crime in the kingdom of the Lord," Moorcock said piously. "We are but doing our duty as we see it."

David saw Mercy spit on her doubled-up fist and knew what was coming. He had seen her do that when she was twelve and Billy Midling, the local bully, had persisted in pulling her pigtails. Billy had come out of that with both eyes blackened. It would be unfortunate if that were to happen to the two religious busybodies. If it did, David was sure he would have a suit on his hands, and with the shipyard just recovering from a long period of inactivity, he couldn't stand that.

Before he could speak, the girl glanced up at him, her green eyes blazing. "Papa, I am going to close both the fat one's eyes and then I am going to squash the young one's nose all over his face if they are not out of here by the time I count to ten."

"Mercy, please restrain yourself."

"Call me Shawna," she said. "That's my real name."

David shook his head. If only he hadn't told her so many stories about her grandfather, who had died at the siege of Quebec before she was born. But how was he to know that the child who had inherited his father's coloring would grow into a headstrong young woman bent on emulating Shawn's wild and impetuous ways?

"One . . . two . . . three," Mercy Shawna was counting, and the two Quakers must have realized that the tall, strapping girl was capable of doing exactly what she had threatened.

"This is too much," Moorcock shouted up to David. "It is outrageous that a female, one of God's gentler creatures, should behave like an ill-mannered churl."

"Four . . . five . . . you are really asking for it!" Shawna hissed. "Six . . . "

The pair began backing away along the dock toward the open front gate of the shipyard.

"We will be back," Moorcock said. "We will be back with brethren who will protest the outrage of arming that vessel to sail against the king."

"If you come back, you better come with bandages all ready to use," Shawna said, "because I am going to arm the workers with ax handles and capstan bars so they can take turns cracking Quaker skulls."

She advanced on them, rolling up the sleeves of her dress. "Seven . . . eight."

The two turned and were hurrying away, muttering threats over their shoulders about having the shipyard closed down.

"Closed down, ye bloody fools!" David had lost his temper now. "How can you jackanape magistrates close down my shipyard when the arming of the *Alfred* was ordered by the Naval Committee of the Continental Congress?"

"We do not recognize the authority of that pack of rebellious subjects of the king," Moorcock yelled back. "We shall see that this pesthole of militarism is closed down at once!"

Those words were a serious mistake, spoken as they were with his back turned as he hastened along close to the edge of the dock with Shawna only a foot or two behind him.

"Nine . . . ten!"

"No, Shawna, no!" David yelled, but it was too late. His daughter lifted her skirt, took careful aim at the Quaker's fat backside and swung her right foot.

The kick caught Moorcock just right to lift him into the air and propel him off the dock into the dirty, icy water of the Delaware River.

"Somebody throw that man a line!" David shouted at the group of shipyard workers who had been following his daughter and the intruders at a discreet distance. Then he turned and hurried down the outside stairs to join Shawna who was roaring with laughter as Moorcock sputtered and splashed in the water while his friend retreated with considerable loss of dignity through the gate of the shipyard.

"Mercy, Mercy, what am I going to do with you?" David said, catching her by the hand and pulling her into the office beneath the drafting room. "Where did I go wrong in raising you since your mother's death?"

"Wrong?" the girl said, turning to watch Peter Untermeyer, the foreman, and two workers drag the wet and enraged Quaker out of the slime and cold of the river and send him hurrying toward the gate. "I don't see anything wrong."

"Your mother would be very grieved by the way you've turned out," David said sternly. "She would have been ashamed of the way you behaved just now."

Shawna tossed her head defiantly. "Shawn would have been proud of me! And proud that I bear his name!"

David sighed deeply. "Aye, but even he would admit 'tis no way for a properly brought up young lady to behave. I never should have tried to raise children all by myself."

"Now, Papa, we've not turned out all that badly," Shawna said with an impudent grin. "Our sweet little Faith is nigh perfect. She has an even disposition, stays home and sees to the housekeeping, makes sure your meals are cooked and your socks mended. Gifford has as strong a sense of responsibility as yourself and is certainly doing his duty carrying a musket with the militia before Boston. Yes, and even Crispin, who hasn't got a drop of Glencannon blood in his veins."

"But why has Crispin disappeared and—"

"Papa, you know in your heart that Crispin has gone to join his own people," Shawna said.

A glint of anger showed in David's eyes. "The Glencannons are his people!"

"No, Papa, he's half Indian; more than half since he spent so much time with Joseph Brant and Shawn's friend Toolah."

"Aye, Toolah was there the night I—" He was remembering that wild night when he and Toolah, along with Robert Rogers and his rangers, had carried fire and death to the Delaware village where his first wife Anne had been held prisoner for over a year. It still shook him to relive that terrible instant when he had fired at a young Delaware chief and Anne had thrown herself in the path of the musket ball, sacrificing her life to save that of her captor and lover.

Disdaining to shoot one of the despised Lenni-Lenape, Toolah had beaten the Delaware chieftain to death with the butt of his musket, and minutes later David had discovered an infant boy in the lodge Anne had shared with the Indian.

"Let me kill it for you," one of the Rangers had volunteered. "I'll smash its brains out on yonder rock and save you the trouble."

"No," David had said. "I'll take it back to Johnstown and we'll raise it, my new wife and I."

Toolah had shaken his head in disgust. "It Lenni-Lenape. You might as well take in weasel."

But the boy turned out to be a joy. With her usual piety, Felicity had decided to call him Christian, but when he learned to read and discovered Shakespeare's *Henry V,* particularly Henry's speech before the battle of Agincourt, he chose to change his name. Since October 25 had been the day of his "birth," as he thought of the time David had rescued him from the burning Delaware village, he picked the name Crispin. Felicity and David had given in and let him have his way, so Crispin he had been ever since.

And now that he was gone, David felt the grief almost as much as he had when he lost Felicity in one of the endemic outbreaks Doctor Benjamin Rush called bilious fever, but which Doctor Edward Bancroft, who was well acquainted with French physicians from the West Indies, called yellow fever.

A year ago David had received a letter from Sir William Johnson, His Majesty's superintendent for Indian Affairs and patron of the Glencannons. It had come, mysteriously sealed, within a letter from David's sister-in-law Aileen. Sir William had said he needed someone he could trust who had extensive experience in the wilderness and he had thought of Crispin. He wanted the youth to carry belts and restraining advice to the farthest afield of the Nations of the Long House, the Cayugas.

Crispin had been eager to go, and because all the Glencannons owed much to Sir William, David had agreed to the mission. Crispin had carried Johnson's message, but its effect was lost once the man Greathouse had murdered Logan's children. The conflict known as Lord Dunmore's War had flared up along the frontier almost simultaneously with the rebellion of the American colonists along the eastern seaboard against the Crown.

Somewhere in the wilderness country beyond the mountains, young Crispin had disappeared. There had come stories of a half-breed leading attacks by Mingos and Cayugas against white settlements, and Shawna had decided that Crispin, horrified by the white man's crimes against the Indians, had joined the red men and become a leader among them.

The fighting had died down along the western frontier even as it had flamed up at Lexington and Concord, but still there had been no word of Crispin, and David sorely longed to hear something of the boy he had raised as his own.

"You know he went with them, Papa," Shawna was saying. "They had justice on their side and he joined them."

David shook his head, unable to believe Crispin had taken up the war ax against white settlers. In his mind he could agree with Shawna that the Indians had right on their side, but emotionally, the slaughter of white men and women, the Indian alliance with Tories and king's officials, was abhorrent to him. All he could really believe was that if Sir William had lived things would be different. As close as he and his father had been to Johnson, they had never known if he favored the colonial cause or that of the king, but David was sure that nothing could have prevailed upon the man to let his Indians become involved in the struggle as his son, son-in-law, and others were doing.

"What are you thinking of, Papa?" Shawna asked. "From that scowl on your face, it must be something bad. Was I that horrid?"

David looked at her, his oldest daughter and the one least like her gentle Quaker mother. "You behaved abominably."

She threw back her head and laughed. "Because I chevied a couple of yellow-bellied Tories who were trying to subvert our workers? I think they got off easily with only one being dunked. The Sons of Liberty would have given them something to remember."

"They were Quakers," David said, "not necessarily Tories."

"I've yet to meet a mealymouthed, psalm-singing Quaker who wasn't a Tory at heart," Shawna said.

"I'm for runnin' the whole bloody lot out of town and giving them a dose of tar and chicken feathers."

"It's very strange, Shawna, that you can feel for the Indians hundreds of miles away but you're ready to use force against a peaceful people."

"If they are so bloody peaceful, why are they always interfering in other people's business?" she demanded. "Why don't they just go off somewhere and be peaceful in a corner instead of constantly striving for political power and minding other folks' morals?"

"Your mother was a Quaker, young lady, and I'll not have you talk about her people that way."

"Why not?" she said, tossing her hair in that peculiarly defiant way she had indulged in even as a child. "You told me yourself how the colony she built far in Indian country was under attack when you and a Mohawk party rescued them."

"I did not tell you that," David said.

The girl shrugged. "Mother told me a number of times. That's why I'm glad I'm more like Shawn than anyone else."

David winced inwardly. There it was again, and the blame was all his. If he hadn't told her so many tales of Shawn's escapades, hadn't built up such an intriguing picture of his roguish father, the girl would not have become so obsessed with him, nor tried to pattern herself to fit his image.

"Your grandfather wasn't always the hero you think," he told her gravely. "Some of the things he did and some of the scrapes he got himself into would have shamed the devil."

"He was a man . . . all man," Shawna said. "The kind of man women long for."

"Oh, aye, he was that! He never gave your poor grandmother a moment's peace with his roving eye and careless ways about his marriage vows."

"Yes, but Papa, think of the women he loved. Think how happy he must have made them."

"For a while, for a very little while until his eyes fell on another pair of trim ankles or saucy smile."

"Well, he's the kind of man I'd be wishing for, if I were a wisher instead of a doer."

"What of Seth Ewart?" David asked. "Is he not enough of a hero and adventurer to please you? After all, sailing a ship to the Indies these days is not the sort of task a mollycoddle would take on."

"Oh, Seth is well enough," Shawna conceded. "In fact, he is coming to call tonight."

"Coming to call and there ye stand with dirty feet and tar-stained hands! Sometimes, girl, I wish I had married again if only to give ye a proper mother to teach ye to wash behind your ears!"

"Oh, I wash behind my ears, Papa, but how can I work around the shipyard and not get tar on my hands? And you know you need me here with Crispin off in the wilds, Billy with Cresap's Rangers and Gifford with Washington's army before Boston."

She was right, of course. Now that she had practically taken over the supervision of the yard workmen, David was freed to work with his half molds, sail plans, and drafting board.

"Not that Seth compares to Shawn, and since I'm Shawn's granddaughter, he's probably not worthy of me."

David swore under his breath and scowled at her when she laughed. Her fixation on the grandfather she had never seen annoyed him.

"Your mother was a woman of great tenderness, loyalty, and sanctity, and so was your grandmother," he said, "but you insist on harping on that old villain of a grandfather. It's almost as though you wish to follow his example, to pattern your life on him."

"If I were a man, I would," Shawna said. "And I do not think it very seemly for you to demean him. After all, he did give his own life for yours."

David's irritation vanished and his lips twisted in a rueful smile. "Aye, there's no denying that, he did."

His mind went back to that day on the Plains of Abraham when the Anglo-American forces under General Wolfe had engaged the French under Montcalm before the walls of Quebec. It was twenty years ago, but David could recall it as clearly as though it had happened yesterday.

The British and American units, supported by a British fleet commanded by Admiral Saunders, had advanced up the St. Lawrence River to the place where the French bastion stood. The city of Quebec was composed of two levels, the lower one close to the river and the upper on the cliff-ringed Plains of Abraham. An attempt to carry the lower town by storm had failed, and the troops had suffered heavy casualties. The bitter Canadian winter was approaching, and that meant the fleet on which the British army depended on for supplies and communications would soon have to withdraw. General James Wolfe, the valiant and ardent British commander whom the Glencannons had reason to remember for his kindness to young Steven during the Forty-five, was determined to make one more effort to take the city before that withdrawal brought failure to the whole expedition.

What was needed was a way up the unscalable palisades that formed a natural protection for the upper city. By chance, while out scouting one day, Shawn, David, and Toolah and stumbled onto a path of sorts that led to the precipitous heights. They had reported the discovery to Wolfe's headquarters, saying that the secret path was guarded only by a handful of not very alert French.

At first the council of officers Wolfe summoned turned down the plan of using the rough steps for an ascent to the plateau above because it was so dangerous. Then a Major Robert Strabo, an American held prisoner by the French since the fall of Fort Necessity, escaped from Quebec and made his way to the army before the city. He, too, knew of the supposedly secret path and had overheard Montcalm himself say that the way up the precipice was so steep that a hundred men could hold it against an entire army. Strabo also had another piece of information to impart. The officer in charge of the group guarding the access route was one Duchambon de Vergor, the man tried for misconduct and cowardice at the surrender of Fort Beauséjour and saved from disgrace only through the intervention of Governor-General Vaudreuil.

"He's a fool and a coward," Strabo told the officers council. "He permits his men to laze around in taverns and keeps no decent watch."

"Once on the Plains," said Shawn, who by then had a major's commission in the ranger battalion, "we will have them by the balls. When Montcalm wakes in the mornin' and sees an army drawn up in position to cut him off from all supplies from the interior o' the country, he'll have to come out and fight."

Wolfe had nodded and his enthusiasm had carried the council. The ascent was ordered, the British camp struck, and troops loaded aboard Admiral Saunders's ships. To the French it must have looked like the British were giving up and preparing to leave before the onslaught of winter.

Colonel Howe of the light infantry then called for volunteers to make the initial climb, assuring them, "If any of you survive, you may depend on being recommended to the general."

Shawn, of course, had been the first to step forward. He couldn't tolerate not being the first man in a fight any more than he could stand being around a woman without trying to bed her. David had followed suit and then Billy Dickenson and Toolah, although the latter was heard to mutter about the madness of the white man in climbing up the side of a cliff to take a city. Who needed a city when there were thousands and thousands of acres of forest to roam around in?

The decision had been made to land the troops at the Anse au Foulon, a small cove less than three miles from Quebec where the crags towered 175 feet above the river and were reached by a narrow trail that had to be traversed in single file.

Shawn was in his glory as he stood beside his son in the leading flat-bottomed landing boat. "Well, 'twill be a fine climb and a bonny starlicht nicht to hae a go at it," he said. " 'Tis this time we'll win our spurs, not for the King O'er the Water but for German Geordie and our own glory."

David had not been in so cheerful a mood. It was cold already on the waters of the St. Lawrence and he had a premonition of disaster that he couldn't shake. He had been on the sloop-of-war *Porcupine* and had heard Wolfe tell his old schoolmate John Jervis, that he did not expect to survive the battle.

The thin, pain-ridden commander had taken from his bosom a miniature of his betrothed and asked the naval officer to return it to the lady if his foreboding proved correct.

Later he heard Wolfe read to the officers gathered around him lines from Gray's "Elegy Written in a Country Churchyard."

"Let not Ambition mock their useful toil,
  Their homely joys, and destiny obscure;
Nor Grandeur hear with a disdainful smile
  The short and simple annals of the poor.

"The boast of Heraldry, the pomp of Power
  And all that beauty, all that wealth e'er gave,
Awaits alike th' inevitable hour:
  The paths of glory lead but to the grave."

"Aye, 'tis sure the general is in a bad mood, laddie," Shawn said. "His humors are gone sour, but as soon as he hears the whine o' musket balls o'erhead, he'll be the same ardent spirit he has always been."

"If the musket balls miss him," David said, "and us."

"Och, they will, lad, they will. The musket ball with my name on it has no been smelted, and besides, I have an assignation for the day after the battle. 'Tis with a seamstress in Pointe Levi. Ye should see her breasts! Like ripe fruit, they are, and every bit as sweet to suck on."

David gave him a dour look. "If she's still waiting when you get back, I'm sure you'll be doing just that."

Shawn chuckled. "Would I not, me lad. I wouldna be a Glencannon if I no had an eye for a plum ripe for the pickin'. And as ye know right well, I'm ne'er a one to get me head blown off when a warm pair o' thighs are waitin' to be spread wi' a pretty nest o' fragrant fur betwixt 'em a' hungerin' to be pierced."

"You're impossible, Father," David said. "You never think of anything but what's under a woman's skirts."

"No true, Davey. I also think o' a full purse and a good lusty battle. How does that bit o' doggerel Sergeant Nat Botwood composed go?" Shawn struck a heroic pose in the bow of the boat as it approached the enemy shore and recited.

> *"'Come each death-dealing dog who dares venture his neck,
> Come, follow the hero who goes to Quebec.' "*

"Aye, I remember," David said gloomily. "And I also remember that Sergeant Botwood fell along with five hundred others when we tried to storm the Beauport lines with our ammunition soaked from wading ashore and the icy rain that poured down on us."

" 'Twas bad luck, but tonight and tomorrow our luck will be good," Shawn said, and then held up his hand for silence. "Hush. We are comin' to the cove. If the sentries be awake, they may hear us."

The cliffs loomed high and dark above them, shutting out the starlight. David gripped his weapon, heard Billy Dickenson cock his rifle and Shawn loosen his claymore in its scabbard.

"Steady, lads, steady," Colonel Howe whispered, and now the muffled oars of the boat seemed like thunder in the stillness.

Then there was a sound on the dock, a creaking of belts and equipment as a sentry awoke to the fact that there was a darker something moving through the shadows cast by the palisades.

"*Qui-vive?*" The challenge rang out sharply.

"Quickly," Howe hissed, "someone who has the French!"

"*La France,*" Shawn called to the sentry.

"*A quel re¹giment?*"

"*De la Reine,*" Shawn replied.

They knew the sentry was expecting a convoy of provisions, and this exchange seemed to satisfy him so that he did not ask for the password.

They moved in past the dock toward the area on the gravelly beach that had been chosen as the landing site for the twenty-four volunteers from the light infantry, the Royal Americans, Fraser's Highlanders, and Glencannon scouts crouched in the boat.

Then again came the challenge of a sentry.

"Be quiet, you fool," Shawn answered in French. "It is the provision boats. Do you want to advertise our presence to the English and draw a broadside from the sloop out there?"

The sentry had to take into consideration that the sloop-of-war *Hunter* was prowling up and down the river with her battle lanterns gleaming and her matches blown up ready to open fire at any moment. Farther downstream the two-deckers and frigates of Admiral Saunders's fleet were raising a hullabaloo fit to waken the dead, and certainly to draw the attention of even the clever Marquis Louis Joseph de Montcalm de Saint-Veran away from the area of the intended attack. Whatever convinced him, the sentry did not challenge them further, so they glided on past again with no alarm sounded and no shot fired. Either action would have brought a hundred or more French pickets running to the scene and ended the chance for surprise.

"I'm cold," Billy Dickenson whispered to David, "cold as the north end of a south bound grizzly with the hair chewed offen his arse . . . so cold I'm a'shiverin'."

"I am too," David admitted, "but I'm not sure 'tis from the cold."

The eerie darkness, the menacing bulk of the cliffs, and the uncertainty of what awaited them at the top was bound to affect all of them. They knew the upper reaches were guarded by French troops, possibly with artillery that could sweep them away at any moment, and that a large detachment of Montcalm's army under the brave and vigilant Bougainville was close at hand; their apprehension grew with every passing minute. The prebattle tension weighed heavily on each man with, apparently, the exception of Shawn.

For he was whistling almost soundlessly, whistling a merry Scottish reel about a miller's daughter with a liking for performing sexual gymnastics while standing on her head. It was very obscene and just the sort of thing Shawn could be expected to whistle when other men were gritting their teeth, holding their breath, and clinging to weapons with sweaty hands.

"A moment more . . . I think I can see the beach now," the coxswain whispered as he swung the tiller slightly. Then they felt a gentle bump as the boat touched bottom.

"Out now, lads, and quickly," Lord Howe said. "Out and up the cliffs to glory or death."

They swarmed ashore, twenty-four men in the red coats of regulars, the kilts of Highlanders, the woods-green and blue berets of rangers. David followed Shawn over the side, and Billy and Toolah were right behind him. When they were all on land, they crouched down and waited while the boat pulled away and a second craft came in carrying Wolfe and fifty more men.

"Go to it, Lord Howe," Wolfe said softly as he climbed ashore, his pain-wracked body driven on only by his indomitable spirit. "God go with you."

Howe drew his sword and waved his hand; the volunteers started forward with Shawn, Toolah, and the other rangers leading the way. The path was narrow and almost hidden by small trees and thick underbrush. They reached the base of the precipice and began the long, dangerous climb, David waiting until his father's figure, clad in hunting shirt, kilt, and beret, was directly over his head before swinging into position behind him.

"Easy, lads, easy," Lord Howe cautioned as the party clambered upward. "Kill the sentries when you reach the top, but no gunfire; bayonets and hatchets only."

Shawn had not yet drawn his claymore. He was using both hands to pull himself up from rock to rock and bush to bush. David had his rifle slung over his back to free his hands for the same purpose.

Halfway up they found the way blocked by an abatis of sharpened tree trunks facing downward. David sucked in his breath. If the abatis were manned by sentries, it would make an almost unpassable obstacle.

Shawn raised his hand for silence and crept slowly toward it. In a moment he was peering behind the defensive position and then turning to wave the rest of them forward. Shawn's shoulders were too broad for him to squeeze through, so Billy, the smallest, and Toolah, the most supple, slipped through first. They fell to chopping at the center stake with hatchets from the upper side while David and Shawn hacked at it from below. The delay was only momentary, but Lord Howe was champing at the bit because he could hear Wolfe and the rest of the attacking force starting up the rough path from the base of the cliff. He also was afraid the sound of hacking would reach the French at the top of the plateau.

"Hurry, men, hurry, for God's sake! The general will be up with us in a few minutes and all of us will be bunched up here, making a sure target for even the drunkest or sleepiest French or Canadian sentry!"

The passage they had chopped through the barrier was big enough now that they could all squeeze between the pointed stakes and scramble on upward. If the sentries at the top had been alerted, they would simply have to deal with the problem when they got there. David took heart in the thought that the thunder of thirty-two and twenty-four pounders of Saunders's battleships battering at the Beauport lines and south-facing walls of Quebec had drowned out the noise they had made.

Then as they came near the crest with Shawn still in the lead, he raised his hand and started to move out onto the plain when there was a sound . . . the clicking of a musket being cocked.

"*Qui-vive?*" came the challenge, and David saw his father's claymore come out. He grasped his own rifle and . . .

"Papa! Papa, what is it?" Shawna's voice brought him back to the present. "What were you thinking, Papa, that makes you look so grim?"

"I was thinking you had best get back to your duties, lass," David said, not wanting to talk about his memories. "The men will be dogging it without your eye on them."

"They wouldn't dare. They know I'll take my tarred rope ends to them."

He frowned. "You're much too free with rope ends and that abrasive tongue of yours. As I said before, you should have had a mother after your own was taken away. I should have married again."

Impulsively, she crossed to his side and threw her arms around him. "Why, Papa, you've been good enough for both mother and father, but if it's marrying you have in mind . . . well, you're still a young and handsome lad, and if you have your eye on a fine lassie, I'll be the first to give my permission. After all, Shawn was still a'lifting ladies' skirts when he was almost fifty, and you've a long way to go."

"Get out of here, you disrespectful little beast!" David said, turning her around and slapping her across the bottom as she fled amid gales of laughter.

2

David strode over to the window and stood looking at the way where the *Alfred* was being worked on. Her bottom had been scraped and some of her spars replaced; now workmen were piercing her sides for gun ports to carry thirty 90-pounders. David had wanted to step her masts farther forward in hopes of getting a little more speed out of her, but the gentlemen from the Marine Committee, Silas Deane and Stephen Hopkins, had refused. They felt it would take too much time and said she was intended to be the flagship of a squadron that was fitting out to sail against the British before they could bring vastly superior forces to bear on this side of the Atlantic.

David shook his head as he look at *Alfred.* "A slug," he muttered to himself. "A perfect slug. She's almost as wide as she is long. They might as well have found themselves a washtub. She'll be run down by the first British frigate to sight her."

He turned and went back upstairs to his drafting table. The plans on it were of a scale of three-eighths of an inch to the foot, making them five feet long and two feet wide, and the ship they portrayed was a beauty. David had worked for weeks on the design, using all the knowledge he and his friend Joshua Humphreys had acquired during their apprenticeship to James Penrose and the additional knowledge they had stored up in working together since.

When they had heard that Congress had authorized the construction of thirteen warships, ten frigates of twenty-eight and thirty-two guns and three ship-rigged corvettes of twenty-four guns, they had worked day and night on the plans to be submitted to the Marine Committee. Since David was somewhat the better draughtsman of the two, he had completed the final plans. To their joy, their design had been accepted for the construction of all five of the thirty-two frigates and one of the twenty-eight gunships.

The colonies needed warships to stand up to the British. And as for the design to break off or separate, it was David's opinion that the die had been cast on that when the first shots were fired at Lexington and Concord, when the fighting at Bunker Hill had been followed by a colonial army besieging General Gage in Boston. There could be no turning back now for either the colonials or the king's forces.

But instead of proceeding with the building of the type of ships that were really needed, the Congress had chosen to permit a group of revamped merchantmen be the first to carry the American banner to sea. Nor were the men chosen to captain the made-over merchantmen much to David's liking.

There were two exceptions to the generally poor quality of personnel in David's estimation. Nicholas Biddle was captain of *Andrew Doria*. The other officer of note was a strange one, a man of mystery who went by the name of John Paul Jones. He had a strong Scots accent and claimed to be the illegitimate son of the Earl of Selkirk. It was rumored he had killed a man on a ship he was master of at Tobago in '72 and had fled trial.

There were even more unsavory rumors about him. David had met a seaman from Martha's Vineyard who claimed to have known Jones before. According to him, one day in '73 a brigantine of rakish lines, showing no flag and with her name painted over, had put in for water. She was manned by swarthy, desperate looking types and armed with three 9-pounders and a Long Tom pivot gun.

"Her captain's name was Jones," the old seaman had told David, "and sure as I've avoided Davy Jones's locker all these years, it was the same man, and that black-painted craft wasn't no peaceful merchantman, not by a long shot."

Be that as it may, David liked the man. He was only about five foot six with arms that nearly reached his knees. He had a sturdy build and was heavily muscled in spite of his small frame. His sandy hair was worn back off his face, and his small sharp eyes didn't miss much. Jones and Biddle were the only two officers David could have sailed with with any confidence. He thought that Shawn would have liked Jones.

Aye, they were alike in some ways, except that Jones didn't seem to have Shawn's eye for a pretty ankle. He did have the same kind of intensity and the same kind of enthusiasm for a cause that Shawn had had. And if the tale the Martha Vineyard's sailor had told were true, they had somewhat the same roguish nature. After all, was Shawn's service with Old Grog when they stormed Porto Bello so much different from the same feat performed by Henry Morgan? Both Vernon and Morgan had been technically in the service of the Crown. Even if Jones couldn't make the same claim for whatever ventures he had undertaken in the black brigantine, David was sure he would make a better captain than the swaggering, loud-mouthed Hopkins or the drunken "Sailor Tom" Hazard who was to command *Providence*.

Well, it was a dangerous course these colonies he now considered his country had entered upon when they followed the advice of that fellow Patrick Henry from down Virginia way.

"I repeat it, sir, we must fight! An appeal to arms and to the God of Hosts is all that is left us."

Certainly every appeal to the government in faraway England had been turned aside, and a tea tax, a stamp tax, and a dozen other duties and obligations meant to help the merchants of the mother country at the expense of the colonies had been imposed without a thought for the welfare of citizens half a world away. Now the talk was ended, and it was war.

The thought of a new war plunged him back once again into memories of that other war and the battle with the French on the Plains of Abraham.

He had seen his father poke his head over the edge of the pleateau, had heard him draw his claymore, and then heard the click of a sentry's musket being clicked. Then the challenge had come.

"*Qui-vive?*"

Once more Shawn had answered in his flawless French gained from his year in the service of the Old Pretender with the French army. "*La France!*"

"*A quel régiment?*"

"*De la Reine.*"

David held his breath, wondering if this time there would be a demand for the password. He cocked his rifle and heard the faintest sound as Toolah drew his scalping knife.

"*Mot de passe?*" There it was, and Shawn had no way of knowing the password.

"Why, here it is, laddie!" Shawn said in English. His hand flicked back and his Highland dirk went sailing through the air to lodge in the sentry's throat, felling the man without a sound.

With a sigh of relief, David scrambled up over the edge onto the top of the palisade. The others swarmed up behind him and then they were running toward the group of tents that housed the guard of the defile.

Everything was a turmoil then as the French came pouring out of the tents, shouting and gesticulting.

"*Aux armes, aux armes!*" some were yelling.

From others another cry arose. "*Sauve qui peut! Sauve qui peut!*"

"On them, lads, on them!" Lord Howe urged.

They were indeed running; militia and colonial marines mixed together in the direction of Quebec which was invisible beyond the low ridge of hills.

Not all of them ran. Some threw up their hands shouting, "*Jè rendre . . . Jè rendre!*"

David spotted the man with a brandy bottle under his arm, wearing the lace-fringed tricorn of a French officer. Still in his nightshirt, he was trying to climb onto a horse being held for him by a *Trois Rivières* militiamen.

"There is de Vergor!" David shouted, recognizing the man instantly from descriptions in letters from his brother Steven about the cowardly and treacherous commander of Fort Beauséjour.

Shawn let out a yell and went for the French commander with claymore flashing above his head.

The militiaman dropped the reins of the horse and started to raise his musket, but David put a ball through his shoulder that spun him around and knocked him to the ground. The horse bolted and de Vergor turned to see a six foot five Highlander armed with a three-foot length of steel bearing down on him. He tried to run, but his nightshirt tripped him up, and then Shawn was on him.

"Scots what hey!" he yelled, catching de Vergor's shirttail on the point of his claymore and dragging him backward to throw him, kicking and yelling, over his shoulder, relieving him of the bottle of brandy with a skillful twist of the wrist.

There was no longer any need for silence, and the rest of Wolfe's army was pouring up the rough path, scrambling over the edge of the ravine and hurrying forward onto the plain. The first shots had alerted the French in Quebec and they could hear drums beating the *rappel*. In the city, the startled citizens heard every church bell ringing out the news that the enemy was attacking Quebec from the rear.

Wolfe and his three brigadiers, Monckton, Murray, and Townshend, were studying a map by candlelight when Shawn approached with the protesting de Vergor in tow.

"I caught him, General Wolfe. 'Tis the lily-livered swine in command here. Do you want to question him or should I toss him in the St. Lawrence?"

He hoisted the screeching Frenchman by a foot and an arm, swung him over his head and strode to the edge of the cliff overlooking the river.

"*Mercy, mercy*, General Wolfe! Spare me! I have much information!" de Vergor howled in terror.

Wolfe and the others laughed and then he called to Shawn, "Restrain yourself, Major Glencannon. Spare the scoundrel so he may entertain us with his lies."

"Oh, pshaw, General! Ye've just ruined a bet I had wi' me son that I could throw the scum halfway 'crost the river." Reluctantly Shawn lowered the collapsing

Frenchman to the ground and shoved him into the hands of the Louisburg grenadiers.

"May I suggest you spare the bottle also, Major," Wolfe said, "at least until the battle is won."

" 'Tis saving it I am for a victory libation, your honor," Shawn replied, "except for a wee sip or two for me rheumatiz."

Wolfe turned back to the map but spoke again as Shawn turned away. "Please stand by, Mr. Glencannon. I shall have orders for you and your rangers by and by."

"Aye, sir, we'll stand by," Shawn said, looking over to where the hundred rangers—mostly Scots from the Mohawk Valley—were drawn up with David. The men were trying to straighten their ranks so they would look less like ruffians beside the perfectly aligned regulars who were forming up all around them.

Wolfe and his staff moved out to reconnoiter while the army fanned out on the grassy plains, which were fairly level, broken only here and there by cornfields, and studded with clumps of bushes. The night had been clear and star-studded, but with dawn, clouds had gathered and a light rain began to fall.

The lines were formed up with the men's backs to the river; when they wheeled to face the *Buttes-à-Neveu* and the city beyond, Bougainville and his 3000 troops a half day's march upriver would be at their rear. This had to be a major consideration for Wolfe as he finalized his battle plans.

It didn't take him long to make his decision. Bougainville would be covered by 1,500 troops, who would also protect the pathway up from the river over which two cannon were being hauled to the heights by relays of seamen from the fleet.

"Gentlemen, we will deploy five hundred yards to where the plains are only a mile wide so that our flanks will rest on difficult terrain and cannot be enveloped," Wolfe told his aides. "For I believe when the marquis deploys, he will perhaps have twice our numbers."

"Good enough odds," said Murray, the youngest of the brigadiers.

Townshend, the son of a duke and jealous of Wolfe's position as commander, said snidely, "If the marquis is as wise as I have heard, he may not deploy at all. He need only wait for Bougainville to join him to make his numbers overwhelming."

Townshend was one of those officers of the British army who not only resented Wolfe's having a command but considered him a madman. When he had been appointed commander of this expedition against Quebec, many of the more conservative officers had complained to Newcastle, the prime minister, who had rushed to George II to protest. But that none too savory individual had one virtue—he was the last British monarch to personally command an army in the field, and he brushed aside Newcastle's objections.

"But, Your Majesty," Newcastle said, "he is mad."

"Mad is he?" the old king growled. "Then I hope he will bite some of my other generals."

On this September 13, 1759, David thought, it was to be proved whether Newcastle and the aristocratic generals or the gouty old king was right. For the sake of all the British and Americans present, David hoped George II was.

Wolfe issued orders rapidly as the light became brighter. The Louisburg grenadiers were to have the place of honor at the fight, the Twenty-eighth regiment and the Forty-third were next with the Highlanders of the Seventy-eighth to hold the center, the Fifty-eighth and the Fifteenth Foot were to compose the left. The Royal Americans and the Forty-eighth were to be held in reserve against the appearance of Bougainville on the field of battle. Howe's light infantry and the six companies of rangers were ordered to cover the flanks against Indian and Canadian woods runners.

"Go get 'em, laddies, go get 'em!" Shawn shouted as the Fraser's Highlanders quickstepped forward and wheeled to face toward Quebec with pipes skirling a pibroch, their red and light green kilts swinging about their knees. "Scots what hey!"

The Mohawk Valley Rangers took up the cry, and then they were moving out at a trot along with two companies of Howe's light infantry in their tailless red coats and jockeylike caps with flaps and neck-pieces to protect the ears and the back of the neck against the rain.

"Look!" Billy Dickenson said suddenly, pointing. "There on the ridge! The French!"

But David was looking back toward the British army. It had fully deployed now, and he could see that it was indeed a "thin red line." There were only enough men for two ranks, and if his seaman's eye didn't deceive him, each trooper was standing at least three feet from the next; there was none of the usual shoulder to shoulder line here. What would be even more noticeable to the French was the forty feet between each battalion.

"Thank God they have no cavalry," David said. "They'd ride right through us."

"Nobody rides or marches through us today, lad," Shawn told him. "I have a lucky feeling this day.

Today we win a whole continent and go home bloody heroes for the lassies to kiss and bed."

Firing was coming from the heavily wooded area ahead of them, and the rangers and light infantry were scattering and running forward, heads down. David saw a flash of smoke on his right toward the cliffs overhanging the St. Lawrence, dropped to one knee, aimed in that direction, and fired.

Still kneeling, he shook the proper amount of powder into the rifle, took a greased patch and a ball out of his ammunition pouch, wrapped the patch around the ball, and drove it home with the ramrod.

"Good shot, Davey, good shot!" Billy Dickenson said. "I saw a Canadian woods runner fall. One day you'll be as good with that rifle as my pa was."

The rangers had all taken cover and were keeping up a steady fire at the French and Indian irregulars who infested the woods, while Lord Howe tried to work his light infantry around to the left.

Shawn had been peering at the French lines, watching them form up and trying to figure out what the extra commotion among them was all about.

"They are comin' on," he said finally. "I do believe they mean to attack."

"That would be foolish," David said, turning to study the situation. "All Montcalm needs to do is wait for Bougainville to join him or attack us in the rear. Why would he fight now?"

"Ah, lad, the mon is a great general but he hails from the far south o' France and they breed 'em impetuous there with none o' the tightfisted, cool-headed way o' Normandy. It appears he's let his hot temperament o'ercome his military judgment, and he'll suffer for it this day, I tell ye, lad."

"They've a couple or three cannon over there," Billy reported, scanning the enemy lines with his hawk's eyesight. "They'll be playin' a tune for us right quick, I'll lay odds."

" 'Tis the redcoats they'll be firin' at," Shawn said, "not us. Look at those Froggies come a'poppin' out o' Quebec. . . . Looks like an overturned anthill."

A torrent of white uniforms were in truth pouring out through the gates of the city, some by way of St. John's and others by St. Louis. Bayonets gleamed in the dull morning light as they rapidly formed up in line with the battalion of Guyenne, which had been patiently waiting for over an hour.

As the regiments came together and their banners were broken out, Shawn recognized them. "There's Languedoc, La Sarre. Bearn was at Oswego and Fort William Henry when the English colonials were massacred; they'll have a lot to answer for today. And there, those big ones in the white coats wi' blue facings and blue vests, that's the Royal-Roussilons."

David watched, fascinated, as the French line shaped up. It was considerably longer than the British line, and officers were shouting orders while sergeants with spontoons measured off distances.

"Almost nine-thirty," said Shawn, "and just about time for the dance to begin."

There was another flurry of gunfire from the woods in front of them, but it died down again, almost as though the flankers on both sides were waiting breathlessly for the main battle to begin.

"If Montcalm decides not to attack, what will General Wolfe do?" David asked his father.

"No need to worry your head wi' that, lad," Shawn laughed. "Montcalm could no more resist the temptation than he could fly."

A puff of smoke arose from the French lines, followed by the boom of a cannon, and a ball splattered mud about twenty yards short of the British lines. They could see the blue-coated, red-trousered artillerymen wheeling a second and then a third piece of artillery into place between the gaps left in the French line.

"The invitation to the dance has been issued," Shawn said as one of the English guns that had been so laboriously dragged up the precipice replied to the French fire.

The British line seemed to dissolve as the order was passed for the men to lie down when the cannon balls began to pass over their heads. The French, however, remained standing in their straight ranks, lending weight to Shawn's opinion that they were going to attack.

Shawn shook his head in disapproval as brown-coated troops began to mix with the white coats of the French regulars. " 'Tis a mess they'll be gettin' themselves into. Montcalm is no at his best today. Those are Canadian militia he's mixin' with the regulars, and it will confuse their advance."

There was much beating of drums and shouting in the French ranks before they started forward, at ten o'clock sharp, in perfect alignment. But as the walk increased to a trot, the long lines began to bend and curve in increasing disarray.

At the first movement of the French, the British guns had opened fire with grapeshot, and the infantry had risen to their feet. Simultaneous with the start of the advance, the French skirmishers, in the woods directly ahead of where Glencannon's rangers lay behind protective cover, began to fire heavily, but more at the British line than at the light infantry or rangers.

The pipes of the Seventy-eighth were beginning to skirl, and the Highlanders on the British left were threatening to rush forward, and were held back only by the shouted commands of their officers. All along the British line other orders were being given, the words drifting on the wind to the ears of David and the others.

"Handle cartridge!"

A ripple of movement ran down the line as the order was obeyed. The French, coming on now at almost a run, fired a ragged volley that showed no visible effect on the British but created confusion in their advance because the Canadians knelt to reload as soon as they had fired.

"Prime!" the British order came. "Load!"

The French were closer now, reloading on the run and letting fly with another volley, and David saw a few gaps appear in the British lines.

"Draw ramrod!" the officers and sergeants shouted. "Return ramrods!"

Billy Dickenson and other riflemen among the rangers were sniping at the Indians and *coureurs des bois* in the woods, the crack of their weapons adding a staccato variation on the refrain of musketry and cannon fire.

But rising above the cacaphonous sound, they could still hear the officers and sergeants in the thin red line calmly calling out orders even as the French lowered their bayonet-tipped muskets and charged.

"Make ready!" The muskets of the British line were raised to high port, and the French came on with much shouting and drum beating.

"Why don't they fire, for God's sake?" Billy rasped. "Are they waiting for the French to be among them?"

"Forty paces is the best range," Shawn said. "They slaughtered us at Culloden at forty paces."

in her green eyes. "And you, Seth Ewart, have you considered that line of work for yourself?"

Seth looked startled. "Of course not. I have my ship and my business is trading. At this time of trouble I think the lines of communication between these colonies and the Indies must be maintained by honest trading voyages. That is more important, I think, than private gain by what is in effect piracy."

Shawna made an impolite sound that brought her a frown from David.

"My grandfather sailed with Admiral Vergon to Panama and followed in the footsteps of Henry Morgan," she said proudly. "He came home better fixed for it than he would have from a dozen 'honest trading voyages.' "

Remembering how poor the family had been when living in northern England, David could only grimace at his daughter's exaggeration. Whatever loot Shawn had brought back from Panama was soon gone, thrown away at the gaming table or in the pursuit of lovely ladies. Shawn had eventually outgrown his taste for cards and dice, but amorous dalliance had remained his prime interest in life up until the very end.

Seth was looking uneasy, seemingly reluctant to be drawn into an argument with Shawna. "There is, of course, a place for naval armament to protect trade," he said. "I believe you, Mister Glencannon, are even now working toward that end, are you not?"

David grimaced. "I'm arming an old tub with nine-pounders that will probably shake her timbers so badly she'll spring a dozen leaks the first time she fires them all at one time. Meanwhile, the keel and timbers of the finest thirty-two-gun frigate ever designed sits rotting while Congress vacillates between begging George the third's pardon for shooting his redcoats at Lexington, Concord, and Bunker Hill or kicking his arse the way it deserves to be."

"Hooray, Papa, hooray!" Shawna said enthusiastically. "That's what I'd like to help do. I'd like to command a fast ship and go in harm's way like that funny little Scotsman John Paul Jones is always talking about doing."

"Instead of which, you should be learning that the proper place for young ladies is in the drawing room, not on a poop deck," David said.

"Why?" she demanded. "Who makes those rules? No one asked me if I wanted to be born a girl. Nobody consulted me before making a rule that females have to be meek and obedient and sit around pining for a hero on a white horse to come carry them off. Why shouldn't I ride the white horse if I've a mind to, or better yet, why can't I sail a tall ship to where I want to go?"

"You can't do it because—" David paused, unable to think of a reason why she shouldn't do the things she was quite capable of doing. He himself had taught her navigation when she was twelve, and she had handled a brig as well as any other man when the family's old friend Captain Amos Pratt had let her stand watches on his *Polly* during a voyage she and David had made to Savannah for a reunion with his younger brother, Steven.

"You cannot do it because it just is not done," David finished lamely.

"You are absolutely right, Mister Glencannon," Seth said, nodding his head in vigorous agreement. "Young ladies simply do not do such things if they want to be welcomed in good circles."

"Then I shall skip the good circles and get into ones where I can be what I want to be," Shawna said defiantly. "That's what my grandfather did."

"Mistress Mercy, surely you cannot mean that," Ewart said, his broad, honest face showing sincere distress. "A young woman of your background and upbringing has a duty to . . . to—"

"To what, Captain Ewart?" she demanded. "To be a proper lady and die of sheer boredom?"

"It is not necessary to suffer boredom to be a proper lady," Ewart said, sounding a little stuffy. "The wife of Mister John Adams is a person of considerable attainment and interests and is still a lady to her fingertips."

Shawna examined her fingertips critically. They were dirty and the nails damaged from work around the shipyard. "I'll never make a lady," she said, "because I prefer to use my fingertips for other things than knitting and pouring tea."

"Nevertheless, I think—" Ewart began.

Shawna whirled and headed for the door. "I have to get back to the dry dock, or those lazy scoundrels will be sitting on their rumps doing nothing."

"Shawna!" David said sharply.

"What is it, dearest Papa?" she asked sweetly.

"We do not use words like 'rump.' "

"Oh? It seems I have heard you use it many times."

"Well, let us say that I may use words like that but you are not permitted to. Do you understand?"

"Oh yes, Papa, I understand perfectly," she said, making him a mocking curtsey before turning to Ewart. "You said you wanted to speak to my father so I will leave you two men to your male talk and get on with my woman's work."

David found himself grinning as she closed the door behind her with such a definite click that it had the same effect as a slam.

"A most spirited young lady, Mister Glencannon," Seth commented. "One wonders if she is too spirited."

David looked at the sober young man, who at twenty-six was already master of a well-founded trading brig, and wondered exactly what it was that had brought him and Shawna together.

"You wanted to talk to me about something, Captain? Are you thinking of hauling the *Venture* out for a good scraping? Or perhaps I can set that mainmast of yours forward a foot or two and add a couple of knots to your speed."

"No, Mister Glencannon, it was not a matter of business I wished to discuss with you. The *Venture* will do for one more voyage. I'm already making ready a cargo for her with calls in Jamaica and Cuba in mind before going on to New Orleans."

"Then what do you wish to discuss with me?" David asked, hoping that whatever it was wouldn't keep him from his drafting instruments for too long.

"It is . . . uh . . . well . . ." Ewart seemed unable to get the words out. "It's that I . . . you see, I—"

"Yes, yes, my boy," David tried to encourage him. "Go on, I'm listening."

Seth Ewart took a deep breath and managed to get it out. "Well, sir, I would be honored if you would give your permission for me to call on Mistress Mercy Glencannon."

For a moment David stared at the younger man, wondering if he had taken leave of his senses. "But, Captain Ewart, you have been calling on her. You call on her whenever you make port in Philadelphia."

"Yes, sir. I mean, no, sir. You misunderstand me. I mean call on her with a certain firm intention in mind."

My God, this tongue-tied young idiot wants to marry my Shawna. My wild, unmanageable hoyden. I was certain pretty, proper little Faith would go first, but here he stands asking for the privilege of taking off my hands the unruly child who since she was five has stuck out her tongue at all convention and kicked up her heels whether I say nay or yea.

Actually, I ought to throw my arms around the fellow and welcome him as one who would deliver me from a troublesome wench whose idea of obedience is to defy her father cheerfully rather than angrily. Yes, this ought to be one of the happiest moments of my life, but instead I would like to tell him to take his ridiculous courtship and find himself a woman more suited to him, one of less fire and ice, one he is capable of handling.

This had been a most unsettling day, a day of memories and of change. Early this morning he had heard it might be months before he could resume construction of the *Randolph*, then had come the unwelcome intrusion of the two Quakers and Shawna's attack on them. That had stirred up old memories of the day on the Plains of Abraham and of his father. And now this young sea captain wanted to take his daughter, his fiercely independent redhead who was also his good right arm here at the shipyard. Could he manage without her? Could he get along without her love and support in his work?

But of course he couldn't stand between Shawna and happiness either, if it was indeed possible for her to find happiness with this conventional young man. On second thought, Ewart would be better than young Bret Morley. Bret had inherited his father's considerable holdings in the Hudson Valley and had promptly squandered a large part of it on the same kind of things Shawn had squandered the gold he had brought back from Porto Bello. Now, although not nearly as rich as previously, he was just as given to breakneck rides through the staid streets of Philadelphia at unheard of hours, to drinking bouts and brawls in taverns, and to scandalous doings with tavern maids and seamstresses. For some reason beyond David's comprehension, probably because Bret was a great landowner and therefore considered an aristocrat, he had been sent by the people of York colony as one of their representatives in the Continental Congress. David approved of the young hothead's call for stronger measures against the British, but he did not approve in the least of the way Morley sometimes looked at Shawna.

Yes, taken all in all, Seth with his broad, pleasant face, stiff blond hair, and honest blue eyes, was far superior as a suitor for Shawna than the too handsome, too long-haired, too wealthy Bret. David knew he should welcome Ewart's request, but he didn't because, quite frankly, he didn't want his beloved redhead to marry anyone. And that was a ridiculous attitude he would have to rid himself of without delay.

"Are you considering my request, sir?"

"Ah . . . ah, yes, of course, Captain Ewart," David said, clearing his throat. "You have my permission to call on my daughter, but you realize there is one hitch in all this."

"And what is that, sir?"

"It is that my daughter has a mind of her own," David said, "and by giving you permission won't

mean a bloody thing. You will have to get her permission as well."

A broad smile lit up Ewart's face. "Oh, I already
have that," he said to David's surprise.

"You mean my daughter has indicated that she
looks favorably upon your suit for her hand?"

The smile faded. "Oh no, sir. In fact, if I remember
rightly, she said something like this: 'Me, marry
you? Why, I'd as soon marry a bale of tobacco or a
hogshead of molasses. They are commodities also
used in the overseas trade just as you are. But you're
welcome as the birds in the spring to try to woo me,
if you want to. I won't stop you, but I will tell you
your chances are about as good as those of a sloop-
of-war against a three-decker.' "

"Ahem." David raised a hand to his mouth to hide
a smile. "And you mean after a broadside like that,
you are still willing to try?"

"Oh, yes, sir," Seth Ewart said. "You see, until then
she had never shown anything but indifference to
me. Now at least I have attracted her attention
enough to irritate her. From there I may move to a
much better relationship, don't you think?"

"Oh yes, to be sure," David said, shuffling some
papers on his desk. "Yes, a rise from indifference in a
young woman's esteem to the level of contempt
would seem to be no mean advance, bespeaking of
great things in the future."

Ewart smiled happily and reached for his tricorn.
"Then with your kind permission, Captain Glencannon, I shall begin my assault on your daughter's affections at once."

"Oh, by all means," David said absently as the
young man left. He was startled at hearing himself
called captain again. Like everyone else who had

served in the French war, he had retained his commission in the militia, but as he achieved success as a
shipbuilder, he was more and more called mister, or
as by the Hudson Valley Dutch for whom he had
built the commodious bluff-bowed craft they favored
for trade, *Mynheer*. So the unexpected title of captain took him back once more to the rain-swept day
on the Plains of Abraham.

"Fire! . . . Fire! . . . Fire!" the order ran down the
thin line of redcoats from general to captain to sergeant, and a sound like thunder roared forth as the
perfectly timed and executed volley hit the charging
French at only forty paces.

For a moment it almost seemed as though the
volley had had no effect on those heavy lines of advancing white uniforms. But when the smoke cleared,
David gasped, unable to believe his eyes.

Whole ranks of French had been swept away by
that single volley. White-coated figures lay still on
the ground or were writhing with wounds and the
whole mass seemed to be recoiling on itself.

The only sound was the shouted orders of the
British sergeants to the redcoats who were taking
several paces forward.

"Handle cartridge!"

"Prime!"

"Draw ramrod!"

The British troops were reloading as they advanced, and the French were curling back as though
in anticipation of another of those thunderbolts that
would be remembered as the most devastating ever
seen by anyone who was there that day.

"Return ramrod!"

"Make ready!"

"Present!"

"Fire!"

The second volley rang out with almost the same precision as the first and with equally deadly effect.

The French army was turned into a desperate mob, shouting, cursing, gesticulating. Some were withdrawing toward the rear, others had thrown down their weapons and seemed to be trying to surrender.

"Draw bayonets!" the order rang out and was followed in quick succession by, "Fix bayonets! . . . and charge!"

A cheer went up that was almost as thunderous as the two volleys that preceded it. Then the red line was surging forward, the British with fixed bayonets and beating drums, the Highlanders with drawn claymores and wildly screeching bagpipes.

"Look, there's Wolfe himself at the head o' the Louisbourg grenadiers!" Shawn said. "He's leading the charge in person!"

"That's no place for a general," David said, ducking down as the Canadians and Indians in the woods beyond opened a heavy fire at the advancing redcoats and their flankers.

"Forward! Forward! Clear those woods!" Lord Howe was shouting. "Cover the flanks of the advance!"

The light infantry and rangers were on their feet. David heard bullets whistling past his ears and fired his rifle blindly into the woods before slinging it over his shoulder and pulling the tomahawk from his belt. He saw Shawn draw his claymore, brandish it overhead, and lunge forward, followed by Toolah screaming a blood-curdling Mohawk war cry, and Billy Dickenson whooping crazily. David and the rest of the Glencannon rangers were right on their heels.

The firing was heavier now on the flanks of the two armies, which had locked briefly in hand-to-hand combat, the French reeling backward and unable to recover from the first deadly volleys.

"My God, the general has been hit!" yelled a young Mohawk farmer serving as a lieutenant in the rangers. David risked a quick glance in the direction the fellow indicated and saw Wolfe on the ground.

"They run . . . see how they run!" someone shouted, and except for the flankers in the woods, the French were panicking and fleeing before the fury of the British charge.

Shawn was into the woods now and David close behind him. They could see Lord Howe and his light infantry in open order swinging toward the left of the advancing army. The firing there was every bit as heavy as that on the right and was being directed at the victorious British center.

David was hacking his way through tangled underbrush, Shawn slightly ahead of him, Billy and Toolah to his right, when he heard scuffling and shouting behind him, but there wasn't time to go back and investigate.

"Keep after 'em, lads! Run 'em off the cliffs if ye have to!" Shawn urged them on after cutting down a buckskinned, long-haired *coureur des bois*.

Toolah grappled with a Mission Indian, the pair rolling around until the Mohawk emerged on top, raised his bloody scalping knife and made short work of his opponent.

Up ahead was the brisk sound of musketry as they came out of the thicket into cornfields with stalks growing so high it was as difficult to see the elusive enemy as it had been in the woods.

There were sights and sounds though of what had become a general rout of the French forces. The roads and paths leading to the bridges were jammed with a frantic mob that included a rabble of militia, woods runners, Indians, and the shattered remnants of some of the finest regiments of the French army. And somewhere in the middle of that mass was the Marquis de Montcalm, mounted on a tall black horse, desperately trying to rally his terrified troops.

"Come on, laddies, flush 'em out! Flush 'em out!" Shawn shouted. "They are sniping at our lads as they advance! They are covering the retreat into Quebec!"

Billy Dickenson picked off a blue-coated Canadian militiaman, and Toolah sank his war ax into the head of a woods runner. Faced suddenly with a war-painted Indian aiming a musket at him, David hurled himself forward, knocking aside the musket with one hand and smashing his tomahawk through the shaved scalp of the red man's skull.

The skull split with a sickening crunch David would never forget, split and splattered blood and gore over his hunting shirt, pants, and leggins. But he had no time to dwell on it as he again heard the rustling sound behind him. The sound was followed by a shout of warning and he whirled to see five French regulars in the white coats and red facings of the Regiment de Berry almost on him with bayonets leveled.

He froze momentarily, the bloodied tomahawk hanging at his side while he stared at the three bayonets pointed directly at him. Then suddenly an arm shot out and knocked him aside, and in a moment of terrible clarity he saw Shawn standing where he had been, turning away two of the bayonets and taking a third in the chest.

There was a deafening blast of gunfire as rangers all around them fired. Four of the five Frenchmen went down, one falling across David's legs and two others on either side of Shawn who still stood clutching the claymore with which he had dispatched the man who had bayoneted him.

For a moment David thought his father had suffered only a minor wound because he was still standing, swaying but standing. He grinned at David. "Ye must keep your eyes open, Davey, and watch on every side if ye mean to be a ranger," he said, and then sank slowly down as though seeking a comfortable spot to sit.

As David reached his side, light infantrymen who had been pursuing the French swept past, and in the distance drums could be heard beating the recall.

Holding his father propped against his shoulder, David shouted, "Billy . . . Toolah . . . go find a surgeon! Shawn's wounded!"

"Not wounded, laddie," Shawn said, "killed. No surgeon in this or any other army will make this blow right."

Billy and Toolah had dashed off, and the young lieutenant from the Mohawk Valley and several other rangers gathered around.

Lord Howe came riding up, tricorn and wig missing, his bare sword in his hand. "Is that Shawn Glencannon?" he asked.

"Yes, he took a bayonet meant for me," David said in a choked voice.

"No, lad, 'twas meant for any man in the way," Shawn said, and fell into a fit of coughing.

"We've had so many casualties, mostly officers," the distracted Howe said. "General Wolfe is dead and Brigadier Monckton badly wounded. Brigadier Townshend has assumed command. We have won a great victory, but the cost has been heavy."

"Ye've lost me too, your lordship," Shawn said with a weak laugh, "and to me that's the most serious loss, although General Wolfe, bless his soul, was a good lad e'en if he ne'er wore a kilt and had no use for them."

Lord Howe shook his head sadly and rode on after his men.

David ordered the men standing around to cut stout branches and contrive a litter.

Shawn coughed and there was blood in the sputum flecking his lips. "Do not bother, Davey. I was wrong for once. The ball wi' me name on it had been cast . . . must a'been a big silver one t'finish the likes o' me, don' ye think? Ah, weel, 'tis a good life I've had wi' plenty o' fightin' and plenty o' fuckin' along the way."

"Father, please don't talk. You must save your strength."

"Nonsense, lad. I've a few things t'say afore I cash in. First, there's that sweet little seamstress back in Pointe Levi. Her man went off to Lake George and one o' Willie Johnson's Mohawks scalped him. I promised t'coom back and ease the ache that left her wi' but noo—"

"Shawn, please don't—"

"Ye're my son, David, my best son . . . the one I've always had the most warmth for. Martin was such a lickspittle . . . sure and I hope he went to heaven 'cause I'd hate to meet him in hell . . . he'd proper disgrace me there."

"Shawn, for God's sake!" David said.

"Ye are a fightin' mon, David, and that's the only kind o' mon I've any use for. Fightin' and fuckin' men are the only ones worth a barrel o' powder t'blow 'em t'kingdom come. But ye think too much, laddie. Ye'd best stop thinkin' and feel. Listen to your blood, not your head. No good e'er came from listenin' to your head. Listen to your blood and your balls, mon. That's what makes the world go round, that's what makes things happen—your sword and your balls."

"Please save your strength until the surgeon gets here," David pleaded.

Shawn shook his head stubbornly. "Won't be here when the sawbones cooms. Never had no faith in 'em anyway, and noo I'm beyond e'en the help o' the great Hippocrates himself." His fingers grasped David's arm. "Promise me, Davey, that you'll go see that wee Celeste in Pointe Levi. That's unfinished business, and you're my son and should take care o' me unfinished business. Do wi' her like I would and gi'e her the few gold coins in my pack. Promise your old father, laddie, so he can die content and at peace wi' the world."

This was the most preposterous deathbed promise David had ever heard of, but it was just the sort of thing that would occur to Shawn.

"Promise me, lad, promise!"

"I promise I'll go see the girl," David said.

"Good lad. And when you get back to Johnstown, gi'e me best to your mother, and that young rascal Malcolm . . . and Aileen, especially Aileen, and her wee lassie. Ye'd best keep an eye on the two bairns, Davey, they're too close . . . and—"

His voice was noticeably weaker and the lieutenant leaned over anxiously. "Would ye like a priest, Major Glencannon?"

"No, ne'er had no use for me," Shawn said, looking up, his green eyes dancing. "Noo if ye was like to find such a thing as a priestess, that ... would be ... more like it. Her I'd ... see wi' a good will and ... "

He was still chuckling as the light faded from his eyes and they closed forever.

4

As the memories flowed through him, David was unaware of the room he sat in or that the weak December sun had fallen low in the sky. He was back in the wake of the most momentous battle yet fought in the century-long war between French and British imperialism, a battle that had decided once and for all that North America would be Anglo-Saxon rather than French, and which in some ways laid the groundwork for the war between the English colonies and the mother country.

They had made a litter from a blanket and two poles made from tree branches and placed Shawn's body on it. Toolah then moved silently to the bodies of the five Frenchmen. Drawing his scalping knife, he lifted the head of the one who had bayoneted Shawn and with a deft movement scalped the dead man. David opened his mouth to protest but closed it without doing so. Toolah had been Shawn's blood brother and he had a right to honor his fallen friend in his own way. So David averted his eyes while the Mohawk lifted the scalps of the other Frenchmen and returned to lay the grisly trophies at Shawn's feet.

"Here are the scalps of your enemies, Brother Bareshanks," Toolah said. "The men who killed you will join you in the hunting grounds beyond the last hills to be your slaves."

Shawn would have preferred the same number of young women to have accompanied him instead of men, David thought, and he had to stifle the hysterical impulse to laugh by swallowing hard.

They carried Shawn and two other rangers slain in the fighting around the flanks of the army to a camp that was being built by the British under the command of Townshend.

Seamen from the fleet were dragging cannon up the steep ascent from the river, burial parties were digging graves, and other men were collecting the wounded to be transferred to the hospital the light infantry had seized while advancing into the meadows along the banks of the St. Charles.

Taking turns digging, David, Billy, and Toolah prepared a much longer grave than those being dug close by. When it was ready, they lowered Shawn's blanket-wrapped body into it. One by one, David removed locks of varicolored hair from a pouch he had found in his father's sporran and deposited them in the grave. Some of the locks still carried the scent of their owners' perfume, but one that was almost blue-black had an outdoors smell about it.

"That is of Non-hel-e-ma," Toolah said. "She they called the grenadier squaw, a priestess and chieftain among the Shawnee. Brother Bareshanks loved her much during his year in Ohio country."

"Yes, he spoke of her," David said and waited while Toolah placed his gory trophies around Shawn's feet before throwing in the first spadeful of earth. They had barely completed their sad task when the drums began to beat assembly.

"What is it?" shouted a Royal North American ensign. "Are the French coming out again from the city?"

"No, it's Bougainville. He's arrived at last and we'll singe his arse just like we did Montcalm's."

The sun was almost directly overhead now, and David who had been awake for eighteen hours and suffered a personal loss that had not as yet begun to sink in, was called on to muster his father's rangers for battle.

The British line formed up with their backs to the city, and this time it was not so thin because there was no need to leave eighteen hundred troops to protect from surprise attack. The surviving generals, Townshend and Murray, were of the opinion that the cowardly, treacherous Governor Vaudreuil, who had held back perhaps half the troops in the city while Montcalm fought a battle, would not dare to come out now.

Nearly out on his feet, David checked the ragged ranks of his eighty-four surviving rangers and was about to order them to take their place on the left flank of the army when Bougainville appeared from the direction of Cap-Rouge. The French general had spent the morning gathering troops from detachments along the St. Lawrence. With an army of only two thousand, he realized as soon as he saw the array on the Plains of Abraham that his force was no match for the army that had already beaten his chief, so without coming any closer he turned and began a retreat toward Montreal.

Governor Vaudreuil also began a retreat, but his was done in panic. He still had an army that was stronger than the one before the city, but he fled from the Beauport lines, leaving the guns in their positions and tents still standing, abandoning Quebec to its fate. While all of this was going on, Montcalm lay dying just inside the city at the home of Dr. Arnoux.

He rallied just long enough to send a message to General Townshend.

"Monsieur, the humanity of the English sets my mind at peace concerning the fate of the French prisoners and the Canadians. Feel toward them as they have caused me to feel. Do not let them perceive that they have changed masters. Be their protector as I have been their father."

Shortly after the message came word of Montcalm's death, and when the fleet moved up to bombard the city and the English army moved to attack, a white flag was seen flying over the citadel. Soon a party of officers were seen approaching with another flag of truce to ask for terms.

With the capture of Quebec, General Townshend had left with Saunders and the fleet, and General Murray had assumed command of the city. That had been a long and bitter winter for the British garrison. Cold and hunger and sickness took their toll, especially among the Highlanders whose kilts were not made for freezing weather. Soldiers and civilians alike were on the verge of starvation when spring brought Saunders's battleships back up the river with supplies in their train and the news that an army under General Amherst had reached the St. Lawrence through the wilderness route. The end of New France was at hand.

David decided then that it was time for him and his rangers to return to the Mohawk valley. They made the trip via batteaux and the Lakes, and left Toolah at Teantontalogo, the so-called upper castle of the Mohawks.

There was sad news waiting for David at Johnstown, and it fell to his sister-in-law Aileen to relay it to him.

"Your mother is dead, David," she told him gravely. "When the news came of . . . of Shawn, she seemed to lose her desire to live. She had never been strong, as you know, and she went into a decline and never recovered despite the best Sir William's physician could do."

Aileen herself was hollow eyed and haunted-looking, her former cheerful manner as subdued as the once lively lilt of her voice. David had wondered at the striking change in her but attributed it to the responsibility that had been forced on her by his brother Martin's disappearance and probable death in the wilds of the Ohio country. And his own and Shawn's absences, hadn't made things any easier for her. With Kate's death, she had also been left with the care of Malcolm as well as her daughter Susan. He could at least relieve her of that responsibility, he thought as he walked toward his own house. He wondered again what Shawn had meant by his warning about Malcolm and Susan. Born the same year, they were uncle and niece but called each other cousin and had been raised almost like twins. But where was the harm in it? He couldn't see any, and dismissed the matter from his mind as he reached his own doorstep.

Love and happy news awaited him within. Crispin, Gifford, and Mercy Shawna had come racing to throw themselves into his arms, babbling all at once, while Felicity stood quietly beaming in the background and holding the newest member of the family, a tiny replica of herself, born seven months after his departure for the Quebec campaign. Delighted as he was to have another daughter, David was sorry that Felicity had had to go through another pregnancy by herself after the difficult time she had experienced carrying and being delivered of Shawna.

"Aye, she was trouble even before she was born, kicking and fighting to get out of her mother's belly," he said, returning from the past with a start and finding it almost dark.

"Papa? What are you doing sitting up here in the dark, you gloomy old thing?" Shawna's heavy work shoes clumped across the hardwood floor, and she had her peacoat buttoned up against the chill winter wind. "And who is it was trouble before she was ever born?"

"Ah ha, so you heard that, did you? Well, 'twas yourself I was speaking of as you know quite well."

She put her arms around him, her cheek wet and cold against his. "Am I really so much trouble, Papa? Would you rather I ran away to sea than stay here and chevy Quakers for you?"

"Your cheeks are cold and wet," he said, ignoring her question. "What have you been about?"

"My cheeks are wet and cold because it's snowing. If this keeps up, we shall have a white Christmas."

"Aye, and the Delaware will freeze over, Hopkins won't get his ships to sea before spring, and by then the British will have fifty frigates on the coasts to snap them up."

"Do you suppose brother Gifford is keeping warm in the lines around Boston?" she asked, helping him into his coat and wrapping his muffler around his neck.

"I doubt it," David said. "If he is, he'll be the first soldier to ever keep warm in wintertime."

He closed and locked the door behind them, and they were going down the outside steps when Shawna returned to her question.

"You didn't say whether you would prefer for me to run away or not."

"I didn't say because you know as well as I do that young ladies do not run away to sea."

"Anne Bonny did. I read about her."

"She was a pirate wench," David said.

"Maybe that is what I would like to be," she said, dancing on ahead of him, graceful in spite of her heavy shoes, long skirt, and peacoat. "A pirate wench with a knife in my teeth, two pistols in my belt, and ready to make any sailor lad walk the plank who refused to kiss me."

David looked up at the leaden sky from which snowflakes were falling steadily. "She is impossible, absolutely impossible!"

"You'll think me even more so when I tell you I told Seth Ewart I did not want to see him tonight after all," she said, slipping her arm through his as he caught up.

"You did what?" He looked at her in astonishment. "Why did you do that after telling him you would?"

"Because he's a sobersided clod," she said, "and because you gave him permission to court me."

"I might have known. I guess I should have forbade him to see you and you'd have fallen in his arms."

"Are you that eager to get rid of me?" she teased. "If I had known that, I would have accepted Bret Morley's proposal and run off with him to New York."

"You'd have done what?" David roared, causing a couple passing in a carriage to turn and stare at them. "What did that young scoundrel ask you to do?"

"To run away with him to New York. There was some talk of marriage later, but it was a trifle vague."

"That young bastard! I'll send Josh Humphreys around to call on him tomorrow with my challenge!"

"No, Papa, no! You're not going to fight a duel with him!" Shawna said with real concern. "He's fought several times and killed at least one man. He's a deadly shot with a pistol, they say."

"Oh? Well, how is he with a long rifle at a hundred yards?" David asked angrily. "Or with a claymore?"

"Papa, gentlemen do not fight with rifles or claymores," Shawna said. "And you're making far too much of this."

"How can I be making too much of an insult to my daughter?"

"I didn't take it as an insult," she said. "I just laughed at him. I think perhaps it was meant as a joke anyway. He is always saying outrageous things to shock people, especially when he's had a glass or two too much of 'kill devil' rum."

"Do you mean he has appeared in your presence intoxicated?" David demanded. "I won't have it! I won't have it at all!"

"Oh, he wasn't intoxicated," she said hastily. "Only a little merry."

"Well, I don't want him around. In fact, the only way I will agree not to call him out is if you promise not to see him again."

He knew as soon as the words were out that he had made a mistake.

"As you will, Father," she said, smiling sweetly. "I won't see him if you promise not to put a rifle ball between his eyes or carve him up with Shawn's old claymore."

David knew from the way she said it that she wouldn't pay the least attention to his words. Well, young Mister Morley would get a cold reception if he came calling, and if he had the gall to resent it . . .

They turned the corner into Walnut Street, passed the livery stables of Israel Israel, the residence of Bishop White, and Christ Church and approached the house where David had lived first as a bond servant to Felicity Briggs. Three years after the French war, David and Felicity had moved back into the house with their children. Using his wife's money plus what he had saved, David had been able to buy the old Penrose shipyard, which he had renamed Glencannon & Sons.

As they neared the house, David and Shawna were surprised to see Henry, their free black servant, coming toward them leading two strange horses.

"Evenin', Miz Shawna. Evenin', Mister David. We's got company," he said. "Miz Faith, she say take the hosses to de stable. I be right back and take care of your boots."

"Take your time, Henry," Shawna said. "We can put our own boots in front of the fire."

" 'Tain't fittin'," the old man said, rubbing his kinky gray hair with a gnarled fist. "No lady oughten take care of her own boots."

"Haven't you forgotten, Henry, that everyone says I'm not a lady because I get tar under my finger-nails?" Shawna said with a provocative grin at her father.

" 'Tain't fittin'," Henry said as he moved off toward Israel Israel's.

"Who do you suppose has come visiting?" David said. "The roads will be next to impossible shortly."

"Aye, and you had plans to spend the evening in your study reading, didn't you, Papa? Now you'll have to put on your best coat, your peruke and—"

"Pshaw! You know I've not worn one of those things since 1770 and ceased to even powder my hair two years ago."

" 'Tis a shame, too," she said, "because you're the handsomest man in Philadelphia, except for Uncle Benjamin. Have you heard he's to leave soon for France to represent the colonies at court?"

David grinned as he scraped the mud and slush off his boots on the device attached to the lower bar of the railing of the front porch. His old friend Benjamin Franklin could not be called handsome by any stretch of the imagination but he certainly had a way with the ladies.

The door of the two-storied, semidetached brick house opened and his younger daughter greeted them gaily. "Father, guess who's here!"

David smiled at her indulgently. She had Felicity's pale blond coloring, but her personality was much more lively and outgoing than her mother's had ever been. She looked particularly lovely tonight in the fashionable pink polonaise ordered from France. The bodice fit her tightly laced figure closely, dipping to a point in front. Two ruffles came from the back of the neck over the shoulders and descended into a rounded, low-cut neckline. The full skirt was looped up with ribbons in the back, forming three festoons with the center one slightly longer than the two at the sides. The petticoat, hooped out from the waist, fell quite vertical, reaching to a little above her ankles; the hem embellished with wide box pleating.

Shawna considered her sister's dainty appearance with some distress. Faith was built on much less generous lines than she was, her features delicate and refined rather than bold and striking. Shawna always felt big and clumsy around the younger girl. Even when they were children, she had loomed over Faith and was painfully aware of the contrast between her sister's porcelain pale complexion and her own freckled, tanned face. And although she scoffed at all those female skills Faith excelled in, she sometimes secretly envied her. Now she was wishing she had let her father buy her one of those new Paris creations also. It would have been nice to wear tonight. Not for whoever the guests were that Faith was being so coy about, but for the man she had an assignation with for later tonight. He was the real reason that she had told Seth Ewart not to call.

"Guess, Papa . . . you have to guess before you go into the sitting room," Faith was saying excitedly. "Guess who is here for the holidays!"

"Would it be Gifford home on leave from the army?" David asked, although he knew how unlikely that was.

"No, no! Guess again!" Faith was so animated and her gray eyes sparkled so that Shawna became suspicious. Her sister was only sixteen but had a very sharp eye for the male of the species.

"If it isn't Gifford, I give up," David said, hanging up his coat and muffler. "Why don't you tell me?"

"Why 'tis Malcolm, of course! Uncle Malcolm, though he seems more like a brother than an uncle."

"Malcolm." David's face lit up with pleasure. "Where is the lad? And what's he doing home from Yale so early in December?"

"He's in the sitting room, and there's someone with him." Faith paused and seemed to notice Shawna for the first time. "And you, my dear sister, must not be seen looking like a wharf rat. I'd be ashamed to have you meet Malcolm's friend in such disgraceful condition."

Shawna tossed her head disdainfully. "Who wants to meet a stupid boy from Yale? I prefer men."

"This is a man!" Faith flared. "A gentleman! And I'm sure that is something about which you know nothing!"

"Stop it," David said. "Sheath your claws and behave yourselves. You are young ladies, not alley cats."

Faith stamped her daintily shod foot. "Father, I will not have Thad Williams see her with tar on her hands and her hair all tangled and pushed back like a boy's! What will he think of me if he sees my sister looking like a longshoreman?"

"And who the bloody hell is Thad Williams and what difference does it make how he sees me looking?" Shawna demanded, hands on hips.

"Don't use that kind of language in front of your sister," David said.

"Thad Williams just happens to be the son of Samuel Williams probably the most important merchant prince in New York!" Faith hissed.

Shawna saw her father frown. So many of the New York merchants were Tories. David Glencannon had always taken being a Whig very seriously and now that the fighting had actually begun, his dislike for those who remained loyal to German George was more and more evident.

"All right, sister, if you think this gentleman friend of Malcolm's is so grand that he'll be shocked by my appearance, I'll go up to my room and bathe and change before he has to face the ordeal of meeting me."

She turned quickly and ran up the stairs, calling for Molly, the Irish lass who acted as lady's maid to both Glencannon daughters. "Molly! Molly, where are you, you bog-trotting beauty? And where's the water for my bath?"

"Comin', Miss, comin'!" Molly's voice drifted up the back stairs from the kitchen.

Shawna tossed off her peacoat and the shapeless dress she had worn at the shipyard. Her heavy workmen's shoes were deposited outside the door for Henry to take care of, and then she went to stand before the fire burning in the grate, holding out her hands to the welcome heat.

"Ah, 'tis that cold I'm reluctant to touch myself without warming my hands," she muttered to herself. "I hope this cold snap doesn't cool a certain gentleman's ardor."

She felt herself blushing at the boldness of her tongue. Her darling papa would be dismayed if he knew she was actually encouraging the storming of her virtue by Bret Morley.

When her fingers felt like fingers instead of frozen sticks, she unfastened and slipped out of the one petticoat she had on. She turned to face the mirror and briefly surveyed herself.

"You're not all that hard to take, my lass," she murmured. "Your snip of a sister may think you look like a wharf rat, but men look at you with a different eye."

Quickly stripping off her shift, she took a closer look, inspecting critically the tall, lithe body with its high jutting breasts, flat and long, smoothly muscled thighs.

"Well, then, Missy, are ye all ready for your bath?" Molly asked as she pushed open the door and came in lugging two buckets of hot water. She was red faced and sweating as she walked over to the round wooden tub set behind a screen near the fire. "Are ye admirin' yourself because o' the young gentleman come home with Mister Malcolm?"

Shawna snatched a dressing gown from the large mahogany armoire, embarrassed that the girl had caught her so brazenly studying her own nudity. "I hope that water is hot," she said shortly.

" 'Tis hot enough to boil lobsters, and that's what ye'll be lookin' like if ye don't wait till I bring some cold to cool it down." She emptied the buckets into the tub. "Don't see why a body has to use one o' these things. Seems like ye could wash your hands and face in a wash bowl."

"Maybe you could but I can't," Shawna said, testing the water with a big toe and drawing it back quickly. "My father learned the value of bathing in the Indies and raised us to value it."

The servant girl sniffed. "Well, since ye get yourself so dirty doin' unwomanly work at the shipyard, it's just as well."

"Go get cold water and shut your phiz or ye'll be gettin' me fist in it!" Shawna said, speaking to the girl in her own idiom.

"Yes, mum, Miss Shawna," Molly said and hurried out without further comment.

"That wench is going to try my temper one too many times," Shawna muttered and fell to gazing at her image in the mirror again, thinking about Bret Morley and the trick he had of kissing a girl behind the ear. She must remember to daub on a drop of the French perfume her father had brought her on his last trip to New York. Yes, that would draw a great many kisses behind the ear, and perchance a few on the lips as well.

Half an hour later, clad in clean shift and petticoat she was going through her wardrobe looking for a suitable dress.

There was the silk sac gown Benjamin Franklin had sent her from England when he was there negotiating with Parliament, but it was a flowered thing, pink flowers at that, and Faith had chosen to wear pink tonight. Besides, pink didn't go well with her red hair. She settled for a green-striped poplin with a quilted petticoat. It was rather too bulky to set off her figure, but Bret had seen her in her riding habit and didn't have to be made any more aware of that.

But right now she had to go downstairs and welcome her young uncle home and meet his friend. She brushed her shining hair into a cluster of curls on top, pinned it back at the sides and let the back fall into a natural cascade. Then daubing perfume behind her ears and between the white mounds of her breasts, which the frock displayed so fetchingly, she quitted her room and went down the front stairs. As she approached the sitting room, she heard her father's voice and knew he was angry. Not that he was yelling, or even speaking loudly; it was the tightly controlled tone of his speech that alerted her.

Malcolm's friend must have turned out to be a Tory, she thought. That could cause problems if Faith had really taken a liking to the young man.

Fixing a smile on her face, Shawna pushed open the sliding door to the sitting room and entered. Crossing to Malcolm, she threw her arms around him. "Well, scholar, are you playing hooky or did they chase you out of the citadel of learning?"

Malcolm Glencannon, the youngest son of Shawn and Kate, looked more like his brother David than like his father. He was tall and slender with the same hawklike beak of a nose, and the same sandy hair, which he wore unpowdered and combed back into a queue. Only the eyes were different. Instead of David's cool gray eyes, Malcolm's were brown with an intriguing shadow in their depths that added to their appeal.

"You grow more beautiful every day," he told Shawna, kissing her warmly. "If they had a school for young ladies at Yale, every male student in the place would be beating a pathway to your door."

"Oh la, sir, your flattery quite turns my poor head," Shawna said, fluttering her lashes at him.

Malcolm laughed and hugged her. "Not yours, little sister. "Yours is as cool as your hair is fiery."

"Don't be too sure of that," David said. "She's a wild one is our Shawna. Her grandfather's very image sometimes."

Malcolm's smile was quizzical. "I've been away too long. "I didn't realize father had come back to haunt us in female form."

"You should introduce your guest, Malcolm," David said, and Shawna could tell from the way he said it that her father didn't care for the young man in the least.

"Yes, of course. Shawna, my dear, this is Thad Williams, my classmate and friend."

Thad Williams appeared to be a year or so younger than Malcolm. He was of medium height and wore his hair in a style known as a "disheveled crop," with a curl or puff carried over the top of the head from ear to ear and a pigtail queue. He was almost too handsome, Shawna thought. His straight nose, full lips, and high cheekbones gave him an almost feminine delicacy. Dressed in the height of fashion, his high-waisted double-breasted dark brown coat had a high stand-fall collar; his tan waistcoat was quite short, cut even higher than the coat. Skintight buckskin riding breeches were stuffed into knee-high brightly polished black boots.

"Your servant, ma'am," Williams said, making an elegant leg.

"I am pleased to make your acquaintance, Mister Williams," Shawna replied and curtsied gracefully.

"Isn't he exciting?" Faith whispered to her sister later when they were going in to dinner. "Handsome, sophisticated, and so intelligent."

"I think he's something of a prig," Shawna said, "and I know Papa doesn't like him."

"Oh, he's just being an old bear," Faith said. "He'll come around. He always does when I work on him."

Shawna had to admit that was true. In spite of the fact that she was much closer to her father, the younger girl could usually manipulate him more easily.

"You can try, but you know how intensely he feels about freedom," Shawna said.

Young Williams had spent the whole time before Henry announced dinner explaining why it was necessary for the colonies to make peace with the Crown.

"My father says we will suffer economic disaster. Our overseas commerce will be ruined."

"It is already ruined by the Navigation Acts," David had replied with that same cool tightness in his voice.

"Ah, but a proper attitude on our part would convince Whitehall that we've learned our lesson. Then there would surely be some relaxation of the Navigation Acts, which were brought about by the folly of some of our leaders."

David's Adam's apple had moved under his cravat, and for a moment Shawna had thought he was going to explode into fury at the arrogant young puppy who was sitting here in his own home telling him that the policies he had worked for were to blame for the situation the colonies had found themselves in before they had taken up arms. But with a self-control she found admirable, but was unable to master herself, he simply turned to Malcolm and changed the subject.

"You must ride over to Germantown in the morning to see Aileen and Susan. They have been living alone there since Susan's husband's death."

Malcolm's face lit up. "How is Susan? It seems like years since I saw her. Was she much grieved over Conrad's death?"

Conrad Hurwitz, the much older man Susan had married following an unhappy love affair about which neither Shawna nor any member of her immediate family knew any details, had passed away the year before. That had been shortly after Sir William Johnson's death and Molly Brent's departure for Canada with her children and Sir John Johnson. Aileen, the long-time companion and secretary to Sir William's Indian wife, had then left Johnstown herself, coming to Germantown to be with her widowed daughter.

After dinner, they returned to the sitting room where brandy was served to the men and port to the two girls. They couldn't seem to keep away from the subject of politics, and David, of course, was firmly opposed to the freely expressed Royalist view of Williams. Faith hung on every word Thad uttered, and Malcolm seemed to more or less side with him. Shawna, having had three glasses of port rather than her usual one, was feeling a bit giddy and wondering how long it would be before she could slip away.

It was nearing nine-thirty and her tête-à-tête was for ten, so she would have to make an excuse before too long. But she was interested in Malcolm's attitude. She knew that in his early years he had been raised almost exclusively by her grandmother Kate and Aileen, both of whom were bitterly opposed to war for obviously personal reasons. Kate had lost three sons because of conflicts between peoples of differing political beliefs: Shawn Junior had fallen in battle during the abortive effort to restore James III to the throne of England; Martin, the oldest and her favorite, wounded in body and spirit at Culloden, had never fully recovered, and finally his mind had snapped completely under the cruel treatment of his master in the new land and he had wandered off into the wilderness to die; Steven, while still alive, she had never seen again after he left with the frontier forces to fight against the French in Acadia. Added to that was the fact that almost her entire married life had been spent waiting for Shawn to return from one war or another only to eventually lose him too.

Aileen had shared her mother-in-law's griefs, and when David had brought Felicity to Johnstown, they had all but adopted her Quakerish beliefs, and Malcolm couldn't have helped being influenced by them.

But was that all there was too it, Shawna wondered. Was Malcolm simply a pacifist, or was he leaning toward the Tory view? He seemed to have considerable respect for Thad's opinions, and from several remarks he'd made, she understood he had become estranged from his old friends Ben Tallmadge, Robert Townshend, and particularly, Nathan Hale and his brother. All of them were ardent patriots, but she could hardly believe that Malcolm and Nathan would have broken up their close friendship over politics.

She hoped they hadn't, but she was more concerned at the moment with her own affairs than with Malcolm's. She had to make an excuse and get away.

When her fourth glass of port was half finished, she got to her feet. "I really think I must retire," she said, pretending to be more affected by the wine than she was. "I . . . I seem to have had a sip too many."

David frowned at her. "I hope that in addition to all your grandfather's less admirable traits, you're not going to take that one up too."

"No, dear Papa," she said, bending to kiss him on the forehead before turning to Malcolm. "And you, sir, I expect to report to the shipyard in work clothes just as soon as you've visited Aunt Aileen and cousin Susan."

Malcolm laughed. "But I'm on holiday, my dear girl."

"From that alleged house of learning, perhaps, but Glencannon & Sons does not close for the Christmas holidays, especially when we have ships to build for the Continental navy."

"The Continental navy? Has it gone that far? If so, I really do not feel I can be of any help at the yard."

"*Have you gone that far?*" Shawna shot back and noticed that her father looked pleased with her. "Have you gone that far toward their side.

"No," Malcolm said calmly. "I am neutral."

"There is no neutral ground between good and evil," David said, "or between right and wrong."

5

Shawna said her good nights and fled up the stairs. Putting the unpleasant situation that was developing downstairs out of her mind, she hurriedly took her warmest cloak and a broad-brimmed felt hat from her wardrobe, turned down the whale oil lamp, and slipped silently down the back way and out the kitchen door.

It had stopped snowing and was a clear chill night with the stars glittering in icy brilliance above her. Shivering and pulling the cloak more tightly about her, Shawna unlatched the gate in the whitewashed wooden fence and went out into the alleyway beyond. It was as dark as pitch in the alley, and the cold wind brought sounds of raucous laughter from the Three Mariners tavern on Front Street. That bothered her; it could be mighty unpleasant for an unescorted young woman to run into a swaggering drunken sailor or two at this time of night. But she was a big strong girl and had only a block to go, so she hurried on down toward the street.

It was lighter in the street but certainly no warmer, the icy wind off the Delaware was stonger here. Fortunately, she didn't have to wait long. As she emerged from the alley, a closed landau pulled by four grays that had been waiting at the corner started toward her, and in a few moments the coachman was helping her through the door.

"So there you are, my redheaded termagant," a man's voice greeted her. "I thought I'd surely freeze before you came to me."

She was pulled unceremoniously into his lap while his lips fastened passionately on hers. The hot, hungry embrace stirred the girl's senses in a way she had never experienced before, but she put her hands against the broad chest and pushed the man away, trying to slide off his lap.

"Bret Morley, you are impossible," she said. "I break all the rules of polite society and my own code of behavior to see you, and you take advantage of it to assault me indecently."

Bret's laugh was reckless. "You haven't seen how I work if you call that being assaulted. You've still all your clothes on, haven't you?"

"Yes, and I intend to keep them on," she said, glaring at the craggy-faced young man whose shock of black hair defied any attempt to keep it tied in a queue.

"Don't say such things or you'll ruin my evening before it begins," Bret said as the carriage rolled over the rough cobblestones. "You promised to me to come to my rooms, didn't you?"

"Yes, and that's all I promised. We can't very well spend the evening riding around in this frigid weather."

"As long as your lips are not frigid, my love," Bret said and captured her mouth with his again.

"No, Bret, please . . . " His tongue stabbed past her teeth as she tried to speak, and the fire it started in her mouth began spreading to the rest of her body.

"Please what, lovely Shawna?" His tone was light but his voice shook a little with the intensity of his lust.

"Please don't do that." His fingers were on her breasts, and she could feel them sinking into her sensitive flesh through dress and underclothing.

"Don't you like it, my darling? Doesn't it make you feel good?" He had located a nipple and was stroking it into life. She could feel it swelling under his expert touch. Until tonight she hadn't realized her potential for passion.

Trying to take her mind off the strange sensations that were flooding her senses, Shawna asked, "Where are you staying?"

"At the Capital Inn on Second between Chestnut and Maple. 'Tis a very fancy place run by a board of directors and advertises that it has a 'Genteel Coffee-Room properly supplied with English and American papers and Magazines.' John Adams and other of my fellow members of Congress stay there. The porter, I have found, is a larcenous fellow and I've greased his palm well, so he'll look the other way when I take a lady up to my rooms."

"And I'm sure he'll think I'm not a lady."

Bret shrugged. "It depends on what you expect of a lady," he said, raising the hem of her dress to expose the rounded calf. "They say the Tory ladies of Boston speed quickly to the lodgings of General Gates and his officers when they crook their fingers, and they are the *crème de la crème* of Boston society."

"No Tory could possibly be a lady," Shawna said disdainfully.

"Ah, such certainty, my sweet rebel. What real difference does it make, Congress or king, Tory or Whig, as long as you've a full table, a strong bottle, and a warm body to love?"

"Why, Bret, and you a delegate to the Congress!" She was genuinely shocked. "What would the people you represent think of such a statement?"

"What do I care what they think," he whispered, his hand moving up her calf to her knee. "All I care about at this minute is what gloriously fleshed legs you have and what a marvelously kissable mouth."

Shawna was fighting the feelings that were threatening to engulf her. His lips on hers were holding her enthralled, and the tingling of his fingers as they trailed higher and higher was almost unbearably exciting.

Some small part of her brain was nagging at her, however, wouldn't let her give way completely. This wasn't the way she had planned it. She wanted to talk, about marriage, about the future, about a lot of things, but Bret was getting her mixed up, confusing her with physical passion to the point where she could hardly tell reality from illusion.

"Such a beautiful child," Bret was whispering as his fingers caressed the soft flesh on the insides of her thighs and his lips pressed kisses down the side of her neck. "Such a lovely, long-legged, satin-skinned child."

"No, please, Bret, not this way," she said suddenly and struggled to regain control of her emotions, to fight off the crazy desire that was causing her heart to pound. "We have to talk, have to settle some matters."

"We can talk later," Bret whispered, nibbling at her earlobe. "There's always time for talking but never enough for love."

He was so impetuous. In that, she thought, he must be a lot like Shawn had been. When Shawn had seen a woman he wanted, he set out to get her, uncaring of any obstacles in the way. She admired Shawn more than any person she knew of, except perhaps her father, and had been amused by tales of his amorous conquests, but now somehow it seemed different. When one was the woman whose affections were being stormed, there had to be some thought taken. She had never considered how the women felt whom Shawn had loved and left. Had they felt cheated? Deserted? Did they pine for him for years, or had they enjoyed the brief fling as much as he had and with as little regret? There was no way she would ever know, but she did know that if she let Bret take her on his terms, she would find out for herself what such a liaison entailed.

But that was ratiocination and had nothing to do with the feelings of wild longing, the need to be wanted the way Bret wanted her, and the desperate yearning his hands and his mouth were arousing in her.

"Stop, please, stop," Shawna gasped as his fingers reached the apex of her thighs and began to glide along the fabric of her drawers. "You can't just touch me any place you please. You can't just take me without my permission. Bret, I must have time to think."

"Thinking is bad for your health," he murmured. "You have to feel . . . you have to follow what your body tells you to do, and, my darling, I can tell exactly what your body is telling you to do."

"How . . . how can you tell?"

"Because your thighs opened to my touch," he whispered. "They didn't even try to close."

"Oh, no, no," she moaned, feeling the truth of what he claimed. The touch of those knowing fingers was like a flicker of fire moving along the crotch of her drawers, tracing the outline of the thick muff and gently probing at the tender flesh of her femaleness.

This had to stop! If it didn't stop now, there would be no stopping at all. She could hear the *clop*, *clop*, *clop* of the horses' hooves, hear the rumble of the carriage wheels on the cobblestones, hear the sound of people's voices in the street, but here in the darkness of the carriage, they were as alone as if stranded on a deserted island. All she had to fight with was her reason and whatever moral strength she possessed.

She closed her traitorous thighs so abruptly and with such force that Bret let out a muffled yelp and withdrew his hand.

"What the devil brought that on?" he demanded fiercely. "I know you liked it. I could feel the response. . . . I could feel the wetness."

"What you could feel does not matter," she said firmly. "What does matter is that I am me. I own my body and I'll make the decision about what to do with it."

"Oh. Well, we're almost at the inn now," he said, hiding his disappointment. "We'll go to my rooms and have some refreshments and maybe you will change your mind."

"It will have to be my mind that is changed," she said. "I am not going to let it be run by emotions."

"Hmmmm. You are a very strange girl," he said. "Very strange. When you agreed to come to my rooms tonight, I thought you . . . well, that you know what I expected."

"What you thought and what I intended seem to be altogether different things," she said. "I may decide not to go to your rooms at all unless you assure me that you will not try to take me without my expressed consent. I want no more of this storming of my emotions, this knowing what my body wants. If we did only what our bodies wanted, we would probably never do a day's work but spend all our time eating and drinking."

"My, my, what a puzzling little creature you are," he said, looking at her as though she were an odd new game animal that had defied his ability to bring it down with dog or gun.

"I, sir, am not at all small. In fact, I stand almost at your own height, and without boots."

"A virago, a veritable daughter of Mars," he said mockingly as the carriage came to a halt before the inn.

"And I've the muscle equal of many a man," she said and raised her fist. "And this is as hard as it looks."

He leaned forward and kissed the fist thrust under his nose, and suddenly she laughed and slipped off his lap as she heard the coachman cough discreetly before opening the door of the carriage.

Bret descended from the carriage and offered her his arm. She drew a deep breath, ducked her head to keep her hat from being knocked off, and descended to the ground. They had pulled up in the rear of the splendid brick building of the newest and finest inn in Philadelphia, and Bret led her through a small private door into a long, carpeted hallway. There was no one in sight and the lights had been dimmed.

"There are back stairs where we may discreetly reach my rooms," he said. "I want no scandal to touch your name."

"Thank you," she said, surprised at the sudden change in his manner from would-be ravager to considerate suitor. "You seem to have undergone a transformation."

"Think of me as having reformed," he said. "Perhaps I have had a religious experience."

Shawna giggled as they started up the stairs. "You didn't need to go that far."

"Don't worry, I haven't," he said, slipping an arm around her until his hand could cover her right breast.

"However, we can do without that," she said and removed the hand. "We must search for the happy mean the Greeks talked about."

"The only Greek I ever knew was a one-eyed boatman who couldn't be trusted with his own daughter," Bret laughed.

"Oh la, sir, you mean you do not have the classics," she said mockingly as he opened the door to his rooms and bowed her in.

"All awaits you, madame, including a chilled bottle of wine, oysters, and other delicacies to tempt your palate. Afterward I shall tempt your other faculties with even sweeter delights."

She looked at him through slitted green eyes. "Remember, it will have to be done with words . . . words and declarations, not with the tactics of a batallion of grenadiers storming a fortress."

She stepped through the door and waited while he turned up the lamp, bathing the room in lovely amber light.

"Your wrap, my lady, and your hat. And then if my lady would be pleased to have a chair." Bret was playing his polite gentleman role to the hilt.

Shawna looked around the room in astonishment. It didn't look at all like a room in an inn. There was the usual fireplace, of course, but the furniture and rugs were more like those of a private home whose owner had exquisite and expensive tastes. A desk, a china cabinet, and bookshelves lined one wall; several chairs and a settee were placed at pleasing angles, giving the whole a rich and elegant air. The furniture all had fretted cornices and latticework, with delicately fretted galleries and distinctive cluster-column legs of almost Gothic inspiration.

"How beautiful," Shawna said. "Is it the custom of the Capital Inn to furnish its rooms so handsomely?"

For the first time since she had known him, Bret Morley looked a little uncomfortable. "No, I must confess the furniture is mine. It was brought from England by my father where it was made by a man named Thomas Chippendale. When I had to sell my father's place in New York City, I saved a few pieces for my own comfort and to impress my colleagues in the Congress. Does it please you?"

"You had to sell your father's house? I thought you had endless stores of money."

"I did, but my luck at the cards has not been as good as it might. Whist, I am afraid, is not my game."

"Then you must stay away from gambling or try some other game," Shawna said.

"I want to try another game, my love," he said. "The oldest and sweetest game in the world, and I want to try it with you."

"That is not a game," Shawna said, although she knew her much admired grandfather had treated it as such. "That is an involvement."

Bret winced. "Do not speak of involvements. That is such a sticky word."

"Not nearly so sticky as being left on the dock after the ship has sailed," she said.

He smiled and turned to a low table where a wine bottle was sitting in a bucket of pond ice. Pulling the cork, which made a popping sound, he poured a golden liquid into a long-stemmed glass. "Here, try some of this. It could alter your whole outlook on life."

She took the glass and sniffed suspiciously at the bubbling amber contents. "What is this?"

"Try it," he said. "I think you will be surprised. It is very mild compared to other drinks."

He lifted his glass and swallowed almost half its fizzing bubbles. Watching him, Shawna decided that it must not be very strong if he could do that, and since he was drinking out of the same bottle, it couldn't be anything that would harm her. The effects of the port she had had earlier had worn off during the ride and the struggle in the carriage, so she wasn't afraid of getting drunk. Besides, hadn't she on occasion downed a tankard of gunpowder-flavored Jamaica rum with sailors from the ships being repaired at Glencannon & Sons yard?

She took a sip of the sparkling liquid and felt a tickling in her nose and a stinging of her tongue. "It tickles."

"Ah, but ever so nicely. It is called champagne and comes from France. My father had several cases in his cellar and I managed to save a few for my own use."

She took another sip and wrinkled her nose.

"Here, let me pour you a little more," he said. "The taste and bouquet have a way of growing on one. There is an interesting story that goes with the wine, about how it was discovered and later introduced at court."

Now that she had drunk a glass of the stuff, Shawna was feeling more relaxed and less distrustful of his motives. The fire was warm and she was beginning to enjoy the tingling in her nose and mouth. She stretched out her legs and sank back in the chair. Through an open door, she could see a large canopied bed, but although its implications disturbed her, she dismissed it with the thought that she was fully in command of her senses and intended to stay that way.

"The story begins with a group of monks in the Province of Champagne in France—"

"Papists?" she asked as he poured them each another glass of wine. "This is a papist drink?"

"Yes, but good wine knows no religion. These monks were of the Benedictine order and by 1668 they had been in the business of making wine for some time and—"

"I thought their business was praying," she giggled.

"True, but even monks can't pray twenty-four hours a day, and they needed to support themselves so they made wine."

"That's better than making trouble like our Quaker friends do here in Philadelphia."

"Well, the wine master was a certain Dom Perignon, and he wasn't satisfied with the wine they were producing. He would say to the other monks, 'Champagne is called the Garden of France and we have the finest grapes, so why should we not have the finest wine?' "

Shawna was staring dreamily into the fire, listening with one ear while thinking about far seas and far places . . . and great tall ships that her father would build to take her to those places where she would find adventure and romance. She didn't notice when Bret filled her glass for the third time.

"So Dom Perignon tried to improve the wine. He set out to blend the best grapes of the area to produce a wine that would outdo everything in taste, color, and fragrance. He finally came up with what he considered a perfect blend. Its color was superb, its taste delicious, and the bouquet like that of the flowers that covered the hills of Champagne."

"But the bubbling, what caused the bubbling?" Shawna asked.

"Ah, I am coming to that," he said, bending over to kiss her and tease her lips with the tip of his tongue.

"One day, what seemed like a terrible thing happened. The wine master was poring over his records when he heard a loud explosion. He rushed down to the cellar and discovered that a bottle of his new wine had exploded."

"Dangerous stuff," Shawna said, looking at the bubbles rising in her glass. "Hope it doesn't do that in my stomach."

Bret laughed as he opened another bottle and filled her glass to the rim. "It won't." He kissed her again and again, long, lingering kisses that sent chills up and down her spine and set her heart to thumping wildly.

"What happened to the Dom?" she gasped when he finally released her lips. He had pulled a footstool close and propped her feet up on it, making room to sit beside them and lean toward her heaving bosom. She knew he must be aware of the way those kisses had shaken her, but he made no mention of it.

"Well, naturally he was astonished and horrified, but as he looked at the shattered bottle, he noticed bubbles in what remained in the base of the bottle. Careful to avoid the broken glass, he tasted the wine. Suddenly he was exultant. He had never tasted anything like it. With a yell he raced up to the refectory where the other brothers were sitting down to the noon meal.

" 'Brothers', he shouted, 'I have been drinking stars!' "

Shawna looked down into the wine glass and watched the bubbles rising upward just the way stars seemed to move on a particularly clear night at sea. "Yes . . . yes," she said in a tone of wonder, "that's what it's like . . . it's like drinking stars!"

6

Several glasses of champagne and many kisses later, Shawna let Bret pull her up out of the chair and guide her over to the beautifully carved and upholstered settee where he settled her down gently, his body warm and vibrant against hers.

"Bret, I feel so vague and unsure of things," she murmured as he began to kiss her neck and work his way down to the upper slope of her breasts, which the striped dress revealed. "I'm so confused. I thought I knew what I wanted out of life but now I'm not sure."

"Perhaps the stars you've been drinking got into your eyes," he whispered, reaching to unfasten the back of her dress and ease it off her shoulders so that more of her breasts was exposed to the burning pleasure of his kisses.

"Please . . . you were going to tell me more about champagne," she said, trying to distract him, to put off for a while longer the inevitable.

"Hmmm, let me see, what else do I know about champagne." He had managed to work one breast free of her corset and shift, and she gazed with the helpless fascination of a rabbit hypnotized by a snake as he kissed his way up one white slope and down the other, letting the tip of his tongue trail across the erect nipple.

"Well, the best champagne . . . they . . . tell me" —he was speaking between licks at her throbbing nipple, which had swollen to three times its normal size—"comes from the area where the River Marne passes the city of Rheims. The grapes Dom Perignon first used were a mixture of black Pinot Noir and white Chardonnay. The wine is matured in the labyrinthian tunnels of the old chalk quarries around Rheims and—"

He stopped speaking as his mouth filled with the whole point of one breast, the hard button of the nipple against his tongue and the rest of the sensitive flesh between his gentle sucking lips.

Shawna moaned and her head rolled from side to side, fanning her coppery hair into a gleaming halo under the lamplight. She felt his hands reaching for hers but had no strength to resist when he moved it to his body.

"Oh, God!" The words were a husky whisper as she touched what he intended her to touch there betweeen his thighs. His skintight breeches were strained to the bursting point by the great thick thing she couldn't believe was real.

"Do you feel that, my darling? Do you feel what you've done to me, how you've made me swell with passion for you? Can you imagine how painful it is in its present configuration? You don't want to deny me the simple remedy that will make it right, do you?"

"But it's not . . . my fault . . . not my fault," she whispered, her head spinning from the effects of the wine and the rush of new and strange sensations that were surging through her. She wanted to take her hand away but found she couldn't. Her fingers insisted on tracing up and down the length of the distended male organ, and her imagination conjured up erotic fantasies of how it might feel to have the monstrous rod invade the secret of her womanhood.

She opened her eyes as she felt him stand, and then he was lifting her in his arms and walking toward the open door beyond which stood the bed she had noticed earlier.

"Oh Bret . . . Bret," she gasped.

"You are not going to tell me to stop," he whispered, "not this time, not now?"

"No, but we have to talk about us," she said. "About love and about marriage."

"Yes, we really must," he said. "Afterward, we'll have a long talk about them and see if they bear any relation to each other."

There was something wrong with that, but somehow Shawna couldn't make her mind figure out what. It was impossible to think about anything with Bret's tongue deep in her mouth and his lips sucking passionate kisses from the depth of her very soul. His fingers were rapidly unhooking her dress as they swayed beside the bed, bodies locked together.

Shawna's resistance was gone and she knew it. She needed what Bret needed, wanted it desperately and passionately.

"My darling . . . my beautiful darling," Bret said huskily as Shawna's dress fell into a pool about her feet. Her petticoats and corset quickly followed, leaving her breasts standing high and free under the silky shift.

Bret's hands went immediately to her breasts, slipping under the loose garment to cup the jutting mounds, fingering the rosy nipples into rock hardness and squeezing the firm white flesh cradled in his palms.

A long shuddering sigh escaped Shawna and suddenly she didn't want to wait any longer. She untied the drawstring of her drawers and let them fall onto the pile of clothing already heaped by the side of the bed. Then she reached for the fastening of Bret's trousers. He had already shed his coat and waistcoat and laughed at the way she was fumbling with the rest of his clothing.

"So eager, my lady. Such a gorgeous, hungry baby."

"Bret, don't laugh at me. . . . Don't tease me," she whispered, pressing close to him, her mouth against the side of his face, breasts pushing into his chest. "I've never been with a man. I want to love you . . . want you to love me."

"Mmmmm," he murmured, tucking the shift up out of the way and running a caressing hand over her belly and thighs before closing in on the curly thatch of red hair between the long, tapering thighs.

Shawna's knees buckled at the touch of those exploring fingers, and at the same instant his trousers dropped, tripping him, so that they fell onto the bed with Shawna on top. She wriggled out of the shift and lay locked in his arms totally nude, her whole body seething with the desperate need he had produced in her.

Bret's lips captured hers again, his tongue leisurely circling her mouth, probing and searching just as his fingers were doing in the lubricous folds beyond the unguarded gate of her virginal valley.

"Tight," he whispered, lips sliding over her jaw to her ear, "so tight I wonder if you can take me."

"I can," she panted as he rolled her over so his lean, hard body was on top of hers. She felt the strong chest crushing her breasts, the flat belly pushing against hers and the strong thighs forcing hers wide apart.

"I hope you remember this night fondly for the rest of your life," he whispered, and she felt the great male thickness of him pressing down onto the mound that marked her womanhood.

"I'll do my best not to hurt you, I really will, even though I am wild to take you as violently as would the stallion you make me feel like."

"Oh, Bret, I love you so much," she husked, stroking her hands across the smooth-skinned, muscular shoulders and back and feeling a yearning to take him to herself and never let him go.

She slipped one hand between them, wanting to touch the awesome hardness of him, wanting to feel the hot, rigid maleness pulse against her fingers. She grasped the turgid shaft, and he lay still to let her explore it, to feel its length and thickness and wonder for the first time if she were really capable of holding so much man flesh.

He didn't give her much time to think about it. Gently he removed her hand and guided the bulging knob of that powerful phallus toward the quivering crevice it sought.

She could hear someone breathing heavily and knew it must be Bret because she was holding her breath almost in fear, certainly in anticipation. She knew he longed to stab deep inside her without thought of the pain or damage he might inflict and was grateful that he was holding back and not using her as a man might have used a woman of more experience. She loved him for his consideration but also longed to cry out that he should batter down the protective membrane and take her completely no matter how painful it might be.

"A little deeper . . . a little deeper each time," he panted, probing and pushing into the tight sheath, "until finally all the way . . . all the way to make us one, to make our bodies a single flame of lust."

"Yes, yes, I want that," she said. "I don't care if it hurts. I have to feel it all."

Then she was clenching her teeth to keep from crying out as she felt the stretching, burning, scraping her hitherto unused flesh was being subjected to. She braced her hands against his upper thighs, trying to hold off and at the same time urge him on. Shifting her hips from side to side to ease the ache of the penetration, she managed to let him sink farther in without increasing the discomfort that struggled with passion for her attention.

Finally he could hold back no longer, his intense passion overcame his sensitivity and he surged all the way into her. Shawna felt a blinding flash of lancing pain as he struck and smashed through the hymen, felt the hot wetness that must be blood and then an easing of the friction as his thrusts continued at a furious pace.

The fury couldn't last long. He gasped suddenly, almost as though in pain, and she felt another flood of hot liquid before he went limp on top of her. She clasped him close, pleased with herself for having been able to take all he offered, but knowing that she had not experienced the same pleasure from the act that he had. If only it had lasted a little longer; she was just beginning to enjoy it when it was over. She wished desperately that they could start all over again because now that the pain was past she was sure she could cooperate fully and attain the same heights of blissful release that Bret had.

As though in answer to her wish, Bret stirred, kissed the hollow at the base of her throat, and began moving, slowly and carefully until his full strength returned, then with more vigor. His hands slid down her sides to hold and position her while he whispered suggestions about how she should move and what she should do to increase the thrilling contact that now was sending her floating upward on a cloud of exquisite sensation. At the end she cried out as all the coiled up sensuality inside her burst loose with such force that it startled Bret as well as herself, leaving them awed and shaken.

When their breathing had quieted and they were about to doze off, Shawna remembered something. "We still haven't had our talk," she said sleepily.

"Later, my darling," Bret murmured. "The night is young. We will take pleasure in each other again presently. There is always time for talk."

She awakened first and reached for him, eager to repeat the experience, to know again the wonder of being loved. Rolling close to him, she strewed feather-light kisses across his shoulders and down onto the dark, crisply curling hair of his chest. His arms came around her even before his eyes opened, and then he was laughing huskily. "My, my, what an eager little virgin."

"No virgin now," she said just before his mouth began to devour hers. "I can still feel the sweet ache of my deflowering."

"And no doubt you're wondering why you bothered to keep it all this time."

"No, I'm not," she said. "I know why. I was saving it for you, the man I love . . . the man I'm going to marry."

She hardly noticed that he made no response because he chose that moment to roll over on top of her, pin her to the mattress and start them once more on their deliriously exciting climb to the gates of paradise.

An hour later she was being helped into the waiting carriage, shivering in the chill air and wishing she hadn't been so foolish as to have let Bret cajole her into letting him keep her lace-edged silk drawers. He had sworn that he would keep them forever in memory of their first night together, just as he would treasure the sheet upon which he had taken her because it was stained with her virgin's blood.

She felt her face flame at the memory and wondered guiltily if somehow the coachman had guessed as he handed her up into the landau that she was naked under her petticoats. That was nonsense, she told herself sharply. There had been no hint at all in the man's manner to make her think such a thing. The only thing he knew was that she was returning from a gentleman's rooms at a late hour, and if he suspected she was a light-o'-love who had been well played during the hours spent there, he gave no sign. When they reached the corner by the alley, he helped her out as respectfully as he had handed her in, tipped his hat, and bade her a dignified good night.

Shawna sped down the dark alley hoping that everyone was in bed and sound asleep. Opening the gate, she stole silently past the woodshed and across the yard to the back door, breathing a sigh of relief as she heard the faint snores of Molly and the cook coming from their room off the pantry. She crept up the back stairs and down the hall to her room, unaware that she was holding her breath until she let it out in a grateful sigh as she shut the door behind her.

Later Shawna was to remember those December days as having been lived in a golden haze of love and lust. During the day she performed her usual tasks around the shipyard with her customary efficiency, but her mind was not really on them. That part of her life she got through automatically and only really came alive during her clandestine visits to Bret's where her lessons in lust continued apace. Every hour she spent with him was an amorous delight, for it seemed he could constantly invent a new way, always had an increasingly delicious confection of passion to introduce her to. She was amazed to find herself changing from innocent, naïve teenager to mature, sexually aroused woman whose life was starting to revolve around a bed and a man and the things they did together in the night.

One of those things had been so radically different from common practice that she had been slightly scandalized at first but had quicky learned the advantages it provided for a woman.

After the ritual glass of champagne and the slow, languorous interval of undressing each other, Bret had stretched out on the bed one night, lying on his back with the erect shaft of his manhood standing up like a tower. Shawna had stared at it and then into his smoldering eyes, not knowing what he intended but eager for whatever joy he would introduce her to next.

"I think we will reverse our approach tonight," he said in answer to her questioning look.

Her green eyes turned puzzled, and with a soft laugh he pulled her to him and whispered in her ear, "You on top, my precious. I shall lie here unresisting but passive while you make love to me."

She sucked in her breath, excited in spite of the feeling of shock at transposing the roles of man and maid. Daring to try anything in her efforts to learn and to please, she moved to straddle him. Then not knowing how else to proceed, she mimicked his actions on prior occasions by supporting herself on hands and knees while leaning forward to kiss him. She teased him with her tongue, flicking it along his lips and darting it between, as she lowered her upper body so that it just barely touched his.

It took only a few moments of that before she began to realize what a new and delicious game this was. She was in charge and could control every aspect of the situation. With rapidly escalating passion prompting every move, she began experimenting with the varied sensations she could produce with her new-found knowledge of physical excitation. Bret remained still, letting her do whatever she wanted, watching her through slitted eyes as she savored every erotic nuance of the way his flesh responded to hers. She was using his sex for her own pleasure, enjoying the opportunity of being in command, of guiding them through the first small ripples of rising lust into the great irresistible waves that buoyed them up and up and up and then sent them crashing into ecstasy's deepest abyss.

Shawna loved that night and often requested a repeat performance, luxuriating in the total freedom of movement it afforded as well as the sense of power it fostered. She was an apt pupil of the art of loving, and Bret was a master of the trade. He had learned well from a great many women of differing classes, ages, and tastes, and was willing to teach it all to this fiery redhead whose appetite seemed as big as his own.

Immersed as she was in her romantic affair, Shawna gradually became aware that something was troubling her father. She wondered if it was the continuing problems they'd been having with the *Black Prince* that had been renamed *Alfred*. Her timbers, it was discovered, were too old and weak to withstand the pounding from the firing of her ninepounders. She was no sooner in the water with her guns shipped aboard than David decided to haul her out and try to strengthen her bracings so she wouldn't shake herself to pieces the first time she engaged the enemy. Since this was not called for in the contract with the Marine Committee, it would have to be done at Glencannon expense, but that didn't enter into David's decision. He simply knew that he could not permit American boys to put to sea in a ship that was not as safe as he could make her, even if the money to rectify her problems had to come out of his own pocket.

"You always seem to have a scowl on your face lately, Papa," Shawna said to him one morning. "Is something wrong at the yard I haven't heard about?"

"No, nothing is wrong at the yard. In fact, I think we may be able to resume construction on *Randolph* quite soon. Congress seems to be giving up on the idea of reconciliation with the Crown and realizing that it is no worse to kill German George's subjects on the sea than on land."

Shawna nodded but refused to be sidetracked into a discussion of government politics. "Then what is it that's troubling you, Papa?"

David sighed, his frown deepening. "It's Malcolm. I'm worried about the lad."

"Why? Because he seems to be leaning toward the Tories?"

"No—yes." He changed almost in midword. "Yes, I am concerned about his political leanings, but more concerned about something else. He's been seeing altogether too much of Susan."

"Susan? Why shouldn't he see her? After all, they are cousins and were raised together. Naturally they are fond of each other."

"Fond of each other is an understatement," David said. "It seems more like infatuation."

Shawna whistled in surprise, then shrugged. "Well, they are cousins so I suppose—"

"They are *not* cousins!" David said. "Malcolm is Susan's uncle just as he is yours."

Shawna opened her mouth to argue but then realized what her father said was true. "Yes, you are right, but you know for a long time I always thought of Malcolm as my cousin too, because he is so close to my age, I suppose."

"Aye, and he and Susan are almost exactly the same age so they tend to believe it more strongly."

"Yes, I can see how they would," Shawna said, "but is that really so bad?"

"Aileen thinks it is. I had occasion to go to Germantown on Committee of Correspondence business yesterday and stopped in to see her. I found her much distressed."

"But why?" Shawna asked, "I do not see what—"

"Malcolm has been there every day. He and Susan go for long walks or even longer rides together, rides that last most of the day. Aileen is tempted to forbid him the house, but, as you know, it is Susan's house so that would be difficult. Neither can I forbid Malcolm to visit. He is an adult and even as head of the family, I cannot control his actions."

"But doesn't he take his pasty-faced fop of a Tory friend with him?"

"Not as often as I would like," David said, sounding almost angry. "Instead, he leaves him here to moon around after your sister and she seems to welcome it."

"Poor Papa," Shawna said sympathetically, putting an arm around him. "You have so many burdens thrust upon you when you should be left alone to do your work. All of your time should be devoted to creating the tall ships that will one day make America great instead of worrying about the improper conduct of younger members of your family."

"Well, lass, at least you have never given me any real trouble," David said, kissing her on the cheek and grinning. "Nothing more serious than booting a fat Quaker into the Delaware."

Shawna laughed nervously, feeling a twinge of guilt at the way she had been deceiving her father. "That pair of busybodies threatened to bring suit. Have you heard aught about it?"

David chuckled. "The magistrates of Philadelphia are now patriots. Your friends were told to take care lest they be charged with trespassing, so I think they will forgo suing for assault."

" 'Tis glad I am to hear it, and pleased to know we live in a country where people cannot interfere with one's business because of quaint religious beliefs."

"I wouldna make quite so broad a statement," David cautioned. "While Quakers are not to be allowed to interfere with the rights of the people of Philadelphia to build ships to defend their interests and those of the United Colonies, I doubt we have advanced so far toward freedom that a Catholic can have full exercise of his rights, or a Jew not have to conduct his affairs with extreme care."

Shawna nodded. "Yes, so 'tis well you gave up your papist leanings long ago."

"With Shawn for a father, they were never very solidly based," David said.

Looking at the plans for the *Randolph* spread across her father's worktable, Shawna drew a finger along the sharp bow. "So now you can build your dream ship."

David's eyebrows rose in surprise. "*Randolph*? Did you think she is my dream ship? She isn't. She's a well-designed ship, mind you, that will outclass most of those she meets and show a clean pair of heels to any she cannot beat, but she is a long way from the ship of which Humphreys and I have been dreaming."

"A long way?"

"Aye. Picture a frigate with scantling like a ship of the line, with long twenty-fours on her gun deck and a good turn of speed."

"Papa, that is a dream! Why, she would have to be like one of those razees the French cut down from battleships. She wouldn't be a frigate at all but a small, weak ship of the line."

"Not if she were 175 feet long and had the lines of a Baltimore clipper. She would be able to run down anything at sea and smash any two frigates sent against her. Given a decent captain and a spirited crew, she would even stand a good chance against a sixty-four."

Shawna's green eyes were shining now. "Could you, Papa? Could you build such a ship?"

"Working together, Joshua and I could do it," David said. "He is as convinced as I that ships like that are what we must have in the long run. *Randolph, Hancock,* and the others will be well enough for now, but not for the future . . . not for the long future of this land of ours."

" 'Tis a grand dream, Papa, but what would be the use of such ships? Surely you would not send them out to lie in line of battle against the might of England."

"No, but the English would learn that their frigates could not make free of our shores as they do today," he said, his jaw jutting out the way it always did when he was very determined about something.

As she went about her duties at the yard the rest of the day, Shawna's mind returned many times to the conversation with her father. She was glad it wasn't the shipyard that was worrying him and wondered if his fears about the relationship between Susan and Malcolm were justified. After all, those two had been so close as children that it seemed only natural they continued to be close as adults. No one had become upset about it then, so why now? Wasn't it possible for a man and a woman to be dear friends without people shaking their heads and whispering that it was unnatural? The fact that they were blood relatives shouldn't enter into it either, in Shawna's opinion. Her father's worry was misplaced, she decided, and let her thoughts return to her own affair. Now that was something Papa would really have reason to be concerned about, if he knew, but she had no intention that he ever know. It was a dilemma she had allowed herself to be caught in and she would have to resolve it on her own. In fact, it was time that she took a firm stand and insisted that Bret discuss the issue he had been so carefully avoiding.

Yes, this very night she was going to bring up the subject of marriage, and she was going to do it while she was fully clothed and in her right mind, not after he had completely addled her mind with his lovemaking. Someone had to carry on the Glencannon line, she reminded herself. Neither her Aunt Deborah in Albany nor Susan had borne any children, and Malcolm and Gifford seemed destined to remain bachelors all their lives. Uncle Steven in far away New Orleans had children, but as far as this branch of the family was concerned, she would have to carry on. Of course, her offspring wouldn't bear the name Glencannon, but they would have the blood, and she was sure Papa would be pleased to have a grandson before he got any older.

But carrying out her resolve proved harder than deciding on it. She was no more than through the door of Bret's sitting room than he was all over her, assaulting her senses with hands and lips that knew so well her vulnerability to his caresses.

"Please, darling, wait," she said, placing her fingers over his mouth as he bent to kiss the tops of her breasts. "I want to talk to you. Please, Bret, I'm serious."

"Thinking and talking about anything serious is bad for one's digestion and morale," he said, trying to evade her restraining hand.

"But not, I believe, for one's morals," Shawna countered, "especially when the—"

"Must we discuss so deadly dull a subject as morality?" Bret murmured, sliding a hand inside her low-cut neckline to cup a warm breast. "I would much rather talk about this and how sweet it tastes."

"Don't you ever think about anything but rutting?" she asked, pushing him away.

"Is there much else worth thinking about?"

"You might give some consideration to your work in the Congress and the fate of your country."

"Oh, please!" He raised a hand to his forehead. "I beg of you, do not bring up a subject so utterly boring and totally fatiguing as the representatives of these Disunited Colonies in Congress assembled!"

"If you find them so wearying, why did you bother to become a member?"

"One has to do something, or at least pretend to," he said. "And that is all any of them do, you know . . . pretend to be doing something. They talk. Oh great Jehovah, how those men can talk! They surely have tongues that wag at both ends, powered, it would seem, by a form of energy superior to the water wheel or the windmill because they never run out of power to keep their mouths going."

Shawna frowned. "But they have important work to do—the problems on the frontier, the decision to build ships to defy the British at sea, not to mention the siege of Boston and the necessity to raise arms and ammunition to support General Washington's army."

"They may have all those and other pressing matters to take care of but they do it not," Bret said with a shrug. "What they do is discuss endlessly whether New York, Pennsylvania, Virginia, or perhaps New Jersey should have preference in this appointment or that, whose merchant captains should command which ships—if the ships are ever built—whose general should have the other commands now that Washington or Virginia has the command before Boston."

As he spoke, he was reaching for Shawna again, but she pulled back, determined this time to force the issue.

"Well, my darling, have you tired of me so soon?" Bret asked, pushing his unruly hair back from his forehead and staring at her with an amused smile.

"On the contrary, my dear," she said. "What I have in mind is a more permanent arrangement."

One of his thick eyebrows lifted quizzically. "What on earth are you talking about?"

"I think you know quite well what I am talking about. If your memory does not fail you completely—

no, stay away! Stay far enough away that I can keep my sanity."

He laughed, flattered. "But why do you want to remain sane in world that is totally mad?"

"Is the world mad, Bret, or is that your view of it is so jaundiced that it seems that way?" She had no trouble sparring with him, but that wasn't what she wanted.

"We cynics have never been properly appreciated by our fellow men," he said. "Perhaps because we manage to tear the veil of optimism from their eyes and let them see the world as it really is."

"You continue to evade my question," she said.

"Your question? I was not aware that you had asked me a question," he said with a perfectly straight face.

She wanted to slap him, but she controlled her anger and said evenly, "Well, if you were not aware that I was asking a question, I will ask it again, and this time I will label it so you will know it is a question and not merely a statement of vague desires."

For the first time he looked worried. "You are not going to ask me something that I might not be able to answer?"

"Not able to answer? Why, what an absurd thing to say. The brilliant young delegate from the Hudson Valley, the scion of one of the richest patrons in the area, the graduate with honors from Oxford, the man of parts not be able to answer a question posed by the daughter of a simple Philadelphia shipbuilder? Of course you will be able to answer. It is a very easy question."

"Very well, go ahead, ask your question," he said resignedly.

Shawna took a deep breath. "I want to know whether you, Bret Van Fleet Morley, have any intention of marrying me, Mercy Shawna Glencannon."

"My answer, my dear, is no."

Despite the fact that she had guessed from his behavior what his answer would be, Shawna was shocked and furious when she actually heard it. Her eyes blazing, she backed toward the door. "Then I am leaving and will never return to this place, nor see you again."

"Please," he said, reaching out a placating hand. "That is only my short-term answer. Wouldn't you like to hear the one for the long run?"

"Frankly, no," she said icily. "Please summon your coachman so that I can go home."

"Not until you have heard me out," he said.

She hesitated, knowing she could not walk home alone through the streets. Because of the squadron being fitted out, there were too many sailors in town for even a stouthearted girl like Shawna to care to chance it.

"Very well, I'll listen, but ring for the coachman first."

"Really, my dear, is that necessary? After you have heard what I have to say, you may not wish to leave."

"I wish to leave right now, and if you do not do as I ask, I will—" She didn't know what she could threaten him with and fortunately she didn't have to. With a shrug, Bret sauntered over to the bell cord and pulled it three times, a signal that would call the coachman away from his warm spot before the kitchen fire and send him out to hitch up the horses to return Shawna to her home.

"Now may I tell you my story?" he asked. "May I tell you my long-run answer to your very direct question?"

"Yes, please do," she said, remaining near the door, tapping one slippered foot impatiently.

"Well, as you know, I am no longer a man of wealth. The estates my father left me are heavily mortgaged to pay my . . . ahem, debts of honor, and—"

"Honor?" Her lips curled.

He shrugged. "At least I paid them. Any other course would have been unthinkable."

" 'Twas unthinkable to run them up in the first place," Shawna said. "You had vast wealth, why did you need to gamble for more?"

"Excitement," he said with seeming honesty. "Excitement. A man cannot live without it."

"So you lost your money. You could go to work, you know."

"Work? Surely you jest! I am a gentleman and a member of the Continental Congress."

"I work," Shawna reminded him, "my father works, my brother worked before he went to Yale. What is wrong with work?"

He grimaced, and then his dark eyes swept over her from bonnet to silk slippers. "Yes, you do work, and I have noticed there is one flaw in your otherwise flawless beauty. . . . There are unsightly calluses on your hands."

" 'Tis better than having them on me arse," she told him, unblushing. "They were got by honest labor."

"Honest labor," he sniffed. "Ladies do not labor; they exist for the purpose of adding a little grace to an otherwise rather grubby world."

"Well, this lady—" She stopped, realizing that he had involved her in a pointless discussion. "You were going to tell me about your long-range plans."

"Ah, yes," He turned and walked over to the delicately wrought small table on which rested the ever-present bottle of champagne in its silver bowl of melting ice. "As I say, I have lost almost everything, but enough remains that I have two choices. I can use my last funds to purchase and outfit a privateer and go a'pirating, or—"

"That would be the right choice," Shawna said excitedly. "Do that and I'll go with you. I can not only navigate but can handle a ship under sail."

"Oh, my dear, such tedious enthusiasm," he said, patting back a yawn. "It is positively fatiguing just to hear it."

Shawna gritted her teeth, seething inside, and he strolled toward her with an indolent smile. He said nothing, just reached out with both hands and pressed his fingers into the swell of her breasts. Instantly her fist shot out, striking him on the cheek and sending him reeling backward.

Rage and astonishment mingled in his expression. "What the hell was that for?"

"That was for being such an insufferably arrogant male," she said.

"You are impossible," he said, holding his stinging jaw. "You are the most beautiful, most sensuous, most satisfying woman in bed that I have ever had, but you are also unpredictable, impulsive, and violent."

She glared at him, hands on her hips as though measuring him for another blow. "Aye, and 'tis best you remember that. Now tell me what it is you have decided on instead of piracy."

He smiled mockingly, his white teeth seeming to light up his face. "Well, there is a lady, not totally unattractive, who has a taste for younger men. Having survived two well-to-do husbands, she is very well fixed indeed, and to put it bluntly, she wants to marry me."

"You . . . you unprincipled cad!" Shawna had difficulty speaking because of the fury rising up inside her. "And what was it you had in mind for me? I think you mentioned marriage in the long run."

"Yes, and I meant it, but it would have to wait for a number of years until the lady—"

"Why, you bloody swab! You longshore rat! You mangy cur! You slimy—" Shawna reached the table in three strides, picked up the bottle of champagne and threw it at his head. Then she turned on her heel and ran from the suite.

When she was halfway down the stairs, she heard Bret's bewildered voice behind her. "She might at least have waited to see which option I had definitely settled on."

She kept going, not caring now what he decided, where he went, or anything else about him. All she wanted was to put as much distance between them as possible.

The next morning she overslept and for the first time since she had been working at the shipyard, she arrived late. David looked up from his drawing board in surprise when she came in.

"Is there something wrong, Shawna?" he asked in concern. "Are you ill?"

"I am quite well, thank you," she said, hoping he would not notice that her eyes were red and swollen from crying. "I have news for you, Papa."

"Good news?"

She smiled at him gravely. "Yes. I have decided to accept Seth Ewart's proposal of marriage."

David's mouth fell open. "You have? I didn't know he had asked you lately. Of course, he requested my permission to call on you for that purpose, and I gave it, but you seemed so little interested that . . . well, I just didn't know he had proposed."

"He hasn't, but he will tonight," she said, "and I'm going to the Indies with him. Suddenly I find that I cannot abide this cold Philadelphia weather and long for the sun-drenched islands."

David dropped his drafting pen and cursed as ink spread across his work.

"I'm sorry, Papa," Shawna said, her chin starting to tremble. "I didn't mean to ruin your morning's work."

David got up and put his arms around her. "It is nothing, my dear, beside your news. I hope you will be very, very happy."

"I will. I know I will," she said, and then to her chagrin found herself burying her face against her father's shoulder and soaking his shirt with tears.

7

Crispin Glencannon lay in ambush in a thick stand of brush outside a tiny settlement on the west bank of the Ohio River, not far from the place where the town of Steubenville would someday rise. His naturally dusky skin tanned to a deep copper tone by exposure to the sun, wind, and rain of the forest country, Crispin was bare chested and wore only a breechclout, moccasins, and a pouch swinging from a braided clout string decorated with scarlet feathers. His hair was braided, and the feather stuck in it was similar to those worn by the Mingos, Shawnees, and others who lay in ambush with him. Also like the others, his face was daubed with war paint.

Smoke was rising lazily upward toward the spring sky from the chimneys of log cabins, and as he watched the white settlers clearing the land, Crispin's mind and heart were filled with conflicting emotions and torn loyalties.

The events that had led to his presence here as a brave in an Indian war party had begun over a year ago with the delivery of a letter from Aileen Glencannon to her brother-in-law David. Crispin and Shawna had watched as David broke the seal and found inside not only a message from Aileen but a mysteriously enclosed communication from Sir William Johnson.

David had reluctantly opened the letter from Sir William and was reading it with a grave expression on his face. "It seems Sir William is much troubled in his mind and feels he can no longer depend on his sons or his deputies in the Indian service. He also blames himself for the removal of the Proclamation Line of 1763, which had kept settlers out of the Ohio country and appeased the western Indians."

"I think the removal of the line was a good thing," Shawna said with her usual impulsiveness. "People need land to settle on, to plow, and to grow their food."

"And Indians need land upon which to hunt or they will die!" Crispin said in a much sharper tone than he usually used with his beloved foster sister. "For once Sir William did not act with wisdom."

David put the letter down and gazed off into space.

"How does Sir William intend to handle the situation?" Shawna asked.

"He has persuaded the Iroquois to make some concessions to the other tribes and wishes to send belts to the Shawnee and Delaware. Since he feels that he needs someone of Indian blood to carry his messages, he has requested that Crispin perform this task."

"Crispin!" Shawna cried. "But he is only a boy and we need him here."

Crispin drew himself up to his full height. "I am part Delaware, as you well know, sister, and I have often hunted in the Ohio country with Thayendanegea and Toolah. I know the languages, and I am not a boy."

His words were so certain and self-assured that Shawna turned to stare at him in surprise. "No ... no, you are no longer a boy. I think he means to go, Papa."

"If he is willing, I am afraid he must," David said quietly. "With the danger of war in New England, we cannot afford to have war on the frontiers."

"I will leave for Johnstown tonight," Crispin had said.

And now he lay here on the banks of the Ohio, face and body streaked with war paint, clutching his musket and tomahawk and watching the white settlers against whom he would be leading his Indian comrades in a short while.

He had traveled to Johnstown by coach and boat up the Hudson and Mohawk rivers. Sir William, looking aged beyond his years, had greeted him warmly but lost no time impressing him with the danger and importance of his mission.

"You are half Delaware, my boy, and already have the bearing of a noble brave. I do not share my Mohawks' contempt for the Delaware, the Shawnee, and Mingo, but for their own good, their chiefs must be persuaded to hold them in check. They cannot fight the white man without the aid of the Iroquois, and the Iroquois will not join in this war as long as I live. The belts and the messages I will give you will make that as clear as I can convey it.

"You must go first to a Mingo village on the west bank of the Ohio River. There lives Talgahyeetah, the chief we call Logan. He has been the white man's friend for many years and he and his people stayed on after the other tribes moved west to avoid too close proximity with the settlers. His mother was a Cayuga, his father a Frenchman, but his loyalty has always been to the English, so much so that during the last French war and Pontiac's Rebellion, he and his family had to flee to Philadelphia for safety. The village he rules over is not large, but he is influential among the Mingos and Shawnee. If anyone can restrain the Indians of the Ohio Valley, it is he, but he must know that he has my support and that of the League."

"What of Cornstalk?" Crispin asked. "I have been told that Shawn Glencannon knew him."

Sir William nodded and said with a faint smile, "Aye, but he knew Cornstalk's sister better and we would do better not to remind him of that."

Dressed in new buckskins and moccasins, and with the belts of peace in his pouch, Crispin had headed for the Ohio country. He traveled over the runways of the Long House, trails that pierced the wilderness running north, south, and west from the strongholds of the Iroquois and guarded always by their scouts. All paths were open to him through the lands of the League because he carried belts and messages from the great Warraghiyagey, the Keeper of the Gateway.

He crossed the towering Appalachians at Crogham's pass, obtained a canoe at a settlement near the headwaters of the Allegheny, and started south, paddling during the day and drifting at night. He timed himself to pass Pittsburgh during the evening hours because of Sir William's warning that agents of the Reverend Connolly and of Governor Dunmore were active there and might well try to stop him if they got wind of his mission.

Safely past that hazard, he headed south and west on the broad bosom of the Ohio toward the village of Logan.

He found it standing in a tree-shaded glade that rose upward from the river, a collection of log huts and a low stockade for horses. At the apex of the rise was a large structure not unlike an Iroquois long house, although built of a different material. Smoke rose upward from two or three dozen cook fires, and the village was just beginning to stir as he let his canoe drift onto a narrow strip of beach. Dogs frolicking at the edge of the water were the first to notice his arrival and in a few minutes their barking brought a brave down the path from the village to investigate. He was a big man with wide shoulders and a broad face and was shielding his eyes against the rising sun with one hand as he came uncertainly forward.

When his canoe touched bottom, Crispin slung his musket over his left shoulder and stepped out, hand raised in the sign of peace. The brave stared at him, slack jawed, and for a minute Crispin couldn't understand what was wrong with the man. Then, as the brave took a few steps closer, he realized with shocked surprise that the Indian was drunk.

"I am Nometha, also called Crispin Glencannon," he said in Iroquoian, "I bear belts from Warraghiyagey, the Keeper of the Gateway."

The man blinked, not seeming to understand. He took another lurching step forward and extended a hand. "You bring rum?" he asked, also speaking Iroquoian but with the words slurred by liquor and a trace of an Algonquin accent.

"No, no, I have no liquor," Crispin said. "I bear belts from Warraghiyagey for Talgahyeetah and for Hokolesqua and the Shawnee sachems."

The Mingo took a couple more unsteady steps toward Crispin, his eyes squinted against the weak sun of dawn. "You Lenni-Lanape," he sneered, peering at the tribal marks Crispin had painted on his face the night before, knowing his approach to the village was imminent.

Crispin was used to the Mohawks' haughtiness toward those who had Delaware blood, but he saw no reason why he should tolerate it from a drunken Mingo so he strode forward until he was almost nose to nose with the man. He regretted it at the first blast of alcohol-laden breath but steeled himself and spoke.

"Yes, I am of the True Men." The words gave only the meaning of Lenni-Lenape; the tone indicated that Mingos, and this Mingo in particular, were less than human.

"You pig of a Delaware, I will—" The Mingo fumbled clumsily for the knife at his clout string and almost dropped it. "I will hang your scalp on my lodge wall, and—"

"I come with belts," Crispin interrupted, disdaining to swing his musket to the ready but letting his hand drift close to his scalping knife. "I am inviolate."

"I will carve up your belts with your hide," the Mingo said, lurching forward, knife ready.

"Do not be a fool, Eisakstehl!" snapped a woman's voice in clear cool Iroquoian. "You are drunk and he is sober. He will cut your ears off and make you eat them. Besides, he bears belts."

The drunken Mingo halted and stared off to his right. A tall slender maiden dressed in an unadorned deerskin tunic and wearing a single red feather in her plaited hair was standing not a dozen paces from them.

"Put away your knife, Eisakstehl," she ordered, "and go to your sleeping pad before I tell Talgahyeetah that you have been at the bottle again. If he finds out, he will choose a new war chief."

The Mingo hesitated briefly, then turned and staggered off up the path to the cabins without a backward glance.

The maiden watched him go, open contempt on her lovely bronze face. "Once he was a warrior," she said. "Now all he does is swill the white man's poison."

Raucous laughter and the sound of splashing water drew her attention and Crispin's to the canoe approaching the beach. In it were four men and two women, one of the latter standing in the bow waving a bottle. Crispin expected to see her pitch overboard at any second, especially with the way the mishandled paddles were causing the canoe to swerve and heel over. But somehow the man sitting beside her managed to hold on and keep the woman from toppling into the river.

The Indian maiden looked at him closely, studying his features. "You are half white. It remains to be seen if you are all white inside. Come, I will take you to my father, we shall feast, you shall be entertained, and perhaps tomorrow you will be asked to present your belts and deliver Johnson's message . . ."

He followed her up the path to the village, anger fading rapidly as his eyes fastened on the clean, strong limbs showing beneath the hem of the simple garment she wore, and noticed the subtle sway of her buttocks under it.

Logan was just coming from his lodge as his daughter led Crispin toward it through groups of staring children, chattering squaws, and sullen-looking young men. A tall, heavyset man, Logan had open, friendly features more noticeably influenced by his white ancestry than those of Crispin.

"My father, this is Crispin Glencannon," Olathe said. "He calls himself Nometha and is part Delaware, but he comes on white man's business."

It was not a gracious introduction, but Logan seemed pleased to see him. "Welcome, friend," he said in almost flawless English. "I bid you welcome to Logan's lodge."

"I bring belts and a message from Warraghiyagey," Crispin said.

Logan's face lit up and he advanced to place a hand on each of Crispin's shoulders. "If you come from my old friend Sir William, you are twice welcome. Any message he would send will be filled with good counsel."

"Counsel on the art of becoming slaves," Olathe muttered, but her father didn't hear in his eagerness to tell his visitor about his friendship with Johnson.

"Sir William entertained me at Johnson Hall when I was forced to flee Pontiac's warriors after the death of my friend Old Britain. And I was with him at Lake George where we defeated Marshal Saxe's old lieutenant and my friend became *Sir* William for his victory. It is good to know he still thinks of me.

"Come, you must be tired and hungry. I will have hot water prepared, soap brought, and maidens summoned to wash from your body the grime of your long journey. And when that is done, you will be provided with fresh buckskins and moccasins while I have a feast prepared fit for the envoy of the great Warraghiyagey."

Crispin had no desire to be bathed and feasted. He wanted to deliver his belts and message and be off to Sinioto with an escort of Mingo warriors as Johnson had instructed him to do.

Logan turned to Olathe. "Will you send maidens to bathe our distinguished guest, my daughter?"

"I will attend to him myself," she said. "It is only fitting that your daughter personally see to the needs of the ambassador from the Keeper of the Gateway."

"As you will, my daughter," Logan said, but the expression on his face told Crispin that the girl was not usually so cooperative in the welcoming of guests.

A tingle of anticipation ran through him and he began to wonder why he had been in such a hurry to get on with his mission to Cornstalk's villages.

"I will leave you in the capable hands of my daughter, who some say is more of a chieftain for our people than I am," Logan laughed, but Olathe's eyes showed no sign of amusement as she watched him go.

"Are you more of a chief than your father, Olathe?" Crispin asked.

"Are you more of an Indian than he is, Nometha?" she demanded, her black eyes boring into his brown ones.

It was the first time she had called him by his Indian name, and he thought it sounded better on her lips than Crispin. "Olathe is a beautiful name and a fitting one for you," he said.

For a minute he thought she was going to lash out at him, but instead she laughed, a brittle, bitter laugh. "My father would have given me a white man's name, but I refused to answer to it. He took his name from an Indian agent, James Logan, who later became governor of the colony they call Pennsylvania, and he would have all his family do likewise. He thinks of himself as being white and would make a white squaw of his daughter, but I will have none of it. My skin is copper and I am copper all the way through. Later I will see if I can find any red man beneath your white skin."

Crispin opened his mouth to protest, but no words would come out; he was too bewitched by the dark mystery of the eyes that held his.

And now he lay in ambush, feeling dizzy from the heat, and silently watched the white men going about their tasks, unaware of the death that awaited them in the nearby brush. He wished for night to come and remembered the last year . . . the year he had spent living among his father's people.

8

The room in Logan's lodge where the huge wooden tub of hot water sat was screened off from the rest of the living quarters by hanging buffalo skins. Olathe had supervised the filling of the tub and then brusquely dismissed the giggling Mingo women who had made it ready.

"Shall I help you disrobe, Nometha?" she startled Crispin by asking as he started to take off his hunting shirt.

"No. No thank you," Crispin said. "I can manage by myself."

"But I insist. Logan's children, like Logan himself, are slaves of the white man, so I must serve you like a slave."

Her perverseness troubled and angered him. It was disconcerting to be treated one moment as though he were an honored Indian guest and the next as one of the whites she hated so savagely. This girl stirred his senses, but she seemed driven by her emotions in ways he couldn't understand.

As though she sensed his mood, she was suddenly friendly, almost seductive in her manner as she came toward him. "Come, let me help you. You have come far in our cause. Your body is soiled and weary from your journey. Let me give it ease."

He was excited at the prospect of her helping him to undress, but at the same time, somewhat embarrassed. His Indian blood and time spent in the forests with Joseph Brant had done little to acquaint him with the customs of individual tribes. He knew that in certain ceremonies among the Mohawks it was the custom for maidens to bathe warriors being prepared to receive an honor or a chieftainship. He recalled hearing stories of how Sir William, on the eve of being made a Mohawk chieftain, had been bathed by several lascivious brown-skinned maidens starved for affection because of the Mohawk belief that warriors blunted their military prowess if they indulged in sex before the age of thirty.

Crispin shivered involuntarily as Olathe's fingers touched his throat and then his chest as she untied the rawhide thongs that held his hunting shirt closed at the neck.

"Are you cold, O great envoy of the Keeper of the Gateway?" she murmured, lips close to his cheek. "You are trembling and surely it cannot be from fear because you have come far and dared much to reach us."

"I am not new to travel in the forests," Crispin said, "and I dared little because none would interfere with a belt carrier from Warraghiyagey."

"Then you did not meet with the agents of the Virginia Land Company," she said, standing very close to him as she drew the shirt off and over his head. "They dare anything. The Reverend Connolly seized Cornstalk's own brother when the Shawnee conducted Pennsylvania traders to Pittsburgh. His Virginia militia have driven out the Pennsylvania sheriffs and magistrates, and he preaches war against the red man, and does it always in the name of the white man's Prince of Peace."

"Are you saying they would actually interfere with a deputy of His Majesty's superintendent of Indian Affairs for all of North America?"

"Connolly, the silver-tongued Bible man, is not alone. He has Lord Dunmore behind him, and with the Virginia militia swarming through this area, none dare oppose him, although I suspect that in a way Logan may deter him."

"But Logan stands for peace. How can he—" Crispin sucked in his breath sharply as the hard apples of her breasts brushed briefly across his chest as she reached to drop the hunting shirt to the floor behind him.

She giggled almost like a normal girl at his reaction, but her voice was like arrow flint as she went on. "Yes, Logan stands for peace, but the man of God— *your* God—wants war! A war that he believes will end in the extermination of the red man and huge profits for the land company that sponsors him."

"Sir William also believes that, Olathe," Crispin said eagerly. "Can you not see that is why we must work to keep the peace? None will gain from war but the land company and perhaps the Tories. We must prevent this war."

"No, we must not. Because I, too, want war. I want war because I hope it will mean the end of the white men in the Ohio country, and even if it does not, it will show that we are not slaves like the poor blacks your people drag all the way from the far land of Africa to do the toil they are too lazy or too arrogant to do themselves."

The shock of her words was nothing like the shock of her fingers trailing, feather light, down his chest, across his ribs and onto his belly before undoing the fastenings of his buckskin breeches.

"Your skin is gritty with the grime of the trail," she said as breeches and leggings joined his shirt on the floor. "I must wash you hard to discover if the flesh under it is white or copper-colored."

"Olathe, I—"

"Be silent for now," she whispered. "I have much to learn about you."

What she seemed mainly interested in learning at the moment was how well endowed he was under the breechclout that was his sole remaining garment.

"You are powerfully built, Crispin Nometha Glencannon," she whispered, those feathery fingers touching his maleness so briefly that it seemed like a memory even while it was happening. But brief as it was, it caused his flesh to engorge with blood and a fever to start in his veins.

Olathe stepped back, gloating over the effect her light touch had had. "Ah, if we needed to build a teepee, we would need only two more poles."

Crispin's emotions were pulling him in different directions. Her open sensuality was arousing lust he wasn't sure he could control, he was angered by her mockery and appalled by her expressed desire to involve her people in what he believed to be a hopeless war. Unused to coping with such diverse feelings, he struggled to make some sense of them, to see them in proper perspective and not let them overwhelm him.

She was smiling provocatively and urging him toward the tub of steaming water when with a quick movement, she jerked his breechclout off. "Get into the tub, my lord, and your serving maid will bathe and anoint you with bear grease in which sweet-smelling herbs have been mixed."

"I would prefer to do without the bear grease," he managed to say.

"Ah, so there is too much white man inside you after all," she said, watching him step over the rim of the tub and sink down into the aromatic but scalding water.

"No more than in you," he retorted, finding the temperature barely tolerable but not wanting to give her any more grounds for mocking him by complaining about it. "No more than in you."

"One-quarter more," she said, "and that one quarter may make all the difference."

His body quickly became accustomed to the heat, and he let it lull him and soothe the tenseness generated by his strangely volatile state of mind. The sense of relaxation didn't last long. It vanished abruptly when Olathe stripped her deerskin tunic off and stepped up on the slab of stone that served as a step by the side of the tub. Only a loincloth remained on the coppery body now bared to his astonished but appreciative gaze. The slim, straight back, smooth rounded shoulders, gently curved arms, and flat belly led his eyes to the swell of hip and softly tapered thighs before they returned to the perfect hemispheres of firm young breasts tipped with nipples of deepest coral.

"What is the matter, Crispin? You look stricken. If you are not careful, your eyes will roll out and boil in that hot water."

"You . . . you are naked," he said and heard the croak in his voice.

"Not quite, but close enough," she said, smoothing the cloth over her loins with both hands. "I did not expect the mere sight of bare flesh to upset you so. Did you not have sisters with whom you swam as a boy?"

"Yes, I have a foster sister. We played together and were comrades, but we never swam together."

"She was white." It was a statement, not a question. "The White Eyes put too much importance on such things." She picked up a chunk of lye soap and rubbed it between her hands in the water to work up suds while he stared, fascinated, at the round smoothness of her copper-colored breasts.

"Does it offend you to see me this way, Nometha?" she asked with a smile that bordered on malicious coyness. "I can wrap a drying cloth around me if it makes you uncomfortable."

"No, it does not offend me," he said from between clenched teeth and then almost choked when she leaned forward to scrub his back and the firm mounds slid along his upper arm.

"That is good because I feel more natural this way, more Indian, knowing that going naked vexes my white blood." Her voice had lost its mockery and sounded almost serious. "If I only knew the exact spot to stab myself so that only my white blood would be spilled, I would do it before the sun sets this very day."

Her long, braided hair dangled down onto his chest and one arm encircled him as she scrubbed vigorously at his shoulders and back. "Beautiful," he murmured. "Beautiful . . . beautiful."

"What?" She drew back to look at him sharply.

"Olathe . . . beautiful . . . is that not what your name means?"

She showed her teeth but whether in anger or pleasure, he couldn't be sure. Returning to her self-imposed task, she rubbed his skin harder and harder. It was beginning to tingle by the time she switched to lathering his chest, and that tingle was forgotten in the stronger one set off when she leaned across to reach his ribs on the far side and her breasts were pressed against his nose and mouth.

He was so stunned and so wildly excited that at first he made no response at all, but then his lips closed over one of the erect peaks and his tongue was tasting the sweet natural flavor of her flesh, savoring its youth and vibrance. Carried away by his raging desire, his hands lifted from the water to clasp her waist, wanting to drag her into the tub with him and do with her what he had once done with Katie, the barmaid at the Blue Bird Tavern in Philadelphia.

That was not to be. With surprising strength, her fingers closed over his wrists and his hands were pushed back down into the water without a word.

After a few more minutes of diligent soaping and rinsing, she spoke. "Where I have washed the stains and grime of travel off you, your skin is as coppery as mine. I find no white there but I wonder about your soul."

"So far even the preachers have not found a way to read that," he said, voice strained by lust and disappointment.

"Ah, but they do not know the way to measure it. They look only in their leather-bound book, but I have a witch woman's ways, ways that were old when the preachers' God was born and Ta-ha-hia-wa-gon, Upholder of the Heavens, was himself a youth."

"Are you a witch then?" he asked.

"Oh yes, but my spells are those that a woman knows," she said, hands far under the water, rubbing soap across his belly and the top of his thighs. She giggled when she came into contact with the swollen shaft of his manhood. "You have not lived among the White Eyes long enough. You do not know how to suppress your feelings the way they do. Have they not preached to you of marriage, of what one may do after marriage that one must not do before?"

"My father is a friend of Ben Franklin and somewhat of a freethinker," Crispin told her, trying not to react to the soap-slippery fingers scouring at his legs and giving an occasional tantalizing touch to his male flesh.

"Your white father."

"My foster father, David Glencannon."

"Yes, I can see the influence of this freethinker on you," she said, "and I much fear these feelings you have will distract you when your mind must be at its clearest, at the time Logan calls to him the chiefs and sachems of the nearby villages to hear your message from Warraghiyagey. Perhaps you should get out of the tub and let me throw cold water on you to relieve you of the painful growth you have developed."

"No, I would not like that."

"Hmmmm. Well, there is a doctor in one of the white villages, perhaps he could be called to lance the swelling and bleed the heat from your blood," she said as though considering a serious possibility.

"Oh, my God!" Crispin cried in alarm.

She laughed. "That idea you do not like either. There is only one other solution I can think of and that will require that I resort to desperate measures."

Crispin stared at her, wondering if this was just some kind of game she was playing to make him seem like a fool. He was in no condition to decide rationally; she had him in such a state of sexual arousal that he hardly knew what he was saying, much less thinking.

"You would not want to deliver the belts to Logan and the others looking as you do now, would you?" she asked.

"I am assuming that as soon as you stop . . . doing what you are doing, it will go away." The soapy fingers were slithering up and down the insides of his thighs.

"Not all by itself," she whispered, lips close to his ear blowing her hot breath into its cavity, and her breasts rubbing against his chin and lips. "It has to have help."

Those beautiful little breasts were nearly driving him insane. Katie, the Dutch tavern girl, had breasts like a milch cow. They had been like twin pillows he could bury his face between while he was grazing her. But these . . . why, they were so small and perfect that he thought they would fit almost completely in his mouth.

"Yes, you need help or you will be unable to face the chiefs and sachems of the Mingo and Cayuga who will be here tonight."

"What kind of help?" he asked in a strangled voice.

"This kind," she said, and he gasped as both soft, slippery hands closed around his penis. "This will make you feel much better and fit to face those who even now gather around the council fire."

Crispin couldn't say a word. It wasn't what he wanted from her, and he wondered about her motives, but he was helpless to resist.

"Does it feel good, Nometha? Ah, it must because it is getting bigger and harder all the time. Oh my!"

Crispin turned his face and found he could catch one of those tormenting breasts in his mouth, pull the rigid nipple inside and perhaps as much as half of the delicious little apple to lick and suck.

"Oh, he's so in need," she breathed, half-sitting on the side of the tub and manipulating his burning flesh with a sureness that could have come from instinct or practice. He didn't know which, and at the moment, didn't really care.

What he did know was that he wanted to touch her the way she was touching him, to make her feel the intense desire she was stirring in him. He reached blindly toward her as her knowing fingers sent liquid fire racing through his veins in place of the blood that had once flowed there. His hand touched the smooth, taut flesh of her leg and started to slide up along the velvet of her inner thigh.

"No!" she said as his fingers just barely touched the wiry tangle of pubic hair. "No, I said no, you white-eyed pig!" She let go of his tormented flesh and clamped her thighs around his hand. "No one touches Olathe without her permission, and I have not given you permission."

"But Olathe, you are touching me . . . you are driving me mad with need . . . with—"

"That is your problem, not mine," she said. "Now remove your hand or I will let you go before the council swollen like a puff adder."

Reluctantly he withdrew his fingers, facing defeat either way and preferring the one that would leave him at least the pleasure she was willing to provide.

Her anger faded as quickly as it had flared, and she murmured against his ear. "Later perhaps you shall have what you want . . . perhaps tonight . . . if you prove yourself a man . . . a red man."

There was nothing he could do but lean back in the tub and let her have her way. Then she gave him just a bit more, apparently feeling generous because he had obeyed her so promptly. She leaned toward him and pressed her lips to his in a white man's kiss.

Crispin found her lips as sweet as wild berries, her tongue dripping honey as it passed between his lips and intertwined with his.

"Soon, Nometha, soon . . . soon your seed will spill into my hand, and you will be mine, body and soul, forever," she whispered, hands increasing their tempo, and in just a few more seconds he groaned as though his soul were indeed being stolen from his body and shuddered under the impact of the violent explosion of pleasure that shook him.

Crispin shook his head to dispel the memory and reality came rushing back. The sun had sunk behind the tall trees, silhouetting them starkly against the bright western sky. Mosquitoes buzzed around his head, and it was no cooler than it had been earlier, although the night birds had already started to sing. He could see a young man in a gray shirt plowing with a spavined old mule, laboriously working his way around the uncleared stumps. A young blonde woman was standing in the doorway of the cabin as though supper had been prepared, and she was waiting for her husband to finish his seemingly endless task. Lights were on in other cabins and most of the whites had disappeared inside them. No guard had been posted, and except for the plowing man and a man chopping wood, there was no one in sight.

In a short time, these unalert people would be mostly dead and scalped. Only a few of the younger women and children would escape war ax and scalping knife. Part of Crispin's mind reeled back from the thought, but the dominant Indian part accepted it as only right. These people had taken the land of his people and must die for it.

Rationally he knew that the fault did not lie with these people but with Lord Dunmore, William Preston, Michael Cresap, Reverend Connolly, and other land grabbers who had lured them here. But those men were beyond the reach of his little band of Shawnee, Mingo, and Cayuga.

"When, O Nometha, when do we strike?" asked young Aoussix, a Cayuga who had joined them only a fortnight ago. "When do the English pay for the blood of those they have slain?"

"Soon," Crispin said, seeing the last village man abandon his plow and head toward the cabin door where the bright-haired woman awaited him. They stepped inside with their arms around each other. Crispin decided he would take the fair-haired woman. He would take her as a conqueror takes a woman of a subject race, as someday all white women would be taken when the red men rose up in one mighty thunder and took back what was theirs.

9

"It was my hope that you would present your belts and message from Warraghiyagey today," Logan said to Crispin the next evening as they sat down to feast on venison, wild turkey, yams, and hoe cake scorched in the embers of the fires that lit up the village, "but it has been decided that we should wait until others arrive."

Crispin noted moodily that there was no mention of who had decided that. He looked at those gathered around the chief's fire and listened to the laughter and shouting coming from the other groups of Mingos. He suspected the delay had been suggested, if not insisted upon, by Olathe, but when their eyes met, hers reflected only innocent uninvolvement.

"Who is coming?" Crispin asked Logan. He was anxious to deliver his message and depart. The longer he waited, the more chance there was that some provocation by the whites who were pouring into the Ohio country, and into Kentucky, might lead to a clash or incident that would set the frontier on fire from the Canadian border to Florida.

"Hokolesqua, Silverheels, and Nonhelema of the Shawnee, Old Belt and Half King of the Seneca, and Michikiniqua and Cold Foot of the Miami. Sacanghtradeye and Shikellimus are already here."

Since the last two were chieftans of the Cayuga and part of the Mingo confederation, it was expected that they would be here, but it surprised Crispin that the Shawnees and Miamis were coming to hear his words. It would, though, keep him from having to travel on to the far Ohio country and so he would be able to return to Johnstown more quickly to report there was indeed trouble brewing in this area.

He had picked up intimations of it all along the way. The Reverend Connolly seemed to have been everywhere warning settlers against the Indians and telling them that a bloody border war was imminent. From information picked up from hunters and trappers during his woodland travels, Crispin formed the opinion that Connolly was not so much warning against the possibility of war as urging the settlers to start one, working on the theory that the sooner it was gotten over with the better. Or did he have another motive? The one Sir William had hinted at. After all, Connolly was Lord Dunmore's agent, and if it came to a clash between the settlers and the Indians at the same time there was a clash between king and colonies . . .

The feasting was well along by now, the food washed down with generous swigs of hot buttered rum. Eisakstehl, the husky warrior who had first greeted Crispin on his arrival, and several of his fellows, were already drunk. Only Logan himself and Olathe were confining themselves to spruce beer, and Crispin thought it prudent to follow their example.

"You are very quiet, Nometha," Olathe said after a while, speaking in the Iroquoian, "and you have barely touched your food. Is our Indian food not good enough for one raised in the palaces of Philadelphia?"

He laughed at her. He knew she must have been in Philadelphia with her father during Pontiac's rebellion and was aware that there were no palaces in that city. And she had spoken to him in the Indian tongue so that everyone around the fire would know what she was saying.

"As you know, O Olathe," he said, "there are no palaces in the City of Brotherly Love, and the table set at my foster father's home is plainer than this."

"Then it is the company that displeases you," she said, eyes glinting maliciously.

"On the contrary, Logan is a most gracious host," Crispin countered. "All men say so, and I have found their words do not praise him enough for the hospitality and friendship he offers freely to one and all."

"If it is not Logan, perhaps it is others here at the fireside who give you offense," she persisted. "Or is it the drinking? I understand that the Quakers of Philadelphia disapprove of alcohol. Are you one who does?"

"Not I, Olathe. I am not of the Quaker faith."

"The Quakers are good people," Logan spoke up. "My great and good friend James Logan, the Indian agent who later became the Father of Pennsylvania, was a Quaker. It was from him I took my name."

"We know that," Olathe said with something less than the respect a great chief had a right to expect from his daughter. "We have heard it many times."

"He felt that rum was a bad thing," Logan said, raising his voice so that all those around the fire could hear. "He thought it was especially bad for Indians."

Olathe's serpent's tongue would not be stilled. "Is that not the way all white men think about Indians? They feel what is good for them is bad for us. I say that is because they think of us as inferior beings. What say you, Crispin Glencannon? Do you feel we are inferior to your white blood? Is that why you are so silent?"

Her words were not lost on the loutish Eisakstehl. He put down the bone he had been gnawing on and glared at Crispin.

"How can anyone not be silent when you talk so much, woman?" Logan rebuked his daughter. "There is no place for another's words because you fill the air with yours."

Obviously the girl was not used to being reproved in public, and the glance she turned on her father was venomous. Beautiful as she was, and much as he was attracted to her, Crispin found her behavior less than admirable. Did she really believe she was working for the best interests of her people, or did she simply enjoy making trouble? He had been disappointed last night when she had not come to his sleeping quarters as she had seemed to promise during their strangely intimate interlude, but now he wondered if it might not be better to avoid any further contact with her except as protocol or courtesy demanded.

He was sure that was the best policy when she returned to baiting him. "You do not drink our rum, Crispin Glencannon, only sip at spruce beer. Is it that your head is weak or that you do not wish to drink with us?"

"You are not drinking rum either, Olathe," he said mildly, hoping to turn aside her barbs by not answering in kind.

"Ah, but I am a woman, and it is known by all that women have weak heads."

"No, you have a strong head," Eisakstehl said, "and this man has insulted you by saying you have not."

Crispin had said nothing of the kind, but Eisak-stehl was far too befuddled to know the difference as he lurched to his feet and glared at the youth.

"There is no need to defend me, Eisakstehl," Olathe said in a sweet, mild, resigned voice.

"I say you need to be defended," the warrior said. "This white man comes saying he brings belts, yet he has not shown us belts, he has not given us message. All he has done is insult us and our ways. Now he has said our women have weak heads."

"Please, Eisakstehl," Logan said. "It is not he who has delayed the—"

"I say he is not a bearer of belts at all but a spy from the man Connolly. I say he has come to see how many of us there are so he can tell our enemies that they may do us harm. I say this man should not leave with his scalp!"

"I have said you are to be quiet, Eisakstehl," Logan said. "We shall have peace around our cook fire."

"Ah yes, Logan always cries for peace," Olathe said bitterly. "He will cry for peace when the White Eyes are trampling on our graves and the graves of our fathers."

"Well, no white man tramples on me!" Eisakstehl sounded a bit more sober and definitely in the mood for a fight. "Do you hear me, white man? I say you are a liar! I say you do not come from Warraghiyagey but from Connolly to betray us! I say you are pig's meat, rotten pig's meat that has laid in the sun so long even the buzzards refuse to pick at it!"

Crispin knew he had to make some reply to this verbal assault, had to show open resentment, or he would lose all standing with these people. He searched his mind for a way that would show these accusations to be lies but still avoid a brawl that would make matters worse.

He got to his feet, having no real hope of avoiding a fight but wanting to make sure no word or action of his would seem to provoke it.

"So he has the strength to stand on his own two feet," Olathe purred. "I was beginning to wonder if Warraghiyagey had sent a woman to carry belts to the Mingos . . . perhaps because we have acted like women."

"I will give you cause, beautiful Olathe, to know that I am a man," Crispin growled out of the side of his mouth in English so that none save Logan and Olathe would know what he said.

He need not have been concerned about provoking Eisakstehl. The big man hardly waited until Crispin was on his feet before hurling himself through the air at him. Not having expected the warrior to move so fast in his semidrunken condition, Crispin was caught by surprise as the two hundred greased pounds of Mingo struck him with the force of a stone from a catapult.

Bowled over backward, Crispin heard the screams from the squaws, the clatter of spilled drinking cups, and a high, mocking laugh he knew must come from Olathe. It was that laughter more than anything else that enabled him to recover from the surprise of the blow and throw up his knees to catch Eisakstehl in the belly as the man bore down on him.

The Mingo grunted and was propelled backward by the thrust of Crispin's legs but recovered quickly and was back with his foot raised to stomp the belt bearer. Crispin reacted instinctively, catching the descending foot in his hands and giving it a sharp twist, toppled the man, then scrambling to his feet.

Eisakstehl regained his feet with all the speed of a catamount and, screeching in rage, came at Crispin with fists doubled up, pounding rather than striking out as a white man would have. One of those hammerlike blows struck Crispin on the head and he felt his knees give way. A second battered against the side of his face and he was knocked sideways even as he was sinking to the ground.

That was almost Crispin's finish. He lay for a few seconds unable to see or think, his head ringing and his eyes unfocused, and Eisakstehl bounded toward him and leaped into the air, intending to land on him with both feet.

A shriek of pleasure echoed above the yells and shouts of encouragement and somehow it penetrated the fog into which Crispin had been sinking. It gave him the will to roll sideways just a fraction of a second before the Mingo landed where he had been. It also goaded him into reaching out a leg to trip up the big man as he crouched there, knees bent, astonished to have missed his target.

Eisakstehl went down, and Crispin managed to get to his feet and shake his head to clear it before the man came at him again, roaring an Algonquin war chant that Crispin couldn't understand.

Crispin had learned Indian fighting from Jospeh Brant and Toolah and white man's fighting on the docks and wharves where longshoremen and sailors did not practice the precepts of the City of Brotherly Love. He needed both kinds now as the huge Indian bore in on him, a killer's rage on his face. Crispin backed away, hoping to clear his head and get the rubber out of his legs.

Logan was calling for an end to the fight, but the rest of the Mingo men were enjoying it immensely.

They were shouting insults at Crispin and encouragement to Eisakstehl as the former backed warily away and the latter stalked him like a panther. But over all the other voices could be heard the shrieks of Olathe suggesting various painful and disabling things Eisakstehl might and should do to his opponent.

Crispin's head was clearer now and he had backed out of the immediate fire area where piles of logs and buffalo robes could cause one to stumble. If he were to win this fight, he needed room to maneuver, and the big man obviously didn't want to give it to him because he kept trying to force him back toward the blaze and the shouting crowd around it.

As Eisakstehl closed in on him, Crispin measured him and lashed out with his right fist. It caught the Indian on the cheek and drew a trickle of blood, but he shook it off and kept coming as Crispin backed away.

"Stand and fight, White Eyes, don't run from me!" Eisakstehl yelled, and Crispin sidestepped a lunge and landed a blow on the side of the Mingo's chin.

"He runs! He is afraid! He runs like Braddock's men did!" Olathe shouted, her voice on the verge of hysteria.

Crispin was in command of himself now and his strength was returning. This time he didn't retreat or dodge but moved in under Eisakstehl's wild lunge. With head down and body half turned to the side, he moved his head just enough to let a blow from the Indian's fist whistle past his left ear, then struck two quick blows at the Mingo's blubbery belly. They sank in, and Crispin heard the explosion of expelled breath and saw his opponent double up.

This was the chance he had been waiting for. He lashed out again and caught the big man on the chin, sending him staggering back toward the screeching Indians. Two braves helped Eisakstehl to his feet, and Crispin followed up his advantage, advancing while the other stood shaking his head.

Crispin started to rain jabbing punches on the Mingo's chest, belly, and head, staggering him to one side and then the other, causing him to reel and almost turn his back to the relentless fists. For a minute Crispin thought he had finished the fight, but he underestimated the recovery power of the sweating, snarling Mingo. As he circled around, looking for an opening, Eisakstehl lifted one heavily muscled arm, swung it without turning and caught Crispin a devastating blow full in the face.

Crispin staggered and went to his knees, and Eisakstehl kicked out with a foot that hit the youth in the chest and knocked him over backward. But the big man was hurt himself and couldn't follow up quickly enough with another kick and a final stomping that would have left Crispin dead, or so close to dead that it wouldn't have mattered.

As the bigger man came in kicking, Crispin tumbled backward, bracing himself on his elbows and aiming both feet at the Indian's middle. He struck him with the force of a battering ram and sent him reeling backward to collapse at the feet of his screaming fellow tribesmen, almost in the embers of the fire.

Crispin bounded to his feet and went after the man, but Eisakstehl still had enough strength to roll over, grab a heavy burning brand from the fire and come raging at him, the flame aimed at his eyes.

Logan shouted a warning, and this time Olathe's scream held more of fear than pleasure. Crispin backed away from the blazing brand as it was thrust at him again and again, singeing the fringe on his hunting shirt, scorching the hair on his hand and lower arm, and brushing briefly across one cheek, leaving a painful but not disabling burn.

Crispin waited for his chance, and the Mingo, now certain of victory, began to beat at his head with the torch. Dodging one blow and then another, Crispin was finally able to crack Eisakstehl's wrist with a quick, slicing chop of his open hand. A howl of pain came from the man's lips and the burning brand went flying.

All through the fight, a rage had been building inside Crispin, a rage he had never dreamed himself capable of, and now it took over. The painful burns on his hand, wrist, and cheek sent anger as hot as the burning brand through him. He wanted nothing short of the death of Eisakstehl now, and even through the alcoholic fumes that swirled in his head, the big Mingo saw that in Crispin's face and began to back away, holding his wrist with the other hand and glancing around as though about to break and run for it.

"Don't let him get away, Nometha!" Olathe shouted, bringing a bloody grin to Crispin's face. For some reason, the Mingo princess seemed to have changed sides. Maybe what she liked was a winner, and now that he was a winner he intended to finish what he had started. He went after the Mingo with taunts on his lips.

Eisakstehl broke and tried to get away. Squealing that his wrist was broken, he tried to break out of the circle of Indians who had surrounded both of them. A dozen hands thrust him back into the center of the arena.

"Stand like a warrior or die!" someone yelled.

"Do not disgrace yourself, Eisakstehl," Logan advised. "Take your beating like you deserve . . . like you would have administered it."

Eisakstehl looked around like a trapped animal, but he found no sympathy in the faces of any of his people. Finally his eyes came to rest on Olathe and he half raised his good hand in pleading.

The princess spat at him. "Fight, coward! Kill him, Nometha! Kill the pig who is not worthy of being called a brave!"

Caught up in his own rage, Crispin barely heard her. All he could see was his enemy standing there beaten, all he could remember was how the man had intended to stomp him to death, how he had thrust the flaming brand at his eyes, and all he knew was that it was now his turn.

Unable to flee, Eisakstehl lifted his hands in an attempt to defend himself, but Crispin brushed them aside and began to batter at the man, landing blows that cut his face and head, that smashed his nose and turned his face into a bloody caricature of itself. Harder blows to the body and belly caused the big Mingo to double and fall to his knees. Then locking his hands together, Crispin brought them down on the back of the Indian's neck, sending him sprawling into the ashes and dying embers of the fire.

Crispin wasn't finished with him yet, and no one in the crowd called on him to spare his fallen enemy when he grabbed him by one leg and hauled him out of the ashes. Straddling the semiconscious man and lifting him by the front of his buckskin shirt, Crispin began to pound him in the face with his right fist until his features resembled a bloody pulp. He might never have stopped while there was breath in

Eisakstehl's body if the voice of Olathe, hoarse with anger and excitement, hadn't come through to him.

"Kill him! Kill him, Nometha! Kill him for me!"

Dropping the man to the ground, he turned to face the girl who stood at the inner edge of the circle of Indians, face flushed and eyes eager. She was enjoying this. She had egged Eisakstehl into attacking him, had cheered him when he seemed to be winning, but now wanted him killed and was urging Crispin to carry out her desire. Suddenly he was sickened by the whole thing. He was damned if he would give her that kind of pleasure. With a shrug, he stepped away from Eisakstehl's limp body and reached to take a jug of rum from a squaw standing nearby. He took a long draught of the fiery liquid and then walked over to where Logan stood looking troubled.

"My apologies, O Chief. I would not have had this happen for anything. I hope it will not interfere with the completion of my mission."

Logan waved a hand. "It was not your doing. The fight was forced on you."

Two squaws detached themselves from the onlookers, one picking up Eisakstehl's feet and the other his shoulders. Crispin watched them carry out the beaten brave and then turned back to Logan.

"I am tired. My body and face are bruised and burned. I ask your permission to retire for the night, O Talgahyeetah."

"Yes, you are injured. There is blood on your face and burns in several places. You must be cared for."

"I will take care of him, Father," Olathe said, coming quickly to Crispin's side. "I will tend his injuries, soothe his aches, and care for him in every way."

Logan frowned but said nothing as Crispin permitted the girl to lead him away.

"You are a great warrior, Nometha, but I still do not know if you have the soul of a white man or a red," she said, guiding him toward a small lodge that stood between the abode of her father and Mishahmiqui, or Council House.

"You battled Eisakstehl bravely and beat him, but why did you let him live?" she asked as they entered the lodge. "You acted like Logan when you did that, Nometha."

"Your father is a great man," Crispin said. "I am not ashamed to be compared to him."

Her lip curled. "You should be. His blood is tainted with whiteness and his spirit with conciliation."

She sat him down on a pile of buffalo hides and brought water to wash his face gently before spreading bear grease on the burns, then repeated the process with his hands and arms.

"You should have killed him. He would have killed you if he had won. Why did you not finish him off?"

"Because I saw your face," he told her the truth. "I saw how you were enjoying it, and it made me ill."

She looked surprised for a moment, but went right on with her questions. "Were you ashamed to have his blood on your hands? Are you afraid of the wrath of the Christian God? Is that the reason you failed to dispose of your enemy when you had the chance?"

"I told you why," he said, and then gritted his teeth at the sting of something she was putting on his cuts. It felt like liquid fire.

"Does that hurt, Nometha? she asked. "It is the liquid extract from the leaves and bark of a shrub. It is called wych-hazel and will prevent mortification from setting in."

"It may also burn off my skin," Crispin said.

"No, no, Nometha," she said softly. "When the time comes to set your skin and the flesh under it on fire, I shall do it all myself."

She was leaning close as she worked at his face, and he could feel those apple-hard breasts and the pressure of hip and thigh against him. It stirred in him the same mad longing it had when she bathed him, and he tried to fight against the feeling, knowing that she was deliberately using her body to befuddle his thought processes.

"Why are you so contemptuous of your father?" he asked to break the spell. "He has done much good among his people and has kept them at peace."

"And he has done the white man's bidding," she said, lips compressed to a thin line. "That is how he has kept our people at peace."

"And you believe peace is wrong for your tribe?" He could feel her body turning slightly so that the flat plain of her belly pressed against his arm rather than hip and thigh.

"When it is the white man's peace, the peace they reluctantly grant us after they take over our hunting grounds, the peace they will take away at any time it suits their purpose."

The sting of the wych-hazel had faded and grease had eased the smarting of his burns. He was much more comfortable outside but excited inside by the warmth of the body under the simple tuniclike garment she favored. This one was made of linen and fringed at the bottom. Olathe scorned the traditional Iroquois squaw dress consisting of a long-sleeved red overdress with blue and white porcupine quill embroidery and white cotton frills at the high neckline, dark blue skirt embroidered in white, pantalets tied at the knees and a woolen mantle. It hampered her movement and was bulky and uncomfortable, she said, and refused to wear it.

She left him briefly to put away her jars and pots, and when she returned, she stood close to him again and spoke in a low, intense voice. "Nometha, you must do what I am going to ask you."

He looked up into her gleaming black eyes. "And what is that, beautiful Olathe?"

"I want you to change the message you bring from Johnson and the Iroquois," she said. "You must not deliver a message that counsels my people to seek peace with the whites. That would be to betray them to the mercy of Connolly and the others, to those who know no mercy."

"Olathe, I am a messenger, a bearer of belts," Crispin said, shocked. "I can no more change the message than I can stop the stars from passing overhead and disappearing from the sky when the sun rises."

"Nevertheless, you must," she insisted. "The Mingos cannot continue the way they have been. We cannot go on extending the hand of friendship while our land is taken from us and our young men and women debauched with liquor and sickened by white man's diseases."

"Olathe, I know your people have been badly treated," he said, trying to ignore the heat of her tempting body. "I know the English settlers have wronged you and probably intend greater wrongs, but I also know that war between Mingos and colonists would benefit none but the Crown. It could mean destruction of this land forever."

"You sound like an echo of Logan! He is constantly telling us that!"

Crispin sighed and shook his head. "I cannot change the message. But this I can promise you—as soon as I return to Johnstown, I will take the matter up with Sir William. I will ask him to go to the Iroquois and request that they use their influence to take pressure off the Mingos in the Ohio country. Mingos are also Iroquois; the League should protect you."

"You do not understand!" she cried fiercely, pounding on his shoulders with her fists. "You cannot imagine what it has been like for me, an Indian princess, an Indian of the heart to watch while my father smiled and bowed and groveled to the white man whose only intent was to first take our land and then destroy us. I shriveled up inside every time I saw Logan embrace a white man. I was so sick sometimes that I had to run off into the woods to vomit when I saw him smiling, laughing, fawning on some white-eyed snake."

Crispin sat silently, listening, sensing that this obsession of hers could have results that were incalculable for herself, her people, and . . . yes, for him as well.

"Ever since I was a tiny girl, I have known that my father was a fool and a coward." Olathe's voice was like a rasp. "Those times we fled to Philadelphia because he dared not take the side of his people against the common enemy, I suffered their overbearing manner, their less than subtle assumption of their basic superiority and our status as savages— tame savages who needed to be indulged up to a point, but savages nonetheless. I suffered through it and my hate became a little white flame deep in my belly, a little flame I have nursed all these years and that someday I will fan into a raging conflagration that will, with your help, Nometha, burn the white man out of the Ohio country."

"Olathe, I am not the Indian commissioner; Sir William is," Crispin protested, trying to keep his senses about him as she began to move her body against him once more. "I know he regrets the signing of the Treaty of Fort Stanwix and thinks it is producing the wrong results, but you must remember that your people, the Mingos, agreed to it."

"We are only a colony of the lordly Iroquois; we had to agree to it." Her bitter words were in marked contrast to the way she was rubbing against him, having maneuvered so that it was not her belly but the plump mound at its base that was rotating against the bare flesh of his arm.

"I can be very good to you, Nometha," she whispered enticingly. "I am much woman and can sear a man's flesh and soul with my love. What are a few words in comparison to that? That's all it would take, O Nometha, just a few changed words. Not outright lies, only a slight change in Warraghiyagey's words to his western wards."

She was pushing him down on the buffalo robes, her slender, lithe body resting on top of his. Taking his unburned hand, she moved it to the apex of her thighs. "There, Nometha, you wanted very much to touch that but I refused to let you. Now I am giving you permission."

"But only through your dress," he said, the excitement of her nearness running through him like a forest fire.

"You want to touch it for real. Is that your price for a few changed words? Those words have to be changed, Nometha. Johnson is no better than any other white man, but these fools, my people, think he is because their uncles, the Iroquois, say he is. If his words are not changed, the Mingos, the Shawnee, and the Miamis will do nothing."

She stood suddenly and peeled her tunic off over her head, standing over him like a copper-skinned goddess in the light from the flambeaux that lined the wall. "Now, Nometha, do you see the things you want from me?"

"I . . . I—" He stared upward at the wonder of her breasts, rising from her chest like bronzed half-moons, the nipples stiff as steeples at mid-arc. His bewitched eyes marveled at the tapering legs and the dark thick brush at their juncture.

"Do you think I am worth a few words, O Nometha? Is the Gatekeeper who opened the Gates more important than I?"

"No . . . no," he muttered huskily.

"Do you want me, Nometha?" Her voice was like the purr of a lioness. "I am a princess of the Mingo, a woman many braves have desired. They have performed feats of daring to win the right to take me to their furs. Do you hesitate to change a few words in a message you bear, to suggest that Mingo, Miami, and Shawnee join together to resist the onslaught of the white man? All you have to do is tell them to defend themselves as best they can. Is that too much to ask for this?"

She bent her legs so that she was half crouching, legs separated widely so he could see the opened blossom of her sex and inhale its seductive perfume.

Crispin's hands were sweating, a pulse was pounding in his head and his heart was beating so hard he was sure it would burst through his chest. He wanted her . . . he wanted her more than he had ever wanted anything in his whole life. But he could not do what she said he had to do. He could not tell the Ohio country tribes to take up arms against the white man. To do so would be a betrayal of his trust to Sir William and a betrayal of his own belief that war now would be disastrous for these Indians, could bring about their extermination. No, he could not do what she asked, but oh, God, he wanted her with an urgency that was like agony.

"Would you like a closer look, Nometha?" she asked and dropped to her knees astraddle his middle. With a husky laugh, she thrust her pelvis to within inches of his face.

The view was devastating, but the musk of her sex was overwhelming, something at once subtle, savage, and totally breathtaking about it. It started Crispin's head to reeling, his heart to thundering, and his entire being to clamoring to possess the woman. It was unbearable, suggesting delights no man had ever experienced, promising moments of pleasure so fantastic that a man might give up his life to sample them.

"What is the matter, O Nometha?" she taunted. "You look as though you are about to swoon, O bearer of belts from the Six Nations. Is it from desire for me?"

"You . . . you know it is," he gasped, barely able to talk. What did the woman want of him? Did she want to turn him into a gibbering idiot groveling at her feet and offering to do anything . . . sell his honor, go against his patron's orders and his own better judgment? Is that what she wanted? Oh, God, was that all? It seemed so little compared to what she was offering. He felt dizzy and could not see clearly. All he could see, smell, taste, and feel was the warmth and fragrance of the goddesslike body she was offering him.

He made a strangled sound in his throat, which she seemed to take for acquiescence because she moved closer.

"You may kiss me, Crispin," she purred. "Kiss me wherever you desire."

Moments later they were on the buffalo robes, bodies locked together, her lips whispering in his ear. "You are going to do what I asked, Nometha. You are going to do what I ask."

Crispin was snapped from his unhappy reverie by the voice of the anxious Shawnee brave beside him. "It is time, Nometha. Give the signal."

It was completely dark now and the mosquitoes and chiggers were worse than ever; even the way his body had been oiled and painted for war didn't help. There in the clearing the settlers' cabins were lit by candles and firelight, and the time had come to test his theory that the best time to attack a white settlement was in the evening, not at dawn.

"Yes, it is time," Nometha said, lifting his head and cupping his hands beside his mouth to give the war whoop that would send the warriors of half a dozen tribes against the unsuspecting village.

10

Lieutenant Gifford Glencannon was standing next to a 12-pound cannon that peered out between two bales of hay in an embrasure near Roxbury, Massachusetts. The gun, which had been dragged on a sledge all the way from Fort Ticonderoga in northern New York through the bitter cold winter of 1775-76 by troops under the command of portly ex-bookstore owner Henry Knox, had its ugly snout aimed at the town of Boston and the British army that lay encircled by a larger army of colonial militia.

Gifford Glencannon was bored. He had thought that being in the newly formed Continental army would be exciting, especially as a part of Colonel Knox's new artillery regiment. That was why he had spent the last of the pocket money his father had given him when he left Philadelphia on a spanking new blue military coat with red facings and gold lacings. He had also purchased a red vest to go with the coat, but that was as far as his funds would stretch so he had no proper sword and was wearing civilian trousers stuffed into the same boots he had worn upon entering the army.

Under the sharp eye of Colonel Knox, Gifford had become quite proficient at handling his small battery of two 12-pounders, but he had nothing to shoot at. The British had learned their lesson well at Breed's and Bunker hills and nary a redcoat had ventured across Boston Neck or out of their lines around Charlestown.

What was the point of being a lieutenant of artillery with fine new guns and reasonably trained gun crew when there was no target for the guns? The war seemed to have settled down into a contest of which army could bore each other to death first. The redcoats would not come out, and the Continentals could not get in. And since Boston held a good many patriotic New England citizens in addition to redcoats and Tories, the new commander, General Washington, had ordered the guns not to fire on the town.

So this tall, husky, pleasant-faced young man with a shock of blond hair and merry blue eyes was bored. He had come to take part in a war and found it an exercise in patience. Gifford didn't have a lot of patience. If it hadn't been for his pride and the Glencannon honor, he would have left after the fighting at Breed's Hill when half the army had gone home, the term of their enlistment having expired.

But here he was with a fancy new uniform coat, a single epaulet, two good cannon and an eye for aiming a gun with nothing to do but gaze glumly at the rooftops of Boston across the Neck.

"What are they waiting for?" Gifford asked aloud, staring at the tall miters of the grenadiers who were mounting guard on the British emplacements. "What do they want, a written invitation?"

"Well, it's like General Green said, Mister Glencannon," said Pachter, the gunnery sergeant from New Hampshire. "We'll be glad to sell 'em another hill at the same price any day. I don't think they hanker for the sort of bargain they got at Bunker Hill."

He was right, Gifford knew. The English had suffered 1,054 casualties, 226 of them fatal, to take a couple of hills neither they nor the Continentals had any real use for. How would the whole thing end? he wondered. They couldn't starve out the British because the harbor was open and ships could come from England with supplies as well as from Nova Scotia and other colonies. Besides, the British small cruisers could raid the New England coast in search of beef and other foodstuffs. Maybe his father was right, after all. Maybe the best place to win wars was on the sea.

"Hey there, Lieutenant Glencannon!" It was tall, lanky Joshua Leech, a private from Newbury, calling to him. He was wearing a flat hat with a feather in it, a shirt that had once been white, and a red vest.

Sergeant Pachter looked up from his constant whittling and watched the Connecticut man hurrying toward them. "I swear, Josh, if'n yew don't quit wearing that red vest, someone is gonna shoot yew for a lobster-back."

"All I got to wear, Sergeant, since I lost my coat at Breed's Hill when the marines came over the barricades," Leech said, taking a subtle dig at Pachter who had been at Roxbury the day the flame of battle had flared briefly between colonials and redcoats.

"Were you calling to me, Leech?" Gifford said hastily to forestall one of their interminable arguments about the relative virtues of New Hampshire and Connecticut men.

"Yes, sir. There's a fellow back at headquarters a'lookin' for you," Leech said. "Sez he's your uncle, but he don't rightly look old enough to be."

Gifford's face lit up. "Oh, that must be Malcolm. He's my uncle right enough, but he's only a few years older. Is he going to come up to the lines?"

"Captain Taplinger says he shouldn't, but Colonel Knox says for you to come back to headquarters 'cause Lieutenant Howard can relieve you in half an hour."

"It will be nice to see Malcolm," Gifford said excitedly. "We were raised together and are almost like brothers. He's a senior at Yale."

"Yup, he talked like one of them educated fellows," Leech said. "Can allus tell them by the way they talks . . . not like real folks at all."

"And Colonel Knox said it was all right for me to leave now?"

"Sure thing. He says the lobster-backs ain't like to stir out of Boston 'fore Lieutenant Howard arrives to take over. You're to come along and see your uncle and afterwards, he wants to talk to you."

"Thank you, Leech. I'll be right along," Gifford said, wishing he had a sword and a pair of buff breeches and military boots. Since he didn't, he brushed off his coat with his hands, picked up a rag used to polish the barrel of the cannon and tried to put a shine on his old boots. Then turning to Pachter, he said, "Keep a sharp lookout, Sergeant."

"Sure, Lieutenant, yew can depend on me," Pachter said and went right on whittling.

Gifford saw Malcolm when he was still over a hundred feet away from the base that served as headquarters. Almost as tall as Gifford, he was somewhat slimmer and dressed in traveling clothes with a long cape. His hat, a tricorn, he held in his hand as he paced back and forth under the large, spreading oak tree outside the colonel's headquarters. There was someone with him, and Gifford was so surprised that he almost came to a halt, thinking he must be seeing things. But no, it was Susan, Cousin Susan. What on earth was she doing here in Massachusetts, much less in Roxbury so close to the siege lines? She was supposed to be back in Philadelphia. Young, recently widowed women had no business wandering around unchaperoned, certainly not in a country at war.

Gifford hurried toward them, waving his tricorn and hoping they wouldn't notice that the braid on it had turned out to be not braid at all and was badly tarnished from the damp air that came up from Boston harbor every night.

"Malcolm! Susan! How jolly to see you!" he shouted, running the last few yards like the good-natured boy he was instead of the staid officer of Continental artillery he was trying to be.

He threw his arms around Susan and swung her off the ground. "My dear girl, how pretty you look! Wait until the officers in my mess see you! I don't believe I'll tell them you're my cousin, just let them think you're my girl."

"Oh, Gifford, you wouldn't!" Susan pretended to be scandalized as she kissed him on the cheek and readjusted her black velvet bonnet his bear hug had knocked askew.

"And you, you overeducated, handsome dog," Gifford grabbed Malcolm by the hand and pounded him on the shoulder at the same time. "Have you come to join the army? You'll find it a precious bore unless you can get into one of the regiments going to Canada under the command of General Montgomery and Benedict Arnold."

"No, I have not come to join the army," Malcolm said with such a definite intonation that Gifford wondered at it.

"No, of course not," he said. "You'll want to finish at Yale before you take up arms. Why, if I had ever gotten beyond the academy and what Papa taught me, I probably wouldn't be wearing this uniform either."

"And very handsome you look in it," Susan said before Malcolm could open his mouth to say anything.

"Thank you, dear cousin," Gifford smiled and took each by an arm. "There's a small tavern down the street just off the village green called the Happy Haven. It has a screened off back room where a lady can be served. Why don't we go there and have a glass of ale or wine and something to eat. It isn't often we get visitors here in Roxbury in the range of the British guns."

Malcolm hesitated, and Gifford, thinking it might have been the mention of the guns that had caused it, added quickly, "Of course, they hardly ever fire. They don't want a return bombardment from my guns. Oh, Malcolm, you should see them. I have two of the most beautiful twelve-pounders you ever saw. Colonel Knox and the rest of us dragged them all the way from Fort Ticonderoga on sledges—eight brass and six iron mortars, thirty iron and thirteen brass guns, and a howitzer. One of the guns is a great twenty-four pounder, some of the others eighteen-pounders, but my twelve-pounders are the pick of the lot. And Malcolm, Colonel Knox says I've the best eye for aiming them that he's ever seen."

Susan clapped her hands, but Malcolm looked more somber than ever. "You take pleasure in killing other men with cannon fire?"

Gifford was somewhat taken aback. "Pleasure in killing men? Well, I haven't yet, you know. I've only fired the guns in practice, but I am sure that if the time comes when I have to do so to defend my country, it will give me a certain kind of pleasure."

"Now, now, Malcolm," Susan said, patting his hand, "we can't all have your ideals."

They had come to the tavern now and Gifford waited until they were seated in the secluded back room and the roly-poly innkeeper had taken their orders before asking, "Just what are your ideals, Malcolm? Are you on *their* side?"

"No, of course not," Malcolm said. "I am not on either side. I abhor this war. I abhor all war."

Gifford stared at his young uncle as though seeing him for the first time. For a healthy young animal like Gifford, war seemed like just one more form of blood sport. How anyone could possibly hate something that brought excitement into life was beyond his understanding.

"Try to understand Malcolm's point of view, Giff," Susan said. "One of his brothers was killed in the Forty-five before he was even born, his father was sold into slavery because he fought in it and finally went mad from the cruelty inflicted upon him. And then, there was Shawn. Malcolm and I adored Shawn as children, and then he went off to Quebec and was killed in another useless war."

"My father served in both those wars," Gifford said, bristling slightly. "And he was with Grandfather when he died. I've never heard him say the war was useless."

"All wars are useless," Malcolm said flatly.

Gifford was not a particularly perceptive person, but looking into Malcolm's brooding eyes, he sensed there was more troubling the man than appeared on the surface. He didn't want to argue with him, but he couldn't let that statement go unchallenged either.

"The French war rid the colonies of the French and Indian troubles."

"And now there are new Indian problems because we constantly push the poor devils off their land and forever mistreat them in other ways," Malcolm said.

"You sound like my mother used to," Gifford said. "Are you becoming a Quaker, Malcolm?"

"No. I admired Felicity very much and now find I agree with her on the futility and horror of war, but I fear I do not have her religious convictions. Perhaps I have no religious convictions at all."

The innkeeper came with the ale for the men and wine for Susan. Gifford gulped at his thirstily, but the other two only sipped at theirs.

"Enough talk of war and such," Gifford said, looking from one to the other of them. "To what do I owe this happy visit? Why are my two favorite relatives here in Roxbury?"

"Why to see you, of course, Giff," Susan smiled at him fondly. "You know we wouldn't pass so close and not come to see you."

"I should hope not, but where are you going? Why are you away from Yale, Malcolm, and you from Germantown, Susan? And what is the news of the family? I have not heard from Papa in six weeks."

Susan and Malcolm exchanged glances and apparently came to a silent agreement that she should do the talking for both of them. They had always communicated better with each other than with other people, Gifford remembered from his childhood.

"Gifford, I think your father has not written because he is most unhappy and does not want to disturb you while you are serving in the army."

"What is it?" Gifford asked in alarm. "Is he ill? Is Shawna, or Faith?"

"No, no, they are all well," Susan said. "In fact, Malcolm and I see no real cause for his unhappiness. You see, far from being ill, both Shawna and Faith have married."

"What? Good God!" Gifford said in relief. "I turn my back for a year and both my sisters get married. But that means Papa is all alone at home and at the shipyard."

"Shawna trained a good foreman for him at the shipyard, and Faith hired a housekeeper before she left."

"That's good. I suppose Shawna married that stodgy ship's captain who was always hanging around, but who did Faith marry?"

Malcolm cleared his throat. "There is the main cause of your father's discontent. Faith ran away with a friend of mine, a classmate named Thad Williams."

Gifford looked puzzled. "Well, Faith is a little young to have married, but I never knew Papa to harbor a dislike for Yale men. After all, he went to the school of hard knocks, not Harvard."

Malcolm smiled but did not break into laughter as he would have in the old days. "I'm afraid it is my friend's politics that has upset David. Thad's father, you see, is a rich New York merchant, and the family is Loyalist."

"They are what?" Gifford exploded and almost knocked over his tankard of ale. "Are you telling me my sister married a damn Tory?"

"Please, Giff," Susan begged. "Thad is a friend of Malcolm's and Malcolm has suffered enough for that friendship without your adding to it."

Gifford scowled. This was shocking news to a young man who saw the current war in black and white, and who considered those who remained loyal to German George as toadies to a vile tyrany.

"Little Faith . . . I cannot believe it." He was distressed for his father and angry at Faith. It seemed to him Malcolm had somehow betrayed the family by having a friend who was a Tory. Then Susan's last words echoed in his head and he looked at her. "How do you mean Malcolm has suffered for his friendship with this Williams?"

Susan put a hand over Malcolm's and gave Gifford a fleeting smile before she spoke. "Malcolm has only a few more months of work at Yale, but his life is being made almost unbearable by those of his classmates who support the cause of the colonies. They refuse to see there is a difference between being a Loyalist, or Tory, and being opposed to war in all its forms. Malcolm is not a Tory, Giff, he is a pacifist in the true sense, just as your mother was. But those horrible young men at Yale refuse to accept that. They seem to feel that anyone who is not for the patriot cause is against it."

"But you have many friends at Yale, Malcolm," Gifford said. "I met some of them when I came to New Haven last summer. There was Ben Talmadge, Robert Townshend, the Hale brothers . . . Nathan and Enoch and you were all so close."

Gifford had finished his first tankard of ale and ordered another, although the other two had hardly touched their first drinks.

Malcolm waited until the innkeeper had gone back into the front room of the tavern, then said, "All of them except Nathan have turned away from me, although they are not among my chief persecutors. That group is led by Sidney Harmon, whose father was an unsuccessful business rival of Thad's father. He seemingly has transferred his enmity from Thad to me now that Thad has left New Haven for New York."

"Well, I am sorry you have these problems," Gifford said after several long draughts of ale, "but you must understand that in times of war men's minds can be closed to the niceties, to the fine line that perhaps should be drawn between the enemy and a neutral."

"My, my, how philosophical my little nephew has become," Malcolm said dryly, and Gifford felt himself flushing.

Susan hastened to fill the brief uncomfortable silence. "Actually, Gifford, these people, who are making it almost impossible for Malcolm to get his degree, are incapable of differentiating between one set of principles and another. They are actively vindictive, and for reasons that cannot be considered political. Harmon, the ring leader, has the personal reason Malcolm mentioned and is determined to drive Malcolm out of Yale before he can be graduated. This would be most devastating to Malcolm's future since he has now decided to read for the law."

"Oh ho, so you are going to be a lawyer, are you?" Gifford said, ordering a third mug of ale. "Well now, that's something the family has always needed, but . . . well, I hope you do not misunderstand this, but there's not going to be much use for lawyers for the next few years, only soldiers, I'm afraid."

"That does not solve Malcolm's problem," Susan said, her hazel eyes full of concern.

"Well, if this fellow is really causing you that much grief, Malcolm, then you must call him out."

"Oh, Gifford, how could you?" Susan cried.

"Does it not seem to you, Gifford, that if I am against war I would be equally against killing a man in a senseless duel?"

"You don't have to kill him," Gifford said. "Simply notch his ears like Shawn did to that bounder before the Forty-five."

Malcolm sighed and leaned back in his chair, giving Susan another of those intimate looks that Gifford was beginning to find disquieting. Apparently he had decided that communicating his problem to a young hothead was impossible and was ready to change the subject.

"Well, we were glad to be able to stop by and see you," he said, "and bring you news of the family."

"Yes, I am glad you came too," Gifford said. "You say Faith has gone off with your friend to New York?"

"Aye, and David has sworn that from that day on, he has but one daughter," Malcolm said.

"Oh, I'm sure he will forget that, sooner or later."

"I am not so sure."

"And Shawna has married Captain Ewart, has she?" Gifford asked. "Never thought she would, but I guess it is well enough. Where is she?"

"Do not worry about Shawna," Susan said. "I suspect she is in her glory. She has browbeaten her husband into taking her along on his voyages to the Indies and by now is probably standing watches on the poop deck and showing off her navigating to one and all."

Gifford laughed. Shawna was about his favorite person in the whole world, although he was a little jealous of the fact that she had picked up navigation much faster than he had under their father's teaching.

"We really have to be leaving soon if we are to catch the stage at Cambridge," Malcolm said, glancing at his pocket watch.

"But you haven't told me where you are going or where you have come from," Gifford said. "And where is Aunt Aileen?"

Susan looked at Malcolm, and he cleared his throat before he spoke. "Well, Aileen is in Gloucester visiting old Captain Pratt and his wife. Amos has been ailing but is better now, and Susan felt she would like to join her mother for a few weeks by the sea."

"Yes, of course," Gifford said, not seeing at all.

"So since I was on my way back to Yale, I volunteered to escort her to Gloucester, and then we decided to stop by to see you."

There was something about the explanation that didn't ring true, Gifford thought, and was still puzzling over it a half hour later after they were gone and he was hurrying to headquarters to see what Colonel Knox wanted of him.

It went completely out of his mind when the tall, handsome, and friendly Knox greeted him.

"Come in, come in, Glencannon," boomed the man. "I want you to meet Commodore Manley who wants to make a sailor out of you."

"A sailor, sir?" Gifford asked, a thrill of excitement shooting through him.

"Yes. General Washington has grown tired of waiting for the Congress to improvise a navy, so he is starting one of his own, and Manley here is to command it. I have recommended you as the best of my young gunnery officers. Do you think you will like that, Glencannon?"

"Colonel Knox, I think I am going to love it!" Gifford said, and all thought of the strange way Susan and Malcolm had acted fled from his mind in the face of his new opportunity for adventure.

11

Gifford arrived in Philadelphia early in February 1776 and appeared at his father's door bundled up in a greatcoat that looked suspiciously like it had once belonged to a British officer. When a delighted David brushed away the snow and helped him out of it, he stared in astonishment at the uniform his son was wearing. It was the blue pants, blue jacket with red facings, and red vest of the new Continental navy rather than the uniform of the artillery.

"I've changed services, Papa," Gifford said with his usual enthusiasm. "You were right, the place to fight a war is on the sea. That's where the prize money is to be won. Look at this uniform—I had it made by the finest tailor in New Jersey—and this fine sword. I paid for it all with the prize money I picked up on a single voyage with Commodore Manley in the schooner *Lee*. With only six small guns we captured the British transport *Nancy* right under Tommy Gage's long English nose at the mouth of Boston Harbor. She might have been fitted out for the very purpose of supplying General Washington's army. She carried a hundred thousand flints, two thousand muskets, and a thirteen-inch brass mortar. Everything our poor general's mouth has been watering for and a negligent Congress has refused to provide."

"Whoa, laddie, whoa!" said David, pouring sherry into two glasses and handing Gifford one. "You do not understand the problems the Congress has."

"No, but I understand the problems they are making for General Washington when they ask him to conduct a war without giving him the means to fight it," Gifford said, and sipped at the sherry appreciatively. This was the first time his father had served him anything stronger than small beer, so he must consider him a full-grown man now that he was a full-fledged lieutenant in the Continental navy. That pleased Gifford more than the lieutenancy itself.

"Sit down, lad, sit down," David urged, gesturing toward the big comfortable chair at one side of the roaring fire and seating himself in the chair across from it. "Tell me all that's happened."

"Well, at first I spent most of my time cooling my heels in the Roxbury line, wondering if the war wasn't going to kill more men by boredom than by gunfire. Then Colonel Knox recommended me for service aboard one of the six fast little schooners General Washington had, of necessity, fitted out to oppose the English on the sea. I was pleased but not really excited about that until I met John Manley and was introduced to General Washington. Papa, do you know he remembered Grandfather!"

"He did? After all these years?"

Gifford nodded, grinning. "Yes. As soon as he heard my name, he showed an interest. 'Are you, by any chance, related to the Major Glencannon who served with me at Fort Necessity and during the unfortunate business of Braddock's defeat?' he asked.

" 'Yes, sir,' I told him. 'Shawn Glencannon was my grandfather, although I scarce remember him since I was so small when he was killed along with General Wolfe on the Plains of Abraham.'

"He sighed and looked sad for a moment, then said, 'I am sorry to hear he's gone. We always lose the good ones, it seems. Well, Lieutenant, may you prove as daring and resourceful a fighter as your grandfather.'"

"Remarkable that he should remember," David said, "but Shawn always did leave an indelible impression on people."

"So it would seem," Gifford said and returned to the subject of his own career. "I tell you, Papa, once I got to sea on the *Lee*, I knew I was in the right service. I was sorry I had wasted time in the army, but when I joined up, there wasn't any navy. Now we have a real one forming up here at Philadelphia. I hear there are to be six ships, one carrying as many as thirty guns. That should really cause some excitement because British cruisers are swarming off the coast like flies."

David smiled wryly. "I'm not so sure there will be much excitement. Congress has chosen an old hack from the merchant marine, Esek Hopkins, as commodore and other not very choice types for most other commands."

Gifford nodded. "I'm to sail with Hopkins on the *Alfred*, and a man named Dudley Saltonstall is flag captain."

"It might interest you to know that Esek Hopkins was picked to command the squadron because his brother was a member of the Marine Committee. Dudley Saltonstall became second in command because he is the brother-in-law of Silas Deane, also a member of the committee."

"Please, Papa," Gifford said, laughing, "you are disparaging my superior officers before they even take their squadron to sea."

"There's one good officer on the *Alfred*," David said. "He's a Scot and—"

"And all Scots are good men, eh, Papa?"

"No, some are the worst kind of scoundrels. I knew one during the Forty-five, a man named Murray, who was not only a thief but a traitor as well. Shawn would have broken his neck if he could have got his hands on him, but the fellow always managed to stay a few steps ahead of him."

Gifford wasn't interested in hearing about the past, so he reminded his father of the subject at hand. "You were going to tell me about one good officer on the *Alfred*."

"Ah, yes. His name is Jones . . . John Paul Jones. He's flag lieutenant. They say he used to be a pirate, but he seems an ardent soul and certainly understands the sea."

Gifford laughed. "So I'm to go to sea with two political appointees and a pirate. Can't say it sounds very promising."

David got up and refilled their glasses. "And you'll be going in an old crock of a vessel as slow and as cranky as any potbellied merchantman I ever saw. She's not fit to carry her thirty guns. I had her hauled out for six weeks but there wasn't much I could do to turn her into a man-o'-war except tear out rotten planking and step her mainmast forward a foot or so in hopes of giving her an extra knot or two."

Stretching his legs out toward the fire, Gifford sipped at his wine, enjoying the warmth both inside and out after the long ride on the top of a stage in a cold wind and snow flurries. "Are there no other good officers in the squadron save this Scottish pirate of yours?"

"Well, there's Nicholas Biddle of *Doria*. He should make a mark if he gets a chance, but she's only a fourteen-gun brig and will be sailing in the teeth of the world's largest navy. Damn it, if only Congress had authorized sooner the frigates we're now building! They could be ready for sea by the time the ice in the Delaware thaws and the ships are ready to sail. With *Randolph, Hancock,* and *Virginia,* our infant navy would not be stillborn as I fear it will with the likes of *Alfred, Cabot,* and their ilk as our only warships."

"But, Papa, that can't be helped, and perhaps the seamen will make up for what the ships lack in speed and the officers in courage and perspicacity."

"I'm not all that impressed by the caliber of the seamen either," David said gloomily. "Congress has authorized the raising of two battalions of marine infantry with the stipulation that they be chosen 'with particular care that none be enlisted in the battalions but such as are good seamen,' but they have also taken a strong line against profane language in the service. It escapes me how men can operate such seagoing museum pieces without needing to do a lot of cursing and praying."

Gifford laughed and said with his customary optimism, "We'll do well enough. I hope they send us directly against the British cruisers who are harassing our coasts."

"Now that I know you'll be with them," David said, rising and crossing over to the solid oak desk in the far corner of the room, "I hope their destination is elsewhere, but I believe the Marine Committee tends more toward your view." He removed a paper from the desk and studied it briefly. "It seems that simpering idiot, Lord Dunmore, has fitted out a flotilla of minor vessels, and they are making life miserable along the shores of the southern states by conducting raids and seizing colonial merchant ships and fishing craft. Having caused a savage Indian war to the western frontier, the Tory swine now proposes to bring war to the eastern seaboard as well. The committee hopes that Commodore Hopkins's squadron will be strong enough to rout Lord Dunmore's vessels, if not to fight the Royal Navy itself."

"Well, that shouldn't prove too great a task for *Alfred*, *Columbus*, *Doria*, *Cabot*, and the others," Gifford said.

"No, not unless Lord Dunmore's privateers are reinforced by British men-o'-war. Assuming, of course, that Esek has the stomach for such action."

"Your opinion of our commodore's courage is not very high," Gifford observed. "I have heard he's an experienced seaman, and that he once captained a privateer during the French war. On one of his voyages, he fought off pirates on the Malabar coast."

"Oh yes, I have heard of his doughty deeds," David said testily. "We have all heard a great deal about them, not only from the man himself, but from the convivial Stephen Hopkins, his brother and the delegate from Rhode Island. Not that the rest of them are much better, mind you. Hoysted Hacker is an incompetent, and Saltonstall is a narrow-minded, shortsighted Puritan aristocrat who can't see over the edge of his Bible to tell if an enemy is in sight or not. No, they are a bad lot—the commodore and most of the captains, except for Manley who has courage, and Biddle who could be the Drake of our navy if he but has the chance."

"Come, come, Papa, aren't you perhaps a little bit jealous? Don't you wish for a command yourself?"

David shot his son a sharp glance, then turned and walked over to the casemented window and stared out at the soft white snowflakes drifting on the wind. "The weather is moderating. I think the ice in Delaware may start to break up before too long. Then we will have a chance to learn something definite about our valiant commodore and his captains."

"You didn't answer my question, Papa," Gifford reminded him.

"No, I didn't," David said, turning away from the window and bringing the decanter of sherry back to refill their glasses. "But the answer is yes and no. Yes, I am a wee bit jealous. I would very much like to command a warship in this struggle for freedom, and I think I could do a better job than the man we've been discussing, but the job I am doing here is more important. I am building *Randolph* to a design of mine and Joshua Humphreys's, and he is constructing *Washington* to the same design. They are larger ships and should be faster than any their rate in the British navy. It will be generations before we will be able to match them in numbers, so we must do so in individual ships."

Walking over to the fireplace, he stirred up the fire and laid a new log in place.

"But those ships must have officers, and I believe I know where they will come from. Not from the political hacks and rusticated marine officers the Marine Committee has seen fit to saddle us with, but from ardent, coolheaded men like Biddle and Jones. And you, Gifford . . . yes, why not you, my lad? If you have half of Shawn's daring and a measure of my own prudence, you should do well . . . very well, indeed."

"Thank you, Papa," Gifford said, touched. "I hope I live up to your expectations because I honestly feel that the sea is my life."

"Good lad!" David said, clapping him on the shoulder. "Now, what are your immediate plans? The *South Star*, Seth Ewart's ship, is due at the mouth of the Delaware within a week and your sister is aboard. If the squadron does not sail before then, you will be able to see her before you go off to the wars."

"I'm looking forward to that," Gifford said, "and I was also hoping to see Faith."

His father's face froze and then a black frown creased his brow. "You have no sister named Faith."

"But, Papa—" she *is* my sister, and—"

"No. She chose to marry a Tory and lives with in New York with the rest of that vile breed who fester there. She is no longer my daughter."

"But, Papa—" Gifford began but didn't finish the sentence. He knew it was useless to point out that in another time and place, Shawn and his sons had been Tories and preferred the old king to the new. If David could change from Tory to Whig, wasn't it possible for Faith to swing the other direction without being considered outside the pale? Not that Faith had changed her politics—she didn't have any to change, if he remembered correctly. She had simply fallen in love and chosen to go with the man she loved.

After a few minutes of silence, during which David stared moodily into the fire and Gifford sipped his wine, the younger man decided it was best to change the subject.

"I forgot to tell you, Papa. I saw Malcolm and Susan."

David looked up in surprise. "With all your other activities, you had time to visit New Haven and Gloucester? You certainly move fast, young fellow."

"No, no, Papa," Gifford laughed. "I didn't visit them. They sought me out in the Roxbury lines."

David frowned again. "Both at the same time? Are you telling me Malcolm and Susan were traveling together?"

"Yes. What's so odd about an uncle escorting a niece to her mother's side?" Even as he posed the question, Gifford recalled that he had thought there was something very odd about it.

David's frown deepened. "Malcolm was escorting Susan to Aileen's side?"

"That's what they said. They told me Aunt Aileen was in Gloucester visiting old Captain Pratt and his wife, that Susan was on her way to join Aileen and Malcolm was escorting Susan there."

"Hmmmm. I could have sworn that Aileen said in her last letter that Susan was with her at the Pratts. When did you say they were in Roxbury?"

"About two months ago," Gifford said. "Just before Colonel Knox recommended me to Captain Manley and I went to sea."

"I see. Well, I think Aileen's letter was dated before that, but I didn't save it so I can't be sure."

Gifford shrugged. "If you're right, why would Malcolm have lied about where they had come from or were going? Do you think she had been to New Haven to see him and they didn't want to mention it lest it be misunderstood?"

David shook his head. "I don't know. They saw an awful lot of each other at Christmas, and for some reason, that upset Aileen terribly. She talked to me about it, but there wasn't much either one of us could do. Besides, there isn't much reason why they shouldn't spend time together, especiall since Malcolm hasn't married and Susan is now a widow."

His father didn't sound very convincing, and from the look on his face Gifford doubted that he actually believed the last statement. The more Gifford remembered what had passed between Malcolm and Susan—the strange intimacy, the unspoken communication, and the glances that seemed to convey understanding beyond mere words—the more disquieting he found the whole situation.

"Well, whatever the problem is, I'm sure they will work it out for the best," he said to reassure David as much as himself. "After all, Malcolm is a level-headed, intelligent man in spite of his odd political ideas."

"What odd political ideas?" David asked absently.

"Why he's a pacifist," Gifford said. "He doesn't believe there is any justice in our cause, or in any cause, that can justify war. I suppose that comes of too much education."

"No doubt," David said, not wanting to discuss the matter any further. It disturbed him that Malcolm felt the way he did, but talking about it wouldn't change a thing. He knew that from his experience with Felicity. A woman of considerable intelligence and overwhelming decency, she had allowed herself to be talked into financing and helping found a ridiculously impractical communal settlement in the forests far northwest of the tribal lands of the Iroquois where settlers were in obvious peril from French-led hostile Indians. The purpose of the settlement, she had assured him, was to promote peace with the Indians. It had, of course, done no such thing, but merely presented a tempting target for raiding bands of Abnakis. The good Christians of Harmony Hill, all Quakers and pacifists, had been unarmed, so the good Christian Abnakis, egged on by their priests, had set out to murder them. Only the timely arrival of David, Billy Dickenson, and a band of heathen Mohawks had stopped the slaughter of one group of Christians by the other.

David sighed, his thoughts still on Felicity. She had been a good wife to him despite their differences, and he knew she had suffered torment during the rest of the French war knowing he and Shawn were still among Sir William Johnson's chief scouts. Her suffering increased when he had fought along with Johnson during the victorious campaign against Niagara, during Bouquet's bloody march to Fort Pitt, and Wolfe's final victory in Quebec. Yes, she had suffered and while suffering had borne him three children, but he had never been sure which troubled her the most—the chance that he might be killed or the knowledge that he was killing other men.

Yes, having been married to Felicity, he could understand Malcolm to a certain extent. He only hoped those pacifist feelings didn't lead him into further folly as Felicity's had led her. Lord, how upset she would be if she knew the *Alfred*, on which her son would soon be going to war, had been repaired at Glencannon & Sons, the shipyard established with the help of her money.

"Papa . . . Papa!" Gifford's voice broke in on David's reverie. "It is getting late, and I'm to report on board *Alfred* at eight sharp tomorrow morning."

"Eh? Oh yes, of course, my lad," David said, rising. "Have you had supper?"

"I ate dinner at the inn in Trenton," Gifford said, "but I confess I could use a bite more."

"Then I'll summon Meg." David reached for the bellpull. "She's as wide as she is tall but a good cook and keeps the maids a'hopping. I suspect Shawna picked her for her ugliness more than her efficiency, but she'll do on both counts, and I shan't be tempted to do anything my redheaded daughter wouldn't approve of while she's away."

Gifford supped on the remains of a beef potpie, cheese, and beer while Meg, a round-faced, jolly Irish woman, hovered over him.

"Eat your fill, Master Gifford," she urged. "You'll not be gettin' decent food aboard that old tub, nor will the Sassenach feed you decent in their prison hulks after the *Alfred* is taken, as she's sure to be."

"Your optimism overwhelms me, Mistress Meg," Gifford laughed as he started on his second helping of meat pie. "Why not think of how we shall feed the British after *we* have taken *them*?"

"Oh, I know how I'd be after feeding them," Meg said. "They'd get hog swill if I had the doing of it!"

"And they'll do the same to us if they catch us," he said.

"Bad cess to the lot of 'em, I say!" was her parting shot. "And you still better eat well whilst you can."

Gifford slept soundly that night, snug and warm in the room and bed that had been his since childhood, protected from the chill wind that shrieked about the eaves by down comforters that smelled faintly of lavender. He was eager to get to sea, but for this night at least, he was glad to be home safe and comfortable instead of huddled in a greatcoat on the poop deck of a warship in the midst of a frigid Atlantic gale.

In the morning, after a hearty breakfast of fried scrapple and eggs and three cups of steaming coffee, Gifford ventured outside at seven. The leaden sky was just starting to lighten in the east as he started down the narrow streets in the direction of the waterfront. The cobbles were hidden beneath a blanket of freshly fallen snow, and the masts of the stranded merchant ships looked like hundreds of branchless tree trunks.

As he had left the house, his father had gripped his hand hard and clapped him on the shoulder. "You'll make a fine naval officer, Gifford. There's no need to tell you to be brave—you're a Glencannon, so 'tis probably better to counsel you to be prudent rather than rash."

"Prudent like you and grandfather were back in the old wars, Papa?" Gifford had asked.

"Prudent as we should hae been," David said, a hint of Scottish burr creeping into his voice as it always did in moments of emotion. "We were no always our own best friends . . . not Shawn, not I, not Steven, nor the rest of us. Faith, 'tis more there'd be of us now if we had been, and remember, laddie, we canna spare you."

"I'll try to remember," Gifford said with a grin, "but you're not rid of me yet, Papa. I shall probably be back for supper since I see no way we can sail yet."

"Not yet, but soon," David said, looking up at the sky.

Buttoning up his coat, Gifford had gone out into Walnut Street and headed for the river on foot, leaving his gear to be brought on later by a servant. A cold wind was blowing up from the river as he passed Bishop White's residence, Christ Church, and the malodorous premises of Israel Israel's livery stable. Walnut Street was wide and much traveled, its cobbles at the moment packed with trampled snow, rutted by Conestoga wagons and filthy with the droppings of horses and cattle that daily passed through even the best streets of the city.

Turning onto Second Street, head bent against the wind that whipped his greatcoat about his legs, Gifford headed toward Market Street, passing one of the new Bettering Houses where homeless folk and drifters were lodged by the city and provided with work and keep while they earned enough money to carry them on their way. The closer he got to the Delaware, the more bitter the wind became, and when he turned onto the hundred-foot wide expanse of Market Street, which led straight to the river, he struggled to hold his cocked hat on his head while trying to keep his greatcoat from turning into a sail that would carry him back the way he had come.

"If this weather keeps up, we'll not sail till the middle of August," he muttered to himself as he approached the ivy-covered, red brick building known as Mechanics Hall, "and the war will be over before we ever see an English frigate."

He eyed the building curiously as he went by, knowing it was there that the Second Continental Congress was sitting, having sworn not to disband until Parliament guaranteed the rights of the colonies. It was there also that the Marine Committee met and would issue the orders for the small fleet assembled in the Delaware to move, or not move, against His Majesty's naval forces.

He was quite a way beyond Mechanics Hall when he heard someone calling his name.

"Glencannon! I say, Giff Glencannon, is that you?"

He turned to see a tall young man running toward him, hatless, unruly black hair blowing in the wind, and handsome features wreathed in a smile.

"It's Bret, Giff . . . Bret Morley."

"Oh yes, Morley . . . didn't recognize you for a minute. Don't think I've ever seen you except in your fancy coach with a footman or two in attendance." Gifford was laughing, but what he said was largely true. Morley was the older by three or four years and they had met through Bret's interest in Shawna, but Gifford had felt he could never know any man so rich very well.

Morley seemed a bit taken aback for a moment, then laughed as he caught up with Gifford. "Always surrounded by the signs of wealth, do you mean? Well, that's been stripped away from me, every last cent of it."

Gifford turned his back into the wind and looked at the other youth, puzzled. "I don't understand."

"It's simple enough," Bret said. "The courts have just finished with me and I now have to get out of town or be thrown into debtor's prison."

"But, Bret, how can that be? You had so much."

"Yes, and I held such bad cards, loved such profligate women, and had so many needy friends," Morley said and held up a piece of paper. "Now all I have is this."

"What is it?"

"This, my fine young friend, is my passport out of Philadelphia, and out of the colonies, for a year or so, I hope. It is a warrant making me a midshipman on the United Colonies ship of war *Alfred*, which is soon to raise anchor and speed away into the frigid waters with yours truly safely on board."

"Oh, good Lord!" Gifford said, breaking into laughter.

"You find my fate humorous?"

"No . . . no, it's just that—" Gifford unfastened his greatcoat and threw it open to reveal his blue uniform with red facings and vest. "It seems we've both taken the same course."

"Well, I'll be! So you, too, are for the life of a sailor. I heard you were in the artillery."

"I was, but I grew tired of sitting in the Roxbury lines doing nothing while Johnny Gage played with half the Tory ladies of Boston."

"And you're a lieutenant. However did you manage? I tried to wangle a like commission out of the committee, but since I no longer have the wherewithal to grease palms, I was lucky to get a middy's berth. They first offered me a sailing master's warrant, but I told them I was still a gentleman, no matter the state of my fortune, and they sniffed through their long New England noses and allowed as how I might be a little old to be a midshipman—the median age is seven and a half, I believe—but they could offer that much."

Gifford laughed. "Most of our midshipmen are older than that. The British navy may take them that young, but ours have to be old enough to wipe their own noses."

"And you are a lordly lieutenant . . . my superior officer. Have I broken the rules of the road, or of naval etiquette, by addressing you as Giff?"

"Not as long as we're not on duty," Gifford said. "At least, I don't think so."

"Thank God. I shouldn't want to be cashiered before I'm even on the muster roll, or whatever it is ships use to keep track of their captive population," Bret said. "How did you get to be a lieutenant? You didn't answer that important question. Maybe I can go back and try again."

"There was no problem for me," Gifford told him. "I had worked my way up to captain in the army and when I transferred to the navy I was given the equal rank, which is lieutenant."

"You mean naval ranks are higher than army?" Bret asked. "If I went into the army, could I be a lieutenant?"

"I don't think so. The navy needs officers, the army needs privates for the most part. You could end up carrying a musket."

Bret shivered. "Dreadful thought. And I should have to walk to do that."

"Now you'll ride all the way," Gifford said, "and roughly on occasion, I'm afraid."

"I've sailed my own yawl on the Hudson, you know," Bret said. "I'm not entirely without experience."

"The Hudson and Atlantic are somewhat different," Gifford pointed out.

"True. Well, perhaps you can help me off to a good start." He showed Gifford the warrant and an order penned in a meticulously neat hand. "This says I am to report to a John Paul Jones, first lieutenant of the *Alfred,* a semiretired pirate they tell me. How does one approach a semiretired pirate?"

"First, I would suggest you get a hat so you can touch it to the quarterdeck when you go aboard; secondly, I wouldn't make any mention of Lieutenant Jones's being a semiretired pirate. Best thing to do is to watch me, I guess, because I am to report to Jones also."

"You are? You mean we are to be on the same ship and you will be my superior officer?" Bret's face was a mixture of dismay and pleasure. "My, my, wouldn't our dear Shawna find that ironic?"

Gifford stiffened. "Would she?"

"Yes, and something else she would find ironic is that I told her I had a way out of my dilemma . . . that there was a very rich lady who was willing to bail me out if I married her. That struck your high-minded sister as rather a low-minded remedy, and she said she never wanted to see me again. Well, what she would find ironic is that when it came right down to it, I could not go through with the bargain. I had to refuse the lady. Which shows, I guess, that even a rakehell like Bret Morley has his limits."

Turning to face into the wind again, Gifford said noncommittally, "I think we had better move along and report aboard the *Alfred.*"

12

Excerpts from log of United Colonies ship *Alfred,* 24, Captain Dudley Saltonstall, commanding Commodore Esek Hopkins flag:

February 17, 1776. Departed mouth of Delaware River with Cape May bearing N.N.W. This twenty-four hours began with cold, foggy weather, light winds E.B.N. Sailing in company with *Columbus,* 20, Abraham Whipple commanding; *Andrew Doria,* 14, Nicholas Biddle commanding; *Cabot,* 14, John B. Hopkins commanding; *Providence,* 12, Tom Hazard commanding. Sailing S.S.E. on port tack enroute New Providence, Bahamas, pursuant to orders of Naval Committee of Congress of United Colonies for the purpose of taking measures for securing and bringing away large quantity of powder stored there. Ship logging five knots. Ten seamen and petty officers much ill with pox. Buried one Samuel Taylor, AB, at dusk.

March 2, 1776. Sighted southern part of Abaco Island, Bahamas. Light winds E.B.N. Flagship fired a gun to starboard to attract attention of fleet, and ships' boats put off from *Columbus, Andrew Doria, Cabot* to bring captains on board for conference with Commodore.

Hornet and *Fly* having failed to make rendezvous, council decided to proceed without them.

Letter from Commodore Esek Hopkins, on board *Alfred*, 24, enroute New Providence, Rhode Island ports, to the Honorable John Hancock, Esquire, Presidt. of the Congress at Philadelphia:

When I put to Sea the 17th Febry. from Cape Henlopen, we had many Sick, and four of the Vessels had a large number on board with the Small Pox. The *Hornet* and *Wasp* join'd me two days before, the Wind came at N.E. which made it unsafe to lye there. The Wind after we got out came on to blow hard. I did not think we were in a Condition to keep on a cold Coast, and appointed our Rendezvous at Abaco, one of the Bahama Islands. The second night we lost *Hornet* and *Fly*. I arrived at the Rendezvous in order to wait for the Fleet fourteen days agreeable to Orders. I then formed an expedition against New Providence which I put in Execution the 3rd March by land, two hundred Marines under the Command of Captn. Nicholas, and fifty Sailors under the Command of Lieutt. Weaver of the *Cabot* who was well acquainted there.

The same day they took Possession of a small Fort of Seventeen pieces of Cannon without any opposition save five Guns which were fired at them without doing any damage. I received that evening an Account that they had two hundred odd Men in the Main Fort (all inhabitants). I then caused a Manifesto to be published, the Purport of which was ('That the Inhabitants and their Property should be safe if they did not oppose me in taking possession of the Fort and Kings Stores'), which had the desired effect for the Inhabitants left the Fort and Governor almost alone.

Captn. Nicholas sent by my Orders to the Governor for the Keys of the Fort which was delivered and the Troops march'd directly in where we found the several Warlike Stores agreeable to the Inventory inclosed, but the Governor sent 150 barrs. Powder off in a Small Sloop the night before.

I have taken all the Stores onboard the Fleet, and a large Sloop that I found there which I have promis'd the owner to Send back and pay him hire for.

The *Fly* join'd us at Providence and gave an account that she got foul of the *Hornet* and carried away her Boom and head of her Mast and I hear since she has got into some port of South Carolina.

I have taken the Governor Montford Brown, the Lieutt. Governor, who is a half-pay officer, and Mr. Thomas Arwin, who is Counsellor and Collector of His Majesty's Quit-Rents in South Carolina, and it appears by the Court Callender that he is also Inspector General of His Majesty's Customs for North America.

Since we came out we have lost Company with the *Wasp*.

I am with great Respct.
Your most Obedt. humb. Servt.
E.H.

Extract from Log of United Colonies Ship *Alfred*, 24:

April 4th. Under way enroute New Providence to New London, Connecticut. First part of this twenty-four hours fair and pleasant, light winds S.S.E., making good 2 knots against headwinds on starboard tack. At sunup sighted sail bearing N.N.E. Made out sail to be HBM Schooner *Hawk*. *Columbus* hoisted request to engage and received permission of Commodore. *Columbus*, 20, Captain Whipple commanding, took schooner *Hawk*, 6 guns, without resistance.

April 5th. Under way enroute New Providence to New London. With Block Island bearing S.W. sighted strange sail. *Alfred*, 24, hoisted Commodore's Pennant and proceeded in pursuit. Overhauled and took HBM Bomb Vessel *Bolton*, 8, after firing three shots. Lieutt. Gifford Glencannon, gunnery officer, exercised his crews at the guns for four glasses under the supervision of Lieutt. John Paul Jones. Night cold, windy and moonless with ships running at four knots on starboard tack.

Gifford Glencannon stood leaning against the taffrail of *Alfred* as the midwatch approached on the night of April 5. He was shivering, the northeaster blowing offshore felt cold after their having spent the last several weeks in the Bahamas. They had left Block Island off their starboard quarter and were heading in toward the Connecticut coast. Gifford was keeping one eye on the quartermaster at the wheel, whose bearded, weathered face was visible in the light from the binnacle, and the other on the horizon. He was glad there was no moon, for as Lieutenant Jones had suggested, now was the time their makeshift squadron was in danger of falling in with British blockaders.

The last two months had been exciting but also frustrating. Hopkins had lived up to David's estimation of him as a fighting officer, but had certainly proved a more than competent seaman and ship handler. Gifford recalled how he had read their orders to the assembled captains before their departure two months before.

" 'When in all respects ready for sea, you will sortie from the Delaware River with your whole force to a rendezvous with *Hornet*, *Wasp*, and *Fly*, which will join you from Baltimore. You then go to Chesapeake Bay in Virginia, and if the enemy are not greatly superior to your own forces, you are immediately to search out and attack all the naval forces of our enemies you may find there.

" 'If you should be so fortunate as to execute this business successfully in Virginia, you are then to proceed immediately to the southward and make yourself master of such forces as the enemy may have both in North and South Carolina in such a manner as you may think most prudent from the intelligence you shall receive, either by dividing your fleet or keeping it together.

" 'Having completed your business in the Carolinas, you are without delay to proceed northward directly to Rhode Island, and attack, take, and destroy all enemy's naval force that you may find there. You are also to seize and make prize of all such transport ships and other vessels as may be found carrying supplies of any kind to, or any way aiding or assisting our enemies.

" 'You will dispose of all the men you make prisoners in such manner as you may judge most safe for North America and least retard the service you are upon. If you should take any ships or other vessels that are fit to be armed and manned for the service of the United Colonies, you will make use of every method for carrying this matter into execution, and to command said ships as soon as they can be made ready for the sea.

" 'For this purpose, you will apply to the several assemblies, Conventions and Committees of Safety and desire them in the name of the Congress to aid and assist you by every way and means in their power for the execution of this whole service.' "

At this point in the reading, Hopkins, his red, heavy-jawed face glistening in the lantern light of the great cabin of the *Alfred*, had paused to blow his long New England nose. Instantly a chattering broke out among the officers of the squadron, with Biddle, Jones, and a few more excited and happy at the prospect of battle the orders seemed to offer.

Others were not pleased at all. Hoysted Hacker, who commanded *Fly*, looked rather green, and Gifford knew it wasn't from seasickness. Whatever *Alfred*'s shortcomings, she was riding far more easily in the swells off Cape Henlopen than the Maryland captain's little one-sticker ever could have.

"Figure I better tell you, Mister Hopkins—" Hacker began.

"That's Commodore, Mister Hacker," Hopkins cut him off.

"Yes, sir, Commodore," Hacker gulped and came close to swallowing the tobacco he was chewing, causing Jones to tighten his already compressed lips and Biddle to snort in disgust. "What I was gonna tell you, in case you and the committee don't know it, is that Lord Dunmore has got hisself reinforced with a real live British frigate."

"How's that?" demanded "Sailor Tom" Hazard of - *Providence*, his tanned face turning pale. "Did you say a real frigate?"

"I sure did," Hacker said. "She's *Liverpool*, twenty-eight, a genuine warship."

"Do tell," Hopkins said, and to do him justice, Gifford couldn't see that the news frightened him. "A frigate for Lord Dunmore, eh?"

"It means naught to us," Jones spoke up impatiently. "*Alfred* will engage her while *Columbus* and the others do in the small fry Dunmore is pleased to call a fleet."

When neither the commodore nor Dudley Salton-stall, captain of the *Alfred*, showed any eagerness to follow the plan of her first lieutenant, Nicholas Biddle spoke up.

"I'll volunteer to fight the frigate with *Andrew Doria* alone," the brilliant young Philadelphian told them. "My gun crews are well trained, and I'll wager we can bring down a mast or two of German George's ship and give the rest of the squadron time to take care of Dunmore. We'll do it even if *Liverpool* sinks us."

To the privateer-trained minds of Hacker and Hazard this sounded like madness, and it showed in their expressions as they stared at Biddle. King's warships you ran away from until you had a chance to pick off a fat merchantman whose cargo would guarantee you the security to sit by your fireside for the rest of your life.

"Well, now," Hopkins had temporized, "I'm sure that you, Nick—Captain Biddle—would be willing to die for the glory, but I'm kinda wondering about your officers and crew."

"I volunteer to sail with Captain Biddle," Jones said eagerly.

"I'll go too," Gifford said and poked Bret, who stood next to him looking uneasy in his new midshipman's uniform, in the ribs.

"And I," Bret said hastily.

"Well, no, gents, that's fine . . . mighty fine," Hopkins said, his nasal accent becoming more pronounced. "I do admire your zeal, but I don't see no real cause for fellas to go risking their lives on no forlorn hopes."

"Why not, Commodore?" Hazard all but sneered. "Iffen they want to git theirselves killed in the general interest, we'll give 'em a proper hero's send-off. No point in all of us getting shot up. Let them fellas have all the glory and we'll git our hides home safe whilst they're at it."

Gifford saw the look of open contempt Jones flashed at the tall, skinny captain and could barely refrain from lashing out at the man himself. But the commodore seemed to be taking it all in stride.

"Like I said, fellas, there ain't no call fer anyone to sacrifice himself for the rest of us, 'cause our orders they don't say we got to go in there and fight Lord Dunmore's squadron."

"Seems to me they do, Esek," Dudley Saltonstall said in his laconic way. "Seems to me we're not only to fight Dunmore but to hunt down any other Britishers out there and let them shoot at us."

"Isn't it conceivable that *we* might be doing some of the shooting?" Biddle asked bitterly.

"Not half what they can do," Hacker said. "Them trained navy gun crews'll blow everything 'twixt wind and water offen our ships 'fore we can say tack."

Hopkins looked directly at Saltonstall. "Our orders don't say that, Dud. And I'll thank you to remember, Dud, to call me Commodore."

"Those orders seem pretty clear and precise to me," said Abraham Whipple. "We may not like 'em, but I think we're bound to follow 'em or we'll be in direct disobedience to the Marine Committee."

"They're sending us to our deaths, that's what they're doing," Sailor Tom whined. "Bunch of bloody landlubbers don't know what they're asking us to do."

"Don't care neither," Hazard added.

"Will you fellas shut your big yaps till I get through reading these here orders?" Hopkins slapped his open palm down on the oak table that dominated the cabin. "Yew ain't heard the whole of 'em yet."

"Well, read 'em, man, read 'em!" Dudley Saltonstall rasped. "We're here to have a conference on 'em and decide what to do."

"They've already decided," Gifford heard Jones say sotto voce. "They can hardly wait for an excuse tae run. All they're thinkin' on is their own skins."

Gifford had to agree with this judgment of their superior officers, although he did feel there were extenuating circumstances. Most of them had previously been privateers and just couldn't conceive of deliberately seeking battle with no material gain in sight.

"All right, boys, this is the rest of the orders," Hopkins said and started to read again. " 'Notwithstanding these particular orders, which it is hoped you will be able to execute, if bad winds or stormy weather, or any unforeseen accident or disaster disable you so to do, you are then to follow such courses as your best judgment shall suggest to you as most useful to the American cause and to distress the enemy by all means in your power.'

"These orders were signed January 5, 1776, by Stephen Hopkins, Christopher Gadsden, Silas Deane, and Joseph Hewes."

Hopkins put the paper down and looked around. "Now, fellas, it seems to me the orders are pretty clear, and it's also clear that this frigate *Liverpool* and her twenty-eight guns is an 'unforeseen accident or disaster' that ought to 'disable' us from following them."

"Yessir, it sure do," Hazard agreed wholeheartedly. "Let's sail back for the Delaware as fast as our sails will fill."

"Or we could try a little privateering alongst the Florida coast," Hacker suggested. "The Spanishers don't hold with British men-o'-war off their coast, and there's plenty of merchantmen for the plucking."

Biddle and Jones looked from one captain to another in total disgust, and Abraham Whipple shifted from foot to foot uneasily as other plans for avoiding action were discussed.

Bret whispered to Gifford, "I think they mean to run for cover without even making a pretense of showing the flag! I'm glad I'm only a midshipman, because I wouldn't be surprised if the Congress had the lot of them hanged for a bunch of poltroons."

"Now wait just a minute," Hopkins was saying as he held up both gnarled hands to silence the rising clamor as the younger officer protested and the older ones argued for safety. "Listen to me! If we do what you suggest, Tom, and sail right back up the Delaware, it wouldn't look right. Folks would talk. The Congress would think we come home with our tails between our legs."

"You're right, Esek," Saltonstall said. "If it warn't for this weather, I'd say we just cruise up and down 'twixt Chesapeake Bay and the mouth of the Delaware for a week or so and then go back to Philadelphia. So far we ain't seen no English men-o'-war in these waters, and if we a week looking for 'em, no one could say we didn't try to find 'em."

"Nope," Hopkins said, shaking his head, "I don't think that's right either, Dud, and the weather is bad. Listen to that wind keening through the shrouds and the ice bumping against our sides. We can't sail up the bay in the teeth of a nor'easter. Besides, I got a plan. Recall what it says in the orders about using our best judgment to do what's the most useful to the American cause and distressing the enemy by all means in our power?"

"Yep," Saltonstall said in his New England twang, "Sure do. Hope yew ain't meaning to do no fighting in these seagoing antiques, Esek."

"One shot through the bilge would sink the *Fly* like a rock," Hazard said.

"No," Hopkins said, "leastways, not much and not at sea. Just think now, what would be really useful to the American cause? Useful, that is, without going so far as to get ourselves kilt by taking on a British man-o'-war?"

Neither Saltonstall, Hazard, nor Hacker had an answer, and by now Biddle, Jones, and Nicholas of the marines were so enraged they could hardly listen to Hopkins's ramblings.

With a crafty look on his long horsy face, Hopkins paused to blow his nose one more time before going on. "Well, I'll tell you what would be most useful. Right now, right this minute, General George Washington is sitting in his headquarters a'wishin' he had more than five or six rounds of powder for every man in his army surrounding Boston. He'd also like powder for them guns Hank Knox brought back from Fort Ti. If he had enough powder, he could run old Tommy Gates right out of Boston into the Atlantic."

"You mean we should sail for Boston and unload all our powder and give it to the general?" Hacker sounded delighted at the prospect of disarming the ships and removing the possibility of ever having to fight.

"No, no, that ain't what I meant, *Captain* Hacker," Hopkins said in a disgusted tone.

"We don't have any extra powder and neither does any of the colonies," Saltonstall said. "Yew know that, Esek."

Hopkins nodded. "I know, but I also know something else. The British have plenty of powder. I know where there's quite a store of it, and I say we go take it away from them."

"Are you talking about the powder stored at Nassau on New Providence?" asked John Rathbun, first lieutenant of *Providence*.

"Yep, I sure am, Lieutenant," Hopkins seemed a bit disappointed that someone else knew as much as he did. "How'd you come to know about it?"

"I traded between Rhode Island and New Providence before the war," Rathbun said. "New Providence has been the seat of British administration for the Bahamas since they run the pirates out a hundred or so years ago. Government House is there and so is most of the store of powder and arms the British have collected in the islands. There are a lot of folks down there who'd rather be on our side than the one they're on now. They depend on the colonies for their trade, especially in salt."

"Do they have British troops and men-o'-war there?" Saltonstall asked.

"I can only speak of what I knew before the war and then there were no troops, only militia. Nor are any British troops stationed there, although I've heard one or two privateers frequent the area."

"Well, we ought to be able to handle a couple of privateers," Saltonstall admitted grudgingly, "but what about the two forts?"

"There's Fort Nassau," Rathbun explained, "built to command the best harbor. A merchant I got to know on my last visit, fellow name of Katcher, told me it has walls twenty-two foot thick and is armed with eighteen-pounders. You couldn't get through the channel into the harbor without those guns blowing you to Kingdom Come."

"A fort!" Hacker was livid. "Esek, you must be going daft! This fleet can't go against a fort like that!"

"I'll thank yew to shut up till you're asked for your opinion," Hopkins said angrily. "I said in the beginning I don't aim to get us all killed for no purpose."

"But what about the fort?" Saltonstall asked. "And what about the other one?"

"The forts are set up to cover the two entrances to the harbor on either side of Hog Island. We don't have to sail in there when we can land someplace else and take 'em in the rear." Hopkins turned to Captain Nicholas of the marines. "How many marines we got in this fleet, Captain?"

Looking very spruce in his green uniform with red facings, Nicholas did some mental calculations before he answered. "We have two hundred men fit for duty, and I guarantee that if you put us ashore with dry feet, we'll take both forts for you and you can carry off whatever is on the island worth carrying off."

The man's confidence and enthusiasm seemed to influence the other officers with the exception of

Hazard and Hacker. Gifford could see there was a world of difference between men like Hopkins, Saltonstall, and even Whipple and the others. They simply didn't see any use in fighting unless there was some profit in it. They had learned during the French war that sea war was a matter of taking chances with your ship and your life in the hope of becoming rich. That philosophy didn't leave room for the dedication to a cause that motivated Biddle and Jones, but neither were they cowards like Hazard and Hacker.

Amazingly enough, Hopkins's plan had worked like a charm despite the fact that *Fly* and *Hornet* became lost during a squall and missed the rendezvous at Abaco Island. The landing of the marines and fifty sailors, under Lieutenant Weaver of the *Cabot*, on the east end of the island had been carried out successfully. Although covered by the guns of the *Providence* and *Wasp*, the protection had proven unnecessary since there was no opposition, and only a few fishermen had observed the landing. Nicholas had formed up his company into two columns and had been about to march toward Fort Montague when an officer appeared carrying a flag of truce. There was also a messenger from Governor Montford Brown inquiring as to the intentions of the landing force and the squadron, which could now be seen off the harbor.

Nicholas had sent back word that the Continentals intended to take all warlike stores belonging to the Crown, but the private property of the inhabitants would be respected and the people would be safe unless the Americans were forced to fire "in our own defense."

The marines had then advanced on Fort Montague where the garrison had fired three shots over their heads "for the honor of the flag," and had then spiked their guns and marched out, two hundred strong, to withdraw to Fort Nassau. They had been dressed in the scarlet coats of British regulars, but it was obvious they were local militia not interested in mixing it with Nicholas's well-trained marines.

Covered by the guns of Fort Montague and out of range of the larger ones at Fort Nassau, the fleet had moved through the channel past Hog Island and been greeted by a message from the governor that the town and the other fort would be surrendered without resistance.

The captured military supplies had been impressive—72 cannon, ranging from 9- to 32-pounders, 15 brass mortars, and 24 casks of powder. There was one bitter disappointment when they learned the governor had sent off 150 casks of powder the night before in a privateer. For that effrontery, Hopkins seized the large sloop *Endeavor* to help carry the supplies, and when the squadron sailed two weeks later, he took along as prisoners the governor, lieutenant governor, and a Crown customs officer.

13

And now they were headed back toward New England, the holds of the ships loaded with military supplies and several prizes sailing along with them. The raid had undoubtedly been useful, but Gifford thought it would have been more beneficial to the colonies to have given battle to Lord Dunmore's ships.

Later that night when John Paul Jones relieved him as officer of the deck, it was clear that the tight-lipped Scot felt the same.

"Well, Mister Jones, we'll sight New London tomorrow," Gifford said.

"Aye," Jones said, his face unreadable in the darkness of the ship's quarterdeck. "And I wager our commodore will be greeted wi' cheers and garlands."

"In spite of having disobeyed the orders of the Marine Committee?"

"Perhaps because of that. With the privateer mentality it is better to avoid hard knocks and turn a profit, but as long as that is the prevailing turn of thought, we'll ne'er ha'e a navy worth the name."

"You're right, but at least we'll make a grand sight sailing into New London," Gifford said, gesturing upward, "twelve ships all flying the flag of the colonies."

He meant the new banner the Marine Committee had entrusted to Jones at the time they had issued his commission; he had been the first to raise it on the *Alfred* before they left Philadelphia. It was composed of thirteen stripes, alternately red and white, with the rattlesnake symbol of Carolina coiled around the pine tree of New England, and stitched underneath it the legend, "Don't tread on me!"

Jones bent over the binnacle one more time, and Gifford could see the scowl on his features in the light of the lantern within it. Then the man straightened and said sourly, "For my part, I canna see how or why a venomous serpent should be the combatant emblem of a brave folk, fighting to be free. I abhor the device."

He turned to go. "Hold to your course, Mister Glencannon, call me if there is any necessity to make more sail or take in canvas, and keep a sharp lookout for English warships. Oh, and keep an eye on the crew. Some of them got to the rum on that last prize and are drinking themselves into insensibility, but the captain refuses to interfere."

A very complete officer was Lieutenant John Paul Jones, Gifford reflected as he scanned the dark horizon with his long glass and listened to the water splashing against *Alfred*'s tubby sides.

When it was almost time for his relief to be coming on deck, Gifford took another turn around the quarterdeck to check the compass and see that the helmsman was steering a true course. Then he made one more swift sweep of the squadron to see if they were holding their stations; the captains had little skill at that sort of thing. *Cabot* was ahead, her two masts outlined against the starlit horizon. Behind to leeward was the *Columbus* with Whipple keeping good station on the flagship. Scattered behind her were *Providence*, *Doria*, and the prizes.

Glancing at his watch, Gifford noted that it was 2:00 A.M. when suddenly there was a hail from the lookout aloft.

"Deck there!"

"Deck, aye!" Gifford shouted.

"*Cabot* making signal for strange sail in sight."

"Can you see anything?"

"Nothing—wait a minute—yes, two sails bearing southeast about twenty cable lengths from the *Cabot*."

Gifford put his glass to his eye and strained to see the sails the lookout had indicated. One he made out to be a three-master, which could mean anything from a merchantman to a frigate or even ship of the line. The other was a single-masted craft, much smaller, perhaps a tender for the larger ship.

"Deck! The *Cabot* is standing down on the stranger to speak her," the lookout yelled, and Gifford could see the brig, captained by the commodore's son John, was indeed tacking toward the strange sail.

Gifford nudged awake the ship's boy who had been sleeping peacefully with his head against the capstan. "Messenger, inform the captain and the commodore that we have raised a strange sail, ship-rigged, and that *Cabot* is approaching to speak her."

A few minutes later, a grumbling, half-dressed Hopkins appeared on the quarterdeck, followed by the instantly alert Jones who took the long glass and examined the stranger.

"Ship-rigged, but not large enough to be a frigate," he said, "or at least I think not."

"When we took the *Bolton*, her captain spoke of a strong British frigate squadron in these waters," said Saltonstall, who had shown up belatedly, still wearing his nightcap on his bald head. "The *Cabot* better steer clear of her."

"My boy knows what he is doing," Hopkins said with a touch of pride. "He's a mite impetuous, but he knows what he is doing. Come up a couple of points, Lieutenant Jones, and we'll move down on them."

There was the sound of stomping feet as the watch was aroused and Jones had more sail bent on. With a fresh wind behind her, *Alfred* began to bear down toward the stranger. Gifford became aware that the palms of his hands were sweaty and he was doubling them into fists.

Why was he so excited? He hadn't felt even mildly tense as the ships had stood into the harbor at Nassau with guns run out and crews at quarters. That had been a snap, but now he felt that something big was about to happen.

The *Alfred* was logging about eight knots, which was fast for her, and Jones was bending on even more sail. The young Scot was eager to come up with the stranger, and that indicated to Gifford that they were approaching not only a warship but an English one.

"Looks like *Cabot* is about close enough to hail," Saltonstall was saying to the commodore who was checking to see if the other ships were following the movements of the flagship.

Faintly on the night wind, they could hear a shout from the *Cabot* and an answering shout from the stranger, which now loomed large against the starry sky, her masts towering over those of the brig.

"Can you make out what they're saying?" Saltonstall asked.

"No, but I—" Hopkins's words were drowned in a sound like thunder, and the night sky around *Cabot* and the stranger lit up with gunfire.

"They've fired a broadside!" Jones shouted. "The *Cabot* is hit . . . she's falling away! Bo's'n, bend on the top sails!"

"Beat to quarters!" Saltonstall shouted. "Mister Glencannon, run out your guns!"

Gifford was already vaulting down the ladder that led from the poop into the waist of the ship where the battery of twenty-four 9-pounders were carried. A boatswain's pipe was blowing, a marine drummer was beating to quarters, and the loud pounding of bare feet, cursing, and shouting were everywhere as the watches below scrambled up the ladders from the berth deck to find the *Alfred* practically flying through the darkness; Jones coaxed every knot he could out of her and kept her close to her best sailing point.

"What the hell's going on, Giff? What is it?" Bret asked, staggering through the darkness looking startled as the battle lanterns were lit and a rolling thunder of gunfire hit their ears as the stranger poured another broadside into the *Cabot*.

"A British ship, maybe a frigate," Gifford told him. "See to the port guns, will you? Half the gun crews are drunk."

He caught a whiff of Bret's breath as he spoke and knew it wasn't only the crew who had gotten to the rum.

When he reached the guns, he saw the crews struggling with the tackle of the nine-pounders, confused by the lack of light, befuddled by the rum and bewildered by the wind and the creaking of the rigging and the flapping of the sails as the *Alfred* rushed into action. One group had managed to get the trunnions of their gun tangled in the lines that restrained them; another couldn't find the hand spikes to lever the carriage round; and a third was so bemused with drink and sleep that they were trying to run the gun out without opening the gunport.

"Get those guns out, damn you!" Gifford bellowed and began running from gun to gun to see that each was loaded first with a cartridge of gunpowder, which was pushed to the back of the barrel and followed by a wad of felt and then the shot, and all rammed firmly home.

They were approaching the enemy ship so that their starboard battery would bear, and Gifford wanted to make sure all twelve guns on that side were ready to fire when the moment came.

" 'Tis the *Glasgow*, 20 guns!" Jones shouted over the sound of the trucks rolling forward as gun after gun was loaded and run out. "We should be able to eat her up!"

"The *Cabot* is disabled!" Saltonstall's voice sounded cracked and strained as it carried to Gifford on the gun deck. "They've shot her all to hell!"

"Stand by your guns, Mister Glencannon, we'll bear in a few moments now." Jones's voice sounded like an island of rationality amid the shouting and cursing and mixed-up orders that were turning *Alfred* into a bedlam.

"Where is the *Columbus*? God damn it to hell, where is the *Columbus*? Why isn't she moving up to support us like the *Providence* and *Doria* are?"

"She's in chains," Jones said calmly but with an edge of excitement in his voice now. "She's to leeward of *Alfred* and the others and we've taken the wind out of her sails."

"Damn! She's our strongest support. We need her!" Hopkins fumed.

"The *Glasgow* has only twenty guns," Jones said. "We shouldna need any support."

"Look at the *Cabot*," Saltonstall said. "She's a wreck!"

"Fire when your guns bear, Mister Glencannon!" Jones yelled, and Gifford was suddenly aware that the dark hull of a ship festooned with battle lanterns was looming through the gunport off their starboard quarter.

"Steady, lads, steady!" Gifford said and went from gun to gun trying to encourage the crews.

Then, before he could give the order to fire, one gun, then another, and finally almost half of them cut loose. He heard no thud of cannonballs striking home and knew instinctively what had happened. The gunners had fired on the uproll and the balls had gone whistling worthlessly through the rigging of the *Glasgow*.

"Fire!" he roared as the dark shape of the *Glasgow* loomed alongside, and even as his remaining guns blazed forth, the enemy ship fired a full broadside, turning the decks of the *Alfred* into a madhouse of flying splinters, wounded men, and a dismounted gun, smashed and shattered by a hit, its empty carriage rolling backward.

"Load! Load, damn it!" Gifford was shouting as he drew his sword and drove the gunners back to their posts. "Load and fire at will!"

One man was down on the deck, his blood showing dark against the holystoned wood, not as obvious as it would have been in daylight but nonetheless a grim reminder that this was war, not just another drill.

One gun after another was hauled back, sponged out, stuffed with powder, wadding, and shot. But before even one could be fired, the *Glasgow*'s batteries roared out once again, and Gifford saw spars falling and another man go down, this one unmoving.

Splinters were everywhere as the British balls smashed into the weak scatlings of the former merchantman, and the expert English crew fired two shots for every one that *Alfred*'s gunners could get off. Then help seemed at hand as Tom Hazard managed to maneuver *Providence* into a perfect position for wracking off *Glasgow*'s stern. But with his customary care for his own safety, and presumably that of his ship, he was popping away at the enemy vessel from beyond range. *Doria,* under Biddle, was much more effective as she ran down on the opposite side of *Glasgow* and began to use her four-pounders against the nine-pounders of the English ship.

For the next few minutes it seemed to the hatless, sweating Gifford that the enemy would surely have to give up, and indeed, as he learned later, the captain of the *Glasgow* had already ordered her signal books thrown overboard in weighted bags.

Because the American gunners were mostly shooting too high, the English vessel was badly cut up aloft and all but undamaged below. All her guns were still in action and she was able to keep up a brisk fire.

"Keep at it, laddies, keep at it!" Gifford urged his men while personally managing to get a nine-pounder back into action and setting wedges to depress the gun so it was low enough to hit the dark hulk from which the galling fire was still being poured into

Alfred. "Keep at it and we've got them! We've got them!"

Touching the slow match to the touchhole, Gifford was rewarded by a solid whacking sound as the gun spoke and leaped back on its trunnions while the ball smashed into the side of *Glasgow.*

A cheer went up from the nearest gun crews, and Gifford ran from gun to gun, checking wedges and supervising the reloading, determined this time to deal a heavy blow that would perhaps bring the English flag fluttering down in surrender.

But he never got that broadside off. There was a sudden crashing sound followed by a scream and several shots. Then there came a violent precipitous movement of the *Alfred,* as though her helm had been put sharply about. Gifford was thrown to the deck, and as he struggled back onto his feet, he saw the ship was swinging away from the *Glasgow,* offering her undefended stern to the enemy who was about to rake her.

Gifford hit the deck again just as a thunderous broadside roared forth from the English vessel and shot whistled through the taffrail, through the windows of the after cabin, and dismounted another gun, leaving several crew members sprawled on the deck.

"What the hell is the matter?" Gifford yelled. "Why did they put the helm about?"

"They didn't," the sailing master told him as he hurried forward with half a dozen seamen toward the mainmast, which had been struck and was tottering precariously, held in place mainly by her standing rigging. "Our wheel block and wheel ropes have been shot away, and if that mast falls, we're goners."

Another broadside lit up the night sky, and suddenly Gifford found himself staring at the headless corpse of the sailing master and splattered with blood and gore as the man's body collapsed against him. For a few seconds, he was so stunned he couldn't move, just stood gaping at the bloody mess of flesh and bits of cartilage dripping down his white trousers in the light of a fire that had broken out amidship.

Fighting off the queasiness and stark terror, he broke out of his trance and began yelling for seamen to fight the fire and try to save the mainmast. The helmless *Alfred* was drifting away from the *Glasgow,* and Gifford could hear Jones and Saltonstall shouting orders that apparently no one could understand over the sounds of gunfire, flapping sails, and the screams of wounded men.

"We're on fire! We'll blow up!" a gunner's mate shrieked and broke away from his post by the port guns that were now swinging to bear as the ship turned. Panic was in the air, and several other men from the battery, unrestrained by Bret Morley, who seemed stunned, were edging toward the hatches that led below.

Gifford moved quickly, smashing his fist into the face of the gunner's mate and sending him sprawling into the scuppers. He drew his sword and struck another gunner on the side of his head with the flat of it, then herded the rest of them back to the portside guns with the threat of his sword and his drawn pistol.

"Back there, you lubbers! Back! I'll kill the first man who leaves his post!" He glanced sideways at Bret. "Mister Morley, I'll thank you to get your men back to their positions and run out your guns. We may get a few long-range shots in yet."

John Paul Jones had come racing forward, shouting orders and rounding up seamen as he came. In a few minutes he had the fire out and the men wrapping cable around the damaged mainmast while Gifford ran the port-side guns out and tried ranging shots at the *Glasgow*. She had made as much sail as her damaged rigging could carry and, ignoring the popguns of *Andrew Doria,* was rapidly withdrawing toward the coast that could now be seen dimly in the first light of dawn.

There was cheering forward, and peering over the bulkhead, Gifford could see the reason for it. *Columbus* had finally managed to catch the wind and was now pounding on past them in pursuit of the fleeing English ship.

"Get them! Get them!" he heard himself yelling.

"Go, you *Columbus,* go!" Jones's voice came from nearby. "Whipple's a good man. He'll run them doon, and cut up the way she is, *Glasgow* will have to surrender."

As the sun rose, the *Alfred*'s crew managed to make emergency repairs to her wheel block and ropes, and she came about to join in the pursuit as *Columbus,* with good light now, began to fire at *Glasgow* with her bow chasers.

Without securing his guns, Gifford ran aft to the poop deck and grabbed up a long glass to have a look at the chase. Jones had also returned to the poop and was watching the mainmast with satisfaction.

"I think she'll hold," he told Saltonstall. "We should be up to *Columbus* in time for the kill."

Hopkins was pacing the deck, hands behind his back. Since the fighting had begun, he had given almost no orders and made no attempt to control

the actions of the other ships by means of signals.
Now he was intently examining the shoreline, which
was becoming increasingly clear as the sun rose
higher.

"Mister Jones, that town over there is Newport,"
the old privateer said.

"Yes, sir, I am aware of that," Jones said.

"Hmmmm." The commodore looked toward *Columbus,* which was doing her best to overtake the
fleeing enemy.

"*Glasgow* is making a signal!" came the shout of
the signal midshipman from his position in the miz-
zen top. "Seems to be to ships in harbor."

"Ahem," Hopkins said.

"Commodore, do you recall what the officer we
captured on the *Bolton* said about a strong British
frigate squadron being stationed at Newport?" Saltonstall asked.

"*Columbus* is making good time," Jones said, as
though to counter the captain's question. "She'll be
in range to fire a broadside in a few moments."

Saltonstall was staring through the glass in the
direction of Newport. "Looks like some of those ships
in the harbor are getting under way. We may have
a whole squadron to fight shortly."

"If they come out at all, they'll be coming out
into the teeth of the wind," Jones pointed out,
"and we'll be able to attack them one at a time. This
might be an opportunity to strike the British a blow
they'll long remember."

"On the other hand, we have the prizes and stores
captured at Nassau," Saltonstall said, gesturing toward the prizes and storeships that were keeping well
to windward. "We cannot risk them just to bring
Glasgow to action."

It seemed to Gifford as though those last words had convinced Hopkins because he grunted and nodded before shouting, "Make a signal recalling *Columbus!*"

Gifford cursed and kicked a water bucket that was lying on the deck. He turned and stalked toward the opposite rail as Hopkins, who previously had given no orders, seemed full of them now.

"Make a signal to *Cabot, Providence,* and *Andrew Doria* to form up on the flagship. Captain Saltonstall, stand down on the prizes and storeships. We're bound for New London."

Whipple in *Columbus* and Biddle in *Andrew Doria* both ran up flag hoists. Whipple's was, "I do not understand signal," and Biddle's read, "Signal incomprehensible with enemy in sight."

"Tell them to follow the movements of the flagship," Hopkins snarled and started toward the companionway leading to his cabin below. "We have better things to do to fight useless battles without any profit."

"We had her," Gifford said, moving to where Jones stood clutching the rail, his knuckles white with the fury of his grip. "Five ships to one and we lost her and suffered the worst in the fighting."

For a few moments, Jones said nothing as he stared hard at the topsails of the *Glasgow,* which were starting to merge with the loom of the coast.

"Never again," he finally said. "As God is my witness, never again will Americans fight without intending to win. Never again."

14

Malcolm Glencannon was lying in a bed in a sunny little room, head resting on his hand as he looked down at Susan asleep beside him, her light brown hair falling softly onto her bare shoulders. Earlier they had made love with such passionate intensity that both had fallen into a deep peaceful sleep from which he had awakened first.

Now he was just lying there looking at her, at the soft pink of her partly open lips, the gentle flare of her nostrils as she breathed, and the luxurious spill of her hair across the pillowcase. God, how he loved her! He didn't care if what they were doing was wrong or not, all he knew was that since the first day they had seen each other after several years' separation he had realized he loved this childhood companion of his more deeply than he had ever imagined loving anyone.

They were in the bedroom of a small cottage Susan had rented on the outskirts of New Haven. Conrad Hurwitz had left her with considerable resources, and as soon as her mother had left Germantown to rush to the bedside of her old friend Amos Pratt, Susan had leased the cottage in order to be close to Malcolm. She had also arranged to have a trusted friend relay her letters to Aileen in Gloucester from Philadelphia by way of Ben Franklin's postal service, so that neither her mother nor David, as head of the family, knew where she was staying.

As though aware that he was watching her, Susan stirred and made a sound so low he could make no word of it, though he bent his head to catch it. Instead, he smelled the sweetness of her breath and the subtle natural perfume of her hair, and that began to excite him again.

"I love you, Susan, I love you," he whispered, but there was no answer, so he leaned closer and traced his lips lightly along her collarbone to her shoulder and down her upper arm. Reaching for the coverlet, he gently pulled it away to expose the full, round globes of her breasts with the flat pink nipples that so intrigued him.

Although almost a virgin because her well-to-do husband had been aging and ill and made almost no demands on her sexually, Susan was an amazingly passionate woman, Malcolm had discovered. Raised in the Anglo-Saxon tradition of a woman remaining passive and rather superior to the sweaty business of sex, she had astonished him by her ardent response to his lovemaking. Now that he thought about it, it had been more than a response; she had met him more than halfway in eager anticipation of his every desire.

She was wonderful. She was like no other woman he had ever known, and during his almost four years at Yale, he had come to know a few. None, however, could compare with the infinite variety and fervor of his rediscovered love. It was almost as though he had searched the world over for a rare flower only to find it growing in his own backyard.

Very gently, his breath stirring a few golden hairs on her arm, he moved his lips to the upper slopes of her breasts, inhaling the fragrance of her body as he strewed kisses across the ivory mounds and into the valley between.

She definitely stirred and said something, but he was too busy to listen. His lips had taken possession of one pink half-crown nipple, worrying it into a hard little peak.

"Feels good . . . could feel it in my sleep," she murmured, twining her long, slender fingers in his hair. "I knew it was your lips and wanted to keep dreaming they would always be there loving my flesh, and I knew if I woke up the dream would be over."

"Why would it?"

"Because in real life nothing lasts forever," she said, and he knew she wasn't talking about dreams and reality in general but about their particular situation.

"Perhaps it could. We could go away somewhere, perhaps to the South, or the West Indies . . . go where no one knows us, assume new identities and marry."

"And give up all your plans and hopes?"

"Yes. War is destroying them anyway," he said. "We could start life anew wherever you wanted to go. Perhaps we could go to France. Would you like to see Paris in the spring?"

"I'm sure it would be lovely," she said, "but what would we live on? Your French is good, but your legal training would be of no use to you in France. Conrad's estate is tied up in property and business ventures which depend on trade. They are shaky as it is with a war raging, and there is no way I could liquidate them without raising questions within the family. And what answers could we give them?"

"That we love each other and what we do is none of their business."

"Malcolm! Would you say that to David who has been more of a father to you than Shawn ever was? Could I say that to my mother who has been alone since my father's madness and death in the wilderness? It's because of me she is alone."

"I wonder," Malcolm said skeptically. "I don't think she ever wanted to remarry."

"Oh, Malcolm, you're wrong," Susan said. "My mother was—still is—a beautiful woman. There have always been men eager to marry her, and at least one of them won her heart, I know, but some strong sense of duty to me made her refuse him. She has devoted her whole life to me, and has a deep concern for me."

"Deep concern about what?" His cheek was resting against her breast as he looked up at her. "I don't understand what you mean."

"Well, I think it is about my mental state. How do we know that my father was driven insane by his sufferings? Perhaps the seeds of his insanity were there all the time and were merely brought to the surface by being confined to the Tower and later mistreated as a bond slave."

Malcolm stirred uneasily. "I've heard Dr. Bancroft, the brilliant surgeon and friend of Uncle Ben's, discuss it with David, but we were able to find out so little about Martin's last years that Dr. Bancroft couldn't even make a guess as to what brought his illness on."

"But the tendency could have been there from the beginning," she said. "After all, Shawn did some pretty strange things."

"Susan!" Malcolm was shocked. "Shawn was wild, but no one ever suggested he was mad."

"No, but at the very least, he was eccentric. Isn't it possible that my father carried some taint, some curse that he could pass on to me, his daughter?"

Malcolm frowned; there was no real way he could deny or confirm that. "But that wouldn't be any reason for your mother not to marry again. She certainly couldn't have passed it on to any other children she might have had."

"No, of course not, but she did most persistently urge me to marry Conrad. Perhaps because he was not only rich but too old to give me children. She must feel that I carry the taint my father had and would pass it on to my children."

"Susan, darling, I won't hear of this! You are the sanest person I know. Tell me, do you personally think you have ever shown signs of being mad?"

She laughed a little. "No, except for the madness you stir in my blood." She rolled against him, but her mind was still dwelling on their discussion. "I still can't help wondering if there is something . . . some mental weakness . . . a taint."

Malcolm decided it would be best to laugh her out of this mood. "All right," he said, "so there is a Curse of the Glencannons. What is new about that? Every old Highland family has at least one curse and at least one mad aunt or cousin who has to be kept locked up in the family dungeon in order to save the honor of the clan. Besides, it's common knowledge among the Sassenach that all we Gaels are as crazy as our mountains are high and our lochs deep and blue."

She giggled, and he thought he had joked some of her doubts away, for when he let his hand glide under the coverlet and down to the warm, silken nest between her thighs, she roused at once, breath quickening, her breasts pushing into his bare chest.

"I really must be getting dressed to take the stage to Gloucester," she murmured. "Mother thinks I am on the way from Philadelphia right now."

"There is plenty of time for love," he said, fingers moving to stir her further.

Her head turned and her lips met his, burning against them while one hand came up to hold the back of his head and the other slid across his flat belly to find his erect, throbbing maleness.

"Oh, my darling," she breathed, "how lovely it is . . . you must be so proud."

"Proud only in that it gives you so much pleasure," he whispered.

"Pleasure so thrilling I can scarce believe it, pleasure I would sell my soul for."

"If I were Satan, I would consider that a bargain," he said as he raised himself over her and felt the tender trap of her thighs open for him in a pattern that had become so familiar during recent weeks that it was like returning home to a beloved place.

"Oh, Malcolm . . . my dearest darling," Susan whispered when he had entered the welcoming gates of her womanhood. "It is so good to know that for now at least you are mine."

"For now and for always," he said, feeling the upsurge of her desire as well as his own.

"Don't say always," she whispered. "Now is enough. Now may be all we will ever have, so it must be enough."

He didn't answer, knowing that any talk of permanence in their relationship upset her, but to his surprise she went on as their passion mounted and their bodies moved together in their own rhythm of love.

"I have always loved you, and I always will," she said. "I have loved you since I was six years old, and I will love you until I'm too old to see or eat my gruel, but being together forever is impossible. Don't even think about it. It's like one of those delightful stories Shawn used to tell us, about how someday we were all going back to Scotland, find Prince Jamie's gold that he sank in the deep waters of a loch and be rich and happy forever. It is a dream, a fantasy that is too beautiful to come true . . . so beyond reach that it is impossible to even hope for."

"No, no, it isn't," Malcolm argued. "I swear to you, it is not impossible."

"Don't talk . . don't make plans . . . just make love," she said huskily, and deeply enwebbed in the full coils of her body, he let desire overpower all else, sure that when the proper time came he would be able to convince her that they could have a life together.

When they had drunk their fill of each other and were lying side by side watching the shadows cast on the ceiling by the sun shining through the vines that partly covered the windows, Susan asked softly, "Is it so awful, Malcolm?"

"Awful? Why it is the most wonderful thing that has ever happened to me. Every time we are together, I think it cannot possibly be as perfect as it was the last time, and then to my astonishment, I find that it is even better."

"I'm glad, but that isn't what I meant," she said, smiling and kissing him on the ear. "I mean our sin . . . our sin against the laws of God and man, our incestuous love."

Malcolm's arm tightened around her. "Love such as ours cannot be a sin. It is as blessed in the eyes of God as it is in our own."

Susan sighed. "Then God must be very good and very forgiving, because what we are doing runs counter to all the laws of man and violates those of God as well, according to every religion I ever heard of. Priests and ministers alike condemn it."

"Bah, what do they know?" Malcolm said. "How do they know who or what God is, let alone what His laws are?"

"Malcolm!" She sounded slightly shocked. "You talk like one of those Deists. They say God exists but we cannot know what His nature is."

"Yes, and some of our best minds share that belief. Tom Jefferson, for example, and Tom Paine."

"But I thought you disagreed with those two."

"Only in that they support this unnecessary war," Malcolm said. "Only in that they support *any* war. I agree with Jefferson about freedom and liberty but disagree that we have a right to take human life to attain them."

"It seems to me things have never been any different. Men like my father and yours could only win their freedom by fighting for it."

"Aye, and they both died for it, as did Shawn Junior. Even Steven has been lost to us because he followed the flag to far Louisiana."

"If I remember correctly, Steven followed his heart to that distant place they call New Acadia," Susan said.

"True he came to love an Acadian girl and when her people were cruelly dispossessed of their homes and farms, he turned his back on the English cause and followed her and her people to their exile."

"Then it was love and not war that led him away," she insisted.

Malcolm nodded. "You're right," he said and then turned and gazed at her, eyes shining with sudden inspiration. "Susan, let's go there! Louisiana is over a thousand miles away, and there is no war there. Yes, I will write to Steven at once, tell him that we are coming, and—"

"Darling, we can't do that," Susan said with a wistful sigh. "We cannot go on even the way we are. I feel that in my heart. Taking so much love . . . so much pleasure, is tempting fate, and if we cannot bring ourselves to give it up, I fear something terrible will happen to one, or both, of us. If it were only to me, I would bear it happily and never leave your side, but I fear desperately for you."

Malcolm held her close and kissed her gently. "There is nothing to fear, my love. While everyone else risks their silly necks in this cursed war, I stay safely at home. Will you be happily married to a coward? That is what they call me, you know."

"Who calls you that? That dreadful Sidney Harmon?"

"Yes, mainly Sidney and his cohorts, but sometimes I'm afraid even my real friends like Nathan Hale doubt my true feelings and think I am either a coward or a Tory like Thad."

"Well, we know better," Susan said and sat up, slipping from his embrace. "The coach will be in New Haven at six. If I am to be on it, we must leave soon."

Malcolm sighed regretfully. "Very well. I'll go saddle the horses while you get ready."

While he went about this task, his thoughts returned to his brother Steven and the idea of going to live in Spanish-ruled Louisiana. No one there would know that he and Susan were related, no one except the two of them and Steven. He remembered what he could about his brother and wondered what he was like now. Steven had been only fourteen when he had gone off to join the New England militia, which had been shipped to Acadia to fight the French. What was he like now? That he was a planter and the owner of considerable property, the family knew from his letters, but what was he like as a man? How would he feel about Malcolm and Susan's relationship? Would he be willing, or able for that matter, to help them get married in Louisiana?

"Yes, I must write to Steven tomorrow," he told himself as he went about saddling the two rented horses. "I will explain just enough of our problem to feel out his attitude, to see if he would be willing to help us."

They reached New Haven too early; the "flying machine" coach from Philadelphia to New York and Boston and beyond was late, as usual.

Deciding to wait at the Blue Boar Tavern, they passed through the common room to a room at the rear reserved for the occasional lady customer. A group of students seated in one corner near the front door were drinking and talking noisily, but Malcolm ignored them and they seemed not to notice him.

After the slatternly serving wench had departed to get Malcolm's ale and tea for Susan, they sat looking at each other contentedly, not touching.

"I noticed the students in front," Susan said, "but you made no move to speak to them. Don't you know all those who attend Yale?"

"Oh, I know them," Malcolm said with a wry smile, "but I'm sure they would rather pretend not to. Most of those at that table are cronies of Sidney Harmon."

"Oh. Was he among them?"

"No, he's probably studying, and a good thing if he is. He could surely use a modicum of education, as well as decent manners."

"If he's that boorish, it is best that you avoid him."

Malcolm's laugh was short and hard. "Don't worry. I do not seek his company; it is somewhat less than pleasant. And since I have studying of my own to do, I shall become somewhat of a hermit." He leaned toward her, his brown eyes filled with love. "I am going to be desperately lonely without you."

"I know, but it won't be for long," Susan said. "If I do not go, Mother will be worried, but I promise not to stay long. After all, I have a house in Philadelphia, and business affairs to look after, you know."

She smiled sadly at her own deceit and sipped her tea in silence until they heard the stage arriving. Over the shouts of the driver, the neighing of horses, and the screech of iron-rimmed wheels on the cobblestones, her voice was barely audible as she got to her feet and said, "This is good-bye, my darling."

"Only for a little while," he said. "You promised."

"Yes, this time it is only for a little while, but remember that someday it must be—" She left the last word unspoken, and it troubled him as he went to get her traveling bag, which he had left strapped to the rented horse.

When he returned she was waiting outside, watching while a groom and stable boy unhitched the six-horse team and ran them toward the stable while a second groom hurried up with a second team. The passengers had descended from the clumsy stage wagon and rushed into the Blue Boar for quick refreshments. Susan and Malcolm were alone in front of the tavern when a tall young man with a thin bony face and a prominent Adam's apple came out the door and approached them.

"I say, Glencannon, are you not going to introduce me to your lovely companion?" The tone was badgering and his manner insolent, and a shiver of apprehension went through Susan that had little to do with his pockmarked face or the tricorn hat perched precariously on the back of his powdered head.

Malcolm hesitated only briefly, then with an almost invisible shrug, he made the introduction. "This is my cousin, Mistress Hurwitz. Susan, my dear, this is Mr. Sidney Harmon, a member of the class of Seventy-six."

Harmon made what he obviously considered a stately leg and looked at Susan with unabated, cold-eyed insolence. "A married woman, are you, Mistress Hurwitz? I presume you are on the way to join your husband."

"No, I am not, Mr. Harmon," Susan said.

"Then perhaps he is with our army, which they tell me General Washington is bringing to New York even now in expectation of a British attempt to take it."

"No, he is not," Susan said coolly, trying to disguise her dislike of the man so as not to cause any further trouble for Malcolm.

"I will be joining General Washington myself as soon as my education is completed," Harmon's voice took on a smug tone. "My father has arranged for me a place on the staff of General Charles Lee, who was the first choice of many knowledgeable men for commander in chief of our armies but was beaten out by Washington."

"I have heard of General Washington but not of General Lee," Susan said, keeping her voice expressionless. The man reminded her of a venomous snake, and while she didn't want to provoke him, nothing could force her to show him any warmth.

"I say, Glencannon, where have you been keeping this charming creature?" Harmon said with false heartiness. "Do you save her for company only for Hale and his kind and deny the pleasure to your other classmates? Tut, tut, my boy, bad manners . . . dreadfully bad manners."

Malcolm's jaw set tightly, determined not to be baited into a quarrel. "She has been with her husband," he said, the lie slipping out before he thought about it. "He asked me to see that she got off on a visit to her mother."

The grooms had finished harnessing the horses, and the passengers were hurrying from the tavern, some still chewing and drinking as they came. Malcolm moved swiftly, lifting Susan's bag into the stage and offering her his hand to board the vehicle. Stepping lightly up into the wagon coach, she leaned to brush her lips against his cheek.

"Thank you for seeing me to the coach, Cousin Malcolm," she said. "I will write you soon." Then she whispered, "Be careful of that man. He has eyes like a snake."

The second his fares were all settled in their seats, the driver cracked his whip over the six horses and the stage was off to Boston, and ultimately Gloucester.

Turning, Malcolm was surprised and displeased to find Harmon still standing in the same place, a half-sneer on his face. "Well, Glencannon, I suppose it will be New York for you when you finish here since that's where most of your Tory friends are and the British will soon arrive."

"I am going to New York," Malcolm said, "but it has nothing to do with Tory friends or the arrival or non-arrival of an English army. I am going only because I have an offer to read law with a man who served with my brother in the French war."

"An Englishman, no doubt."

"An American from Pennsylvania and a longtime associate of Ben Franklin," Malcolm said, and continued with a grim sense of pleasure, "Uncle Ben, as we call Mr. Franklin in our family, has recommended me quite highly to his barrister friend."

"Hmmm. Well, brilliant as he is, I suppose even Franklin makes a mistake now and then," Harmon said in a deliberately insulting tone.

"I hope not in this case," Malcolm said evenly and walked on past his tormenter to loose the horses from the hitching post and lead them off toward the livery stable a short way down the street.

As he came out of the livery stable and turned in the direction of his room, he saw someone else he knew, a slender young man with pleasant even features and light brown hair dressed in the regimentals of a captain in the Continental army.

"Nathan! Nathan Hale!" Malcolm called, running toward his friend and former fellow student.

Hale smiled and shook hands warmly. "How are you, Malcolm? I hear you are going to read for the law."

"Yes, and here you are back at Yale," Malcolm said, thinking he detected a reticence in the other despite the friendly greeting. He wondered at it because he and Nathan had never fought over their differing beliefs. From the outbreak of fighting at

Lexington and Concord, the young would-be school-teacher had been just as calmly determined to join the army as Malcolm had been to remain neutral, but where the others cursed Malcolm for a Tory and a traitor, Hale had defended him.

"What are you doing in New Haven now that you're out of the place and on your way to a career?" Malcolm glanced at the uniform and added hastily, "After the war is over, of course."

"I've come to see Enoch, naturally, and to meet with Ben Talmadge and Robert Townsend," Nathan said. "You know, a kind of get-together before we all go off to the army."

"Do you suppose I could join you?" Malcolm asked. "I'd like to see all of you again, I really would. No matter what our disagreements of the past, I would like to—"

"You see Enoch all the time," Hale said, looking embarrassed. "It might be better if just the three of us get together, say at the Blue Boar later tonight?"

"Done," Malcolm said to cover the hurt he felt as he realized Nathan was trying to spare his feelings. Apparently he thought Townsend and Talmadge wouldn't want anything to do with him. And these were men who had been his classmates in the class of seventy-three until he had been forced to drop out for three years because of setbacks at the shipyard.

"I'll see you later then," Malcolm said.

"Yes, later," Hale said and walked on as preoccupied by his own thoughts as he had been when Malcolm hailed him.

Malcolm watched him go, wondering what it was that so filled his friend's mind that at first he hadn't seen him. Was it the war? He was in a unit called Knowlton's Rangers, Malcolm knew, and judging by his uniform, had quickly advanced to the rank of captain. Did he have doubts about a colonial victory, or was it something on his mind? Knowing Hale, Malcolm was sure he wouldn't let the prospect of personal danger faze him for a moment, much less send him walking down a New Haven street so lost in his own thoughts that he would fail to recognize an old friend.

15

At the Indian Queen Tavern on Fourth Street in Philadelphia on the Fourth of July, 1776, Benjamin Franklin stood up at his table and raised his tankard of toddy. "Gentlemen, I propose a toast to our new Republic!"

Richard Henry Lee, Thomas Jefferson, Stephen Hopkins, John Adams, and David Glencannon rose to their feet and lifted their drinks in answer to the toast as the outside sounds of saluting cannon, exploding fireworks, and cheering and singing crowds penetrated to the dark but cheery room in which they had gathered.

"To our new Republic," Adams said. "Long may it live!"

"Aye, it will live," Jefferson said, "if the British do not succeed in cutting it into thirteen pieces before it is fully weaned."

"Then, sir, it shall rejoin itself like the snake of legend," Dr. Franklin responded, "and strike them still with its fangs."

"I was hoping, Dr. Franklin, that you would propose a toast to all thirteen parts," spoke up Stephen Hopkins, a noted imbiber.

"Why not?" Franklin said. "Tonight is a time for toasts to celebrate the birth of a republic that will outlive old England and all the tyrants of Europe. Why not thirteen toasts to each of our United Colonies?"

"States, Benjamin, states," Jefferson suggested. "Call them United States, as I shall propose to the Congress ere long."

"Very well, thirteen toasts to thirteen states then," Franklin said agreeably.

"Temperance, Benjamin," John Adams counseled, his face of New England granite showing disapproval of the uproar coming from nearby tables where other members of the Continental Congress were making merry after having placed their necks in George III's nooses by signing their names under that of John Hancock. "Temperance in all things."

"Temperance out on it!" Hopkins said. " 'Tis a glorious night, is it not, Dr. Franklin?"

"Aye, a glorious night indeed," Franklin agreed. "Which prompts me to remember a little poem I wrote a few years back on the subject of temperance."

"Not you," David Glencannon laughed. "Surely not you, Benjamin."

"Yes me, David, and I'll recite it to you all in celebration of this glorious day and happy night.

"There is but one Reason I can Think
Why People ever cease to Drink
Sobriety the Cause is not
Nor Fear of being deem'd a Sot
But if Liquor can't be got."

There was general laughter at the table, and, encouraged, Franklin recited another verse.

"If on my Theme I rightly think
There are Five Reasons why men drink:
Good Wine, a Friend, because I'm dry,
Or lest I should be by and by,
Or some other Reason why."

That does not scan," Adams declared soberly. "Friend Franklin, you will never threaten Mr. Shakespeare's laurels."

"All right, then I'll try a drinking song on you that I composed." Franklin was irrepressible amid the conviviality of the tavern celebrations.

> " 'Twas honest old Noah first planted the vine
> And mended his morals by drinking its wine;
> And thereforth justly the drinking of water decried;
> For he knew that all mankind by drinking it died.
>
> Derry down, derry down, derry down, derry down."

To the refrain of "Derry down" everyone at the table except John Adams emptied their tankards, and Hopkins called loudly for a serving maid.

Amid the general merriment, Adams turned to David. "How comes the *Randolph*, Mr. Glencannon? We shall be needing her the more now that we are a nation."

"Well, quite well," David replied, sipping at his fresh toddy, "although I could use a few more good hands in the yards. Most of those I had, including my good right hand, my daughter, are away at sea or in the army."

Adams's thin nose flared slightly. "Your daughter is away at sea?"

"Aye, she married a merchant captain; they sailed for the Indies and are considerably overdue coming back." Some of the worry he had been feeling crept into David's voice.

"The winds and seas have their own ways," Adams said, "but in time most ships come home. When do you plan to launch *Randolph*?"

"As quickly as possible," David said. "Sometime during September, I hope."

"Hmmmm. Well, the sooner the better. General Washington tells us that he expects a British fleet and army to attack New York this summer. He is gathering his forces there even now."

David didn't quite understand what Adams was getting at. Early in March, General Washington had performed a brilliant feat of strategy by occupying Dorchester Heights overlooking Boston Harbor, where the guns brought from Fort Ticonderoga by Henry Knox were looking down Gates's throat. The British hurriedly made plans to storm the heights, but a gale preventing it gave Gates time to remember Bunker Hill and the horrendous casualties that "victory" had cost, and he decided withdrawal from Boston was the better plan. While Washington withheld his fire to spare women and children, Gates had loaded his troops, and sailed for Halifax.

Now the war seemed almost stalemated. An American invasion of Canada by Generals Montgomery and Arnold had taken Montreal, and Arnold, following Wolfe's old route up the cliffs of the Plains of Abraham, had placed the Americans in position to perhaps capture Quebec. The death of the valiant Montgomery, in an attempt to storm the gates of the city, had sent the Americans reeling back and finally driven them out of Canada completely. It seemed to David that the new republic they had proclaimed that day was in as much danger of an invasion from Canada as from attack by sea, but Adams was telling him differently.

"Washington tells us that a British fleet under Admiral Howe arrived off Sandy Hook, New Jersey, on June 25; the fleet accompanied by transports sailed into New York Bay and they have now seized Staten Island."

"And you think they intend to attack New York?" David asked.

"General Washington thinks they do, and I think that if they take New York, they will next strike at Philadelphia with the purpose of capturing as many of the Congress as they can as well as taking over our second greatest port."

"So it would be better for the *Randolph* and all the other ships being built here if they could get to sea as quickly as possible," David said.

"Aye, and I had hoped to have a mission for *Randolph* as the finest of our frigates," Adams said. "We plan on giving her to Nicholas Biddle. Do you know him, sir?"

"Yes, a most excellent officer who saw service in the British navy. My son writes me that in the fleet they speak of him in the same breath with John Paul Jones."

Adams nodded and then they both turned to listen as Ben Franklin struck up another of his drinking songs, this one having to do with love and wine.

"Fair Venus calls; her voice obey
In beauty's arms spend night and day.
The joys of love all joys excel
And lovin's certainly doing well

Oh! no!
Not so!
For honest souls know
Friends and bottle still ring the bell."

The others joined in the chorus of the great philosopher's slightly *risqué* song then listened while he regaled them with the second verse.

"Then let us get money, like bees lay up honey;
We'll build us new hives and store each cell.
The sight of our treasure shall yield us great pleasure
We'll count it and chink it and jingle it well."

The chorus was repeated to much slapping of tankards on the table and Franklin continued.

"If this does not fit ye, let's govern the city;
In power is pleasure no tongue can tell,
By crowds though you're teased, your pride
   shall be pleased,
And this can make Lucifer happy in hell."

Adams had almost smiled at the pleasure of governing, but as the chorus roared out once more, he frowned and turned back to David.

"Our happy friend, Dr. Franklin, does not know it yet but he will soon be taking a long ocean voyage. Mr. Silas Dean has done us little good at the Court of Versailles, and the French know nothing of any Americans but General Washington and *le Bon Homme Richard* there. We can't spare the general so our jolly philosopher must go to plead our case with fat Louis against German George."

"And he must go by warship," David guessed, "the faster and stronger the better."

"Well put, Captain Glencannon. The seas swarm with British cruisers, and we cannot spare *him*, even in his cups."

A short time later, David excused himself and went out into the streets and found them filled with celebrating Whigs, plus a few scowling Tories and Quakers. Pushing through the crowds, he made his way to the Tun Tavern on the east side of Water Street. It was there in 1732 that American Masonry had been born, and in 1775 that the first marines had been recruited for the new country's navy, but it was neither of these claims to fame that drew David. He went to the Tun because it was noted for its food and served "rump steaks, cut with the grain, and only one brought in at a time always hot."

He was hungry because in the excitement of the day and the press of work at the yard, he had skipped both breakfast and the noontime meal. Tomorrow, he told himself, as a laughing, flirting serving girl brought a sizzling steak to his table, he would be working even harder. Tomorrow he would be taking his men off every other task and put them on the completion of *Randolph*. She would never fall into British hands if he could help it, and neither would his shipyard—he'd rather burn it to the ground with his own hands.

After he had polished off the steak, broached potatoes and boiled cabbage, David left the Tun, heading for Chestnut Street and home. With none of his children there, it was not a cheerful place but he preferred it to the noisy celebrating going on around him.

As he entered the house, he received a pleasant suprise. The housekeeper had been watching for him and hurried down the hallway to intercept him.

"Here's a letter came for ye, sir. 'Tis from your son, him that's in the navy. Paid for it out o' me own purse, I did, when the post come."

"I'll see that you're reimbursed," David said, taking the missive from her and turning toward the sitting room.

"Don't matter much," the woman said with a shrug. "'Twas just scrip . . . not worth a Continental, as they say."

David nodded, not really listening as he opened the letter and started to read.

Dear Papa,

I hope this finds you in good health, and be assured my health is excellent despite indifferent food and hard work. I am happy to report that I am now 2nd Lieutenant of the U.S. *Providence*, a one-masted sloop of 12 guns, John Paul Jones commanding. It was with a great sense of relief that I learned my friend Paul Jones was to take over command from that notorious poltroon "Sailor" Tom Hazard, who was found to be a "cowardly incompetent" and dismissed from the service. Jones is the very opposite of Hazard, indeed of most of the officers in this squadron. He is energetic, efficient, and gallant, and has inspired all of us in this ship (except perhaps the First Lieutenant, John Peck Rathbun, a gawky New Bedford fisherman, who, while competent and courageous himself, simply cannot get along with Captain Jones).

You will be happy to hear that we in the *Providence* have been out from under the dead hand of that national disaster who styles himself Commodore Esek Hopkins. I will tell you of his disgraceful and ridiculous behavior later; for now I will quote Colonel Henry Knox who calls him "an antiquated figure, like the illustrious

Dutchman." Our Captain is even more contemptuous of him, having written to the Maritime Committee of the congress: "There is a fellow here who calls himself a commodore, and who keeps us all at an awful distance by wearing an English broad pendant. He had lately the honor of being a stick officer, vulgarly called boatswain's mate aboard an English man-of-war, and was duly equipped for that high station, if Fame speaks true, by his deigning to read English. That such despicable characters should have obtained commissions as commodores in a navy is truly astonishing and would pass for romance with me unless I had been convinced by senses of the sad reality."

Papa, you can see our captain is not one to spare his invective, but however well deserved his condemnation of our commodore is, I fear me it will win him no credit with a Committee of which said commodore's brother is a member. Papa, you must use your good influence with other members of the Committee to push Paul Jones's advancement, which despite his merit has been slow because he is not only a prickly Scotsman and hard to deal with, but because he comes from South Carolina, which has supplied no ships to the navy.

Once having been appointed to the *Providence*, a fast and handy little vessel, Paul Jones immediately made shift to get her to sea, although Esek Hopkins swore the lack of manpower and supplies made it impossible for the ships to move. *Providence* was shorthanded, and those of the crew who hadn't deserted to privateers were near mutinous, but with the help of Lieutenant

Rathbun and myself, Captain Jones soon impressed them it would be better to mend their ways (there were only two broken bones and one cracked skull after we had convinced them to attend to their duties). Jones then managed to recruit a dozen more stout fellows, and one night in the teeth of an Atlantic gale, we sortied from the harbor, leaving Hopkins nursing his broad pendant and his pride, looking like a very fool for saying it couldn't be done.

We had a fairly uneventful cruise in that we convoyed a detachment of General Washington's troops from Rhode Island to New York where they were needed to help in the defense of the city, which I understand is in imminent danger of being attacked by large English forces under the command of the brothers Howe.

On our return we found that Commodore Hopkins still had not sailed despite having been joined by two fine new frigates built in Rhode Island yards, *Warren*, 32, and *Providence*, 28. (This makes two ships in the navy named *Providence*, but as you know, the old sailors' superstition prevented changing the name of our sloop.) We learned also that Hopkins had received orders to go out and fight, but he still refused and found a thousand reasons why he could not sail and not one why he could. But Captain Jones allowed of no excuses to keep him from fighting the enemy and was back out to sea in short order, as was Captain Biddle in *Andrew Doria*. Meanwhile, Hopkins sat on his broad pendant and did nothing but flog sailors on the slightest pretext and, one officer said, "set the most impious example to his officers and men by profaning the name of Almighty God and declared that the Continental Congress was a pack of ignorant lawyer's clerks."

Our second cruise was more productive and exciting, Papa. Having taken in stores, Captain Jones ordered us toward the good hunting grounds of the Bermudas. In a week's time we had taken three fat merchant ships and put prize crews on board. Then we sighted what we at first assumed to be a fourth merchant ship and bore down on her. She showed her colors and a row of gunports, and a man who had served aboard her recognized her as *Solebay*, 28. Even Paul Jones was not fire-breather enough to wish to fight a frigate with a tiny sloop, so we fled. *Solebay* bent on everything her masts would carry and showed such a turn of speed on her best sailing points that it looked as though she were about to overhaul us, and we could hear shot singing in our rigging. But Captain Jones, as fine a seaman as he is an officer, had been gradually edging to leeward until the wind stood just forward of our beam. Then with perfect timing, he suddenly ordered the helm hard over, and breaking out a cloud of light jibs, we spun our heel oh so sleek and went hurtling past the dumfounded English on our best point of sailing. *Solebay* let fly with a broadside, but *Providence* was moving so fast that they hit nothing but wind and water, and before they could come about we were over the horizon.

Since our presence off the Bermudas had led to a scarcity of enemy shipping, we headed north again toward the British fisheries where we harried them most unmercifully, burning some and taking others. Once off Cape Sable we were struck by a gale stronger than anything I had ever seen, but our valiant captain proved the master of this also. When most ships might have deep-sixed their guns to survive, Paul Jones ordered ours dismounted—and rather fearsome work it was with white water over our decks, and with myself, as gunnery officer, and my men lashed together to keep from going overboard as we carried out the orders to move them be-low decks. Papa, if you have never seen a four-pounder swinging free on the end of a line, dangling from the rigging in the midst of a gale and threatening to smash into mast or bulkheads at any moment, you have missed one of the most fearsome sights on this old globe. But when it seemed that all was lost, a young lieutenant (modestly I must confess that it was I) managed to swing on another line and wrap his legs around the harness of the loose gun and maneuver it carefully down the hatch.

Having captured another six English fishing craft, we headed once more for our base and our stationary commodore and his embalmed squadrom. The closer we got, the more aware we became of increasing numbers of English vessels, most of them men-of-war, and some transports in convoy. Paul Jones had his glass to his eye constantly, hoping for a chance to cut out one of those fat transports and carry a battalion of redcoats into American captivity to exchange for our tormented seamen prison-ers, but the chance never offered itself. We speculated much about the destination of all those British ships, and Lieutenant Rathbun suggested that this was the long-expected invasion fleet aimed at New York.

Captain Jones didn't think so. "No, there's a lot of them but not enough to take New York from Washington's army. I suspect their destination is closer at hand—Newport, perhaps, or Providence where our exalted Commodore waits for Divine Guidance to reveal to him a way out of Narragansett Bay."

"Well, Captain," I said, "you have to remember that there are only four useable passages out of the place. We can't expect the poor man to be able to do with so few."

Paul Jones laughed but Lieutenant Rathbun looked down his long New England nose at me, and I knew, good officer though he is, he tended to side with Hopkins because they were both Rhode Islanders and both disliked our captain.

We were standing in through Muskeget Channel, with Martha's Vineyard on our port quarter and Nantucket Island on our starboard, when we raised a sail. I immediately called the captain who came topside, glass already moving toward his eye to study what I could now see was a large ship approaching us.

"How do you make her, Mr. Glencannon?" Jones asked a few moments later.

"Warship built, Captain," I said. "Almost certainly British unless Congress has managed to set a fire under the Commodore."

"Quite correct," Paul Jones said, "and if I ken her right she's as slow as a penguin in the air."

Since I was aware that penguins have no wings to speak of, I realized this ship must be a sluggish sailor indeed, but I couldn't understand how he could tell and asked him.

"Look ye there, laddie," he said, pointing toward the rigging of the frigate, which from her colors we could tell was indeed British. "Look at the press of her sail and the swing of her yards. . . . She's a slug for sure."

Rathbun had come on deck and Jones turned to him. "I'll have the sail shortened now, Mr. Rathbun, if you please."

Rathbun stared at him as though he had taken leave of his senses, and I must confess I didn't understand the order either.

"That is the *Milford*, 32, by the cut of her jib, Captain," Rathbun ventured. "She will eat us up if we try issues with her."

Now, Papa, for all his admirable traits, Captain Jones is not a commander who welcomes arguments from from his lieutenants about orders, and I expected him to, at the very least, detach Rathbun's head from his shoulders and hand it to him. But to my surprise, he merely grinned one of his tight little grins and said, "I want sail shortened to give him a wild-goose chase and tempt him to throw away powder and shot."

So we continued to bear down on *Milford* as though we were a line of battleship and she a cockleshell. Then when we were only a few cable lengths away, and she was beating to quarters and running out her guns, Captain Jones ordered us to break out the Rattlesnake flag and run out our popguns. But instead of closing as the surprised English seemed to think we were mad enough to do, we came suddenly about and skedaddled with only part of our sail set.

Milford let fly with a full broadside and came lumbering after us, plowing through the combers while we danced over them, yawing to and from to fire a full broadside every ten minutes. Shot passed to starboard of us and to port of us, it passed over us and perhaps some of it passed under us because most did surely fall short and none really came near.

"What's this . . . what's this?" Captain Jones said after half a glass of this throwing away of German George's precious powder and shot. "I do believe we are being fired upon by that vessel back there, Lieutenant Rathbun."

Even Rathbun had to smile, although I feared it would crack his face of New England granite.

"Yes, sir, I do believe they are shooting at us," he said.

"Then by all means we must reply for the honor of the flag," Jones said, looking up at the Rattlesnake banner he despised. "Call Marine Captain Trevett, if you please, Mr. Glencannon."

"Yes, sir," I said and passed the word for John Trevett, captain of our marine detachment of twenty men.

Trevett arrived on the double, strapping on his sword as he came and perching his little round marine's hat with the turned up left brim on his head. "You wanted me, Captain Jones?"

"Yes, Mister Trevett, I did. Have you noticed, sir, that that warship is firing at us?"

Trevett gawked for a minute, then nodded. "Yes, sir, I must say I have."

"It is my feeling, sir, that we must make some sort of fitting reply, and yet I don't care to be as free with our powder as is the gentleman in command of that frigate."

"Yes, sir." None of us had any idea what was coming, but I was beginning to enjoy the captain's charade immensely. "I expect we should make some reply."

"Then I want you to post one of your marines on the afterdeck," Jones said, stretching out his orders deliberately because he knew all officers and most of the crew were listening intently. "I want this marine armed with a musket, and each time the *Milford* fires a broadside, I want the marine to return the fire with one musket shot."

"Yes . . . yes—" I thought John Trevett was going to collapse from laughter right there on the deck before he could obey the order, but Paul Jones kept a perfectly straight face as he waited for the marine captain to recover himself. "Yes, sir, one marine . . . one marine . . . one shot in . . . ha, ha, ha . . . in reply to each broadside."

So we sailed merrily along, Papa, with German George's ship shaking the seas with the thunders of her useless broadsides and the U.S. *Providence* replying to each with a single musket shot while our crew rolled in the scuppers over the fun of it.

But all good things come to an end, and a rain squall bore down on us as we rounded Cluttyhunk Island and the poor *Milford* lost us in the haze and ruined our game.

Then, Papa, there was more serious business at hand. As we approached Narragansett Bay, we spoke the *Andrew Doria*, who had made good her exit from the bay shortly after we had. With megaphone in hand, our captain hailed her. "Did you have good hunting?"

Nicholas Biddle, who I'm sure you remember, Papa, as a most excellent and energetic officer, was on the poop deck of the 14-gun brig. "The best!" he shouted back with his megaphone. "We took dozens of prizes, including two transports loaded with Scotish troops bound for milord Howe's army. But we have other news not so pleasant."

"What is it?" Jones called.

"Newport is taken, and the mouth of Narragansett Bay is blocked by British warships. Howe detached General Clinton with 6,000 troops and sixteen warships. Hopkins is under blockade at Providence."

"That must make him very happy," Jones shouted.

"As pleased as Punch," Biddle replied. "He's hoisted his flag in *Warren* and sits there with three strong frigates and half a dozen other ships and does nothing while they capture one of our best ports right under his long nose."

"Suggest we put into New London," Jones shouted. "Take on supplies and work out some way of getting to Providence and putting some backbone into them there."

"Concur," Biddle said. "See you in New London."

And that, Papa, is why we are currently in New London while our valiant Commodore and the rest of the squadron is snug abed in Providence with the Hopkins's reputation safe courtesy of German George's frigates, one a two-deck, 44-gun called *Diamond*. I'll wager, though, the next time you hear from me we'll be either in Providence or sailing up the Thames bombing the houses of Parliament, because the two best officers in our navy, or anyone else's navy, are ashore even now with their first lieutenants, putting their heads together, while I stand anchor watch and write you this letter.

> Your dutiful and affectionate son,
> Gifford

David put down his son's letter slowly. He had been thrilled and excited by Gifford's account of the part the infant American navy was playing in the winning of the independence he had drunk toasts to earlier that night. But he was enraged at the knowledge that his country's ships could fall into the hands of men like Esek Hopkins and "Sailor" Tom Hazard. God, how he wished he could be at sea again and in command of a fast ship. He knew that with the need for experienced officers, and with the influence of Benjamin Franklin, he would have no problem in getting a command. It was then that he recalled John Adams's warning that Philadelphia might be in danger of falling to the British if they took New York and then pushed up the Delaware to strike at the nation's heart.

"No, I must not think about getting to sea now, not while *Randolph* still sits helpless on the stocks. My duty is to get her launched and ship her masts as quickly as possible. Then after I turn her over to someone like Biddle or Jones, I can look for a command of my own."

Yes, *Randolph* had to come first, and he knew that as he tried to rush her to completion, he would sorely miss Shawna and Crispin. Crispin had been his right-hand man around the yards just as Shawna later had been his right-hand woman.

16

"Nometha . . . Nometha . . . Nometha!" It was the voice of young Aoussix, the Cayuga, that came through to Crispin as though from a long distance. "What is wrong? Why are you lying there staring at the cabins?"

Just moments before Nometha/Crispin had raised his cupped hand to his mouth to give the war whoop that would have sent a dozen eager braves of the Mingos and Shawnees racing across the open fields toward the handful of cabins to carry death to the white people. But now he couldn't move; the memories had come surging back in a wave that had paralyzed his will. The memories of Olathe and the other white woman who had yellow hair like the one he had glimpsed in the doorway.

"I have seen a vision," Crispin said. "A vision that tells me we must not go on, that we must return to Logan's village."

"Return to the village? I don't understand," Aoussix said. "Why would you be sent a vision like that?" Indians had great respect for visions but felt they should serve some purpose. "The whites are here. They are unaware and can be killed easily."

Shingas, a brave who had been with Nometha almost from the beginning, crawled closer and spoke. "Why do you falter, Nometha? Even when Logan decided on peace, you led the young men in battle. Why do you falter now?"

Aye, I led the young men after Logan said his honor was satisfied and there should again be peace. But it wasn't I . . . it was a puppet who dangled from the girdle of Olathe who led you.

He had to get away from the other braves, these men he had led in bloody battle against the whites he had once considered his people, or at least the people of the family he loved. He had to get away from them so he could think.

"We must not attack, we must return," he said. "I have had a vision. I must leave and return to Logan's village. Something is happening there, something I must prevent."

Before he said the words, he had not felt something was happening, but suddenly he felt there was, as though he really had a vision. The premonition was caused because Olathe was there and so, God help him, was the white girl with the golden hair. Olathe hated him, but even more she hated the girl he had brought to the village. Olathe, whom he had loved more than his own soul, now hated him, hated him with the mad intensity she saved for all those who had white blood, including her father and herself.

"You will take command, Shingas . . . take command and recall the braves. There is danger if we go on. I must return to the village at once."

Then he was on his feet and running, flying through the early evening as though his feet were winged, while memories poured in on him and the guilt that was riding him like an evil jockey whispered in his ear.

"You did it, Crispin. You betrayed your trust. Sir William trusted you and sent you with the message of the Iroquois to their little brothers, the Mingo, and because of that woman you did not deliver the message as it was given. You betrayed your duty as a bearer of belts."

His moccasins were noiseless on the soft moss and leaves of the trail he followed, and the sting of branches and vines against his face was nothing to the sting of the whip of guilt.

You betrayed everyone—Sir William, your adopted tribe the Iroquois, your white family, and the Mingos—and all for the caresses of a mad woman."

"No, no, no!" he shouted into the night as he ran. "It was not my fault! It was the fault of Dunmore! It was the fault of the Reverend Connolly! It was the fault of Greathouse and the others who murderd Logan's children!"

But he couldn't stem the flow of memory, and scenes of the great council meeting flashed through his head, pictures of those who had gathered to meet with the belt bearer of Sir William and the august "uncles" of the Mingos, the Iroquois League. Hokolesqua had been there, and Nonehelema, his sister, a tall, stunning woman with a handsome, intelligent face; Little Turtle of the Twigtwees, who had carried on after Pontiac had massacred Old Britain and destroyed his town of Pickawillany; and a dozen other chiefs of the Ohio country.

And most importantly for Crispin, there had been Olathe. Olathe like a burning torment in his soul, Olathe whose words were always in his ears.

"Are you white beneath your copper skin, Nometha, or will you save your people and help them in the war they must fight against the white man?" she had demanded the night before the council meeting.

They had been alone in her lodge, and she had stripped him of his clothes, bathed and freshly anointed and painted his body for the coming meeting. She had laid out a bucksin shirt of such finely worked material that the decoration of beads and shells had glimmered in the firelight like a multicolored fantasy. She had stood before him almost as naked as he, wearing only moccasins and a breech cloth.

"Look at me, Nometha. Will you give up the enjoyment of my body for the cheap loyalties the white men have taught you?"

"My loyalties are also to the Long House," he replied. "The Long House desires peace."

Her lip curled. "Johnson says the Long House desires peace. How do you know what the Long House wants?"

"Thayendanegea was at Johnstown. He knew the hearts of the Iroquois and the message they would send to their little brothers the Mingos, and to their nephews of the other Ohio tribes."

Her black eyes flashed with anger. "You are such a fool! Do you not know that Thayendanegea is a creature of William Johnson just as all the other Mohawk leaders are? He lets Johnson use his sister as a harlot as he has used other Mohawk women."

"No, you lie," Crispin protested, but his senses were being overwhelmed by the musk of her body and the excitement her presence generated in him. "Mistress Molly is the most respected person in Castle Johnson."

"That is what is seen on the outside," she said. "How is Degonwadonti treated when no one looks on? As a slave, I'll wager."

She was wrong, he knew she was wrong. He was not an outsider at Castle Johnson. He knew the place and the people as he knew the house and family he'd been raised in; William Johnson and Molly Brant were as much a part of his life as were David Glencannon, Shawna, Gifford, and the others. He also knew it would do no good to argue the point with Olathe.

Besides, he was too awash with desire, too beguiled by the sight of the round, coppery globes of her breasts, tipped by the dark cherry nipples that he knew from experience could burn in his mouth like hot coals.

"I do not ask that you change the word of the Long House entirely," she was whispering. "Just keep them from urging peace at any price. Counsel the Mingos and others to fight if they are forced to the edge. I know they will be, and so will the Iroquois someday, mighty lords of all though they think themselves. Advise self-defense . . . or revenge for crimes the white man has committed and those he will commit against us. The Iroquois would not deny us that right, would they?"

"The Long House has voted for peace," Crispin insisted. "Olathe, perhaps you do not understand what is behind this seizure of your land."

"Oh, I know what is behind it. The white man is greedy for the land and the Iroquois for money. They have sold our land to the white man and now urge us to let it go without a struggle."

"No, not really. That is not the message," Crispin said, his head swimming with the scent of her in his nostrils and the heat of her flesh on his bare body. "Sir William urges Logan and the other chiefs to think on the fact that Lord Dunmore wants to bring on an Indian war to aid the cause of King and Parliament against the colonies, that Connolly and perhaps Cresap are his agents, deliberately trying to provoke the western Indians in order to set them up for slaughter."

"I believe anything of white men," she said, "but they could also mean to provoke the western Indians so that the colonists can be slaughtered; caught between redcoat and red man they will make a fine screaming torture fire to be enjoyed by all."

There was a wild glint in her eyes and he realized he had put an idea into her head. He should not have spoken at all, but she was so close and the sensual lure of her so strong that he barely knew what he was doing or saying.

She put her hands on his shoulders and let the hardened peaks of her breasts touch his chest. "You will do as I ask, will you not, Nometha?"

There was as much fire in her eyes as in the flesh touching his. Twin points of dancing flame held his eyes captive even as the hot points of her nipples welded his flesh to hers.

"No . . . no, I cannot," he said on a ragged breath. "It would be betrayal."

Her tone changed subtly, and she shifted her weight so their bodies were no longer touching. "You have to if you ever want me between the furs with you again, Crispin-known-as-Nometha. If you do not do what you must do, you will never posses me again . . . but . . . other men will—men who are willing to take up the hatchet and lift blond hair, willing to burn white flesh at the stake, willing to kill for the rights and freedoms of the red man. If you do not do what I tell you, I will give myself to them, one after the other, and I will tell you every exquisite detail of each encounter. I will start with Eisakstehl, he whose face you forever marked. . . . Yes, I could even face his loutish lovemaking, his drunken fumblings, because at least he is a man willing to fight. What are you, Crispin/Nometha, a man or a trembling rabbit who shakes like a leaf before the wind of the Long House's breath?"

"It is not fear, Olathe. I am not afraid."

"Then you will do it . . . you will do it," she murmured, the burning pools of her eyes making it almost impossible for him to look elsewhere.

But he could feel her hands moving, and what she was doing made the mist into which he was drifting thicker and shut out the rest of the world, leaving only the small space in which they stood.

He heard the soft rustle as the string of her loincloth came loose and the garment fell to the ground.

"You are going to do it, Nometha . . . you are going to do it," she said, her voice as monotonously repetitive as the droning of bees on a hot summer day. "You are going to do it . . . for *this* if for nothing else."

This was the steaming forest that was being pressed against his tumescent manhood. *This* was the torrid, moist flesh slithering along the length of his throbbing erection. *This* was pushing him down onto the bearskin on the floor of the lodge and rolling on top of him with his maleness already entrapped. *This* was the most thrilling sensation in the universe, his reason for being and the black magic she used to bend his will to hers.

Later that same night he had stood before the assembled chieftans, still half in a daze, and drawing the belts one by one, had delivered the message Sir William had charged him with delivering to the western tribes, the message containing the advice of Sir William and the Long House. He delivered it almost as it had been given to him, making only the changes Olathe had demanded that he make.

The message caused consternation among the chiefs and sachems who sat around Logan's fire, Crispin could see it in their usually impassive faces. There was no reply that night, of course. The wisdom of Indian councils was that a message received should never be answered at the same session. The feasting would continue and afterward the chiefs would have time to think and consider every point that had been presented. Most of the points had seemed to counsel peace and were represented by black and white belts of wampum. The new one, calling on the tribes to defend themselves if attacked, had been accompanied by a red belt, a war belt, sewed by Olathe herself. She had not forgotten anything.

The next night the assembled chiefs had expressed themselves concerning the word sent by the Keeper of the Gateway and the members of the Long House. Even then it had not been a unanimous decision for war. Olathe had not stacked the deck that obviously, not so much that word would get back to the Long House that someone was lying in their name.

Hokolesqua and his subchief, Shemeneto, of Kispoko town, were in favor of war now. Little Turtle, who had fought against Pontiac on the white man's side, wanted war but suggested waiting for a provocation that would bring all the tribes to their side, provocation that would make it impossible for even the lords of the Long House to stand aside.

The other chiefs were also for war, save Nonhelema, the Grenadier Squaw, sister to Hokolesqua who ran her own village as she saw fit, and Logan.

Logan was speaking quietly but with great eloquence when the thing happened that Olathe had been depending on, the incident that would be the final straw in tipping the delicate balance between war and peace.

"Dead . . . they're all dead! Oh great chieftains, they are all dead!"

The screams echoed through the village, rebounding from the log and mud walls of the lodges, bouncing back from the tall, dark trees that looked down on the council fire, sounding and resounding like the blare of trumpets.

"Dead! All are dead! Their bodies lie in bloody pools behind the tavern of Greathouse!"

An old woman came stumbling into view, her voice a wail of anguish. "Hear me, my chief! Hear me, the mother of Logan! My children and my sister's children —Logan's aunt and his cousins have all been turned into mindless, rum-swilling wrecks and then deliberately murdered! Look—look at the blood on my hands! It is their blood from where I touched them!"

The council meeting dissolved into wild turmoil with only Logan trying to calm the people.

Olathe instantly took advantage of the situation to raise a cry for revenge. "War! War now! Men of the tribes, will you take up the hatchet now?"

A party of braves gathered to cross the river to confirm the horrifying news that Logan's mother had brought after going in search of a daughter and a grandson.

"We must wait," Logan was saying. "We must be sure that this is true and that it was actually done by white men."

"Do you also call for patience, O Nometha?" Olathe was suddenly beside Crispin in the madness of the village, where warriors shouted and ran to and fro while women and children cried and screamed all around them.

Crispin didn't know what to say. If the news that had come like a thunderclap were true, then there was no justice on the white man's side and Olathe was right, the Indians must fight and he must fight with them, not against them. Some kernel of doubt, some remaining touch of reason made him turn to her and ask, "Is this what you expected?"

For once she looked surprised. "This? No, how could I? If it is true, my own sister is dead, my aunt and my cousins. No, it was not this particular crime I expected from the white man, but I knew, given his nature, that there would be a crime to force us to war so we can be destroyed. Horrified as I am by this, I welcome it! I am glad it comes now when there will be no redcoats to aid the colonists and we can kill them with the permission, even the blessing, of their own king!"

Crispin shook his head. "I cannot believe that murder has been done."

"You shall see it with your own eyes. Look, even now the warriors return and those bundles in the bottoms of the canoes must be bodies."

They were. As several hundred Indians of many tribes gathered on the banks of the river, the braves who had gone across to the tavern slowly unloaded the canoes, laying the blood-soaked blankets on the narrow strip of sand so the horrified throng could look down on the open eyes of the dead and their slashed and mutilated bodies.

A sound that was a roar of fury combined with a scream of agony rose up from Logan's village, and Crispin's voice joined with the others. The sound echoed and reechoed, seemingly against the silent heavens themselves, and then was slowly replaced by a keening as the women began to wash and tend the bodies while the chieftains gathered once more around the council fire.

Hokolesqua made the first move. He took a belt from h's pouch and threw it down in the firelight. It was red, for war. One by one, the other chiefs followed,the red belts piling up while the warriors war-whooped and Olathe danced among them, screeching like one of the Furies from Greek mythology that Crispin remembered from his schoolroom.

"War! War! Revenge! Blood for blood!" she was shrieking, hair swirling about her head and eyes glittering madly. "Take up the ax!"

When it came Logan's turn, Crispin saw the old man take a belt from his pouch and move toward the pile. There was still regret as well as rage on his face as he tossed his red belt on top of the others.

Finally only Nonhelema and Crispin remained. Crispin didn't hesitate. He picked up the red belt Olathe had woven, stepped forward and dropped it on the pile. Nonhelema cast the only vote against war when she threw a black and white belt to the ground beside the stack of red belts. Then she turned with great dignity and left the council fire to return to her assigned quarters.

Later that night Olathe was a fury of lust in Crispin's arms; she writhed, clawed, laughed, and cried, and her body gave him pleasure such as he had never imagined a man might receive from a woman.

"It has happened," she said once during a pause between their frantic couplings, "They have finally done what I knew they would do, and now they shall die screaming by scalping knife and torture, trapped by their own acts between redcoat and red man. It is good. O Great Spirit, at last it is good!"

The next morning war parties had burst forth from Logan's village, and from a dozen other towns, and struck at the Maryland settlers. For days death and destruction rained down on the area; burning cabins and fleeing whites were everywhere.

Nometha, having forsworn the name of Crispin, accompanied the other warriors. He shot, axed, and scalped along with his red brothers, feeling no pity and showing no mercy. Any momentary qualms he had Olathe seared from his mind as though it were a loathsome disease.

"Kill, kill, kill!" she whispered as her body heaved and thrashed beneath his.

"Burn, burn, burn," she husked as he kissed her scented flesh, delighting in every secret curve and indentation. "Torture, torture, torture. Show no mercy . . . never again show mercy."

And Nometha showed none. Soon he was a leader among the younger braves, noted for the most daring and destructive raids, for doing the most damage to white settlements, for killing the most savagely. Caught up in a vortex of unleashed violence, Nometha spun out of control and could no longer recognize himself.

It was Logan who declared a truce. His heart had never really been in the war, although he had killed his share, and he arranged a truce through John Gibson, a universally known and liked Indian trader who was married to Logan's sister, and through Nathaniel Gist, another trader married to an Indian woman. These two convinced Patrick Henry, an ardent Virginia patriot, to present Logan's case against the white man's government, and Logan had agreed to go to Pittsburgh so a hearing could be held.

"You must go with me, my son," Logan said to Nometha. "I will need you if my English fails me."

Knowing that Logan's English was almost as good as his own, Crispin doubted his motivation, wondering if it wasn't a device to remove him from the influence of Olathe.

She certainly saw it that way. She screamed and yelled that Logan, whose heart was white, wanted to take away her Nometha, the most effective of the war chiefs of the Ohio country in spite of his mixed blood.

Logan listened to his sister and proclaimed a truce, and when Olathe's rages went beyond what his patience could endure, he finally denounced her and publicly declared that he no longer had a daughter.

Not in the least perturbed by this action, Olathe simply moved her furs and other possessions into the lodge Logan had given Crispin and announced that she was now his wife as well as lover.

Nometha didn't know whether he was ecstatically happy or frightened by her pronouncement, and her parting words to him didn't help.

"When you return, bring me many scalps," she said, "or do not return at all."

It reminded him of the story of the Spartan mothers who had sent sons off to battle saying, "Return with your shield or on it." At least, he comforted himself, Olathe wasn't his mother, and he could be glad of that.

17

So Crispin, dressed once more in white man's clothing supplied by Gist, had gone to Pittsburgh with Logan and the two white traders in search of justice for Logan.

"Is it true you were Sir William Johnson's messenger to the western tribes?" Gibson asked as they rode along the King's Highway toward the stockaded walls of the town where the Momongahela and Allegheny rivers came together to form the Great Ohio.

"Yes, but that was before Logan's children were murdered," Crispin replied. "Now I am Logan's war chief."

"And a most brave and able one," Logan said with the grave sadness that now marked his every word.

"Your message to the western tribes," Gibson said, "was to remain neutral in event of war between king and colonies, was it not?"

"Yes, but—"

"You know," Gist said to Gibson, "even with Sir William dead, I think his words might carry weight with both settlers and Indians."

"Sir William dead?" Crispin asked, shocked.

"Yes," Gist said, his shrewd eyes swinging toward the youth as he caught the note of pain in his voice. "He was stricken and died shortly after addressing a council of the Six Nations and strongly advocating peace."

Crispin's first feeling was resentment at Gist for using the sorrowful news to try to impress Logan and himself with the peaceful intentions of at least one white man, but knowing Sir William as he did, he realized that counseling such a conclave in that manner was exactly what Sir William would have been doing with almost his last breath. He grieved for the kindly Scotsman and knew that the loss would be felt even more deeply by Johnson's wards, the Indians of North America.

"Could you not also speak to Lord Dunmore and his council?" Gibson said. "He and Connolly are trying to throw the whole blame onto Cresap, but we believe it was Connolly and his deputy Murdy who enflamed the others to murder."

"I have finished talking to white murderers," Crispin said coldly.

"Think of it as a way of helping your adopted people," Gibson urged.

Crispin didn't reply and they rode on in silence. Logan had had very little to say after the first few days following the killings when he had led the warriors himself and fought with the courage of despair. It was almost as though all the words had been drained out of him by his grief, or perhaps he was saving them for one great outburst against his tormentors.

Patrick Henry met them at the Virginia Arms Tavern where rooms had been reserved for them. Logan and Henry spoke quietly together for some time, and after the exhausted old man had gone off to sleep, Henry spoke to Crispin.

"I had thought to help him put his grief into words, but I think it will not be necessary other than a word here or there," the orator said. "His sincere emotion will have a stronger effect than all my artifice."

Logan was to be allowed to speak before Dunmore the next day. Word had been put out that Cresap, the leader of the Maryland colonists whom Dunmore had sent into the Indian lands, had been relieved of his post and might be tried for murder.

"The whole thing was intentional," Gibson said. "Dunmore knows war is coming and he wants the Indians of the west on the side of the Crown. How better to accomplish that than by pitting settlers and Indians against each other?"

"The settlers were eager enough for it on their own," Crispin pointed out.

"Aye, they were," Gist agreed, "but they might have listened to reason if Dunmore hadn't succeeded in provoking the incident he wanted."

Logan said nothing as they made their way to the structure called Governor's Hall. It stood inside the limits of the old fort, having been built by the French in 1755. They had referred to it as "La Fortresse de la Reine," and with the exception of Castle Johnson, it was the only formidable and solidly fortified edifice of stone west of the Hudson. When the British had taken Fort Duquesne in 1758 and razed it, they had spared this building, had indeed added to it, making it more grim and forbidding than before.

The hall was now used as courthouse, temporary jail, and on rare occasions, ballroom. The upper floor served as residence for the governor of Virginia when he visited. Below the white and gold decorated apartments where Dunmore was in residence, stretched a long, empty stone hall with a wooden balcony running around its walls halfway between the flagstone floor and the massive buckeye beams of the ceiling.

It was in this bare and gloomy hall, damp and rank with the penetrating odor of mortar and dropping moldy plaster that Lord Dunmore had consented to receive the great Mingo, Chief Talgahyeetah, known as Logan, the White Man's Friend until the white man had proved he wanted no Indian for friend.

The hall was filled when Logan arrived, the floor packed with folk in homespun and buckskin, the balcony crowded with merchants and those who passed for gentry in this out of the way corner of the world. Candles had been lit and their glow softened the dreariness of the hall a little.

Logan spoke not a word as he entered with Crispin, Gist, and Gibson, nor did he look to either side as a buzz of excitement arose at his appearance, broken by several catcalls and shouts of anger.

Gist led the way to a bench at the front of the hall facing a small dais upon which shortly thereafter Governor Dunmore, resplendent in blue silk and powdered wig, took his place, flanked by Virginia's superintendent deputy, Captain Murdy.

"Virginia has no right to come in here and usurp the Pennsylvania magistrates," Crispin said bitterly, "and she certainly has no right to have a superintendent of Indian affairs. George Croghan is Sir William's deputy for Indian affairs in the southern colonies."

"Sir William is dead," Gist said.

"Aye, and because of that mincing fop up there on the dais, thousands will die!" Crispin rasped.

"Be silent, my son." Logan broke his own silence to say, "You have been too much in the company of the woman who is no longer my daughter."

A tipstaff had advanced to the front of the dais. "Now rise for His Lordship the Earl of Dunmore, Royal Governor of His Majesty's colony of Virginia," he intoned. "God save the King!"

The crowd struggled to its feet, some persons with extreme reluctance, and listened while Dunmore announced that as His Majesty's Royal Governor for Virginia and the Ohio Territory, he was graciously consenting to permit the Indian chief known as Logan to speak for himself concerning the murder of his family.

"I should like to point out first, however," Dunmore said, a smirk crossing his rouged and powdered face, "that by the vigilance of His Majesty's government, the chief perpetrator of this foul deed has already been arrested, and I call upon the tribes to lay down their arms and return to their peaceful ways now that justice has been done."

"Chief perpetrator, bah!" Gist muttered. "Cresap was fifty miles away, engaged in persuading George Rogers Clark and his followers from attacking the Shawnee. Clark will testify in detail to that."

Still Michael Cresap was the man who had led the Maryland settlers into Mingo country, Crispin reminded himself. If not directly responsible for the murders, he had conspired to arrange the circumstances that led to the deaths.

At a signal from Gibson, Logan had risen and was standing before the dais, the candlelight making his noble, hawklike features look more mysterious and impressive than ever. For a few minutes he stood wrapped in his blanket, the single feather of chieftainship fallen slightly to the left. Then slowly his eyes swung to rest on Connolly, then on Murdy, and finally on Dunmore. For what seemed an eternity,

Logan's gaze remained fixed on the extravagantly dressed governor.

That his stare troubled Dunmore soon became evident as he began to squirm in his chair and finally raised a hand and gestured. "You may speak, fellow," he said with a lisp in keeping with his London fop appearance.

"Yes, have no fear, Logan," added the Reverend Connolly. "You are among friends. As a man of the cloth, I give you my word you will not be molested if you choose to denounce Cresap and his henchmen for their crimes."

Crispin felt rage flow through him. He clenched his jaws and dug his fingernails into his palms to keep from shouting out at the hypocrisy of it all.

"Speak up, man, speak up," Dunmore said, growing noticeably more nervous under the Indian's silent, accusing stare. " 'Pon my word of honor as an English gentleman, you have my full parole to say what you please about Cresap and Greathouse."

"Nice of him to include Greathouse," Gibson whispered. "Next I suppose Connolly will announce a vision from God telling him Cresap did the actual murders from fifty miles away by witchcraft."

Logan slowly raised his arms and spoke.

"Brothers!"

The word echoed through the drafty building, the irony of it impossible to ignore, and there was an audible sucking in of breath from the listeners.

"Through that thick night which darkens the history of our subjugation, through all the degradation and reproach which has been heaped upon us, there runs one thread of light revealing our former greatness, pleading the causes of our decay, illuminating the pit of our downfall, promising that our dead shall live again! Not in the endless darkness whither priests and men consign us that thread of light to be lost; but from the shadowy past it shall break out in brilliancy, redeeming people's downfall, and wringing from you, our subjugators, the greeting—*Brothers*!

"Brothers; for Logan, that light comes too late. Death darkens my lodge; my door is closed to sun and moon and stars. Death darkens my lodge. All within lie dead. Logan is alone. He, too, is blind and sightless; like the quiet dead his ears are stopped, he hears not, nor can he see darkness of light.

"For Logan, light or darkness comes too late."

The old man paused, his eyes moving around the hall, half accusing, half pleading with those who watched and listened with breath almost held. Then his eyes returned to the dais, passed over Connolly and Murdy with the briefest flicker of contempt and settled once more on Lord Dunmore, who started up in his chair as though he expected to be physically attacked.

"I appeal to any white man if he ever entered Logan's lodge hungry and he gave him not meat; if he ever came cold and naked and he clothed him not!"

The governor's painted face looked more clownlike by the moment as Logan continued in what seemed to everyone in the hall to be a direct accusation.

"Such was my love," the chief said slowly. "Such was my great love for the white man! My brothers pointed at me as they passed, and said, 'He is the friend of white men.' My eldest daughter mocked me as a traitor to my own people, and while she, of all my children, still lives, I have put her aside and no longer have a daughter."

Crispin winced. There could no longer be any doubt that Logan meant what he had told Olathe, and under her spell as he was, Crispin could still see that her father's judgment was justified.

Logan's voice was rising, and his raised hand was almost, but not quite, pointing at Lord Dunmore.

"Such was my love for my white brothers that I even thought to live among you rather than among those of my own blood. But how was my love returned . . . how was the friendship I extended rewarded?"

The voice was strong and vibrant but infinitely sad as the old man made the hall resound with his words.

"What was the return I received from my white brothers? The return was in blood. Unprovoked, in cold blood, they have slain all my kin—all!—all! not sparing woman or child. There runs not a drop of my blood in the veins of any living creature!

"Harken, brothers!" Logan's voice had fallen until it could scarcely be heard, and Crispin saw the ladies in the balcony leaning forward to catch every word. "Harken! I have withstood the storms of many winters. Leaves and branches have been stripped from me. My eyes are dim, my limbs totter, I must soon fall. I, who could make the dry leaf turn green again; I, who could take the rattlesnake in my palm; I, who had communion with the dead, dreaming and waking; I am powerless. The wind blows bare! The old tree trembles! Its branches are gone! Its sap is frozen! It bends! It falls!

"During the course of the last long and bloody war, Logan remained idle in his cabin, an advocate for peace. But now all the relations of Logan have been murdered, not a woman or child was spared. There runs not a drop of my blood in the veins of any living creature. This called on me for revenge, I have sought it: I have killed many! I have fully blunted my vengeance. For my country, I rejoice at the beams of peace; but do not harbor a thought that mine is the joy of fear. Logan has never felt fear. He will not turn on his heel to save his life. Who is there to mourn for Logan? No one! Logan cries for peace. . . . Logan cries for justice . . . justice and peace."

Abruptly the old chief sat down and covered his face with his blanket, leaving a silence like that of the grave. It lasted for several moments and then was broken by the sobbing of a woman. Looking around, Crispin saw several women, even officers' and officials' wives in the balcony, wiping at their eyes, and also a few men were seen to brush away an unaccustomed tear.

On the dais there was consternation, Dunmore whispering loudly to Murdy, and Connolly consulting his prayer book to avoid making a comment.

"Wait, there is one more here who would speak," Gibson addressed the dais after a short conference with Gist. "We have here the representative of Sir William Johnson."

"Sir William is dead," Connolly said.

"Let him speak, let him speak," Dunmore said, slumping in his chair as though from fatigue. "We might as well hear all of it."

He hopes to draw off the sting of Logan's words, Crispin thought, to cover them with legalisms to take people's minds off what the old Indian had said. Well, he would get his legalism, get it thrown right in his face.

He was on his feet then, facing the dais while the crown grew quiet again.

"Who are you, young man?" Connolly demanded.

"I am called Crispin Glencannon, the adopted son of Captain David Glencannon of the Committee of Public Safety of the Continental Congress."

There was a gasp from the Tories in the balcony at mention of that most radical of colonial groups.

"I am also the representative of Sir William Johnson, His Majesty's superintendent of Indian affairs for North America. Is there any here who dares deny me the right to speak?"

The last was aimed at Connolly who was leaning forward as though about to summon the guard to silence this defiant upstart who could but mean more trouble for an already discredited governor.

"Why are you here?" Connolly demanded. "Sir William is dead and a new superintendent has not been appointed."

"Then I speak for the dead," Crispin said. "I am here to speak of that chain which links the governor of Virginia with the corpse of Logan's youngest child!—not to mention the links of the chain backward from Greathouse to Murdy to Connolly to—"

"Treason! Treason! Stop this at once!" Connolly shouted.

"Take that man out of here! Guards, eject him!" Murdy was yelling, but the crowd on the floor had closed around Crispin, and men in tricorns and coonskin caps alike were shouting that he be allowed to speak.

"Let's hear what he has to say!" shouted a big frontiersman. "It's our people who are dying out there."

"Let him speak! Let's hear the truth!" yelled a woman standing on a bench in the rear. "My man is dead and scalped! I want to know why!"

"I am here to ask one question of Lord Dunmore!" Crispin shouted over the uproar. "Why this war, falsely called Cresap's War, should not be known to all as Lord Dunmore's War? I am here to deliver the words of Sir William from beyond the grave, to ask the one question he would ask if he still lived. The question is this: where are my children? Where are the tribes I, as Keeper of the Gate, swore to protect? Where are those Cayugas called Mingo who are wards of the Long House? Where are they, Lord Dunmore? Where are the Shawnees, the Wyandottes, the Lenni-Lenape, the Senecas, who keep the western portals of the Long House? Answer, sir! For this was the mission Sir William sent me on. Answer! lest the Long House ask in terms of war instead of words after their children, lest the king say to you, Lord Dunmore, 'O thou unfaithful steward!' "

The place was a bedlam now. Patrick Henry had led Logan out, and ladies were scurrying down from the balconies to make good their withdrawal. There was milling in the crowd as guards, directed by shouts from Murdy, tried to push through to Crispin. An officer in the gallery above leaned over the edge with sword pointed at Crispin. "Arrest that man, he has spoken treason!"

"Come on, lad," Gist said, grabbing Crispin by the shoulder. "I knew your Glencannon grandfather well, and he couldn't have done better."

Crispin wasn't sure he wanted to be compared to Shawn, but before he could argue the point, Gibson spoke from his other side. "It's time to leave Pittsburgh. You can do no more here, and they might decide to take Logan hostage if you stay."

"But Logan has declared for peace. The tribes would fight to the bitter end without him, killing and dying until there were no more to die or kill."

"Perhaps that's what *they* want," Gibson said, jerking thumb at the dais that resembled an upturned beehive at the moment.

Crispin hesitated. "I don't know . . . I—"

"Go, go now," Gibson urged. "I was as close to those who were killed as anyone, but I do not want war. I do not want more revenge, and neither does Logan. You must take him back to his people. Gist will go with you."

Back at the Mingo village they found that the news of Logan's speech and his declaration for peace had preceded them. The chiefs of the other tribes had gathered to hold council.

Olathe raged at Crispin as he had known she would. "You fool! You coward! You white eyes! I sent you with him to keep him from the surrender that has always been in his heart!"

She took him by the shoulders and shook him violently. "You are as bad as he is! Worse! I want nothing more to do with you ever again! Get out of my sight! I will go to the furs of Eisakstehl tonight!"

"No, no Olathe! It was not my fault! Even if Logan makes peace, I will fight on!"

She sneered and tossed her head. "We shall see, but until we do, you shall not touch me, Eisakstehl will, in any and all ways he wishes. He may be a rum-sodden fool, but he will not kiss the white man's ass!"

And then she was gone. Crispin had turned to follow her, but a hand, a strong brown hand, had restrained him.

"Wait, please," a woman's voice said in English, and he whirled to find himself face to face with the woman the English called the Grenadier Squaw. "Olathe is evil. You must not follow her."

Nonhelema stood almost six and a half feet tall and carried herself with great dignity. Her calm assurance impressed him, as did the quiet friendship in the level dark eyes.

"I have only just heard your white man's name," Nonhelema said. "I knew you only as Nometha before."

"That is my name. I have rejected the other and cast aside my white heritage."

"Do not be so quick to let that woman change you from what you are. Beware of her, Crispin Glencannon, she is a witch who brews evil medicine."

Some of what Nonhelema was saying was true, Crispin knew. There were bonds that held him to Olathe even when he knew she was wrong, even when he could see she might lead her people to destruction to satisfy her own deep hatreds. He could see it, but he could not fight it and he would not admit it to anyone else.

"She is right," he said now. "The Indian must fight or he will die."

"The Indian will die if he fights," Nonhelema said. "I am not a person who dodges danger. I have faced it in peace and in war, but I saw the power of the white man when his armies came to the country around the Scioto when the French fought the English. I know the Indian cannot win against the kind of odds he will face. I know the only way is peace, and of that I have tried to convince my brothers."

Listening to her, Crispin knew she spoke the truth, but the memory of Olathe's kisses, of her lithe body joined to his, of the fire that burned in her eyes was so strong that he was unwilling to believe the truth.

"I know, Crispin Glencannon," Nonhelema said. "I am a priestess, and I have sometimes seen into the souls of others. I know that the soul of Olathe is a cauldron of festering evil."

He wanted to be angry but could not be, not at this calm, quiet woman.

"I must do what I must do," he said finally.

She shrugged and started to turn away, then turned back, smiling a little for the first time. "I knew a Glencannon once. His name was Shawn."

Crispin nodded. "He was the father of the man who adopted me."

He saw the hurt in her eyes. "You say 'he was.' Then he is—"

"He died very bravely on the Plains of Abraham, died saving my father's life."

"Aye, that would have been his way," she said. "Then he shall never know that I have a daughter whose hair is red."

She said no more but Crispin, knowing Shawn's reputation, understood. He also understood the woman's interest on learning his name. Shawn had that effect on people. They hated or loved him, but they never forgot him.

When the council met, Logan and Nonhelema voted for peace. Hokolesqua and other chiefs hesitated, while still others voted for war. Without waiting for the decision, a band of hotheaded young warriors painted and armed themselves and went out seeking more white men's scalps. Nometha, driven by the thought of Olathe in the arms of Eisakstehl, desperate to wipe away the vision of her writhing in passion beneath the gross drunken brave, went with them, fanatically determined to win her back at any cost.

But the thirst for blood, the desire for revenge was gone as he took over the leadership of the war parties and led them in raid after raid. His only aim was to please Olathe, to somehow win her back, to deserve her love.

And now on this foray, Nonhelema's words had been haunting him constantly. They came back time after time as he lay in ambush, and when he had seen the white woman with the yellow hair calling to her husband from the lighted door, memories had come flooding back . . . memories of Olathe and another white woman, the one whose husband he had killed, the one he had taken prisoner and kept in his lodge. And with the memories had come fear, a terrible certain fear of something only he could prevent.

And so Crispin Glencannon was running through the night, running as fast as he could go toward Logan's village and Olathe . . . Olathe and a girl named Joan Parsons.

18

David threw himself into the completion of the *Randolph*, and with the aid of workmen lent to him by Joshua Humphreys, the construction moved apace. As she neared the time for launching, David gave up going home in the evenings; instead he slept on a bunk in his office and had a cookshop send in meals he often left untouched.

By August news came that a British fleet had appeared off New York and that General Washington was expecting the arrival of an army commanded by General Howe to attack the city.

Randolph slid down the ways on August 10 and was immediately warped around to the fitting-out docks, and John Adams wrote David that orders had been sent to Captain Biddle to hand over command of *Andrew Doria* and report to Philadelphia to raise a crew for the frigate.

The day after that David received other news that was not so welcome. It came in a letter from his sister-in-law Aileen and concerned his brother Malcolm and her daughter Susan. She had come to believe, she said, that her daughter was lying to her. Letters from the girl were coming from Germantown, but when Aileen replied to them, there was no actual answer to anything she said, only another letter that made no reference to the one she sent to Susan.

"I must know if Susan is actually at the house in Germantown when she is not with me," Aileen wrote. "She left here Saturday a week past and should by now be home. Would you, dear David, be kind enough to look in on her there just to reassure a mother's mind?"

David had felt a bit like a heavy-handed uncle in a bad play when he had gone to the house in Germantown that Hurwitz had left his young wife. But once he had ascertained from the servants that Miss Susan, as they persisted in calling her, had not been there since shortly after Christmas, he was concerned himself. He went so far as to question one or two of the neighbors and learned that a young gentleman had called for Mrs. Hurwitz in a phaeton, loaded several bags and a trunk into it, and driven off with the lady, heading northeast.

Feeling more and more like a nosy relative, David had asked for a description of the young gentleman and was struck by the resemblance to Malcolm.

Now what were those two up to, he wondered. In all the excitement of Shawna's wedding and the distress over Faith's, he had entirely forgotten Aileen's worry about how much Susan and Malcolm were seeing each other. What if she had been right? What if their childhood affinity had indeed ripened into infatuation? His mind flinched from the unhappiness and perhaps the tragedy that could result from such an attraction. Uncle and niece was far too close a family connection to be accepted as a proper alliance, no matter how near an age the two principals were. Tongues would wag, the scandal would spread, and the family name would be besmirched, not to mention the ostracism the pair involved would suffer. Perhaps Shawn's dying warning had been valid after all. Who knew more about the irresistible urge to indulge one's carnal nature, or had a quicker eye to spot a budding romance?

David tried to shake off the unpleasant turn his thoughts had taken. He was jumping to conclusions, he told himself. He should reserve judgment until he had more facts. But he had to inform Aileen what he had discovered; it was her right to know. He disposed of that unwelcome task as soon as he returned home, and received a frantic letter back begging him to go to New Haven and find out what, if anything, Malcolm knew of Susan's whereabouts.

By then it was the middle of August and he was faced with a hard decision. Gifford's ship and the squadron it was part of was due, and Seth Ewart's ship, with Shawna aboard, was long overdue. David knew enough about the vagaries of wind and tide not to expect any ship to arrive on the scheduled day, or even the scheduled week, but Shawna's ship was months overdue and he was greatly troubled over the fate of his beloved child.

On the other hand, as head of the family he did have a duty to Aileen and Susan, and for the first time since Crispin and Gifford had gone away he was in a situation in the shipyard where it might be possible to get away if he had to. *Randolph* was still fitting out, it was true, but she was progressing well and Joshua Humphreys was available to keep an eye on her rigging. He also had an excellent foreman, a squat French Canadian Shawna had hired who had the ability to swear in three languages. And David's sister Deborah had sent her husband's nephew, an admirable clerk with some shipbuilding knowledge, to help out. So one summer morning, David mounted his favorite horse, stuck a pair of pistols in his saddle holsters, and set out for New Haven, hoping that his mission would prove needless and his fears groundless.

He was approaching Tarrytown, New York, when an incident occurred that was to have a profound effect on his future life. General Washington's army had taken up positions around the city of New York to defend it against the anticipated attack, and he had run into frequent pickets of militia and, occasionally, Continentals. He was approaching one of these that guarded the ferry across the Hudson when he saw that the pickets had stopped one of the most elaborate coaches he had ever seen. Superbly built and richly decorated, it was drawn by a matched team of sleek black horses. Up on the driver's seat was a coachman in livery, beside him a footman, both looking down haughtily but nervously at the group of homespun-clad militia blocking their way. A sergeant in a plumed cocked hat was talking to someone inside the coach.

"I don't care what kind of pass you got," he was saying. "I have my orders right from General Colonel Sullivan, and he says not to let anyone pass this point who ain't personally authorized by him, and—"

"But that is ridiculous!" The woman's voice issuing from the coach was well bred and imperious in a strikingly English way. "I have a pass personally signed by General Putnam. I have his permission to leave New York."

"Where are you going?" the sergeant demanded.

"That does not happen to be any of your business, young man!" the voice snapped.

"Waal, I'm just gonna make it my business," the sergeant said. "I can't see no reason why no English lady wants to leave New York lest it's to plot with Tories and help old Howe take the city."

"What utter nonsense! If you must know, I am on my way to join my husband who has been ill," the woman said.

Somehow her voice was familiar . . . familiar in the way a favorite childhood song is familiar. For some reason it sent a faint surge of excitement through David as he urged his horse closer to the carriage and the militia confronting it.

"I demand to be permitted to pass!" the woman was saying as he halted a few feet away. He could see her leaning out the window of the vehicle. The hood of her blue velvet traveling cloak was pulled up over her head and she wore a face mask to protect her complexion from the rigors of travel. David could see nothing that gave a clue to her identity but there was an air about her, a regal tilt of the chin, a touch of aristocratic arrogance that reminded him of someone.

"You ain't in no spot to be demanding nothing, lady," the sergeant told her. "Matter of fact, you just might find yourself on the way to the provost marshal, that's what."

"You have seen my pass, you stupid oaf! Is it that you do not recognize General Putnam's signature, or is it simply that you are too much of a jackass to know how to read?"

"You ain't got no call to talk that way to me. I'm in authority here, and I say you ain't going nowhere. You better just git down out of that high and mighty carriage o' yourn and come on over to the house where Captain Radin can tell you what's for around here."

"I shall not under any circumstances get out of my carriage," the woman said disdainfully.

"If you don't, I'll drag you outa there and have you carried to headquarters."

"You wouldn't dare! Even an insolent rebel wouldn't behave in so beastly a fashion to a lady of quality."

"I sure would, and just to show you, I'm going to—"

"Stand easy, Sergeant," David said as the man reached for the door of the carriage.

The militiamen had been so absorbed in the conversation between their sergeant and the lady that none had noticed David's approach. Now two of them turned quickly and lifted their muskets to the ready.

"I am Captain David Glencannon of the Philadelphia Committee of Public Safety," he said with authority. "What's going on here?"

"Don't rightly know, Captain," said one of the two, a boy of perhaps sixteen. "You better ask Sergeant Tully. He's got himself into a argumentation with that there fancy lady."

David pushed past the pair. "Sergeant, what is going on here?"

The sergeant turned and stared up at David, squinting against the afternoon sun. He seemed about twenty and spoke around the wad of tobacco in his mouth. "Who might you be, Mister?"

"I am Captain David Glencannon of the Committee of Public Safety," David said. "If you want to know, more about me, you might ask General Washington. He knows me well."

"General Washington, huh?" Sergeant Tully took off his broad-brimmed flat hat and scratched his straw-colored hair. "How do I know you're telling the truth?"

"Send a runner to General Washington's head-quarters or summon your own officer. I'll speak to him."

The sergeant looked uneasy but he stood his ground. "If you are who you say you are, then you can pass, but—"

"Here are my papers," David said, taking from an inner pocket a letter from Benjamin Franklin appointing him to the Committee and another from the chairman of the appropriate committee of the Continental Congress.

Sergeant Tully stared at the letters for a few moments as though trying to make up his mind about something. Then he handed them back.

" 'Pears like they are what they say they are, but since I can't read so good, I can't be sure."

"Then you should summon your officer at once," David said, letting impatience creep into his voice.

"Can't do that," Tully said. "Captain Radin, he don't take kindly to having his afternoon snooze interrupted. 'Sides, he can't read much better'n I do. I guess you had better just go on through. Don't suppose you got General Howe's army in your pocket anyhow."

"And the lady?" David demanded, putting his papers away. "What about her?"

"She don't get by no way," Tully said.

"Why not if she has a pass from General Putnam?"

"That's what she says, but I can't read it, and 'sides, she's an English one."

"I'll take a look at her pass," David said, taking over with the ease accumulated in long years of command on sea, land and shipbuilding.

"Yessir, yo do that," Tully said with obvious relief. "She's one o' them sassy black-headed women with a tongue like a firebrand. I thought she was like to claw my eyes out."

"I'll take care of it, Tully," David said, sliding from his horse and striding to the door of the coach.

"And who in bloody hell do you think you are, another of those hayseeds playing soldier without a fit uniform, or a musket with bayonet?" The woman had settled back inside the carriage and her voice came from the relative darkness of its interior.

"Madame, I am a member of the Committee of Public Safety. I understand you have a pass from General Putnam. May I see it, please?"

"Why should I show it to you? I've already shown it to one illiterate rebel so why should I show it to another who can't read either?"

"Madame, I assure you that I can read," David said, leaning down to look inside the coach. He heard a gasp of surprise and a strangled giggle.

"Do you find something amusing?" David asked stiffly, staring at the masked face.

"No! Oh my God, no! You are . . . I couldn't believe my eyes, but you are!"

"I am what?" David was growing irritated.

"You are David Glencannon," she said and raised her mask so he could see her face.

It was David's turn to gasp. "Elspeth!" He was staring into the face of the woman he had loved more passionately than any other in his life, staring into a face he hadn't seen for twenty years and realizing it was, if anything, more beautiful than the one of the eighteen-year-old girl he had known.

There was a lovely maturity to it now which made it more appealing than he remembered, and when she threw back the hood of her cloak, he saw that her hair was still the shining blue-black she had inherited from her Celtic ancestors.

"A few strands of gray and a few wrinkles, David," she said, "but I can sit a saddle with the best of them. I ride every morning when I'm in England and can dance the night away when I've a mind to."

"You are beautiful," he said. "More beautiful than ever."

She laughed, the sweet, tinkling sound he had never forgotten. "And you, David, except for a bit more broadness to the shoulders and a lot more wisdom in your eyes, are still the same . . . handsome as ever and, of course, still as much a rebel as ever."

David smiled. "I never thought to see you again and certainly not under such circumstances. What on earth is the wife of a peer of the realm doing wandering around America in the midst of a revolution?"

"A long story and you shall have the full of it in good time, but what about these yokels? Can you possibly handle them?"

David turned back to the pickets. "Sergeant Tully, I'll take responsibility for passing this lady through your lines. I know General Putnam's signature and this is authentic."

"Yessir, Captain, sir," Tully said, sounding relieved to have the matter taken out of his hands.

"Where are you bound, Elspeth?" David asked. "I have to be in New Haven as soon as possible, but perhaps I can escort you part of the way."

"That would be wonderful. I have had a terrifying vision of myself wandering the roads of this incredibly large and uncivilized land without ever finding my destination. I'm sure you can direct me by the shortest way."

"I would be most happy to, Lady—I'm afraid I've forgotten your husband's name."

"Westcott," Elspeth said with a smile that had a tinge of sadness in it. "It doesn't matter that you don't remember the original name, because Cedric changed it twice since we married."

"Changed it twice?" David's eyebrows rose questioningly. "Has he fallen on evil times and had to dodge his creditors?"

She laughed. "No. In fact, he has fallen on very good times, at least he had until this preposterous civil disturbance broke out."

David frowned at her. "We consider it more than a mere civil disturbance."

"Oh, David, you always were a rebel at heart. I suppose if you lived in Paradise, you would be in opposition."

"What was it Lucifer said in Milton's *Paradise Lost*? ''Tis better to rule in Hell, than serve in Heav'n.'"

"No, I don't believe you have that kind of ambition," Elspeth said, touching his hand with her soft one. "It's one of those things they say about the Irish, that they are always against whatever government is in and for the one that is out."

"I am a Scot," David said.

"Oh, well, it's the same thing."

"I'm afraid the Sassenach will never understand the Gael, even when, like you, they are half Irish," David said. "But to get back to your husband, why did he change his name twice?"

"The first time was when his uncle, Lord Muir, died and Cedric inherited his estates; the second when his father passed on and he came into his lands in Ireland."

"Then you must be incredibly rich."

"Oh, we are, we are, and incredibly stifled by it all sometimes," she said with a twinkle in her amber eyes.

"You still haven't told me what you are doing in America, or where you are going and why."

"Well, I left London before it was known that actual war had broken out. Dear Cedric was wounded in that monstrously bungled affair at Breed's Hill, and by the time we reached the coast off Boston, we learned that the rebels had taken the city. The ship I was on was rerouted to New York and by the time we reached here, your people were already in control of it also. I am now on my way to Newport, which, I understand, we still hold."

"Yes. At least there is a squadron of English frigates there so I would assume they still hold the shore facilities."

"Well, that is where they tell me Cedric is, so I must go to him."

"You must love him very much," David said, unable to keep a note of wistfulness out of his voice.

She gazed up at him, amber eyes full of mystery, and shrugged. "I thought it my duty when I heard he had been wounded, but apparently he has recovered and been seconded to a marine regiment serving with the frigates in Newport. Having come so far, I couldn't turn around and go back without seeing him, so I set out on this adventure."

"Well, I will set you on your way. I must go to New Haven, and Newport is beyond that up the coast. I will see you that far and perhaps can arrange for an escort for you from there to the British lines."

"Thank you," she said. "Oh, David, our two countries are really at war, aren't they? It's such a dreadful thing, Englishman fighting Englishman."

"Aye, it is," he said, "but it has happened before, in the Civil War, in Monmouth's Rebellion, in the '17 and in the '45."

"Yes, I know," she said, "but we don't have to be enemies, do we. I have such fond memories of you."

"And I of you," he replied. "No, we shan't be enemies. I will mount up and ride with you as far as I go."

"No, David. Your horse can be tied to the coach, or the footman can ride him. You must sit in here with me so we can talk."

"Yes, of course, Elspeth," he agreed, his pulses racing. The prospect of being alone in the relative intimacy of the carriage was exciting, almost as exciting as it had been all those long years ago in London.

"Now, isn't this better?" she asked a few minutes later, moving over on the luxuriously upholstered seat to make room for him. Under the cloak she wore a pale blue redingote gown with a velvet jacket, tasseled sash, satin revers, cuffs and train. A lingerie tie and jabot showed at the throat, made of gauze with a scalloped edge and checked embroidery. Her figure, he noted, was as slim and trim as it had been when she first came aboard the *Betsy Worth* at Madras.

"It has been a long time, Elspeth," David said. "Or do you prefer that I call you Lady Westcott?"

"Of course not, David. You know very well I have never been one to stand on formalities, or been that much of a lady, if the truth were known."

She was laughing as she said it, but to him she had always been and always would be a lady. Arrogant at times, strong-willed always, and passionate to the point of total abandon in bed, but never anything less than a lady.

"You are married of course, David," Elspeth said after he had given the coachman directions and his horse had been tied to the rear of the carriage. "Married and by now the patriarch of a family, I would assume."

"I have married twice," David told her. "Before I left England, I married Anne Parrish . . . I'm sure you remember her."

"Oh, God, no!" she exclaimed. "You didn't! Not that fatuous little milksop!"

"It was not a very happy marriage," David admitted, disconcerted as ever he had been in his youth by her forthrightness. "She was taken in an Indian raid and died in one of their villages. I then married another lady, the one to whom I was bonded, in fact, and who had showed me great favor."

"In bed as well as otherwise, I hope," Elspeth said, eyes gleaming wickedly.

"She was a very pious person . . . a Quaker. We were wed practically on the battlefield, and she bore up well under my military caress. She made me a good wife and I loved her well."

"Doesn't sound like the type for you, but who knows? You didn't think I was either."

"Of course I did," he protested over the sound of the coach's rumbling as it rolled along the rutted roadway. "There were just too many obstacles in our way. You were promised to Lord Derry—that was his name then, wasn't it?"

"Yes, but that promise I held rather lightly compared to what I felt for you."

"Did you, Elspeth, did you really?"

"Oh yes," she said with quiet sincerity. "Could you not tell?"

He shook his head. "It seemed you valued me partly for my shock effect on your friends and partly for my ability to please you in bed. Perhaps I was blinded by my youth and stubborn pride."

"I meant you nothing but good, but I tried to interfere in your life, tried to turn a would-be rebel into a devoted servant of the king. I would never do that again."

David was startled by her choice of words. Was she implying there might be something between them again? No, he was imagining things. They were merely traveling a few miles together after a chance meeting, old friends reminiscing about the past, each with a life and a family to return to when the trip was ended.

He cleared his throat self-consciously. "I . . . well, you certainly have come a long way to be with your husband."

She looked out the window on her side of the coach. "I . . . if you remember, he was over forty when I married him, David. It was not a marriage of love, but of convenience, and now he is over sixty. I felt it was my duty to join him because he sounded so unhappy after he was wounded at Breed's Hill. After all, he is the father of my daughter." She turned back to him, eyes alight with pride. "I have a daughter named Jessica, David."

"Is she as beautiful as you?" he asked, as relieved as she to get away from the subject of her husband.

"Oh, much more so. She is quite the reigning belle. I was always a little too . . . ahem, astringent, to be really popular with the majority of men."

"I always thought of it as being of an independent mind."

"Oh, dear David," she said with a throaty laugh as she touched his hand lightly. "You were so good for me."

Her soft fingers pressed his and the contact sent a tingle of desire through him which he found very unsettling. It was pleasant but at the same time alarming; he was no longer a callow youth to be stirred by a gesture and an expression of appreciation. He cast about in his mind for a way to get onto a less intimate footing.

As though sensing his mood, she removed her hand and said, "You haven't told me yet, do you have children?"

He grinned. "Three, a boy and two girls. And in addition I raised my youngest brother and a half-Indian boy I adopted." His grin faded and he added somberly. "They are all scattered to the four winds now, but I am on my way to see my brother and hope to see two of the others soon."

"You are indeed the patriarch of a family," she said. "And where is that devil-may-care father of yours that you were always talking about?"

"Shawn? Shawn died at Quebec with Wolfe."

"Oh. I am sorry, but at least he was on *our* side that time. He was, wasn't he? Surely he wasn't fighting for the French."

"We were both fighting for England," David said, "as we did all through the French war, first with George Washington, later with Sir William Johnson, and finally with James Wolfe."

"How interesting. I met your Colonel Washington, you know."

"General Washington," David corrected.

"I was not aware that he ever attained higher rank than Lieutenant Colonel in his Majesty's forces," she said a trifle haughtily.

"Perhaps not, but your General Braddock trusted him more than any officer in his command, and our Congress has made him a Lieutenant General."

"I see. Well, he really is quite charming in an austere way, and handsome, too, despite the pock marks. He was most accomodating to me. So was another officer, a Colonel Lord Sterling. Feature a lord serving with a riff-raff army like yours."

"I believe his title to his father's estates are somewhat in doubt," David said, "but they tell me he is a good officer."

"He was extremely nice to me. In fact, all of your officers were," she smiled. "I was surprised to find so many gentlemen where I was expecting a rabble in arms."

"We have that too," David said, looking out the window and noting that they were drawing near to Bridgeport. They would not be able to reach New Haven before nightfall, much less Newport which was still almost two hundred miles away. "We have good officers, however, and valiant men. We will not easily be put down."

Elspeth looked distressed. "Then there will be a long war. I talked to Lord North before I left London, and he is most determined to subdue this rebellion, although Pitt and other Whigs like the Howe brothers would prefer accomodation with the colonies."

"It is the Howes who are in command here in America," David told her.

"Yes, but they are honorable men," she said. "They will do their duty."

"Aye, they will," David agreed, "but men of two minds do not always make the best commanders in the field."

"That is true, but we have a trained army. Yours is a hodge-podge of—"

"Elspeth," he broke in, "there is something more pressing we have to consider at the moment than our respective armies and their chances of winning the war. We are still a long, long way from Newport and it will soon be dark. This embarrasses me, but I am afraid we shall have to stop for the night and—"

"Why does it embarrass you?" she asked with a puzzled expression.

"Well, you are a married woman and it would not be proper for you to be seen traveling with another man. If you will please have the coachman stop, I will ride into town some time after you and find a room at a different inn. In the morning, we can meet on the road a few miles the other side of Bridgeport and continue on our way."

Those amber eyes glowed as they rested on his face. "David, I know you are the soul of honor, and I see no reason why we should not stop at the same inn, enjoy a good dinner—if such a thing is to be found in this barbarous country—and talk of the past . . . the past that I believe is very precious to both of us."

19

David and Elspeth sat gazing at each other across a candlelit table in the best room available at the Blue Dolphin Inn on the coastal road just outside Bridgeport, Connecticut. The inn was perched on a bluff overlooking the Atlantic, and for once it had been a sunny, happy Atlantic they had looked out over during their early evening dinner. But with dusk the draperies had been drawn, leaving them in a setting of intimacy that both were keenly aware of.

At first the innkeeper had been reluctant to let them have rooms when David had approached him in the taproom, but the moment he had seen Elspeth and heard her title, he had changed his tune.

"But of course, Lady Westcott . . . of course we have rooms for you and your . . . ah, traveling companion," he said with an ingratiating smile and a clumsy bow. "It is seldom we have guests of your high station and our finest accomodations will be made ready for you at once."

Behind Elspeth's back, David scowled at the man, convinced he was a Tory or a toady of the worst kind. An American gentleman traveling with a lady got the cold shoulder, but an English noblewoman accompanied by an American gentleman was as welcome as the queen herself.

"You shall have the best chamber, the Rose and Star, which hasn't been used since Governor Tyrone passed through here a year ago," the innkeeper said, rubbing his hands together gleefully, "And if I do say myself, who shouldn't, we can offer you a meal that might do justice to the finest London hostelry."

The fellow was so glad to see a genuine English lady that David expected him to start waving a Union Jack, and the blank space on the wall over the man's head had almost certainly been occupied by a portrait of George III a few months previously.

After showing Elspeth to her quarters with great fanfare, the man leeringly showed David to a room next to hers. "There you go, sir. Smaller, but convenience is sometimes more important than size, I always say."

David could have strangled him, but he knew there was no point in making a scene. A man and a woman traveling together invariably aroused suspicion but it infuriated him that the man should assume what he was assuming.

When he mentioned it to Elspeth, however, just before they sat down to dinner, she laughed and shook an admonishing finger at him. "Oh ho, he saw something devilish about you, my lad. You're not the true-blue, straight-as-an-arrow young Scot I knew as a second mate in the Indian Ocean. Now that you've a spot of gray in your hair and a few lines of experience in your face, you've developed the look of a rakehell."

David smiled in amusement. His life of work and child raising had left little time for hell raising or amorous escapades.

"I'm afraid ships have been my main passion over the years," he told her.

"Ha! They were when I met you but I weaned you away from them for a while."

"Yes," he admitted, looking at her over the rim of his glass of Madiera. "I loved you very much, you know."

"And I you, David," she said, eyes wide and serious. "Too much to have been really happy with any other man, but over the years I've learned to respect and admire Cedric. How many men his age would have bought a commission in a line regiment after having served in the guards, just because he thought the king needed him?"

"He is a man of principle then," David said with reluctant admiration. He had been hoping there would be more reason to dislike Elspeth's husband on grounds other than being on opposite sides in a war. One really couldn't hate a man for that; he reserved his hatred for American Tories, whom he considered traitors. The English officers fighting against the colonies were simply men doing their duty, although in his opinion they were serving tyranny.

"Yes, Cedric is a man of principle," Elspeth said. "Very much like my father actually—a bit arrogant, a bit vainglorious, and awfully stuffy at times, but he is far superior to most men of his class in England. He is not a drunkard, a wencher, nor a gambler. I have not been actively unhappy with him."

David couldn't help wondering how satisfactory a lover Cedric had proven, but that wasn't something a gentleman asked a lady, especially not a lady whose bed he had shared before her marriage.

"Tell me about your children, David. You said there were two girls and a boy, plus an adopted son. Are they all near you in Philadelphia?"

"No, none of them are. My son Gifford is at sea in the *Alfred* under the—"

"At sea? How dreadful! He shall most certainly be captured by our navy, and as you know, we sometimes treat rebels rather harshly."

"From what Gifford writes me, there's not a ship in the British navy from three-deckers down that could outsail and outfight the new captain of the *Alfred*, John Paul Jones."

"Oh, you rebels are all alike when it comes to bragging about your officers," Elspeth chided. "All I heard in New York was how great a general George Washington is."

"I don't know if he is a great general," David said, "but I do know he is a great man."

"Well, I will say he is a gentleman with excellent, even courtly, manners. I had no idea you were developing an aristocracy in this wild Indian land of yours."

"We are doing a lot of things here that may surprise you. I hope you note them carefully and relay the information to your leaders when you get back to London."

She waved a hand airily. "Oh, they are all for you anyway—my Lord Chatham, Mr. Burke, and that awful Mr. Foxe. He rather reminds me of our old acquaintance Johnny Wilkes. Do you remember Wilkes, David?"

"I do indeed." As wild a rake as any England has produced, Wilkes was nevertheless a politician of considerable skill and insight who had been persuaded to aid in the rescue of Anne Farrish when she had been kidnapped by the wastrels of the Hell's Fire Club.

"Well, he's sympathetic to you bloody rebels also," she said cheerfully, holding out her wine glass for a refill. "Johnny Wilkes always was for the underdog." She broke into an unexpected giggle. "Strange he never worried about the underwoman . . . ooops, did I say something risqué?"

David smiled. The wine she had consumed was making her more talkative and a trifle giddy. In spite of her earlier declaration that it was perfectly all right for them to have dinner together and stay at the same inn, the situation seemed to be making her a trifle nervous and causing her to drink too fast.

A knock had come on the door at that point, and the innkeeper, his buxom wife, and his daughter had entered bearing steaming platters of food. They had dined well on oysters on the half shell, an excellent joint of beef, potatoes, succotash, and squash.

"What is this?" Elspeth asked, indicating the mixture of green and yellow vegetables.

"It's called succotash. Kernels of corn cooked with beans and seasoned with green and red peppers. Do you like it? It's considered an American delicacy."

"And this?" she stirred the squash with her fork.

"Indian squash," David said. "It was one of the foods that saved the lives of the early Pilgrim colonists."

Elspeth tasted it and made a face. "Poor souls. One would think they might have preferred death."

He noticed, however, that she ate the succotash with relish and devoured the beef and potatoes as well. When it came time for dessert, she had two pieces of pumpkin pie along with the nuts and sweetmeats that topped off the meal. How, he wondered, could a woman with such a healthy appetite have kept her figure so well?

She seemed to sense his thought and patted her flat stomach. "Riding. I ride constantly, summer and winter. It helps keep me trim and gives me something else to think about than what might have been but wasn't."

Her voice was sober as she finished speaking, and her eyes met his as she sipped at a glass of port.

"Yes," David said, "I have my work and my life has been full, but I remember."

She sighed. "And so do I. But come, you haven't told me about your other children. What of your girls?"

"Well, my older daughter is also at sea, on her husband's ship, which trades with the West Indies. They are overdue by many months and I am beginning to worry about their whereabouts. The Indian lad I adopted has been away for almost two years. He was sent on a mission by Sir William Johnson, the late Indian commissioner, an old friend and comrade-in-arms of mine. His continued absence also greatly disturbs me."

"Ah yes, being a parent is not an unalloyed joy," Elspeth observed. "Where is your other daughter?"

David scowled and his lips tightened. "I would just as soon not discuss Faith. She married a bastard of a Tory and has gone with him to New York or hell, and it doesn't make any difference which as far as I am concerned."

"David Glencannon!" Elspeth was shocked at his reaction. "That doesn't sound like you. Do you also hate me because I am on the king's side?"

"No, of course not. I could never hate you. Besides, you are English born, you haven't turned against your native land as Faith and her husband have."

Elspeth shook her head. "I think war rattles the brains of even the most sensible of men."

"And women?"

She sighed again and said wistfully, "I think it would be nice if everyone could get along together and restrict our fighting to the French as Englishmen have always done since Adam and Eve were evicted from the Garden of Eden."

Having recovered his good humor, David smiled and refilled their glasses. "Well, we don't have to talk about that tonight."

"No," she agreed and once again their eyes met and held. "What shall we talk about tonight?"

"Us," he said impulsively. "Us . . . how we were and how we are now."

A flicker of alarm crossed her face. "David, I—I think there are some things better not discussed."

"Why?" he asked, knowing full well why but stubbornly insisting anyway.

Elspeth stirred in her chair and looked uneasy. "Some memories are too volatile to stir up . . . like sleeping dogs they should be left in peace."

Again he asked, "Why? We can't change the past by ignoring it or pretending it didn't happen."

"No, but we cannot let it rule the present either," she said, shifting her glance to the flickering candles, then rising abruptly to cross the room and sit on a small settee upholstered in an elegant rose brocade that made a striking background for her dark hair and pale skin. "We cannot let it rule us and hurt others."

David's excitement at having been reunited with her so unexpectedly had been steadily rising since they reached the inn, and now, curiously, it was being intensified by her reluctance to talk about their earlier affair. Getting to his feet, he walked slowly to the settee and seated himself beside her. "Would others have to be hurt?"

"We might be able to hide what we were doing from our families but we could not hide it from ourselves," she said, "and that in itself would change relationships."

David wasn't listening. "I have thought of you so often," he said, putting his arms around her. "I have gone over every detail from the day you came on board the *Betsy Worth* until I left London to join my father in the uprising."

She giggled nervously. "We did rather add to the already overheated climate in the Indian Ocean, didn't we?"

"We did more than that." He was pulling her closer, eyes on the soft moistness of her lips. "We knew real love for the only time in our lives."

"That's only an assumption you're making," she whispered just before his lips touched hers, lightly at first and then with increasing passion.

"Is it?" he murmured without releasing her. "You say that but your lips are telling me something altogether different."

"Well, I cannot be held responsible for what they say," she said, sounding breathless. "They are notorious hussies."

"You ha'e no control o'er them?" he responded to her jesting. "Good, then I'll just be using them as I please."

"Oh no . . . no . . . please . . . " His mouth silenced hers with long, seeking kisses, and he felt her stiffen and strain away from him at first but then gradually melt against him, breasts crushed into his and the beat of her heart matching his.

She moaned as his lips parted hers and his tongue tasted deep of the sweetness of her mouth. Her fists pounded his shoulders, but he ignored the intended rejection and moved one of his hands to the swell of her breast in a firm caress, stroking the fullness and savoring the vibrancy of it through the layers of cloth.

"I love you, Elspeth," he whispered. "I know now I have always loved you, everything else was only illusion. I was such a fool to let you go, such a fool not to realize there had to be some way for us to be together."

"There could have been then," she said in a voice trembling with emotion, "but now there can never be."

"Why not? You do not love your husband." He kissed her again. "You do not love Cedric, Lord Wescott."

"I—" For a moment he thought she was going to lie, but she shook her head. "No, I do not love him, I do respect and admire him. Strange as it may sound coming from a person of my class, I have a sense of honor and responsibility and it would make my life miserable if I betrayed him."

David gave her a long appraising look, knowing that among the aristocracy husbands and wives had a strong disinclination to let ordinary rules of morality govern their conduct. Was Elspeth really different from the rest of them, or was it that she no longer loved him, was not attracted to him physically as she once had been?

No, he could not believe that. He had felt her respond to his kisses and her face was flushed and her eyes glowing with desire. Even as she was refusing him, it was clear that she wanted him as much as he wanted her.

"Elspeth," he pleaded, "it isn't as though this were some passing fancy. I am not a jaded English milord looking for a light-o'-love. I'm the man who loved you years ago and still loves you."

She pushed away from him, as though the close contact shook her resolve. "No, David, not 'still.' Perhaps you could love me again, given time and the right circumstances, but what you are feeling now is simply passion aroused by remembrance of our youthful romance. Since then, you have been married happily to a woman who gave you three children. You must have loved her very much."

"I—" Of course he had loved Felicity, but never in the way he had loved Elspeth. Perhaps poets and other romantics were right about first love. "Yes, I did love her very much, but it was a different kind of love, and you were forever out of my reach. Life goes on and one settles for what one can get."

"That is true, but the fact is you did love her and you can learn to love someone else," Elspeth said, getting up and pulling the drapery aside to look out at the moonlit Atlantic beating against the rocky shore. "Men do not love one woman to the exclusion of all others, nor were they made to live alone."

David smiled and went to stand behind her. "How philosophical."

"Not really," she said, "but I have not lived this long without learning a few things about men."

"Well, Madame Professor, since you know so much, tell me what I am thinking right now," he said, putting his arms around her from behind and cradling her breasts in his palms.

"That is not hard to guess," she said, standing rigid in his embrace. "But I am too much of a lady to say it."

"Or too afraid?" he suggested.

"Perhaps that too," she admitted and tried to pull away only to have him press closer until her uncorseted bottom was tight against his lower body and he knew she could feel his arousal.

"Oh, David . . . please, I beg you, do not—"

"What is the matter, my darling? Does it upset you to know how much I want you?"

She drew in a sharp breath. "Yes, it does. My memories are quite clear on how well and passionately you make love."

' "Then let me add to those memories for both of us," he whispered against the delicate curve of her ear.

"No!" she gasped. "Why must you torture me so? You are not being fair, David! I told you my reasons. It was one thing when we were young and without responsiblity, but now . . . no, it is impossible! It can never be, not ever again!"

She pulled free of his clinging hands and turned to face him, pale and strained. "I think you had better go now. We are leaving early in the morning and—"

"Elspeth, please . . . "

"No, David. Please do not make it any harder for me. I cannot do it and live with myself."

He gave up then, said good night and left the room. Outside in the hallway, he leaned back against the door while anger, disappointment, and despair fought for possession of his emotions.

' "I should have taken her anyway," he muttered under his breath. "She wanted to as much as I did. Maybe if I had just taken her, it would have been all right because it would have been on my conscience rather than hers."

But even as he said the words he knew they weren't true, that he could not have done what he had said. He could no more have forced himself on Elspeth than she could allow him to make love to her. Suddenly the bitterness that had been starting to churn inside him ebbed away, the feelings of rejection and anger faded, replaced by something else —not exactly a pleased sensation, but one of satisfaction, perhaps, to know that Elspeth was what she was. Her refusal told him she was worth loving, that she did not hold herself cheap as so many women of her class in London society did. With a sigh of rueful resignation, he opened the door to his own room and went in.

He stood for a moment staring at the bed, thinking that sleeping alone had not been the way he planned spending his evening but knowing he would rest easier with the knowledge that if Elspeth had refused him she had almost certainly refused a number of other men in the past.

He slept well that night, dreaming contentedly of Elspeth, even though she was always just slightly beyond his reach.

They were away early next morning, and the horses made good time. David and Elspeth sat close together, hands clasped between them, but not saying much. Everything of a personal nature had been said the night before, and when they did speak it was of more ordinary matters.

Once as the road curved almost to the coast, David saw the long, low silhouette of a man-o'-war on the horizon with all sails set and a strong wind on her stern quarter.

"Look at that!" he exclaimed. "She must be logging ten knots if she's doing one."

"Is that good, David?"

"Not in that kind of wind," he said. "My friend, Josh Humphreys, and I have designed a frigate to carry forty-four guns on two decks that will, we hope, turn out nearer fourteen knots."

"Isn't that quite a lot of guns for a frigate?" she asked.

"Aye, especially since she'll carry twenty-four-pounders on her gun deck. Those are battleship guns, but she will have battleship scatlings as well, so why not?"

"But ships overloaded with guns tend to hog, do they not?" she asked.

He looked at her, pleased that she knew the term, and then remembered that she had always been knowledgeable about ships and the sea. "Aye, they do, but we have worked that out too."

Elspeth seemed diverted and amused by his confidence and enthusiasm. "And how have you done that?"

"Oh, we haven't done it yet, except on paper, although I'm putting all of our ideas that I can into *Randolph*,which I'm building now. She will be nothing like the ship I have in mind, but she will be bigger, stronger, and faster than any ship of her rate in the world."

"Then the other ship so far is only such stuff as dreams are made of?"

"Dreams and good solid plans that I have drawn up since I am the better draughtsman. More of the ideas, however, must be credited to Joshua."

"I see. And how did you two happen on this idea?"

"Well, it is Joshua's contention that in the foreseeable future, a navy built by the Colonies must of necessity be inferior to that of the mother country or any of the major powers. So it is his theory, and I agree, that since we shall never have as many ships as our enemy, each ship must individually be bigger and stronger."

Elspeth looked at him questioningly. "But how can you do that? The French are the best ship designers, and the ships we capture from them are especially prized, but they have not done anything like that."

"Ah, but they have," David said, "in one feature at least in their razees. The word means 'beshaven ones' and they are ships cut down from old line-of-battleships, which have been worn out in service. Their upper decks are cut off and their masts shortened, leaving the floor plan of their original configuration and thus producing a large, roomy frigate that can carry battleship guns on her gun deck and fight anything but a three-decker. But because of their size, the razees are frightfully slow and we want speed."

Elspeth grinned at him. "So you can run away from our ships?"

"No, so we can catch your ships when they run," he said.

"Oh, David, must our countries fight each other?" she said, clutching at his arm. "Once we were all Englishmen and now—"

"Once we were all Scots, Welsh, Irish, and Cornishmen," he pointed out. "Peoples change, even as individuals do."

"I do not change," she said. "What I was, I still am; the man I loved, I still love."

"Oh, darling—"

They were interrupted by a shout from the coachman and the slowing of the carriage. David leaned out the window and looked down the road. It was blocked for nearly a mile by long columns of militia moving in the opposite direction. The men, dressed mostly in homespun, were wearing civilian tricorns or round hats. Three officers near the head of the column were mounted, and one was in uniform. David recognized him at once.

"Hank Skerles!" he called, getting out of the coach. "Colonel Skerles!"

The officer addressed was heavy with age, his gray, unpowdered hair tied at the back of his head.

He kneed his spavined old horse toward David, who was standing in the road with columns of young boys and old men of the Massachusetts and Connecticut militia marching past on either side of himself and the coach.

When the old soldier was within a few feet of David, he leaned forward and stared at him nearsightedly. David smiled as he noted the colonel was dressed in the same blue and red regimental he had worn in the French War, and that they bore evidence of some hasty repairs made by his wife to ready them for a new campaign.

"Davy? Is that you, Davy Glencannon? Well, I'll be hornswoggled, it shore is! Why, it must be fifteen years since Fort George and Fort Ti. How's your pa?"

"Dead these fifteen years, Hank, at the Plains of Abraham."

The old New Englander took off his tricorn and held it against his chest for a minute. "God rest his soul. He was as good a soldier as he was an old reprobate."

"That he was," David agreed and then gestured at the dusty columns of militia. "Where you taking all these old men and little boys, Hank?"

Hank Skerles peered at him closely and then at the luxurious carriage. " 'Pears like you've come up in the world, Glencannon, and them that do tend to be Tories. You of our persuasion or not?"

David laughed and placed a hand on the elegant coach. "Not this far up in the world. This belongs to a lady I am escorting as far as New Haven. As for myself, I am a member of the Committees of Safety and Correspondence. I am also a ship builder and currently am constructing a frigate for the American cause, if that's what you mean by 'our persuasion.' "

"Ha! That's exactly what I meant, by thunder, and welcome you are to the good cause, my boy," Skerles said and leaned farther forward and spoke in a stage whisper, blinking in the dust raised by the marching men. "The British is landed at New York from a great fleet. Gen'l Washington, he fit 'em a battle on Long Island and lost, he fit 'em another in Harlem Heights and come out even but had to retreat jes' the same 'cause Lord Howe's got more regulars than a dog's got fleas. So he's called up the militia of New York and the New England colonies to help him run old Howe back into the sea and rescue the city from the red-bellies and the yella-bellied Tories."

David looked at the hay-foot, straw-foot militia straggling by and thought Washington would have been better off with the more experienced, better-trained Continentals alone.

Skerles lowered his voice to an even lower pitch. "Say, we lost a lot of men killed and wounded, but lots more of 'em jes' up and went on home."

"Deserted?"

"Wouldn't put it that strong," Skerles said, cutting a chew of tobacco from a plug he took out of a pocket in the tails of his uniform, offering it to David, and then popping it into his own mouth when David declined. " 'Spect it's more like plantin' time and lots of fellas gits a powerful urge to feel a plow in his hands this time of year."

"This is August, Hank," David said. "Any planting or plowing that needed doing is long since done."

Skerles shifted the tobacco from one cheek to the other before saying laconically, "Well, there's lots of things to be done 'round a farm in summer too, Davy."

The rear guard of the column of militia was in sight as David introduced the Colonel to Elspeth. Skerles bowed graciously, if somewhat stiff-necked, to her and then went trotting off after his men. The pipes and drums, playing "Down, Derry, Down," were fading in the distance when David climbed back inside the coach.

"Your Lord Howe seems to have given us a beating," he told Elspeth. "He has captured New York."

"I hope that means this war will soon be over," she said with no trace of truimph in her voice.

"Never!" David said. "Even if the British take all our cities, we will go on fighting, from our forests and mountains if we have to."

She gave him a bewildered look, and then apparently decided to drop that aspect of the subject. "I suppose this might affect my position. If our army has occupied New York, perhaps Cedric is no longer at Newport. It may by that he would have come to me if I had waited where I was."

David had no answer to that and they lapsed into silence, each preoccupied with thoughts of their own.

When they reached the quiet little college town and were driving through its shady streets, David directed the coachman to take him to the boarding house near the Yale campus where Malcolm stayed.

Then he said to Elspeth, "There is a respectable inn a few minutes drive from my brother's lodgings called The Mohawk Maiden. It is run by a cousin of my brother-in-law, Henrik Bemus, and I can arrange for a room there, if you like. Perhaps by tomorrow we'll know more about the English forces in Newport."

"Yes, that would be best," she said. "I'll wait in the carriage while you see your brother and we can go on from there."

20

Mrs. Siddons, the lady who ran the boarding house, paled with shock when David went to her door inquiring for Malcolm.

"Good God," she gasped, "for a moment I thought it was himself come back to life, or leastwise to consciousness."

"*What?*" David roared. "What are you talking about, woman? Has something happened to Malcolm?"

The woman sputtered and backed away. "I . . . I hate to be the one to tell you, sir, but . . . well . . . "

"For the love of God, what is wrong?"

Hearing David's voice raised, Elspeth got down from the coach and hurried to his side, evoking a stare and further delay in replying from the landlady. Finally she summoned up the courage to blurt out the news.

"He's been shot . . . wounded . . . killed maybe. This morning at dawn . . . out by the Oaks . . . a duel. Them friends of his from the college, they took him to Dr. Manley's place in Hope Street."

"The address," David snapped, almost beside himself with shock and fear. Malcolm was more like his son than a brother and this on top of the concern he'd been feeling ever since Aileen's letter had come was overwhelming. "Give me the address!"

"Let's see—it is 432, or 324, or—anyway it's in Hope Street, but they say there's no hope for him."

But Elspeth was hurrying him back to the coach and he barely heard the last words. His mind was a whirlpool of conflicting impressions and confused emotions. Malcolm in a duel? Impossible! The youth was a confirmed pacifist, hated violence of all kinds, even the justified violence of a struggle for liberty. There was nothing David knew of that would make him take part in the criminal idiocy of a duel.

"David, darling, I am so sorry," he heard Elspeth say and became aware that she was holding both his hands in hers. "Perhaps that woman is mistaken. . . . Malcolm's condition may not be as bad as she says."

David took a deep breath and tried to calm down. "The thing is, Malcolm would never have fought a duel. It isn't in his nature."

He was glad of her presence; it was having a steadying effect on him, enabling him to get a grip on his emotions.

They did not find the doctor's house at either 432 or 324, but it was the right street, and the footman and coachman, walking down each side of the street, quickly located a doctor's sign on the dwelling at 455 Hope.

There were three young men in the sitting room when David and Elspeth entered. One of them, dressed in the dark green uniform with yellow facings of a dragoon regiment, stood up immediately.

"Captain Glencannon, how fortunate that you should come," he said. "I am Ben Talmadge. Nathan Hale is with Malcolm and the doctor. I'm afraid Malcolm's condition is bad, very bad, but Dr. Manley is the best to be had. He was apprenticed to Dr. Edward Bancroft."

David felt a slight relief at knowing Malcolm was in such good hands. Bancroft was a friend of Ben Franklin's, and next to Benjamin Rush, was probably the best doctor in Philadelphia.

The other young men were Nathan's brother Enoch and Robert Townsend. David knew that his brother had been at odds with some of his old friends because of his pacifist views, but it seemed they had all rallied around him now.

"What happened?" David asked. "What is all this about a duel?"

"It wasn't a duel at all, it was murder," a voice said from the doorway to the doctor's examining office. David turned and saw Nathan Hale and was surprised to note that he was not in uniform. He had heard the young man was already a captain in the Continental army.

"How is Malcolm? I want to see him." David said.

"The doctor will be out in a moment," Nathan said. "Malcolm was shot at six o'clock this morning and Manley does not think he will recover, although he may linger for some time."

"Why did you say it was murder?" Anger and grief made David's voice harsh and Elspeth put a sympathetic hand on his arm.

"Because he was shot with deliberate malice by a fellow named Sidney Harmon," Enoch Hale spoke up.

"I don't understand," David said. "How did Malcolm get involved in a duel? He is a pacifist and would consider a duel evil; it would go against all his beliefs to take a human life under any circumstances."

"He had no intention of killing Harmon," Nathan said. "He simply meant to stand the man's fire and let it go at that."

"We didn't realize that, of course," Townsend put in. "We thought he had finally had enough of Sidney's beastly bullying and chose the field of honor as the place to have it out with him."

"We were all partly to blame," Tallmadge said. "We saw what was happening from the beginning but because we thought Harmon was a patriot and began doubting Malcolm's loyalty to the American cause, we stood aside and said nothing."

"That was better than most of the students did." Enoch said. "They egged him on."

"Please," David said to Nathan Hale, "tell me from the beginning exactly what happened."

"I'll tell you what I know," Nathan said. "I don't think we properly understood Harmon's enmity toward Malcolm. We assumed it was based on his contention that Malcolm was a Tory. That rumor got started because of Malcolm's friendship with Thad Williams, who we have heard has married your daughter, sir."

"Yes, he did, but without my permission," David said tightly.

"Yes, well anyway, Sidney, who professed to be the patriot of patriots, began to hector and bully Malcolm. At first all of us defended Malcolm against Harmon and his cronies, but gradually as feelings became more heated over the controversy between Crown and colonies, we . . . well, we failed to stand behind Malcolm as we should have."

"Most of us, that is," Enoch broke in. "But Nathan never faltered in his loyalty and friendship to your brother, Captain Glencannon."

Nathan ignored the interruption. "We did not support Malcolm and he became isolated and all but friendless once Thad had left. Sidney and his crew badgered him relentlessly, taunting him for his failure to rally to the cause of the colonies and insinuating he became pacifist because he was a coward. Malcolm bore all this with a certain stoicism, but I knew he was suffering inside, and then finally—" Hale hesitated, looked around at the others and then at Elspeth. "Uh . . . the subject is a little delicate for a lady's ears."

"Feel free to continue, sir," Elspeth said. "I am a married woman with a grown daughter and not easily shocked."

David was less sure he wanted to hear what Hale had to tell him but he saw no way of avoiding it, and with Malcolm lying at death's door, it was his duty to get all the facts that had led to this terrible event.

"Of late," Nathan went on, "Sidney's chevying had taken on a more personal tone. As I understand it, it involved a young woman Malcolm was seen with frequently here in New Haven as well as in nearby North Bedford. Apparently Harmon jumped to the conclusion that there was something suspicious about their friendship and had begun to make insinuations about it. Malcolm did indeed seem secretive about her . . . perhaps protective is a better word . . . and never introduced her to any of us. Sidney assumed the worst and was determined to make trouble."

Hale paused again and looked around at his brother and friends, his expression slightly reproachful. "I have been away with the army and few classes are being held because of the summer recess, so Malcolm was alone and being harassed incessantly. I came up for a weekend from Brooklyn prior to leaving on an assignment for General Washington, and Malcolm and I were having supper at the Blue

Boar Tavern when I was called away by the arrival of a courier from headquarters. While I was talking to the man who brought a dispatch, I became aware of angry voices raised in altercation. I turned and was astonished to see Malcolm engaged in a violent dispute with Sidney.

"I have known your brother for a number of years, Captain, know him very well, but I have never seen him as enraged as he was then. His face was scarlet and he had Harmon by the throat, and I honestly think if I hadn't intervened, he would have strangled the man. It was a most extraordinary way for Malcolm to behave and I am sure it had something to do with this young woman he's been seeing. Perhaps Harmon, in his typically nasty way, cast aspersions on the young lady's character and on her relationship with Malcolm."

David sighed heavily. "You never met this young woman, Nathan?"

"No, Captain Glencannon, I never did."

"None of us did," Townsend said, "which seems strange because the only other girl Malcolm was briefly interested in, the daughter of a lay Quaker preacher, he introduced to everyone."

"Can you tell me what the lady looks like?" David asked, doggedly determined to dig out the facts leading to this tragedy, no matter what the personal cost.

"I have only seen her from a distance," Nathan said. "She is of medium height and quite slender. I don't know the color of her hair because she had on a hooded traveling cape the few times I saw Malcolm putting her on a stage."

"Her hair is brown, light brown, and she has a sweet face," Townsend offered. "As I entered the tavern one day, I almost ran into her. She smiled when I bowed but Malcolm made no move to introduce us."

David's expression was grim as he listened. There was no doubt in his mind that the girl was Susan, but he had no intention of revealing her identity to these young men, or to Elspeth, for that matter. This was strictly a family matter.

The door of the examining room opened, and the doctor, a tall, balding young man whose wig had been cast aside, appeared. He was coatless, had his sleeves rolled up, and looked weary and discouraged.

"This is Captain David Glencannon," Nathan said, "Malcolm's older brother."

"It is well that you are here, sir," the doctor said, stepping to one side and gesturing for David to enter. "Your brother is in a deep coma, and I must tell you frankly that I doubt he will ever regain consciousness, or that he will live long."

Chilled by the man's words, David entered the room and slowly approached the table where Malcolm lay, pale and still, head swathed in white bandages. Heart heavy with anger and grief, he stood looking down at the youthful features so like his own.

"Is there no hope?" David asked as the doctor came to his side.

"There is always hope, I suppose," Dr. Manley said and pointed to the side of Malcolm's head, "but the ball struck him here, driving a splinter of the skull inward to press against the brain. That is what has caused his unconsciousness."

"Is there no way to relieve the pressure?"

The doctor hesitated. "Well . . . it is just barely possible that if the damaged piece of skull were to be cut out—and this is a most difficult operation—

and the resulting incision were trephined, that is, a piece of skull taken from a fresh cadaver carefully inserted, your brother might eventually recover."

"Yes, I've heard of that operation," Elspeth said from the doorway. "There are one or two surgeons in London and three in Edinburgh who have performed it."

For a minute David thought wildly of obtaining a ship and transporting Malcolm to Scotland, but Dr. Manley quickly squelched that idea.

"Even if it were possible under war conditons to make such a trip, young Mr. Glencannon would not survive an Atlantic voyage."

"But there must be some way," Elspeth said. "Money is no objective. My purse is not bottomless, but it is deep and—"

"No, no, I couldn't allow you to use your money," David said. "This is not your problem."

Those remarkable amber eyes met his levelly. "If you have a problem, David, it is also mine."

In that moment he knew she truly loved him and that his love for her was equally strong, but here in front of the doctor and with Malcolm's friends listening was no place to tell her.

Deep in thought, Dr. Manley paid no attention to their brief exchange. "There is one man here in these colonies who might be able to help. He has performed a similar operation, although one much less complicated."

"Who is he?" David asked eagerly as Manley herded them back out into the waiting room.

"My own mentor, Doctor Edward Bancroft. He performed the operation on a child who had been injured in a Conestoga wagon in Philadelphia. It was only partially successful as the child remained partly paralyzed. He is, however, the most accomplished surgeon in North America. If you could consult him, and if he were willing to attempt surgery with so strong a chance of failure . . . well—" he shrugged his shoulders eloquently, "there might be a slight chance of recovery."

"Contacting Doctor Bancroft would be no problem," David said. "He is a longtime friend of Ben Franklin who looks on Malcolm as almost a son."

Manley brightened a little. "Of course, it would be almost as difficult to transport your brother to Philadelphia as to cross the Atlantic. He would have to be lying down all the way and carried in a vehicle with excellent springs so that he would be bounced and joggled as little as possible."

"You shall take my coach," Elspeth said at once. "I will continue my journey by public stage or on horseback."

"Elspeth, you are too generous. I cannot allow you to—"

"You not only can, you must," she said. "It is the only practical way of getting Malcolm to Philadelphia."

"We could take him by sea," David said.

"Surely not, sir," Tallmadge said. "The British blockade is getting more dangerous by the day. Only warships or extremely fast merchantmen are getting through. To take a ship from here and try to get into the Delaware and up to Philadelphia would not only be dangerous but downright foolhardy."

"And from a medical point of view, I must offer the same objection to a short sea voyage as to a long one," Manley said. "If your brother is to have any chance for survival at all, I'm afraid you must accept the offer of this lady's coach."

"Very well," David said. "I do not know how to thank you, Elspeth, and I shall worry about your traveling the rest of the way alone even with safe conduct passes from General Washington and Lord Sterling."

"Where is the lady going?" Robert Townsend asked.

David looked around at the intensely patriotic young men and wondered how far he could trust their discretion. But since he had no choice, he explained as best he could.

"Lady Wescott is an old family friend who is trying to rejoin her husband, a British officer, on Newport Island. We are assuming they still have their foothold there."

"They do, sir," Townsend said, swallowed hard and went on, "I'll take it on my own responsibility to provide Lady Wescott with an escort of dragoons to see her within sight of the British lines."

"Thank you," David said and turned to the doctor. "How soon can my brother leave?"

"I will have to prepare him . . . devise a protective bandage and perhaps a wooden neck brace to hold his head immobile during the trip. He will be ready by tomorrow morning at the earliest."

David nodded. "Very well. That well give me time to take care of another matter."

He turned back to the four young men. "Before I go, I would like you gentlemen to describe the duel in which my brother was wounded so seriously."

"Well, after the incident in the tavern," Nathan said, "Sidney naturally sent a challenge. Sooner or later he would have done so anyway; he was only waiting for an excuse. He hated Malcolm and one way or the other was determined to goad him into a duel. When the challenge came, we all urged Malcolm to turn it down, but he would not."

"He had a perfectly good reason to refuse," Townsend said. "Everyone knew of his Quaker-like beliefs, which do not countenance duels or other violent acts."

"No, he wouldn't listen," Hale said. "He was absolutely determined to go through with it, so I offered to stand with him and Townsend was one of the witnesses. Dr. Manley was there as attending physician. Harmon brought two of his cronies with him, and we met at dawn in a little grove outside of town. You know the formalities, I suppose. The rules were laid down and Harmon as the 'injured' party had the choice of weapons. He picked pistols."

"Did Malcolm examine the pistol he was given carefully?" David asked.

"He refused to even look at it," Nathan said. "He disliked the thought of even touching it."

"I checked it," Townsend said. "It was primed and loaded; no irregularity that way."

"I didn't think there would be with you gentlemen there," David said. "I was merely trying to judge his mental attitude."

"We went through the usual preliminaries," Hale continued. "The firing was to be at thirty paces and these were stepped off and then the men turned to face each other."

"I took the opportunity at that moment to urge both of them to desist from what is an illegal activity," Manley said.

"Neither man would agree to withdraw," Townsend said. "Harmon was beside himself with joy at the opportunity to kill Malcolm, and Malcolm seemed driven by some strange compulsion."

"I thought he might have a chance because he had right on his side," Enoch said.

Townsend shook his head. "No, he had almost none. Harmon is an experienced duelist and has killed his man before. I should have gone to a magistrate, but one lives by a code, you know, and is reluctant to break it."

Nathan took up the tale again. "They faced each other and Dr. Manley began the count. Malcolm was standing with his pistol in his hand, letting it hang loose at his side as though he hardly knew what its purpose was."

"I don't think he did, or at least he didn't care," Tallmadge said. "I know he would never have raised that weapon and pulled the trigger even if he had realized it was the only way of avoiding certain death. I cannot understand him but I can at least admire his consistency."

"When the handkerchief was dropped and the word to fire given," Nathan continued, "Malcolm did pull the trigger, but he fired with the weapon still hanging by his side, discharging the bullet into the ground. Harmon laughed. As long as I live I will never forget the diabolical grimace of pleasure on his face when he raised his pistol and leveled it at Malcolm."

David's fists clenched and his jaw set rigidly as he tried to contain his anger.

"I remember thinking that surely he wouldn't fire," Nathan said. "If I had not been so sure, I might have rushed in between them. I reasoned that having seen Malcolm disarm himself, he would fire harmlessly into the air or into the ground. And the longer he stood there without firing, the more convinced I became that he would not shoot an unarmed man in cold blood. I should have known from the look on his face that he was simply prolonging his enjoyment at having Malcolm at his mercy."

"And all that time, Malcolm just stood there," Enoch said. "Stood there without flinching, waiting for the ball."

"Your brother was . . . is . . . a very brave man, Captain Glencannon," Townsend said. "I have been in a battle and three skirmishes, but I could not have just stood there and waited to be shot down."

"Then before I could cry out as Harmon's intentions became crystal clear, he finally pulled the trigger. I saw Malcolm's head jerk back and then he fell. I ran toward him but Harmon was closer and quicker. He covered the thirty paces in several rapid strides, stood over Malcolm, who was crumpled facedown, and rolled him over with his foot to look at the bloody head. Then he smiled and walked away without a backward glance. I am sure he thought, and still thinks, that he killed Malcolm."

"How horrible," Elspeth said. "How utterly vicious. I hope the magistrates will see that he does not go unpunished."

"He will not go unpunished," David said flatly. "I can assure you of that."

"I wish I could be as sure of that as you are," Townsend said. "With the disruption caused by the war and the fact that Sidney's father has important friends in the Connecticut legislature, it will be—"

"I wonder if you could find a carriage for Lady Wescott as well as the escort you promised," David asked.

"Of course. I would be delighted," said the young major of dragoons. "It is always a pleasure to be of service to a beautiful lady, even a beautiful enemy lady."

"You are most gallant, sir," Elspeth smiled and took the arm he offered, then turned back to David. "I will see you again before I depart, will I not, Captain Glencannon?"

"Oh, yes. If you will take your coach to the inn and have your luggage transferred into the hired vehicle, I will join you there before you journey on."

Elspeth studied his grim face, a worried frown creasing her brow. "That is a promise, is it not? I will see you?"

"Yes, I will be there soon," David promised. He knew what he had to do and didn't want her present when he did it.

Reluctantly Elspeth allowed Townsend to escort her out of the doctor's house to her coach. She sensed something in David's manner that alarmed her but knew she had no right to question or protest whatever action he was contemplating. It would be best to do as he asked and perhaps later she could be of more help.

As soon as the door closed behind Elspeth and Townsend, David turned to the three remaining young men. "I assume, gentlemen, that this Sidney Harmon is still in New Haven?"

Nathan Hale eyed him silently, but Enoch spoke up. "Yes, he's still here. He has done a lot of talking about going off to join the army but never will, I'm sure. It is just talk."

"Excellent," David said. "Nathan, I will have to ask you to stand with me as you did my brother. I intend to kill Sidney Harmon in a duel tomorrow morning at dawn. He may have his choice of pistols or sabres."

"Captain Glencannon," Nathan said, "I must ask you to reconsider. Harmon is an expert shot and an accomplished swordsman."

"He is a bully and therefore a coward," David said. "His cowardliness and guilt will unnerve him."

The two Hales, Tallmadge, and Dr. Manley all tried to dissuade him, but David would have none of it. Overriding their every objection, he finally said to Tallmadge, "Will you please deliver my card to Mr. Harmon and suggest that he make his will. You might also suggest that, if he is a religious man, he make his peace with God."

21

"I do not like the look of it," Seth Ewart told his wife as the brig *Venture* headed north along the North Carolina coast toward Cape Hatteras with a fitful wind off her stern barely filling her sails. "There's an oppressive feeling in the air and the barometer has been falling for two glasses."

"There isn't a cloud in the sky," Mercy Shawna said, irritated by his constant fretting about one thing or another, "and the sea is so calm it is almost glassy."

"That may be," he said, looking aloft at the fluttering of the topsails, "but a storm can come up out of nowhere in these waters, and rounding Cape Hatteras is no place to be caught in a blow."

Shawna held her peace but sighed inwardly. Seth was a good, steady man and would always make her a dependable husband, but their marriage was anything but ecstatic. Not only was he a long way from being the consummate lover Bret Morley was, but he showed little more enterprise as a merchant captain than he did in bed. Not that he was a bad businessman; he had managed to wangle advantageous trades for salt in Bermuda and rum in Cuba and they were heading home with a full cargo. But although the Bermudans had cooperated with them fully in spite of the island still being British held, Seth had been skittish. At the sighting of a sail he thought could be a man-o'-war, he had sought shelter in a small lagoon and taken down his top masts. That had cost them two weeks lost, and even after the rum had been loaded in Havana and the Spanish authorities had assured them that *guarda coastas* had seen no British warships off the coast, he had still clung to harbor, hoping for the arrival of a Spanish frigate rumored on the way. He had reasoned that if the expected ship would convoy them through the Straits of Florida, they had a good chance of getting away scot-free.

Shawna had been impatient with his caution because, on the cruise south, they had not sighted a single British man-o'-war, nor heard of one except the frigate *Liverpool* 28, said to be operating with Lord Dunmore's squadron of small craft against the Virginia and Carolina coasts. Feeling that the sooner they made home port the better because the people in the colonies were beginning to feel the shortages caused by war, Shawna had wanted to sail at once and used all her powers of persuasion on Seth, even pointing out to him that no Spanish warship had stood up to an English one of equal or near equal strength since the Days of the Armada. She couldn't convince him, however, that the Spanish frigate wouldn't be much protection, and he had hung in Havana Harbor hoping for a convoy until the nearness of the hurricane season forced him to make the decision to sail.

"I'll take in the t'gallants now," Seth said, "then if we are hit by a sudden blow we can snug down more quickly."

"You can't spend your whole life snugged down," Shawna muttered to herself, but aloud suggested, "Why not bend on everything she will carry and try to weather the Cape before the blow comes?"

"Good Lord, Shawna, that would be suicide," Seth said. "You don't know what it's like to be caught on a lee shore. You cannot imagine how many ships have been lost trying to round Cape Hatteras in bad weather . . . it is a veritable graveyard of ships and men."

Shawna knew the reputation of Cape Hatteras quite well, and it seemed to her the bolder course in a situation like this might be the safer one as well.

Aside from the importance of getting a cargo of salt back to the colonies as quickly as possible, Shawna had another reason for urging speed. Even more than salt, the patriot cause needed gunpowder, and she believed she had information that might lead to their obtaining an enormous hoard of it. American ships had already raided the Bahamas and made off with what stores they could find, and Shawna had learned from the many Bermudans who favored the American rebellion that the barrels of gunpowder, shipped out for safekeeping prior to the raid on Fort Nassau by Commodore Hopkins, had been returned to the arsenal along with newer supplies of ordnance. The fort was strong but rather than being manned by British regulars, it was guarded by local militia, which was something less than alert she learned by judicious questioning and a casual stroll along the road past the gates.

Anxious though she was to convey her knowledge to the proper authorities so that action could be taken to appropriate the English cache, there was nothing she could do to hurry Seth along. Telling him about the powder would be useless; he was a trader by profession and at heart. To him the possibility of the colonies coming into the possession of a large store of gunpowder with which to carry on the war would be of small consequence compared to a safe voyage and a profitable cargo.

"Mr. Radin, will you come aft, please!" Seth was calling to the sailing master. "I want to take in sail and change course."

Elias Radin, a burly, tattooed individual, who had worked his way up from the lower deck, came swaggering aft. His shoulders were so wide he had to turn sideways to get through the hatchways on the ship, and his heavy arms dangled apelike well down past his knees. His teeth gleamed whitely in his swarthy face and the golden earring in his left lobe jingled as he came up the ladder from the main deck to the poop and casually touched his forelock to Seth.

"Yes'r, Cap'n, what'll it be" he asked, letting his black eyes linger appraisingly on the way the breeze molded Shawna's dress against thighs and buttocks.

"I want to take in sail and come about to give Hatteras a wide berth," Seth said.

"Yes'r, Cap'n, I'll call the hands," Radin said, and let his glance slide over Shawna again before he swung back down into the waist of the ship and began to bellow profanely at the hands.

"I do not like that man," Shawna said as soon as he was out of earshot.

"Don't like him?" Seth looked surprised. "He's competent, knows how to give orders, and has the ability to handle the ship. What is there to dislike?"

"He is insolent and has a sly manner I do not trust." She couldn't be any more explicit without mentioning that the looks he gave her were not the kind a hired seaman should bestow on the wife of his captain and owner of the ship.

"Well, my dear," Seth said mildly, "as long as he does his job well, I don't think we have anything to complain about. After all, we do not have to entertain him socially, or even have him at our table in the great cabin."

Shawna turned away, listening to the pounding of the bare feet of the seamen on the deck and watching as men swarmed aloft like monkeys to the whine of the bosun's pipe. No, she thought, she didn't have to face Elias Radin across the captain's table, and she could be grateful for that. In fact, she and Seth had been eating alone since the first mate died of yellow jack in Havana and they had been unable to find a trustworthy replacement. But truth to tell, she was getting tired of looking at Seth's complacent face three meals a day while he methodically chewed his food without expression or comment.

Shawna was beginning to realize that in her fury at Bret Morley she had probably made as big a mistake as she had in getting involved with the rich young member of the Continental Congress in the first place. What she had taken for shyness and reticence in Seth she now saw as stodginess and lack of spirit.

If she had been in charge of the ship, she would have rounded Cape Hatteras even in the teeth of a gale, would have taken the ship inshore of a group of outlying rocks upon which several craft had been sunk. Old Amos Pratt had told her that it was possible, with heavy enough seas running, to clear the rocks.

"Barometer's rising a bit now, ma'am," said Benwich, the white-bearded quartermaster, from his place at the helm. He always treated her as a kind of cocaptain, entitled to all the information the captain received. "Thar's gonna be a blow but 'twon't amount to all that much."

Seth had paced restlessly to the front of the poop deck to watch the sails being taken in and was paying no attention to what the man said.

"Aye," Shawna answered him, "and we'll be sailing halfway across the Atlantic to avoid Cape Hatteras and a little bit of wind and water. We'll waste a full day, if not more."

The man grinned at her. "Cape Hatteras ain't no place to fool with though, Mistress Ewart. 'Member the old *Sandwich,* as fine a full-rigged ship as ever sailed in the coastwide trade. She was caught by a sou'wester 'bout half mile off the rocks and couldn't weather the Cape. Cap'n tried to come about and run before the storm but she carried her mainmast out and was on the rocks before they could cut away the rigging of the fallen mast and claw their way off."

Shawna stepped closer to the helm. "You've sailed these waters before, quartermaster. Tell me, have you ever heard of a way a ship this large can cut inside the outer rocks of the Cape and, passing over those inshore, pass through the Pamlico Sound and out again to the north?"

Benwich glanced up at the sails that were filling rapidly, and then at the barometer, and finally at the breakers swirling whitely on the reefs to port. "Seems like I heared 'tis been done, but seems like I also heared a lot of folks who tried it ended up aground. You can sail through Ocracoke Inlet—ain't no trick to that, 'cepting to avoid the sand bars in Pamlico Sound once you get in. You can sail in Hatteras Inlet and do the same, but going north toward Albemarle Sound and out again 'round Roanoke Island takes some doing. With lots of water under your keel, you might maybe have a fifty-fifty chance

—wouldn't want to try it, though, lest 'twas a matter of life or death."

"How about life or capture by a British frigate?" she asked. "That coaster we spoke two days ago said the *Liverpool* and British light craft are very active around Hatteras and northward."

"Well, ma'am, I don't hanker to end up in no lobsterback prison hulk," the quartermaster said. "Yes'm, I sure might chance it that way."

"If we run into *Liverpool* by standing out too far past the cape, we might have to try it," Shawna said.

Benwich carefully gauged the wind and spat his tobacco cleanly to leeward, missing the taffrail by almost a foot. "Don't expect Cap'n would want to risk it even then. Careful man, the Cap'n."

"There's such a thing as being too careful," Shawna muttered rebelliously as she watched the hands swarm aloft to take in the topsails. "You spend so much time looking for trouble that you find it."

The quartermaster chewed reflectively for a few moments, but before he could frame an answer, the round, black face of the cook appared above the coping of the galley.

"Chow down, Missie," Cookie said. "Chow down in aftercabin."

"I wonder what would happen if he said dinner was served," Shawna said, heading toward the after-companionway.

"No one would know what he was talking about," Benwich called after her as she disappeared down the ladder into the main cabin where the midday meal of lobscouse, a delicacy of salt beef and potatoes hashed together, cabbage, ship's biscuit, and a tot of rum had been set out for her and Seth.

About halfway through the afternoon watch, with the *Venture* beating to seaward against near gale winds and with most of her sails reefed in, the fore-top lookout let out a bellow loud enough to wake the watch below.

"Sail ho! Sail ho!"

"Where away, man, where away?" Shawna shouted, grabbing the long glass out of Seth's hand.

"Four points off the port bow! Full-rigged ship!"

"Damn!" Seth fumed. "We almost made it around the cape!"

Shawna spared a disgusted look and clamped the long glass to her eye to stare at the sail that could be seen from the deck now. It was indeed a full-rigged ship, and in these waters of lobster boats, coastwise brigs, and Baltimore schooners, a full-rigged ship could mean trouble.

"How do you make her?" Seth asked, not taking back the glass because he knew Shawna had sharper eyes than he had.

"Not sure," she said, "but I think we should make more sail and stand by to come about."

"We can't come about with these gale winds coming up and with Hatteras off our port and—"

"She's a big ship." Shawna was straining to see if there were gunports along the distant vessel's sides, but it was still almost hull down and the scurrying clouds were casting shadows on the white capped sea. "We can come about and run toward either Hatteras or Ocracoke Inlet."

"We'll be trapped in Pamlico Sound," Seth objected. "They will send boats in to cut us out."

"Not if we can work our way through the reefs and sand bars and come out of the north."

Seth shook his head. "That's too dangerous, if not impossible. I'll call the sailing master and see what he thinks."

"You better make up your mind quickly," Shawna told him, "because that ship shows a line of gunports and she's making more sail."

Radin swung up onto the poop with one long apelike pull of his hairy right arm. "We could run south till we shake her or can put into Charleston or Savannah."

"That could mean weeks and money lost while our cargo rots," Shawna pointed out.

Radin's predatory teeth gleamed whitely in his swarthy face. "Better that than us rotting in an English prison hulk, Missie."

"She's broken out her t'gallants and is running 'fore the wind," Shawna reported. "She'll be in range of her long tom in half a glass."

"Hands to the braces!" Seth shouted. "Stand by to come about!"

"Let's bend on everything she'll carry," Shawna said as the topmen went up the braces hand over hand and the closely reefed sails began to flatten in the wind as they were shaken out.

Shawna's red hair was whipping about her face, and she clung to the rail with one hand, still holding the long glass to her eye with the other. The *Venture* heeled over and started to swing around, the wind striking her first on the starboard bow and then almost abeam, causing her to roll in the heavy troughs and seem to hesitate before swinging on around to fill her sails with the wind on her quarter.

"That's the *Liverpool*," Shawna verified as the *Venture* began to fly before her pursuer. "She's a witch for speed . . . they've broken out the Union Jack and run out the guns."

His ship's sails were filled, but Seth was still hesitating over whether to enter Pamlico Sound or run on south and try to shake the warship as they went down the coast.

He hesitated too long, and as the foamy water marking the entrance to Hatteras Inlet passed astern, Shawna cursed under her breath, using all the words she had picked up around the shipyard and aboard ship, words her father had threatened to tan her bottom for using if he ever heard them coming from her lips.

"Why does that frigate have to be so fast?" Seth fretted. "Most lime-juicers are slow as barges."

"French built, Cap'n," the quartermaster said around the wad of fresh tobacco in his mouth. "Captured in the French war."

"If we head inshore we might be able to reach Charleston 'fore she can overhaul us," the sailing master suggested, "or we can beach her and take to the boats."

"And lose ship and cargo?" Seth said testily. "Damned if I will!"

"Better than being locked up on a prison hulk," Radin argued.

"No. I am captain here," Seth said. "We're going to save both ship and cargo."

Radin turned away, but Shawna saw the ugly look in his eyes. Despite his bluster and strength, she sensed that the man was afraid. A frightened man who was also mean could be dangerous and she determined to keep an eye on him.

"We're a peaceful merchantman," Seth said to Shawna. "There's no reason to think they'd take us prisoner. Why, I doubt they'd even detain us for long."

"We've a cargo of contraband on board," Shawna reminded him. "We've been trading illegally with the Bahamas and Cuba. We have no license from a royal governor, couldn't have gotten one if we'd applied. No, Seth, we are rebels and we will be treated like rebels."

She had stated the facts calmly, hoping they would spur him into making a decision but it only seemed to dishearten him more. His shoulders slumped and he walked to the taffrail and stared disconsolately at the *Liverpool* looming larger and larger behind them.

"There's still time to turn in at Ocracoke Inlet," she urged, keeping an eye on the sailing master who had gone forward to supervise the layout of running tackle that had become snarled. "We could feel our way north through the sound with a good man in the chains to take soundings."

"*Liverpool* could follow us there," Seth said dejectedly.

"I imagine just the sight of her off the coast has caused the North Carolina militia to turn out, and they mlust have some artillery. The British will think twice before exposing their only genuine warship on this coast to shore guns and artillery."

"I still think it's safer to run south, even if they are gaining on us," Seth said. "A stern chase is a long chase, they say."

"Yes, but—"

"The frigate has opened fire!" came a hail from the lookout, and they both whirled to see a puff of smoke rising from the side of the *Liverpool*.

"What the devil?" Seth asked in surprise. "They're too far away to—"

" 'Tis a signal, Cap'n," the quartermaster said, pointing. "Look . . . just coming around the headlands south of Gore Sound."

There was a sail, and it took only a quick glance through the glass to tell them it was a brig, that it flew the Union Jack and had several guns mounted amidships.

"Another one, by God!" Benwich said. "One of fancy-pants Lord Dunmore's private ships that's been ravaging the coasts."

"We're blocked off," Seth said in despair.

"A stern chase won't be a long chase now," Shawna said, watching the brig, which was showing a surprising turn of speed although sailing almost directly into the wind. "Yonder is a handy craft. She's reaching and will be on us before we can come about unless we do so quickly."

Contrary to popular belief, a handy ship sailing within several points of a head wind, a practice called reaching, could often sail as fast, or faster, than one sailing with the wind dead astern.

"Perhaps we can come about and head out to sea and—" Seth's voice trailed off without finishing what even he knew was an impossible proposal.

"Stand by to come about!" Shawna shouted, taking matters into her own hands. "We're heading for Ocracoke Inlet!"

For a moment Seth looked as though he were going to countermand the order, or at least reprimand her for taking it on herself to make the only possible decision. But he merely shrugged and told the quartermaster to start coming about and to steer for the mouth of the inlet that was hard on their lee now.

Bare feet pounded on the deck and there was the cracking of sails being hauled by sweating, cursing men as the ship's boom came swinging overhead and the other sails were trimmed. *Venture* heeled over sharply and began to pitch as the heavy ground wells, brought on by near-gale weather, caught her. For one heartstopping moment, the sails hung loose as they changed course, and Shawna thought the ship was about to be caught in chains with both enemy vessels bearing down fast. But, with a shudder, she caught the wind again and with white water over her bowsprit, plunged through the heavy seas heading toward the narrow channel into Pamlico Sound.

In coming about, they had given the *Liverpool* a chance to draw closer and now she opened fire for real. Her bowchaser spoke and a 12-pound ball splashed into the turbulent seas a cable length short of *Venture*.

Shawna laughed, grabbed a line and swung up on the taffrail with skirts and hair blowing in the wild wind. She shook her fist and shouted at the frigate, "Hey, you bloody bastard of a lobsterback, you missed! You couldn't hit the House of Parliament from the Thames River on a clear day with a wind behind you!"

The next shot whistled close overhead, missing the masts and rigging but splashing near enough to wet their decks.

"Don't tempt 'em, Missie, don't tempt 'em," the quartermaster laughed and from his expression she knew he was enjoying this wild run for freedom as much as she was.

"Come on, come on!" she shouted to the deck crew. "Get those lines secured! Keep those sails free and we'll show the lot of them a clean pair of heels!"

They were perhaps a mile from the entrance to Ocracoke Inlet and both British ships were gaining on them by the moment. The brig also had opened fire and one of her 9-pounders passed through a flapping sail on the foremast, causing consternation to the crew who were forward but doing no damage.

Shawna swung down off the taffrail and was walking toward Seth, who had the long glass to his eye examining the boiling froth of water churning around the entrance to the channel for which they were heading, when a ball from one of the enemy ships struck home, smashing into the hull of the *Venture* just below the poop deck. Splinters flew in all directions and with unbelieving ears and eyes, Shawna heard Seth scream and saw him go down, hand gripping his thigh where blood was already staining his white canvas britches.

"Keep on your course!" she shouted to the quartermaster and leaped to Seth's side, turning him onto his back so she could see the extent of his wound.

"Splinter . . . thigh . . . hurts . . . bleeding," he mumbled, his blood seeping into the holystoned planking.

Shawna knew from the brief training Dr. Rush had insisted she have in emergency medical practice that it was imperative that she staunch the flow of blood or her husband would die. She snatched the sheath knife out of his belt and began hacking at her petticoat to get bandaging.

"Water . . . bring me water and rum!" she shouted to the cook whose head had popped up above the coping of the companionway.

Kneeling beside Seth, she cut away the heavy canvas of his pants to lay bare the wound. What she saw made her suck in her breath. The flesh had been gashed all the way across the fleshy part of the thigh to a depth of at least two inches and blood was pouring from it. She had to get that stopped and quickly.

"Seth, I'll have to apply a tourniquet. Can you roll over onto your other side . . . onto the good leg?"

"I . . . I guess so." He struggled over onto his left side with her help, and Shawna cut away the whole pants legs. Twisting the canvas into a long strip, she got it around his leg above the wound and looked about for something to tighten it with. A loose belaying pin came clattering toward her with the rise and fall of the ship, and she grabbed it up, slipped it through the loop of canvas, and twisted it tight.

By then Cookie had arrived with a kettle of water and a bottle of rum. She used part of the material cut from her petticoat to swab out the wound, sprinkled the rum liberally onto the raw flesh, and started to bandage it. Finding that she needed more cloth, she hiked up her skirt to cut off more, not caring that she was displaying the length of her long, shapely leg in the process.

At least she didn't care until she looked up and saw Radin standing at the top of the ladder from the main deck leering at her. But she didn't have time to worry about him or modesty. She was still trying to stop the bleeding and complete the bandaging, but every time she let go of the belaying pin to do something else, the tourniquet loosened and fresh blood soaked the wadded up muslin.

"Cookie, come here," she called to the cook who had backed away and was staring horror-struck at the wounded captain. "Can you hold this belaying pin right where it is?"

"Yes'm," the Cookie said, kneeling beside her and taking hold of the pin. Then she was able to finish the bandaging and ease Seth's head onto a coil of rope. His eyes opened briefly and he half smiled at her before passing out.

Then she had to think about the ship. "Cookie, stay here and keep that pin tight for fifteen minutes . . . a quarter of a glass . . . Then loosen it for a few minutes and tighten it again. Do you understand?"

"Yes'm," Cookie nodded vigorously and settled into a comfortable squat beside his fallen captain. "Ah takes care ob de cap'n."

Shawna got to her feet and looked around. "How far to the inlet?" she asked the quartermaster, noting that the ship was ducking her bowsprit into green water and that both pursuing ships were still firing.

" 'Bout half a mile," Benwich said, spitting less successfully than before with the wind roaring across their decks and *Venture* pitching, yawing, and rolling all at once. "Think we're gonna make it if they don't bring down a mast. They're aiming at 'em now."

"Keep her steady on the entrance," Shawna ordered, forbidding herself to duck as a ball whizzed past her head so close she could feel the breeze of it. There were half a dozen holes in their sails, and several ropes had been shot away, but the crew under the boatswain's orders were repairing them almost as fast as they were damaged.

"It's time we came about," Radin said, pulling himself up onto the poop and standing just in front of the ladder. "Stand by to come about and strike your sails. We're going to surrender before we're blown to pieces."

"What was that you said, mister?" Shawna demanded, advancing on the man with hands on hips.

"I said we're going to come about, anchor, and strike our flag," Radin said. "There's such a thing as taking reasonable chances, but this is too much."

"And who in hell gave you the right to make decisions here?" Shawna said.

"The captain is out of it. I'm the sailing master and second in command, so of course I make the decisions."

"The hell you do! I'm half-owner of the *Venture*, and I'm relieving you as sailing master and appointing myself captain of this ship, and we're jolly well going through Pamlico Sound, out the other end and on to Philadelphia, come hell or British man-o'-war!"

Radin laughed at her, his voice mocking and his eyes leering. "I'd like to see you do that, little lady. I'd sure like to see you try."

She was moving closer to him, determination in every step, but he didn't notice that. All he noticed was the long, white expanse of leg where she had cut away dress and petticoat and the way the wind was plastering her clothes to her statuesque figure.

"You and me will be havin' some fun later on, Missie," Radin said, "but right now I got the ship and our lives to think about."

"I'm giving you a legal order right now, Radin," Shawna said steadily. "You are relieved of your post and I am in command of this ship. If you disobey, you will be tried for mutiny when we get to Philadelphia."

Members of the crew, including the boatswain, had come aft and were staring up at the poop deck as though waiting to see whom to take orders from. Shawna knew she had to enforce her will now or everything would be lost.

With no sign of the fear she felt of the man, she moved to within a foot of Radin. He grinned and the lust on his face sickened her.

"I told you, Missie, I'll get around to you later. Even with you prancing 'round half-naked on deck, I still got to—"

She stepped closer and he reached for her, either to push her aside or pull her to him. She didn't wait to find out which. Hooking a foot behind one of his, she shoved with both hands. Radin let out a bellow of surprise and went tumbling head over heels into the waist of the ship, landing with a loud thump on the deck below.

Before anyone could move or say a word, there was a crashing sound forward as a ball buried itself in the side of the *Venture*, and another carried away a spar.

Shawna's eyes took in everything at once. If the spar weren't tended to it might carry the mast with it. "Boatswain, get that spar cut away! Put a good man in the chains to take soundings and—"

"We're into the channel!" the quartermaster shouted. "I can see militia setting up a gun on the headlands yonder. That'll give the lobsterbacks something to chew on."

"Aye, it will," Shawna agreed joyfully as she saw the *Liverpool* starting to come about. Her attention snapped back to Radin as he groaned and sat up, holding one shoulder with the other hand. "Oh, and boatswain, have a couple of men carry Mister Radin below. He seems to have fallen down the ladder and injured his shoulder."

With a final barrage of shot, the *Liverpool* had turned away, and after a puff of smoke rose from the artillery piece on shore, the brig had done the same.

Shawna had time now to move back to where Seth lay unconscious on the deck with the cook hovering over him.

"He breathin' bettah, Missie, and de bleedin' is stop."

"Yes, he does look better, doesn't he?" she said, sinking to her knees beside her husband as the shouts from the leadsman were relayed back to the poop deck.

"He's going to be all right, and we've got water under our keel," she said. "We're going back to Philadelphia with ship and cargo intact."

22

At 6 o'clock of a bright August morning, with the sun shining and birds singing, David Glencannon, shipbuilder of Philadelphia and member of the Committee of Safety of the United States, shot a man dead in a wooded area outside of New Haven, Connecticut, and avenged what appeared to be the fatal wounding of his youngest brother.

Nathan Hale had been forced to leave abruptly on a mission about which he was very reticent, and could not stand as David's second. Major Benjamin Tallmadge of the Second Regiment, Continental Light Dragoons, took his place. Enoch Hale and Robert Townsend carried David's challenge to their former classmate, Sidney Harmon, who at first had been inclined to laugh at the note they handed him.

"You mean this old gentleman proposes to face me in a duel? What does he want, two funerals in the family instead of one?"

"Malcolm is not dead," young Hale said, trying to keep the loathing out of his voice.

"Oh? Too bad. I had hoped I'd put that philandering Tory away once and for all," Harmon said, taking a pinch of snuff.

"Captain Glencannon offers you the choice of weapons," Townsend told him.

Harmon waved a careless hand. "Let him pick his weapon. I can kill him with equal ease using pistol or sword."

"I suspect Captain Glencannon will choose Kentucky rifles," Hale said. "He is quite adept with them, he and his father having founded Glencannon's Rangers during the French War."

Harmon's eyes flickered slightly. "Long rifles? Surely you jest. Nobody would ever use rifles in a duel."

Hale had caught the flicker and decided to play on it. "Captain Glencannon does, and he once shot five Ottawas in a row, each one hit in the left eye."

"Hmmmm." Harmon reconsidered. "Perhaps it should be swords."

"Captain Glencannon will be delighted," Townsend said, recalling something he and David had talked about the night before and not hesitating to expand it a little. "He still has his father's six-foot long claymore."

"Six feet long?" Harmon scowled. "There must be rules against using such things in civilized warfare."

"In the far highlands of Scotland, or on the Kentucky frontier, no one ever heard of such rules," Hale said.

"Pistols then . . . pistols by all means," Harmon said, tightening the cord of his dresssing gown. "I've killed my share with the sword, but the pistol is my real weapon."

"Captain Glencannon will be delighted," Townsend said again and bowed his way out with Hale following.

As soon as David laid eyes on Harmon the next morning, he knew the young man was nervous. He kept glancing at David as though he had expected him to be wearing horns all the time the seconds were laying down the ground rules.

"What's wrong with the fellow?" David asked. Deeply concerned though he was over the outcome of the duel, and depressed by Elspeth's tearful farewell, he had his nerves well in hand as became an old campaigner. "He keeps fidgeting and peering about."

"I think he expects a band of Indians to burst out of the woods and scalp him," Townsend said with a wry grin. "I'm afraid, sir, that we exaggerated your prowess in battle and on the field of honor."

David shrugged, remembering the day long ago in Scotland when Shawn had so terrified his opponent that the man had panicked and had been barely able to stand still as his earlobes were shot off. David had no time for such flamboyant gestures. He simply intended to kill Harmon for the coward and bully he was.

"Gentlemen, are you ready?" asked Dr. Manley who was acting as neutral observer.

"Ready," David said, testing the weight of the pistol he held in his hand. He had never fought a duel before, but to a man who has waited patiently in a group of Highlanders for a battalion of British grenadiers to open fire, who later waited in a British line or a French regiment to roar forth a massed volley, and who had fought redskins in their woods and *courer de bois* along their rivers, facing one man with a gun seemed like no new experience.

"Take aim," Manley said, his voice a bit unsteady.

David raised the pistol, leveled it, and aimed between the eyes of the man who had shot his brother and now stood thirty paces away. There was a trickle of sweat under his collar, which he attributed to the warmth of the early morning sun. He could see the youth quite clearly despite the slight haze that had drifted in from the sea during the night and still hung in occasional wisps about the ground.

Then as he looked at the other man, David became aware of a reluctance to take a human life. In the heat of battle, he had never hesitated, but here with the birds singing and the sun shining, it seemed a cruel and unnecessary thing.

"Fire!" the doctor called, and almost in the same second, Harmon's pistol spoke.

David felt a sting on his cheek and a trickle of something he knew must be blood down over his chin. His finger tightened automatically on the trigger, and as though in a dream, he saw Harmon go over backward and lay still. Even before Manley reached the man's side and bent over him, David knew he was dead and turned away.

"Well done, Captain Glencannon," Townsend said, pounding him on the shoulder. "Well done, indeed."

"Right between the eyes," Tallmadge said. "I've never seen such shooting . . . never seen such coolness."

David took no credit for his cool nerves. That was the way Shawn Glencannon had expected his sons to behave. To David's knowledge, Martin was the only one who had ever failed to live up to his father's demands. Even Malcolm, pacifist though he was, had never shown any personal cowardice. David remembered a time when Crispin, then a boy and not yet able to swim, had fallen into the Delaware. Malcolm had plunged into the river and swum almost a mile downstream to rescue the lad. Shawn himself had been perfectly capable of running when he thought a battle lost or of avoiding a fight if it was hopeless, but he had never felt a cowardly emotion. So David didn't feel he had done anything exceptional. Neither did he feel good about what he had just done; he would never feel good about it— couldn't—no matter what Harmon had done.

"Thank you gentlemen for your help," he said, "and now I must impose on your friendship for one more task, the crucial one of transferring my brother from Dr. Manley's place into Lady Wescott's carriage for the trip to Philadelphia."

They rigged boards between front and rear seats of the coach and placed a feather bed on them, then carefully lifted Malcolm's limp form through the door and laid him on it, feet facing toward the front. Dr. Manley provided David with extra dressings for the wound and medicine to be used only if Malcolm should recover consciousness for even a few moments.

"But I do not expect that, sir," he said. "I do not expect him ever to recover his senses, and doubt he will be alive when you reach Philadelphia."

With those less than sanguine words lingering in his mind, David took his place on the narrow portion of seat not taken up by the improvised ambulance bed and instructed the coachman to drive slowly and with extreme care.

Just before the coach started on its way, David leaned out the window and said to Enoch Hale, "Please convey my regards and thanks to your brother when he returns to New Haven. I will be eternally grateful for his many kindnesses to Malcolm."

"I will do that, sir," Enoch said with a worried frown, "if he returns to New Haven."

Later David was to recall those words, but at the time he thought they portended nothing more than the fact that Nathan perhaps did not intend to come back to the university town, or might have duties elsewhere.

The trip was long and slow, but since it was summer, the roads were in fairly good condition, and Malcolm seemed to weather it without noticeable change in his already desperate condition.

En route David received the news that Washington had been defeated on Long Island by General Howe's troops and had been forced to give up the lines on the Harlem Heights and had retreated into New Jersey. There was talk that Philadelphia might be in danger, but the city seemed calm enough on the hot day in early September when the carriage reached there. David directed the coachman straight to the Glencannon house on Walnut Street.

On reaching home, David hurried inside to get a manservant to help him carry in Malcolm. He had just entered the parlor, which was semidarkened against the heat of the day, when he heard a pleased exclamation.

"Papa! Papa, you're home!"

There was the rustle of skirts, and then he was engulfed in the whirlwind that was Shawna.

"My darling girl, how wonderful to see you," David said when he caught his breath. "I was terribly worried about you, you were so long overdue."

It wasn't until then that he noticed there was a man in the parlor and he was bending over someone on the settee. To his astonishment, the tall, thin, dignified man was none other than Dr. Benjamin Rush, the city's most famous physician.

"Dr. Rush, how fortunate that you are here, but what brings you?"

"It's Seth, Papa," Shawna said. "He was wounded when we outran a British frigate and brig-of-war off the North Carolina coast."

"Good Lord! How is he?" David crossed the room and peered down at Seth Ewart's pale face.

"His wound developed pus so I called in Dr. Rush," Shawna explained.

The doctor was taking off his spectacles and putting them away. "It is mere laudable pus, Mistress Ewart. His humors are rendered out of adjustment by the wound and must seep off the poisons. I shall send Pickens the barber around to bleed him this evening."

"Dr. Rush, I have another patient I would be grateful if you would look at," David said. "He's outside in a coach. I'll fetch the manservant and we'll bring him in."

"Who is it, Papa?" Shawna asked. "Crispin?"

"No, it's Malcolm. He has been wounded, perhaps mortally, in a duel."

"In a duel? Malcolm?" Shawna said in disbelief and then realized this was no time for such comments. "Come, Papa, I'll help bring him in and Dr. Rush can examine him on the dining room table."

The examination didn't take long and Rush's diagnosis was the same as Manley's. "Desperate . . . almost certainly fatal. These wounds where part of the skull has been ruptured and is pressing on the brain are almost always—"

"Wouldn't it be possible to operate?" David asked, "to relieve the pressure and perform a trephine?"

"Theoretically possible," Rush said, "but an operation of such risk that I doubt any doctor would be willing to accept the responsibility."

"But he's going to die without it, isn't he?" Shawna asked.

"Doctor, I was told that Dr. Edward Bancroft of this city once performed such an operation," David said.

Benjamin Rush's thin nostrils twitched and his manner became perceptibly cooler. "I have heard that he did . . . once."

"And the patient lived?"

"She lived," Rush said, "but there are times, sir, when a person might be better off dead?"

"What do you mean?"

"I don't believe the young lady has ever said a sane word since she quitted Bancroft's operating table." Rush was rolling down his sleeves with the sort of decisiveness a professional man might assume when talk turned to witchdoctors and shamans as practioners of medicine.

"You haven't a very high opinion of Dr. Bancroft then?" David asked.

Rush hesitated as he put on his coat and looked about for his hat, then he turned back to David. "Let me say this—I know him to possess an M.D. and an F.R.S., to be a friend of Dr. Franklin and a strong patriot. I do not know of any other recommendations I can make for him."

Nevertheless, as soon as Rush had departed, David sent his free black servant, Henry, for Bancroft. Then he went out to tip the coachman and footman and give them instructions on how to return to New York through the American and British lines.

"I hope the young gentleman recovers, sir," the coachman said, touching his laced tricorn and then driving off. David watched the coach disappear, regretting having it go because it seemed a part of Elspeth and likely the last contact he would ever have with her.

Dr. Edward Bancroft came quickly, a bustling, neatly dressed, friendly little man in an old-time periwig and spectacles especially designed for him by his friend Benjamin Franklin. He exuded and inspired confidence, but his words after examining Malcolm were not hopeful.

"It would be an operation of the most desperate kind," he said. "One would hesitate to perform it under the best of circumstances, and his present condition would make it impossible. The loss of blood and present debilitation of the patient are all against success, and there is the additional difficulty of obtaining a fresh cadaver."

"Perhaps, given a little time, he would grow stronger," Shawna suggested.

"With nourishment, perhaps, but trying to feed an unconscious person is extremely risky because of the danger of choking him or getting food into the windpipe. And if I am to perform the operation, we do not have too much time."

"Why not?" Shawna asked bluntly.

Bancroft looked around as though to assure himself there was no stranger in the room who might overhear him. "You are a friend of Dr. Franklin, Captain Glencannon, and a member of the Committee of Public Safety, so I see no reason why you should not know—Benjamin will tell you himself, no doubt, as he pays no attention to such things as secrecy in diplomatic matters."

"Diplomatic matters?"

"Yes. No doubt you have seen the *Reprisal*, which recently came up river and docked."

"Yes, Captain Wickes commands," David said. He had seen the low freeboard, rakish black-hulled craft with her three tall masts before he had left for New Haven and thought she looked more like a privateer than a man-of-war in spite of her eighteen 6-pounders.

"She is waiting to take Ben to France," Bancroft confided. "The Congress feels there is a real possibility that France may take up arms against Britain as our ally if things are handled properly, and Mr. Adams and others are convinced that only Franklin can handle the delicate negotiations."

"Yes, Mr. Adams mentioned that to me himself," David said, "but I don't see what that has to do with—"

"Mr. Arthur Lee and myself are to accompany Franklin, and we will join Silas Deane of Connecticut there as American commissioners."

"I see, and are you leaving at once?"

"Probably in early October."

"Then we have approximately a month to try to build Malcolm's strength so he can survive the operation. Would he have a chance then?"

"One in ten perhaps," Bancroft said. "I've only performed the operation once and it . . . well, it was not completely successful."

"This one will be," Shawna said with her inborn confidence and optimism. "And we will see that he's strong enough."

Weary from the events of the last few days and the strain of the trip home, David felt a thousand years old and was glad for the presence of his cheerful, energetic daughter.

As soon as Bancroft left, she set about finding out how and what to feed her unconscious uncle. David had already discovered that with care Malcolm could be given small amounts of water which he swallowed without any problem, so Shawna decided broth, chicken or beef with all meat and vegetable strained out, would be best. That and milk would have to be their chief weapons in the battle for Malcolm's life.

But taking care of Malcolm was only one of the things that needed their time and attention. Seth, while recovering, was still not up and about, and the housekeeper had not hired out to be a nurse. David had his work at the shipyard and Shawna had to dispose of the cargo of the *Venture* and get the ship ready for sea again.

"She needs to be hauled out," David told her after inspecting the brig. "We should do it as soon as you get the cargo sold."

"Will you have time to do the work at the yard?" she asked.

David nodded. "*Randolph* is ready for sea. I discussed that with Humphreys this morning. She is only waiting for Captain Biddle and his crew to come aboard."

"But don't you have other work?"

"Only the *Delaware* now," he told her. The *Delaware* was a 24-gun light frigate, and it along with the *Washington* and *Effingham* were the last of the frigates Congress had authorized to be built in Philadelphia. Somehow the *Delaware* didn't have the appeal for David that *Randolph* had, probably because he considered her too light for modern warfare. But he did want to get her launched because General Howe's army was driving Washington's forces across the Jerseys and there was a possibility that the British might turn toward Philadelphia at any moment.

The days passed quickly, with David and Shawna struggling to make time for everything they had to do. They took turns nursing Malcolm and Seth, to the extent that he needed it, and they labored along with their crews at the shipyard and on the *Venture*. The brig's cargo sold at a handsome profit to Boston merchants and then she was hauled out. The *Delaware* changed slowly from the bare ribs of a ship to a hull and her decking over began.

Shawna fed the unconscious Malcolm with extreme care three times a day, broth or milk sopped up on a clean cloth and slipped gently into his mouth where his tongue and throat muscles instinctively responded and sucked at it. It was a slow process that took over an hour each time. When even the ebullient Shawna began to look tired and wan, David decided they needed help. Since Deborah's husband Henrik was ill and she had the tavern to take care of, the only ones he could think of to call on were Aileen and Susan. He wrote to Aileen in care of Amos Pratt at once.

The letter he got back was shocking and disturbing in the extreme. She addressed David as though he were a stranger and from there on grew more hostile by the sentence.

"Dear Captain Glencannon,
   I am in receipt of your recent communication saying your brother Malcolm is unconscious and in need of constant care and requesting that Susan and myself return to Philadelphia to help. I will start right off by stating that I do not care what Malcolm Glencannon's condition is, and I have no intention of telling my daughter anything concerning him. We will not be returning to Philadelphia in the near future. We have taken a small house on Cape Cod and will stay there to await the birth of her child, which is due sometime in the Spring. I will not detail the circumstances of the conception, but I am sure you will understand why my feelings for your brother are of a nature that precludes my extending any help to him or his family. It is my devout wish that

I had never met or had anything to do with any Glencannon.

> Aileen O'Hara"

David let the sheet of paper flutter out of his hand onto his desk, astonished and shamed by its contents, although somewhat prepared for the unwelcome news by his own discovery of the relationship between Malcolm and Susan. And now there was a child on the way and Aileen obviously blamed the entire Glencannon family for that circumstance and not just the young couple themselves. She felt so strongly, in fact, that she had used her maiden name to repudiate her whole connection to them . . . Aileen, who had always been more of a Glencannon and more fiercely proud of their heritage and tradition than any other of them.

"Thank God Martin didn't live to see this," David said to himself. "Aye, and 'tis just as well Shawn didn't either. He was most fond of Aileen and spoke of her and Susan with his dying breath."

Deeply grieved though he was, he decided not to discuss this turn of events with Shawna or Gifford. Maybe someday he would write to Steven in faraway New Orleans and tell him, because he and Aileen had worked together to keep the family intact after the transportation of the men, had endured much to bring them all safely to the new land and reunion in the colonies. But David would speak of it to no one else. He unlocked the secret drawer of his desk and deposited the letter with other family papers.

The days of late September dragged by endlessly, David and Shawna working so hard they hardly noticed the gorgeous colors of the turning leaves

or the slight chill in the air. Things eased up a bit
when Seth was able to get up and hobble around the
house and sit with Malcolm occasionally, and when
the *Venture*, her bottomed cleaned of weed and
barnacles, was floated out again. Her masts were
restepped in place, David taking particular care to
make the improvements in them he had in mind to
increase her speed from the first time he had seen her.

Malcolm never stirred, but color came back into
his cheeks and he had ceased to lose weight. Finally,
just ten days before he and Franklin were due to
sail, Bancroft announced himself satisfied with his
patient's ability to withstand the operation. Then
there was the matter of locating a suitable cadaver,
which entailed more waiting.

Only five days prior to the scheduled departure
of the *Reprisal*, Shawna came rushing into David's
office at the shipyard to report breathlessly, "There's
been an accident on Chestnut street. A drayer's assistant was crushed under the wheels of a Conestoga
wagon. He is still breathing, but the man who
brought the news says there is no chance for his life.
I have already checked and the body can be purchased for twenty-five dollars."

"Send one of the workmen for Bancroft," David
said. "Who is the money to be paid to?"

"I'll take care of it," Shawna said and hastened
off before he could question it further.

Bancroft came the next morning with his assistant
and a coarse, bawdy-looking woman named Sara to act
as nurse during the operation. David took one last look
at his expressionless face as the dining room table was
made ready and three lamps arranged around it on
stands to throw the best possible light. Malcolm was
carried in by the doctor and his assistant, and the

sheet-draped cadaver was brought in from the wagon outside by an undertaker and his gravedigger.

"Are you sure that cadaver is fresh?" Bancroft demanded.

"He warn't dead yet when we put him in the wagon and headed this way," said the undertaker, "but he is now. Feel him, he ain't even cold."

Bancroft lifted one corner of the sheet, then stopped and stared in surprise. "My God, the man is black! He's a nigger!"

David looked at Shawna. "He was a slave," she said. "I bought his body from his owner. What difference does it make?"

"It could make considerable difference," Bancroft said stiffly. "Savants are of the opinion that the Negro skull is much thicker than that of white men. There is also doubt concerning whether the black race is completely human and the compatibility of—"

"Have you personally measured the thickness of a black man's skull?" David asked.

"No. All the cadavers we handled at Edinburgh were white. I doubt that the medical students would have cared to—"

"Proceed with the operation," David said. "It is the only chance we have."

Bancroft shrugged and turned to his assistant. "We shall have to be quick about this, Crowell. You must cut away the skin of the corpse while I prepare Mr. Glencannon's head. Then I will make the incision in both skulls. Sara, you stand by with a damp cloth for my brow and the brandy in case either of us need it."

There was nothing for David and Shawna to do but wait and pray. They sat in the parlor with Seth, whose healing leg was propped up on an ottoman.

"You two have done everything you could possibly do," Seth said. "It is in the hands of God now."

"God and Dr. Bancroft," David amended.

"Aye," Seth agreed, "and may the Lord Jehovah guide the good man's hand and keep his little saw and scalpel from slipping."

"Even the tiniest slip and it will be all over for Malcolm," Shawna said.

"Let's hope he doesn't resort to brandy to keep his hand steady," David said.

"Surely he wouldn't do that," Seth said. "Dr. Bancroft is a godly man, unlike some of our local physicians. I have the utmost confidence in him."

That was very well for Seth, David thought. It wasn't his brother lying in there helpless and unconscious. He couldn't keep from going over in his mind what Dr. Rush had told him of Bancroft's previous attempt at trephining or of the unfortunate young woman who had survived the operation but was left a hopeless idiot. He shuddered inwardly, knowing Malcolm would prefer death to that fate and that he would prefer it for him. But he had made the decision and now he would have to live with it, no matter what the outcome.

"Did I hear the doctor say the cadaver was that of a black man?" Seth asked. "Do you think it wise to use his skull? If Malcolm should find out that he had . . . well, you know . . . part of the skull of a nigger implanted in his own skull, it might—"

"If Malcolm survives and recovers, I think he will be grateful to the dead man whose skull he shares, and will not concern himself with the color of the man's skin," David said.

So they waited, and the waiting stretched into hours of suspense. David knew that if the operation had failed, they would have been notified promptly, and took some comfort from the passage of each additional minute.

They waited and, to occupy their minds, they talked about the *Venture* and the possibility of getting her a cargo for trading in the Indies. They talked about Gifford, but David carefully avoided any mention of Aileen and Susan.

They talked about the war, how Glover's brigade had fought a day-long battle with Howe's advance forces at Pell's Point to cover the withdrawal of Washington's army. They talked about Colonel Haslet's regiment surprising the camp of Rogers's Queen's American Rangers and dealing them a strong blow.

"Rogers," David said, shaking his head, "back in the old war, Rogers used to be a friend and hero of ours; now he's a hated enemy. How times change."

"He deserves to be hated," Shawna said. "He's American born, yet he's leading that treacherous gang of Tories in raids against his own people."

The long morning faded into early afternoon before the door to the dining room finally opened and Bancroft appeared, looking tired and a little grim. But as he saw their anxious faces, he smiled faintly and nodded.

"The operation is finished, and your brother is still alive, Captain. If it is to be, he will recover consciousness within the next forty-eight hours. I can say that the operation was not a failure, but only time will tell if it is a success."

"Thank you, Doctor," David said. "Thank you very much."

"I will not, of course, be able to stay on to care for young Glencannon."

"I think we can prevail upon Dr. Rush to step in now," David said, "although I believe he disapproves of operations of this kind."

"Dr. Rush is an excellent man, but some of his ideas are less advanced than those of the Edinburgh school where I was trained."

The undertaker and gravedigger were carrying out the corpse when David turned to them on impulse. "I would like to see that he gets a decent burial. I will pay whatever is required."

The undertaker looked scandalized. "A decent burial for a nigger? Never heared of no sich thing."

"Well, you've heard of it now. See to it, and if he has any family, I would like to help them."

"I'll see what I kin do, but folks won't take kindly to it," the undertaker said sullenly. "How could he have a family, slaves don't have families."

" 'Scuse me, Mr. Downey, sir," the gravedigger said. "This here fella was name of Toby, sir. He was workin' fer the drayer part time. Ole Miz Marshall was his real owner, and he had a woman you might call his wife out to her farm and was tryin' to raise the money to buy her freedom."

"Well, then there is something we can do to show our appreciation, isn't there, Shawna?"

"Yes, indeed, there is, Papa. We can buy the girl's freedom and maybe give her work."

" 'Spect ole Miz Marshall welcome a chance to sell the wench sir," the gravedigger said. "She don't really have nothin' for her to do."

"We'll take care of it then," David said and turned back to Bancroft. "Thank you again, Doctor, and I wish you a safe trip and a happy return."

As soon as the doctor and his assistant had left, David, Shawna, and Seth went in to see Malcolm who was lying on a cot that had previously been prepared for him. His head was bandaged and his face pale, but he seemed to be breathing easily.

"Thought I saw his eyelashes flutter once when I was washing the blood off his neck and shoulders," Sara said. "Think maybe he's going to be all right.

David grinned at the woman in happy surprise. Ugly hag she might be, but right then he could have kissed her.

"Of course he's going to be all right," Shawna said. "He's a Glencannon, and the Glencannons are fighters."

23

On August 22, 1777, a huge British fleet appeared in Chesapeake Bay. It covered transports carying the larger part of Lord Howe's army, which had embarked in New York. Washington's army, after suffering through a long winter at Morristown, had fought half a dozen battles, including the astounding victories at Trenton and Princeton, but in the end it had always been forced to fall back before the superior training of the British and the dilatory strategy but excellent tactics of Howe. The long-expected invasion from Canada had come with an army of British, Hessians, and Indians spreading terror as they advanced down the Mohawk Valley. Men, women, and children had been put to the tomahawk in a deliberate campaign intended to terrorize the country into returning to the Crown. Of all the attackers, the Tories commanded by such figures as the Butler brothers and Sir William Johnson's son, Sir John, were the worst.

"Sir William would have died before raising a hand against his neighbors," George Crogham told David as he passed through Philadelphia on his way to the frontier to help make peace with the Indians.

"He would have suffered torture before letting his Mohawks become involved in a war between two groups of Englishmen," David said.

"Not Englishman against Englishman anymore, Captain David," Crogham said.

"True, but we've been Englishmen for so long that it is hard to remember sometimes that we are now Americans."

The British plan had been a good one; Burgoyne's army attacking from the north was to have been met by Howe's moving up from New York to cut the country in half and leave that hotbed of rebellion, New England, severed from the rest of the states. But Howe, with the strange ambivalence that plagued his whole conduct of the war, decided that instead of marching to meet Burgoyne, he would attack Philadelphia and travel most of the way by sea.

Now his army was disembarking at the place called Head of the Elk, about 45 miles from the city, and all Philadelphia was in turmoil. The Congress itself was nervously thinking of packing up bag and baggage and departing for points farther west. The fighting in the north, however, resulted in Burgoyne's forces believed checked at the battle of Bemis Heights by a colonial army commanded by Generals Gates and Arnold, with Daniel Morgan's riflemen and the Mohawk Valley militia playing a large part.

A few months previously Malcolm had declared himself well enough to make plans for the future.

"David, I've had a lot of time to think since I first recovered consciousness," he told his brother, "I am still a pacifist by nature, but after what happened to Nathan, I feel I must do something to help in this struggle."

During the first months of his recuperation, David had managed to keep from Malcolm the heroic death of Nathan Hale, who had been hanged as a spy by the British occupation force in New York, and also the fact of Susan's pregnancy. He had finally had to tell the younger man that his best friend and classmate was dead, because it was universal knowledge and his brave, defiant words were on everybody's tongue.

"I feel I must somehow make up for what they did to Nathan," Malcolm said. "I would like, if I can, to take his place."

"You mean you wish to become a spy?" David asked in surprise.

"I could never fight, kill other men on a battlefield, but I think I could serve . . . fight, that way. Ben Tallmadge, Robert Townsend, and Enoch Hale are all at Morristown with Washington. They have commissions and ostensibly serve in the Second Regiment of the Light Dragoons, but are actually Washington's intelligence corps. Thanks to Bancroft's miracle, I am now able to join them."

David had hoped to keep Malcolm at the shipyard with him, but he could tell from the look on his brother's face that no argument of his would be heeded.

"Very well, Malcolm," he had finally said. "All I ask is that you be as careful as your dangerous new profession will permit."

"Within the limits of serving our cause, I will be," Malcolm had assured him, and days later had ridden off, still unaware that he had fathered a child during his illicit romance with his niece Susan.

In the months that followed, there had been no word from him, and David, struggling to complete the *Delaware* and help Joshua Humphreys with his work on the *Effingham*, had consoled himself with the thought that Malcolm's type of service didn't permit the writing of letters.

The first news of him had come from a surprising source, a letter from Gifford aboard the U.S. sloop of war *Ranger*.

David had read the letter aloud to Shawna.

"Dear Papa,

You will be surprised to hear that I am no longer on the old *Alfred* but on a brand-new ship particularly chosen for Captain Jones by the Naval Committee until the line of battleship *America*, 74, shall be ready for him. We had some high old times on *Alfred*, dreadful slug that she was, but when John Paul Jones sails the seas there is always excitement. Now we are ready for greater things because *Ranger*, by her lines, is sure to be the fastest thing on the oceans, and we are bound (and this, Papa, is MOST SECRET!) for France where we are to take orders from none other than Ben Franklin and hope to aid him in bringing the French in on our side in this war. But for now we sit idle because the Congress in its august majesty has seen fit to provide us with a ship of fine lines, eighteen guns, and a set of sails that would shame a river barge. They are not good canvas, as one might expect, or even mediocre duck, but disgraceful hemp and jute that bags are made of. Captain Jones was furious and refused to sail, so we wait here at Portsmouth until our good commander can locate a sailmaker gullible enough to take a Congressional warrant in payment for a set of sails. Are there any such gullible New Englanders?

"Now comes the surprise, Papa. Three days ago we received a passenger aboard whose identity will surely flabbergast you as much as it did me. I will not keep you in suspense any longer—it is, of all people, our beloved Malcolm. Papa, this is an even BIGGER SECRET than the one before. Malcolm is for France on a matter of secret intelligence. Mr. Arthur Lee, one of Uncle Ben's commissioners, has written to Mr. Adams and President Hancock that he believes someone in the embassy at Passy is a traitor, or spy, who is betraying all the good Doctor's secrets to the British and much hampering his efforts to cement the French alliance. General Washington, on the recommendation of Major Townsend, has picked Malcolm, who is now a captain in the Continental Dragoons. So when we sail for France, hopefully within a week or so, Malcolm goes with us, and that is not to be revealed even to Uncle Ben. We hope also to take news of great moment. The fighting around the city of Saratoga has been most heavy and sanguinary, and it would seem so far that our forces have had much the best of it and have hemmed in the British and their Hessian and Tory allies. If Burgoyne should be taken before we sail, what grand news that would be to take to France. Surely that would decide them on the alliance we need so badly to win our freedom. For now, I will close, hoping to write again before we sail and to urge Malcolm to do the same. But he seems moody and downcast for some reason, perhaps brooding over the importance of his mission and the necessity of deceiving our best and oldest friend, Ben Franklin. Give my love to Shawna.

> Your obedient, if wandering son,
> Gifford"

So now they knew that Malcolm was safe, at least for the present, but both he and Gifford would be sailing into waters dominated by British men-of-war. As for Malcolm's moodiness, David didn't think it had anything to do with his mission but was in some way connected with Susan. Perhaps he had tried to see her only to be scathingly condemned and driven away by Aileen, or maybe the girl herself had turned against him because of her condition. Whatever it was, David couldn't discuss it with Shawna, and made light of it when she speculated as to Malcolm's unhappiness.

In any case, there was nothing to be done about it and there were other things to be thought about. The British, having landed at Head of Elk, were advancing toward Philadelphia, and David began to make plans to prevent his shipyard from falling into enemy hands.

"Shawna, you and Seth must get a crew on board the *Venture* at once," he told her.

"Papa, you know crews are as scarce as hens' teeth in this city. When General Washington called for Pennsylvania to mobilize to help stop the British advance, almost every ablebodied man in the area disappeared."

"Then hire those who are not ablebodied. I don't mean enough men to get her to sea, just enough to take her upriver and hide her in some inlet if the British take Philadelphia."

"I don't want to run away, Papa. I want to stay and fight. There are six 9-pounders and a dozen 6-pounders left over from the *Delaware* and *Randolph*. Let's cut gunports in the *Venture* and join the Pennsylvania and Continental navies in defending the Delaware."

"Shawna, there are also several sets of fine sails, enough cordage to equip several frigates and thousands of fittings of various kinds in our shipyard. They would make a valuable haul for the British, and I will destroy them if I have to, but I would rather save them for use on later ships we'll build. Load them on the *Venture* and make ready to sail as far up the Delaware as you can with those naval stores."

"Yes, Papa," Shawna said, rather meekly for her. "What about the cannon?"

"Take them too. Cut gunports in your ship, if you must, but don't risk her and those stores by fighting overwhelming forces."

"You talk as though Seth and I are to go alone. What will you be doing?"

"I'll stay here and burn the shipyard," David said. "I'll stay with the workers who are willing and we'll burn the place down to the last shed and pile of lumber."

"And be taken by the British in the act! They might hang you as they did poor Nathan."

"I'll take my chances on that," David said.

"Then I will too," she said. "Seth can take the *Venture* up the river."

He took her by the shoulders. "Shawna, you're my daughter and you're a Glencannon. You'll do what you should do."

"Yes, Papa, but—"

"I'll join you on board the *Venture*. I'm not going to sit around and wait to be captured, believe me. I've spent time in British prisons and I'm not hankering to try another."

Marching his army overland to throw it between Howe and Philadelphia, Washington paraded through the capital on August 25. David, Shawna, Seth, and

Henry, the black servant, were among those who watched the 14,000 Continentals march. It was David's opinion that Washington had planned the display more to restore the morale of the Congress and the people than for any practical purpose, and as he watched the troops go by, he thought it would probably suceed in doing that.

The general himself rode at the head of the parade and, as always, made an impressive figure in his buff and blue uniform, mounted on a white charger. Beside him rode a handsome young French officer, whom gossip said was the Marquis of Lafayette recently arrived from France to offer his sword in the American cause.

Cheers rose for Washington and cheers rose for Lafayette from the throats of thousands of patriots who had turned out to see the spectacle. Most Quakers and Tories had stayed indoors; the few on the streets went about their business trying to ignore the presence of the troops, the Quakers even turning their eyes away, as though their holiness might be compromised by the sight of guns and marching men.

Washington recognized David as he passed by and waved his hat. "We are going to win a victory, Captain Glencannon. You had best come join us."

"I will as soon as I get my frigate to safety," David called after him, *and burn my shipyard*, he added silently, having no real hope that Washington could stop the vastly superior British forces.

Behind the general and marquis came several bands and clattering mounted troops led by Colonel Theodore Bland's First Virginia Dragoons, and then the guns of Colonel Knox's artillery. The divisions of infantry in which the Continental army had been formed came next, led by Major General Nathanael Greene and his First Division, the best organized of them all. Following them came the unit of William Alexander, Lord Stirling. The Irish milord was a sturdy, red-faced man who was said to be often in his cups but who never shirked a battle and never let drink interfere with his ability in the field. Behind Stirling's division was that of Adam Stephens, a Virginian whose troops were the most frequently uniformed but who, according to rumor, used liquor to fortify his courage on the battlefield. Bringing up the rear was the division of Major General Benjamin Lincoln, commanded in Lincoln's absence by a young brigadier called Mad Anthony Wayne, who had yet to make a name for himself.

"Oh, Papa, ain't they grand?" Shawna said, squeezing David's arm in her enthusiasm.

"*Aren't* they grand, my dear," David corrected. "You've been spending too much time in the company of sailors."

"Ha!" she said with a toss of her gleaming red locks. "You should hear me swear and you'd be sure of that, but I still think they look grand and very soldier-like."

"I wonder about that, Mistress Ewart," said a cool, precise voice from behind them, and turning, they found John Adams standing there. "Our soldiers have not yet quite the air of soldiers. They don't step exactly in time. They don't hold their heads quite erect, nor turn out their toes exactly as they ought. They don't all of them cock their hats; and such as do, don't all wear them all the same way."

"But surely they will win and save Philadelphia, won't they, Mr. Adams?"

Adams gazed around at the crowd and at the city, the largest in America, second largest in the British empire, and shook his head. "There are more people lurking in their houses than have come out to see the troops parade by. Sometimes I wonder if saving this nest of Quaker cowardliness and Toryism is worth it."

"Surely, sir, you are too harsh on us," David said. "Colonel Knox himself, one of our best officers, is a Quaker."

"*Was* a Quaker, Captain," Adams said. "He was read out of his meeting for supporting the cause of freedom. Do you know, sir, that a few days ago General Washington sent Alexander Hamilton here to Philadelphia to requisition shoes for his barefoot army, but he could find none because the Quaker merchants had hidden them all so they could sell them for British gold when the city falls?"

Adams, obviously, could see no good in the Quakers and their pro-Royalist views. Having been married to a Quaker woman, David had tried to understand her views, but as he watched the grim-faced Adams walk away, he could see how Adams and most other patriots felt about people who not only refused to fight for freedom but helped those who would destroy it.

A week later news came of a battle where Washington had made a stand on the Brandywine in an attempt to block the British advance on the city. Howe, with his usual good strategic sense, once he had shaken off his indolence, had managed to flank Sullivan's division and had driven the Americans from the field. But Washington's troops had not fled as they had at the battle of Long Island, but had fought stubbornly and withdrawn in reasonably good order. The general had informed the Congress that he still intended to impose his army between the capital and the British.

Then during the night of September 25, David was awakened by the sounds of hoofbeats and a babble of excitement in the street. A glance at the clock told him it was three in the morning. But something was going on. He got up, dressed quickly, and was headed downstairs when he was met by Henry on the steps. Henry was in his nightshirt but had pulled his pants on over it.

"Theah's a gent'man here, Mr. Davey, what says he's from Mr. John Adams with 'portant news."

David hurried into the parlor and found a booted and cloaked dispatch rider waiting.

"Compliments of Mr. Adams, sir," the horseman greeted him. "Mr. Adams says he has just received dispatches from Colonel Hamilton that General Howe is in possession of the Schuylkill fords and might be in Philadelphia by noon."

"What of General Washington?"

"Washington's army stood to make a last fight of it, but a terrible thunderstorm broke over both armies, ruining the American's powder and forcing Washington to fall back on his depot at Reading Furnace. General Wayne has been surprised at Paoli and many of his troops were bayoneted as they lay unarmed or tried to surrender. Nothing can stop Howe now."

"Thank you. Tell Mr. Adams that I will wait on him later in the morning," David said.

He ran back upstairs and pounded on Shawna's door. "Shawna! Seth! Wake up! The *Venture* must sail at once!"

The door opened and Shawna peered out at him, sleepy eyed but still inclined to argue. "Papa, let me stay with you and I—"

"That's an order," he snapped. "Get your clothes on. We're leaving for the shipyard at once."

As they hurried through the streets, panic was already spreading through the patriot segment of the population. Congressmen were being summoned from their beds to the State House to hold an emergency meeting at six to hear the news. General Putnam at Peekskill was called upon to send down 1,500 Continentals at once; Philemon Dickinson in New Jersey and Smallwood and Gist in Maryland were asked to send militia, and all Pennsylvanians who had not already turned out were told to do so at once. Then they appointed Washington virtual dictator for three months and began to make their own plans to flee to Lancaster.

Having laid tinder around the buildings, the lumber sheds and the ways of his shipyard, David met briefly with Adams at daybreak.

"We are going to Lancaster," Adams informed him. "General Putnam and Colonel Gist will meet us there with their troops. We will continue the war from there. You had better come along."

"I've made plans to burn my shipyard," David said. "The *Delaware* is upriver with the *Washington* and *Effingham*, but I'll burn everything else the minute the British enter the city."

"Don't wait too long," Adams cautioned. "You are a member of the Committee of Public Safety and they just might hang you if they catch you."

"I'll get out in time," David assured him, determined not to burn his yard prematurely nor to let it fall to the British.

As he was hurrying through the streets again, he passed smiling Quakers all along the way. For once their faces had lost the expressions of gravity they liked to cultivate and some were actually beaming, as were the known Tories.

"We should have hanged or burned out the whole bloody bunch while we had the chance," David muttered to himself, heading for the house to pick up the cash he had on hand and the personal papers he had neglected to send on to the *Venture*.

He was passing a bookstore when he saw the proprietor, a mousy little man in a musty wig and dirty vest, putting up a plaque that had obviously been written well before this morning.

The bubbling pot of patriots
Has boiled above the brim,
*   And down the sides*
*   In glory glides*
The sediment and skim.

Lawyers and louts, pig-noses and snouts,
Congressmen all in a row,
*   Mind how you act;*
*   You're plain distract;*
Howe! Clinton! command here below.

Shades of our sires, our soul inspire
*   Their threat'nings to despise,*
Let's do what God, what laws require,
*   And laugh at Congress lies.*

But Oh! God bless our honest King;
*   The Lords and Commons true*

The rage that had been building in David all morning burst loose and he grabbed the bookseller by the shoulder.

"Where did you get that trash, you scoundrel?" he shouted.

" 'Tis all over town. Everybody's posting it. 'Tis the way the people feel." The man was frightened but ready to stand his ground as several laughing youths and a couple of Quaker merchants stopped to watch.

"It may be all over town," David said, "but it is not going to be where I can see it!"

He kicked out the glass window to which the plaque had been posted, turned the bookseller around, and kicked him through the broken window. Then turning, his wrath like an armor about him, he pushed his way through the group of louts and Quakers and continued on his way home for what might be the last time.

When he got there he found that the women servants had fled; only Henry remained, and his lined face brightened when he saw David.

"Mr. Davey, I'se glad you come. The redcoats be here in a couple hours, but I got hold ob a wagon and done loaded the grandfather clock, the spinet, and some othah things, and I drives you out of town. Cain't let yourself git took, suh."

"Good man, Henry," David said, patting his arm. "But you go on. I have work to do. I don't want them to catch you. They might sell you off to the Indians or something."

"Mr. Davey, I is a free man, ain't no one gonna make me a slave. I picks up a musket and fights for freedom if they let me, but since they don't, I takes care of my folks and thet's you and your chillun."

"I know, Henry. Shawna is on board the *Venture* and I'm going to burn the shipyard before the enemy arrives. You get out of town while you can and I'll meet you in Lancaster."

Hastily, David gathered up his papers and money box and left, trusting Henry to do as he was told.

Bad news awaited him at the shipyard. The workmen he was depending on to help him set the fires were gone, every last one of them, including the French Canadian foreman who had seemed so dependable.

"Papa, Papa, the men are all gone," Shawna called as he trundled a lumber cart loaded with the plans and the model of the frigate he and Joshua Humphreys dreamed of building someday to the dock where *Venture* was tied up. "I'll land the crew and help you fire the yard."

"You'll obey my orders, lass, like I did your grandfather's," David said, piling the plans, models, and things from the house into the arms of Seth and the old quartermaster.

"No, damn it, I'm not going!" Shawna shouted and started down the gangplank.

"Captain Ewart," David shouted to Seth. "Detail two men to drag that woman on board and then cast off!"

Seth stared at his father-in-law aghast for a moment before turning to the boatswain and another hand. "Please assist my wife back onto the ship."

Shawna was cursing and kicking as she was taken back on board. "Papa! Papa, damn you! They'll hang you! You can't burn that yard all by yourself . . . you haven't got time! A picket boat just passed heading upstream and they said there are Brunswick Jagers in the outskirts of the city! Come with us!"

"Haul in your gangplank, Captain Ewart!" David shouted, picking up an ax. "I'm going to cut your lines!"

If there were picket boats abroad, he didn't want them to take the time to cast off, so he hacked at the lines while Ewart ordered the hands to the braces to make sail.

A quarter of an hour later, *Venture* was in midstream, her sails filling, and David was waving goodbye as she started upstream carrying with her much of what he held dear.

But he didn't have time to waste staring at the departing ship. He had his work cut out for him. The sun was getting higher and higher in the sky, and the British might even now be entering the city. Fear gave his feet wings. The kindling had been laid ahead of time and in the building that held his office were two lanterns and tar-covered sticks to use for torches. It would have been simple with the help of the yard crew, but now he had to do it all alone.

Hurrying to the office and sail loft building, he picked up the first lantern, turned the flame high and hurled it among the hay and kindling piled against one wall. It burst into flames, and he left, carrying the torches and the second lantern.

In the street in front of the yard he saw militiamen running along the wharf to one of the Pennsylvania galleys. An officer on horseback saw David and shouted to him. "Captain Glencannon, the Hessians are at Drexel Hill! The militia has broken! The city has fallen! Flee while you can!"

"Look to yourself!" David called back. "I have work to do."

As he spoke, he dipped one of the torches into the fire taking hold around a pile of scrap lumber.

Smoke was pouring through the yard from the burning office and sail loft, but as he looked around, he knew he wasn't going to have time to finish his work. There was just too much to be done by one man. The three ways, the dock, the sheds at the fitting out basin and the mold loft were untouched, and British patrols would even now be spreading through the city.

In desperation he shouted to passing militia and seamen heading north, most of them carrying what must be loot.

"You men, help me! Help me burn this shipyard so it won't fall into British hands!"

They ignored him and kept on going.

"I'll give a hundred dollars to each and every man who helps me!" he shouted again, but he might as well have saved his breath for the work in hand.

He raced through the smoke, torching everything as he went, but it wasn't going to be enough. He didn't have the time and he was tiring as he pushed himself to the limit. Soon he was gasping for breath, tears of exhaustion and anger and frustration running down his cheeks.

"Damn it . . . damn! I've got to do it, got to!" he panted as he groped his way to the mold loft and threw the second lantern into it. The burning whale oil splashed on the tinder and flamed upward.

Stumbling and almost blinded by the smoke, he started toward the ways and knew he wasn't going to make it when he heard the sound of drums . . . drums that could only be those of the British, coming from somewhere close at hand.

"Papa, Papa! Where are you?" The voice that came to him through the fire and smoke left him momentarily thunderstruck.

"Papa! It's me, Crispin! Where are you?"

Then suddenly a tall, copper-skinned youth in buckskins appeared ahead of him, and David felt a surge of joy even in the midst of his despair. "Crispin! You . . . where? . . . how? Where did you come from?"

As they embraced, Crispin said, "From the Ohio country where Sir William sent me three long years ago, and from the Walnut Street house only a few minutes ago where Henry told me you were here."

"Henry? I told him to get out of town."

Crispin took one of the torches from David's hand. "Come on, Papa, let's finish the burning. We can talk later." Then he was off on Indian-quick feet to set fire to the slips and the wharf.

They had finished when they saw the first of the black-coated Brunswick Jagers, carrying short German rifles, coming into the yard with British sailors with buckets and wet blankets running behind them to try to put out the now unquenchable flames.

"Run for it, Crispin," David urged. "You're a woodsman, you can make it. I'll surrender."

"No, don't be a fool, Papa! It's you they want!" Crispin grabbed him by the arm and started to pull him toward the other side of the yard that was completely obscured by smoke.

"But the city has fallen," David said. "There will be pickets everywhere. We can't get out."

"Henry has a plan," Crispin told him. "He's waiting with a wagonload of hay. He'll hide us in it and play the dumb black man and get us through the lines. He thought of it himself and was determined to come with me. He would have come to help us burn the yard, but I told him to stay with the horses lest they panic."

They were running then, with the flames all around them and the shouts and an occasional shot coming from the Jagers.

"They're firing blind," David panted. "They caught a glimpse of us but not enough to take aim."

Henry was sitting on the seat of the wagon David had seen previously loaded with furniture. Now it was filled with hay. Sitting beside Henry was a tall, light-colored Negro woman.

"This is the wife of thet fella who give Mr. Malcolm his skull piece, the one you bought freedom for," Henry explained. "She want to leave de city so I figure we might's well take her with us."

"I wants to thank you, suh, for what you done did," the woman said with a shy smile.

"It is we who owe you thanks," David said, climbing wearily into the wagon and burrowing under the hay.

As the wagon rolled along, he fell into an exhausted sleep. He had no idea how many times Henry was stopped by patrols searching for the "scoundrelly incendiaries who fired half the waterfront." He never knew what devious means the black man and woman convinced those who stopped them that they should be allowed to pass. He didn't wake up, in fact, until they were somewhere on the Lancaster road and the morning sun was shining and loud voices were demanding that Henry get down so the wagon could be searched.

"Cain't do thet, suh," Henry was saying. "This heah hay belongs to Squire Marswell. Squire, he a Quaker and powerful partial to his gracious majesty, the King, and this hay foah his horses what he goin' to present to General Howe foah his staff to ride on."

"I don't give a hang who the hay belongs to!" This voice had the impatient snap of a British subaltern about it, and there seemed to be others present. Someone was urging that the wagon be pushed out of the way, someone else demanded that it be searched.

David risked a look out from under the hay and found himself staring into the window of a large, expensive carriage, a carriage he recognized, and the face staring back at him was that of Elspeth Wescott. Her amber eyes opened wide in surprise, but she seemed to take in the whole situation in that one glance. Her coach was partially blocked by the wagon over which the British pickets were arguing. Her eyes caressed David for another moment and her mouth formed what he was sure in his bemused, half-awake state was a kiss.

Then she settled back in her seat and he heard her voice, her unmistakable voice, as he ducked back under the hay.

"You there! You, lieutenant!" she called in the voice of command only the sons and daughters of the aristocracy could use. "I am Elspeth, Lady Wescott. I am on my way to join my husband, Brigadier Wescott, in Philadelphia, and I am in a hurry. I simply cannot brook this kind of delay."

"I am sorry, your ladyship, but my orders are—"

"Get that wagon that is blocking my carriage out of the way, Lieutenant, so that we can pass."

"But your ladyship, I—"

"I shall be dining with General Howe and General Cornwallis this evening, my good man. I doubt you would care to have me mention that you had been rude to me on the King's highway."

"No, your ladyship, of course not. Move on, fellow! Move on quickly! Get your blasted hay out of my sight!" the officer yelled, and Henry, nothing loath, was cracking his whip.

When the wagon was rolling along briskly, Crispin asked, "What's the matter, Papa? What is it? What are you laughing at?"

"Laughing . . . oh, well, because something wonderful just happened."

"I agree. If that rather unpleasant lady had not been so impatient, we would have been found out for sure."

"She was not impatient, Crispin. She was in love."

"In love, Papa? I don't understand."

"Neither do I, Crispin," David said. "No more than I understand where you came from so suddenly."

"I told you, from Ohio country. I have a lot to tell you, Papa, but I think it had better wait. There is a girl waiting for me in Lancaster. She has been terribly wronged and I have to make it up to her, but I'll explain all that later."

David was too tired to argue, and he was smiling as he drifted off to sleep again and dreamed of a pair of amber eyes telling him the lady loved him and lips that had formed a kiss.

When he awoke again, he was lying on the hay staring up at a starry sky. "Where are we?" he asked Crispin.

"Lancaster, Papa. It's on toward morning and you've slept all the way, laughing in your sleep every once in a while."

"Lancaster, eh? Didn't you say something about a girl?"

"Yes, she's waiting for me here and —"

He broke off at the sound of a town crier's voice booming through the dark streets of the little Pennsylvania town whence the Continental Congress had fled. "Four o'clock and all's well! Four o'clock and Burgoyne is taken! Four o'clock and Burgoyne is taken!"

David sat up. Suddenly he felt wonderful. Elspeth loved him and Burgoyne had surrendered. The *Ranger* would be carrying the news to France and surely the French would enter the war now.

"Do you hear that, Crispin? Do you hear that, Henry? And you, my good woman? Burgoyne has surrendered! We are going to win the war! We are all going to be free! Henry... Crispin... we're all going to be free, and it's a glorious night for America ... a glorious night for America and the Glencannons!"